ONE MINUTE TO MIDNIGHT
BOOK EIGHT OF THE GUILD WARS

Tim C. Taylor & Chris Kennedy

Seventh Seal Press
Virginia Beach, VA

Copyright © 2020 by Tim C. Taylor & Chris Kennedy.

All rights reserved. No part of this publication may be reproduced, distributed or transmitted in any form or by any means, including photocopying, recording, or other electronic or mechanical methods, without the prior written permission of the publisher, except in the case of brief quotations embodied in critical reviews and certain other noncommercial uses permitted by copyright law. For permission requests, write to the publisher, addressed "Attention: Permissions Coordinator," at the address below.

Chris Kennedy/Seventh Seal Press
2052 Bierce Dr.
Virginia Beach, VA 23454
http://chriskennedypublishing.com/

Publisher's Note: This is a work of fiction. Names, characters, places, and incidents are a product of the author's imagination. Locales and public names are sometimes used for atmospheric purposes. Any resemblance to actual people, living or dead, or to businesses, companies, events, institutions, or locales is completely coincidental.

Cover Design by Brenda Mihalko
Original Art by Ricky Ryan

Ordering Information:
Quantity sales. Special discounts are available on quantity purchases by corporations, associations, and others. For details, contact the "Special Sales Department" at the address above.

One Minute to Midnight/Tim C. Taylor & Chris Kennedy -- 1st ed.
ISBN: 978-1648550645

I would like to thank the three 'M's who helped to make this book possible: Melia, Melissa, and the McPherson clan.

– Tim

For Sheellah.

– Chris

Prologue

Hotel Jim Bowie, Houston, Texas, Earth

Sansar Enkh woke in a sweat. The sheets were on the floor, as were her pillows. She didn't notice as she ran to the window and threw open the curtains. The sun, halfway above the horizon, greeted her, and she stared at it for several moments while her breathing slowed.

It wasn't growing—it definitely wasn't flaring out of control in a massive explosion—nor was it shrinking to oblivion. It looked the same as it had every day that week—the harbinger of another scorching day in eastern Texas. Hot? Yes. But roast the planet to cinders hot? Definitely not.

When it didn't blow up after 30 seconds of intense scrutinization, she finally felt safe enough to consider her surroundings, and she realized several people were looking at her from the street two floors below with their mouths open.

She looked down. At some point during the dream, she'd torn off her clothes as Earth's star went nova. Her face ignited in a flush, and she snatched the curtains closed, then she went back to sit on the bed.

The dream had been the most vivid she'd had since the one where the Tortantulas had overrun the former Golden Horde base in Uzbekistan. The fact that she'd now had it twice was terrifying.

She had asked her scientists about it after the first dream, and they had tracked down every helioseismologist thought to be a leader in the field and asked for their opinions. While all agreed that the sun would eventually explode, not a single one of them had said it would be anytime soon. The earliest was six billion years from now, so she had put it down to bad Tex-Mex and happily earmarked it as "someone else's problem."

But now…a second time. And so intense…

Something was coming. Something awful.

* * * * *

Chapter One

Near the Starkiller Inner Chamber, Aneb-4

From: Major Sun, Aneb-4
    To: Assembly Member Ayean, McPherson-3
    Message Body: Type/Universal Text/Human/Eng4
Message Text: Ayean, I shall return to McPherson's Star as soon as I can, but this cannot wait. I request you investigate any signs of unexplained activity on the planet. I have learned there may be weapons of fearsome potential which have been hidden away in the nebula for tens of thousands of years. Endless Night has learned this too. We can't allow them to control such power.

    Shipments to nowhere. Offworlders being brought in and taken to remote locations. Power generators being imported—big ones. That kind of thing. And take another, deeper look at what those Besquith were up to. I think we may have missed something.

    As the local Spine Patriot commander, I have requested the same of Keriwoot. Keep him apprised, but please send your response directly to me.

    Good luck.

Sincerely,
Major Sun.

* * *

There 'may' be weapons.

That was a lie. Sun knew damned well there were two more starkillers hidden somewhere in the nebula. At least Hopper had believed so, and the Jeha scientist hadn't been wrong about her science so far. Only in her choice of employer.

What was the point of contacting the Jivool miner on McPherson-3 if she gave him only half the story? Better to not contact him at all.

She opened her eyes onto the gloomy cavern.

Trust was becoming a scarce resource.

She knew the Patriots were riddled with Endless Night spies. The Scythe had been lurking for centuries, so deeply compartmentalized even they had no idea of the extent of their operations.

And there had been growing signs of another organization operating out of the nebula's shadows. Observing but not yet acting.

Who were they? If pushed, she'd say the F11 conglomerates closing in on the source of the Goltar's so-called Infinite Flow of credits. But that was just a guess.

Damn it!

If she jumped at every shadow, she'd never achieve anything.

Sun sent the message packet. Her pinview reported a viable network path had been established. Within fifteen minutes, it would be queued up with other data packets for transmission with the next ship out the local stargate.

With a few modifications, she sent a similar request for information to Keriwoot.

"Problem?" called a man's voice.

She turned around, wearing her sweetest smile, and stared into the face of one of the precious few people in the galaxy she could trust.

She'd thought him dead. These past two hours had proved he was still very much alive.

Her smile grew more genuine with every moment.

"A problem?" She shrugged. "I think so."

She shuffled over to him, trying not to think about the origins of the jumble of blankets and garments they had requisitioned and bundled into makeshift bedding material. Or whether they had ever been cleaned.

They were in a mineral-encrusted storage compartment inside the battle-torn inner segment of an ancient underground war machine. Sometimes you just had to take your pleasures wherever you could find them.

Branco waited patiently for her answer while she gently ran her fingertips through his hair.

"I was so desperate to get back to you, my love, that I think I might have brushed aside some warning signs." She looked down, distraught. "We all did."

"You know where one of the other starkillers is located."

It wasn't a question. "I think so. I thought the Besquith we encountered in the McPherson system were a distraction to keep us away from Aneb-4, but now I'm not so sure."

She thought back to the cavern hacked out of the rock in a deep gallery of the Gelheik Sands Mine and shuddered at the memory. Alien bodies had been smeared over every surface. A powerful detonation in that enclosed space had practically liquidized everybody in the blast zone.

At first, she'd thought it had been Besquith ammunition cooking off, but Ayean had insisted the explosion had come from blasting charges.

A lot of them.

Certainly more than the Besquith had needed to make a distraction. The longer she thought about it, the more she decided they had been planning to do some tunneling of their own.

"I just sent a message to my contacts on McPherson-3," she explained. "We need to look again, and harder."

"If you're so certain it's there," Branco said, "we should be marshalling our forces and heading there immediately."

"You're right. But our forces here are mostly aquatics. Unless we can flood the mines, they'd be useless, flapping like a landed catch on the bottom of the mine floor."

"Fair point," Branco admitted. "We're beneath an island right now, but Aneb-4 is essentially a waterworld." He rubbed his chin. "Most of the forces don't have rebreathers, but what if we could manufacture them? Shouldn't be too hard."

She sat on her haunches and rested her hands on his shoulders, looking into the face she'd missed so badly. He looked so haggard. Splotches of scaly green skin were spreading over his throat and down his chest, but Branco was alive. For now.

He gave her his boyish smile and winked. "To the devil with being sorry, Sun. We snatched two hours for ourselves. Earlier today, I was cowering on the ground as a barrage of kinetic torpedoes rained down over my head. That's two hours more than I thought I'd get. Let's be grateful and accept that now it's time we got back to work."

She held his gaze mournfully, regretting that their time together would be so brief.

And then brightened into a smile. Branco was right. That was why he was so good for her. She should forget about what they couldn't have and be grateful for the precious gift of time together.

But it was hard to think that way. He looked so damned ill.

She mashed her lips against his and then dressed herself with speedy efficiency.

As she laced her boots, she paused and looked a question at Branco, who was still lying on the makeshift bed.

He grinned back at her, but his expression looked forced this time. "I'll follow later," he said. "I need a rest. I've had a busy day, and you've worn me out."

She laughed. "It *has* been a busy day."

With a final kiss, she left him behind, adding under her breath, "And it's not over yet."

Sun was still making her way to the surface when she received news from McPherson-3.

It was Keriwoot. From the timestamp, the Gliboonian had sent his message eight days ago. And, from the fragmentary wording by the normally bloviated alien's standards, Keriwoot had been in a hurry to send it.

"Ayean is dead. We're under attack. Besquith and…Major Sun, I have learned there are things worse than Besquith. All is chaos here. I shall send an update once the situation clarifies. Keriwoot."

A freighter arrived from McPherson's Star the following day.

And the next.

But there were no further updates from Keriwoot.

* * * * *

Chapter Two

Golden Horde American Headquarters, Houston, Texas, Earth

Someone tapped on her doorframe and Sansar looked up to find Nigel Shirazi. *Why didn't someone tell me he was in the building?* "What are *you* doing here? I didn't know you were coming. Are you here with good news? We can begin taking contracts again?"

"No, sorry," Nigel said, looking down. "We keep trying," he said, his gaze coming back up to meet her eyes, "and I mean *all* of us are trying—but the Speaker is against doing anything that might split us up while the Kahraman are at the doorstep."

"How about the fact that while we sit around on our asses, we're not getting any good training? Working on tactics and techniques? Remember those things?"

Nigel hit her with his boyish smile. "I remember them well, and we keep reminding the Speaker about them, too." He shrugged. "Still…I've got nothing. Well, nothing you'd be interested in, anyway."

"What do you mean?"

"Well, right before I left, the Speaker approached me about a job that was very much off the books. A friend of his wanted some help in an out-of-the-way place."

"What's it pay?"

"He didn't know. Said it was negotiable. The thing is, they're looking for CASPer troops, and it sounded like some sort of assault mission. Didn't think you'd be interested in it, especially since you'd be on your own dime to get all the way out there, and might not find the job worthwhile once you did."

"Where is it?"

"Out on the ass end of the galaxy somewhere. Place called the Spine Nebula or something like that?"

"*What?*" Visions of the Sun exploding clouded her eyes.

"You know about the Spine Nebula?"

"Never heard of it until today," she said. *But the reaction I just got tells me it's involved.* "But I'll take it."

Nigel shrugged. "The contact info is to meet Gloriana at Station Five in the Beta-Caerelis system."

"Could the Speaker have been any less specific? I wonder how many Glorianas there are there."

"I don't know. That's all he said; sorry."

"That's fine," Sansar replied. "So really, why are you here?"

"I'm here to pick up a new transport for another off-the-books mission I picked up."

"Another one? Maybe I need to come to Capital Planet. It seems like all the good contracts are happening there. They sure aren't happening at the merc pits…"

"I'll continue to work on that. Also, when I get back from this mission, I may have some new toys to play with."

"Toys? What kind of toys?"

"I can't say yet. It's a surprise." Nigel glanced at his watch; he was late. "Sorry, I have to go. Say hi to Jim for me when you see him."

* * * * *

Chapter Three

**Patriot/Midnighter Command Post,
Inside the Great Engine, Aneb-4**

"You have incoming," announced Blue from her orbital eyrie. "Two old dropships and what looks like a commercial passenger shuttle. Oh, and there's an executive yacht making a suborbital hop over to your little party island that I wouldn't mind for myself. You want *Midnight Sun* to take them out?"

Sun wasn't sure whether her sister was joking. There were a lot of things she wasn't sure about anymore.

She sighed. Branco had shown her that she could be more than the straight foil to her sister's antics, but it was a pattern Sun found difficult to break.

"Negative," she said. "Galactic law prohibits firing at atmospheric craft from orbit."

"Seriously?" Blue's laugh sounded genuine. "After releasing a bombardment of kinetic torpedoes over your heads, a few shots from *Midnight Sun's* lasers is hardly going to make any difference."

"You will not fire," Sun insisted. "And that…"

"And that is an order? You forget yourself, *Major* Sun."

Difficult words were left unspoken but somehow still seethed along the comm link between the sisters and draped an uncomfortable silence over everyone in the room.

Sun glanced awkwardly at Lieutenant Colonel Mishkan-Ijk. Her superior officer stared back impassively through his bony Goltar eye sockets. On the Midnight Sun Free Company TO&E, Sun was two levels below her sister, but she had since assumed command of the Spine Patriots, an organization with a distinct agenda that had been at war with the Midnighters only a few weeks earlier.

Events had careened forward so aggressively that Sun had managed to bypass the question of where her loyalties lay.

For now.

But that was only possible because the CASPer contingent she nominally commanded had mostly been wiped out, and First Sergeant Albali was more than capable of commanding the survivors.

When Gloriana arrived with reinforcements, all that would change.

Neither sister chose this moment to speak on the matter. It was a question to kick down the road for a little while longer.

"Easy, Bad Dog," said Blue.

"Dog?"

"Sorry. Been reading texts by early mech combat theorists while I've been cooling my heels waiting for you to take the planet."

"Captain Blue!" said Mishkan-Ijk with a sharp snap of his beak. "Major Sun."

The Goltar didn't say anything more. He didn't need to. Sun burned with shame at the Goltar's disapproval of the sisters' conduct.

"If we may return to the present situation," he said, "this base still has significant antiair defenses, but the fire control systems have been sabotaged. Captain, we need to release our dropships from orbit now to intercept and either shoot down the bogies or force them down."

"Agreed," said Blue. "Dispatching First Flight now."

"Receiving signal from bogies," reported one of the Goltar in the signals team. "They identify themselves as the Anebian system government."

"Unlikely," said Branco.

Sun swallowed hard at his voice. He sounded like a brittle husk.

"I've not set foot inside the capital," he continued as he walked over to the Tri-V on prosthetics Sun had retrieved from the bottom of the base's inner chamber. "But I did set up resistance cells around Port Chinto. Endless Night was busy taking over."

"But you said you established resistance cells?" said Sun gently.

"Perhaps they...*resisted?*"

"I don't know." He stabbed fingers at the crown of his head and dragged them down. "I haven't yet reappraised myself of the situation."

"Dropship flight issuing instructions to bogies."

A Tri-V holo-display appeared at the floor. "What's going on?" asked the image of an angry HecSha. It wore a silken green scarf stained with blood.

"The transmission is coming from the yacht," supplied the signals team.

Branco peered at the alien. "I know you," he said.

"And I know you, Gleaming Fool."

"Gleaming what?" asked Sun. She cast a querying glance at Branco, who shrugged back.

"What can I say? I've made a name for myself in this world."

Branco spoke to the HecSha. "I greet you, Rievskegg. It's good to see you. We're still racing to keep up with events, which is why you're getting the military escort. I can tell you've come a long way from Port Chinto City Hall, but can it be true that I am speaking with a representative of the planetary government?"

"My friend, I am now the prime representative of this world. Endless Night has withdrawn. The old establishment is in hiding, and the Patriot resistance has taken its place. I have been selected as the prime representative of this system until such time as we have eradicated Endless Night and have time to think of—" he growled, "—*alternate* forms of representation."

The prospect of relinquishing power clearly didn't appeal to Rievskegg. Typical HecSha.

"You vouch for him?" she asked Branco.

"I do. He's one of mine."

"No, Branco," said the HecSha. "I am one of *hers*." He bowed. "I pledged fealty to Major Sun as commander of the Spine Patriots. I am her servant."

Sun didn't know whether to groan or cheer. The Spine Nebula had been a dumpster fire for so long that its people were desperate for leadership. Everywhere she went, aliens kept going all feudal on her, wanting her to be some kind of medieval queen.

That wasn't Sun's style at all.

Still, she needed all the support she could get.

"Thank you, Rievskegg. You've done well."

She paused. Unable to help herself, she went ahead and asked, "What was the process by which you were selected? I inquire because political legitimacy could soon become an important factor."

"You don't have to worry on that count, Major. My selection was fair and completely above reproach. We didn't have time for anything as complicated as an election, so we decided leadership in a wrestling contest. No weapons. No armor. Clad only in hot, oiled mud, as is the HecSha way."

"What about the other races?"

"Few survived the opening round. And that is good, because these difficult times require strong leadership."

"Looks like the HecSha way it is," she said. "At least for now. I'll meet you shortly."

Mishkan-Ijk gave the inbound delegation landing coordinates on Romalin Island and cut the link.

"This world is on our side," said Sun. "At least that's one headache out of the way."

She froze, noting Branco's pained expression. But then, he always looked drawn these days. She decided there was a lucid intelligence behind his concern. "What is it?"

"The Tyzhounes forced Endless Night to abandon the island and the great engine," he said. "I understood that. But as soon as *Midnight Sun* arrived to retake Romalin, the Night didn't just withdraw from the battlezone to let us slug it out with the Tyzhounes. Rievskegg is from Arizcazar, the landmass on the other side of the planet. Why did the Night abandon that? I think they've evacuated the entire system. We'll need to use our contacts to verify that, but this looks like an evacuation. They aren't coming back."

"Scorched Earth," said Blue from orbit.

Sun shuddered. She cast a recording of the destruction of the Unthor system to the Tri-V disc. The violated star pulsed every color in the spectrum under the lash of the starkiller, sending out deadly waves of destruction at two percent of lightspeed.

Unthor had been home to a third of a million people. Aneb-4's population was 120 million.

Of course. It made perfect sense. If her guess was right that Endless Night had located one of the other starkillers on McPherson-3, and they were prepared to use it, then what better target could there be than Aneb? It was, after all, the system where the Night's deadliest foes were currently concentrated.

"Holy shit," said Mishkan-Ijk.

Heaven knows, there'd been enough interspecies misunderstandings between Goltar and Humans. Not this time.

None of the Humans dirtside or in orbit could add to the Goltar's words.

Holy shit, indeed.

* * * * *

Chapter Four

Med-Bay 13, *Midnight Sun*, Orbiting Aneb-4

"Stand still!" Sun demanded.

Since the day she'd been born, Blue had rarely shown signs of paying attention to her big sister, and that wasn't about to change now. If anything, her pacing outside the med-bay door grew more frantic.

"I said, stand still, dammit. You're like an expectant father from the days of yore. Should I bring you a fat cigar and a glass of cognac?"

Blue looked up and gave a grin. "There's an idea. Swap the brandy for a decent Scotch and I'm in."

Sun grabbed her sister by the shoulders and shook her.

Entropy! When had Blue lost her muscle tone? She was bones wrapped up in pallid skin.

Sun released her grip. Blue had always been small, but Sun had never thought of her as frail until today. Not that any of that would make Sun go easier on her sister.

"You never liked Branco. Why are you suddenly acting so concerned?"

Blue looked away. "He's slowly rising in my estimation."

"Bullshit! He'll never be good enough for your big sister. That's what you think of him. Deny it!"

Blue stared back fiercely. "It doesn't matter what I think. You love him."

"You know I do."

Blue bit her lip. "I need you to tell me that. Don't ask me why."

What game was she playing?

"Please," said Blue, a word that came rarely to those lips.

The fight drained out of Sun. "Fine. I love him, all right? He means the universe to me."

"If you could, say, give up your legs in return for having him whole and healthy again, would you do it?"

Sun frowned as she peered behind her sister's reddened eyes, trying to make sense of the chaotic mind behind them. She didn't understand what was going on here, but she did recognize her sister was at a crisis point. Blue wasn't playing games.

"Would I allow myself to be mutilated?" Sun mused. "I can't see myself ever rolling over and letting something like that happen to me. But, yes, I would sacrifice everything to see Branco well again. I've spent my entire credit balance seeking a cure. I won't stop there."

Blue nodded slowly as if having arrived at a fateful decision.

Sun waited, watching Blue as she assembled her words of explanation.

But before they came, Doctor Decima DiMassi emerged from the med-bay. With a dearth of Human patients, Med-Bay 13 had spent much of the past two years as Branco's personal residence.

DiMassi took a deep breath before she began, but her somber expression told Sun all she needed to know.

"I've given Branco every test and analysis available to me," the doctor began.

Sun held up a hand to stop her. A priority message was coming through her pinplants.

It came from the Spine Patriot observation network. The Endless Night ship, *Crazy Notion* had emerged at the Wahrner's Grise system. It was traveling under a false name and an altered engine signature, but those old smuggler tricks wouldn't fool the Patriot observers. Half of them were smugglers too.

According to their best intelligence guesswork, Hopper was on board *Crazy Notion*. Since the Jeha scientist understood the starkillers more than anyone, her location carried enormous significance.

If Endless Night had seen fit to take her to Wahrner's Grise, then Sun had a new odds-on favorite for the location for the last of the three starkillers.

"My apologies, Doctor," Sun said. "Please make your report."

"This Selroth aquatic herb Branco's been taking. *Ribbwah*. It's fascinating. I want a larger supply for my analysis. And not just for Branco. This herb could prove invaluable to Earth's pharmaceutical industries. It's given him another burst of life. Without it, he'd be dead. The disease Branco picked up in the jungles of Rakbutu-Tereus is still progressing, but it's significantly slowed by the *ribbwah*. However, the herb is highly addictive and is causing poisons to accumulate in his body. I'm unsure whether the disease or its treatment will kill him first."

"And his mind?" asked Blue. She shrugged guiltily at her sister. "Branco said himself that he's been having unsettling memories."

"Yes," said DiMassi. "His brain chemistry's misfiring. I'm no expert in neural meshes, but those in his head are working outside of pattern norms. He told me that it hurts to access his pinplants. I'm afraid that is not a good sign."

"Let's summarize," Sun said. "Branco is going mad, he needs alien seaweed to survive, and the cure will kill him. Copy that. How long has he got?"

DiMassi gave a palms-up shrug. "A lot of this is guesswork. But I'd measure his lifespan in weeks. Sorry. Normally, I would say I could do something to ease his pain, but to be honest, there's nothing I can do for him that the Selroth herb can't do better."

Sun moved to enter the med-bay, but the doctor shot out an arm to bar her way.

"Some of the tests were invasive, which is why Branco is sedated. You'll be able to speak to him in a few hours."

"Thank you, Doctor." Blue's dismissal was strangely curt. "You may leave us."

Sun took a deep breath as the doctor retreated from view. The war continued with or without Branco, and Blue needed to know the intel update. "I have a possible location for both Hopper and Starkiller-3."

"Screw that," said Blue. "We're here about Branco. Tell me again, would you sacrifice a limb if it made him whole? Does he really mean that much to you?"

"He does, and I would. Why do you keep asking that?"

It was Blue's turn to grab Sun by the shoulders. She'd lost muscle mass, but there was nothing weak about her grip. "Keep him alive," Blue said. "He needs to hang on until Molina gets here."

"The Wrogul? How did you…?"

Years ago, Blue had snuck into startown to get herself an alien-tech morphogenic tattoo. It hadn't taken properly, leaving Blue completely hairless and with a skin tone several notches paler. Sun often forgot about her sister's appearance—she'd love her however she looked—and worried instead about the deep damage to her mental state.

Every so often, though, Sun saw her sister's visage afresh and freaked the hell out.

Blue's face had gone as pale as a blood-drained carcass. The blood vessels cutting through her cheeks glowed like flowing lava.

She'd witnessed Blue's demon impersonation on a handful of occasions. Most ended in violence and death. Either Blue was thunderously angry or petrified with terror.

Sun swallowed hard. "Molina…What price will we have to pay?"

"Leave that to me," Blue replied in a trembling voice. "God knows you've sacrificed plenty to look after me. Now it's my time to return the favor."

* * * * *

Chapter Five

Endless Night Base, McPherson-3

"Out, slug, before I turn you into lunch!" the Besquith roared.

"Yes, sir. Right away, sir," Jombon said, keeping his head down and backing out the door. "Just trying to straighten up the place." He bowed, turned, and fled the area, hoping the Besquith wouldn't sweep the room again. If the Besquith did, his life would be forfeit.

This was the chance he'd been looking for ever since his last trip to Station 5 in Beta-Caerelis. While there, he'd met with the Human known as Beowulf, Jombon's long-time source for Sparkle. Lately, though, Beowulf had been less interested in Jombon's money than what he knew.

Beowulf's organization was looking to push deeper into the Spine Nebula, but they were worried about the ongoing turmoil between the various factions with interests there. The one they were most worried about—obviously—was the Endless Night, who Beowulf, quite rightly, saw as competition, and who Jombon worked for as a low-level minion.

He'd offered Jombon a hundred thousand credits and free Sparkle for a year if he could find out any information on their plans. It had seemed like an easy enough task, and with that kind of wealth, Jombon could leave the Spine Nebula forever. The free Sparkle was a bonus. All he'd have to do was plant a few listening devices and pass on the information.

When he'd heard that someone important was coming, Jombon had known this was his chance. He'd gotten access to the VIP quarters and injected the listening devices into two of the pillows in the room. He'd almost gotten out unnoticed. Now, however, his life was forfeit. The Endless Night monitored for transmissions from inside and outside the base. When the listening devices transmitted, someone would find them, and the Besquith was sure to remember who'd been in the room.

He had to flee.

* * *

Shove 'n' Done Tavern, Station 5, Beta-Caerelis

"Need something?" the Blevin waitress asked.

Beowulf looked up. "No, thanks," he said, picking up his half-full drink. "We're good."

"She comes around a lot," Sha'Gar noted.

"She does," Beowulf agreed, watching the Blevin sashay over to the next table. "Almost too much." He waited until she was headed back to the bar, then slid the slate over to the Zzardar. The small lizard-like alien picked up the slate. "What's this?"

"Transcript of a conversation between two of the leaders of the Endless Night. It was very interesting because the two people who we thought they were, obviously aren't."

"What does that mean?"

"We thought the local Endless Night leaders were a female elSha named Coron and a male Zuparti named Retenex. As it turns out, though, once they got talking, we found out they are actually a female Lumar named Grael and a male Oogar named Jankel, based on the languages spoken and the names they used with each other. It took some time to parse this out, and it ended up burning two of our operatives within their organization. They call each other sister and brother, which threw us for a time until we could get verification of the people who'd been at this meeting. We think the elSha and Zuparti are covers for the people really in charge."

"How does this affect me?"

"It probably doesn't," Beowulf said. "It is background info for when you read the transcript."

Sha'Gar looked down, and Beowulf followed along on a second slate.

Jankel: *"Good seeing you again, sister."*

Grael: *"And you as well, brother."*

Jankel: *"And it is always nice when we can put aside Coron and Retenex."*

Grael: *"Truth."*

Jankel: *"I have been giving the use of the starkiller some thought."*

Grael: *"And what have you come up with?"*

Jankel: *"I think we need a demonstration of it before we blackmail the guilds on Capital Planet."*

Grael: *"A demonstration?"*

Jankel: *"Yes. We need to show them the power of the weapon. If we just tell them about it, they will send mercenaries to try to wrest it from us. If we show them the power, they will be worried that we will fire it when we see their forces appear."*

Grael: *"So, keep them in awe, and allow them to pay?"*

Jankel: *"Exactly. I don't think 4% is too much to pay us to not destroy all their headquarters buildings, do you?"*

Grael: *"Four percent of what?"*

Jankel: *"Four percent of everything. If the major corporations and guilds paid 4% of their revenues in return for a guarantee that Endless Night would not obliterate their stars, the wealth would be unimaginable. Four percent. Surely that's not too much to ask?"*

Grael: *"It doesn't seem so to me, but I know what the starkiller can do. Of course, if the weapon fired successfully last time, so do the people of the Tau-Rietzke system. At least, they did…briefly."*

Jankel, chuckling: *"I'm sure they did. Unfortunately, that system is too far outside the cognizance of the Galactic Union for it to be a good example."*

Grael: *"You've changed your attitude, brother. It was you who persuaded me to power down after we targeted Aneb. To wait, watch, and consider before being so bold as to shake down the guilds themselves. Such caution was so unlike you that I listened. What's changed?"*

Jankel: *"Just a little detail in the latest public update from the Cartography Guild. They've listed the Tau-Rietzke stargate as temporarily out of service."*

Grael: *"Out of service! Melted to slag in starfire more like. Excellent. We know the weapon works. So why not target our enemies at Aneb-4?"*

Jankel: *"Because they are but an irritation, their strength infinitesimal compared with the guilds. We must think bigger, sister."*

Grael: *"You have a better target in mind, I presume?"*

Jankel: *"I do, and one that no one will miss."*

Grael: *"Are you going to tell me, or are you going to make me beg?"*

Jankel: *"Of course I will tell you. The Mercenary Guild just fought a war, right?"*

Grael: *"Against the Humans, yes."*

Jankel: *"One which they lost, right?"*

Grael: *"The Peacemakers intervened and stopped it. No one really won or lost."*

Jankel: *"But the Merc Guild wouldn't mind if the Humans all of a sudden disappeared, would they?"*

Grael: *"No, they would not."* Grael chuckles. *"There are probably many people and guilds which wouldn't miss the Humans overmuch."*

Jankel: *"Exactly. So they will be happy to have the Humans gone and paying us won't seem so bad. The alternative is their star goes nova and everyone dies. Four percent doesn't seem like much at that point, does it?"*

Grael: *"No, it doesn't."*

Jankel: *"When should we do it?"*

Grael: *"As soon as possible."*

Jankel: *"And no one knows about it?"*

Grael: *"No one. A Jivool was sneaking around in the tunnel system, but he was found and eliminated, and the tunnels filled with sand burrowers. No one will be venturing down there anymore."*

Jankel: *"Good. Good."*

"There was more," Beowulf said, reaching over to take the slate, "but it was inconsequential to the matter at hand."

Sha'Gar raised a scaly eyebrow. "Which is?"

"I want you to go take a look at this starkiller and let me know where it is for sure, so we can put together a strike team and eliminate it before they destroy Earth."

"You really think they can do that?"

"I don't know whether they can do it or not, but *they* obviously think they can." Beowulf shrugged. "I don't get back there very much anymore, but I'm sure our bosses don't want to have their star go nova."

"I suspect they don't," Sha'Gar said with a chuckle.

"Do we know where this is? I didn't see a planet, much less a location on one."

Beowulf tapped his slate a couple of times then handed it back. "We think it's in the Gelheik Sands Mine of McPherson-3."

"Looks like it," Sha'Gar said. "'*Local Jivool miner goes missing; feared eaten by sand burrowers.*'"

"That's what we thought, too."

"Sounds dangerous. What's in it for me?"

"One hundred thousand credits if you can confirm/deny that the starkiller is in the mines there, and bring back targeting information."

"So I don't have to destroy it? I just have to find it?"

"Correct."

Beowulf could see the Zzardar thinking about it. "Sand burrowers?" the Zzardar said. "Adults can eat someone my size in a single bite."

"So don't let them see you."

"They can't see for shit. They have great senses of smell and touch though."

"So don't let them smell or touch you."

"Yeah, if it were only that easy."

"If it were that easy, I'd go myself and save the organization 100,000 credits."

"I'd like to talk to the spy who captured the conversation you showed me."

Beowulf shook his head. "He didn't make it out of the Endless Night base. How do you think I came up with the 100,000 credits so easily? They would have been his."

Sha'Gar seemed to think about it some more. "Okay," he finally said. "I'll do it." He held up a claw. "*But,* it's going to cost you

500,000 credits. If I do this, I want to be able to retire to a nice warm planet somewhere, preferably outside the range of this starkiller thing."

"I can give you 250,000," Beowulf said, "but that's as high as I'm authorized to go." He shrugged. "I'm sure Sandoval would go for 250,000."

"I'm sure he would, too," Sha'Gar said. "And he'd probably get caught. He can't evade sand burrowers, nor can he camouflage like I can."

"A quarter million. Take it or leave it."

"Oh, come on, Beowulf, you know I'm going to take it, just like I know you could go to a half million if I really insisted. I also know that you'll do something else for me when I return from successfully completing the mission that will make it worth my time."

"What's that?"

"I don't know yet. I'll tell you when I return."

"Fair enough," Beowulf agreed. "Sold."

Sha'Gar handed back the slate as the Blevin waitress returned, then he stood. "I'll get right on it."

* * * * *

Chapter Six

Speaker's Chambers, Merc Guild HQ, Capital Planet

There was something foul in the water. Effluent that was also carried on the breeze.

Ever since she'd debarked her shuttle and swum into the blunt urbanization that housed the guild headquarters on Capital Planet, the place had seemed off to Gloriana.

When she passed into the air-breather zones that dominated the place, she'd put a name to the taste.

Desperation.

It was the merest hint, but there nonetheless.

Two months? Was that all it had been since she'd last been here to see Toyn-Zhyll? So much had happened since then. She ground her beak at the memory of losing a large slice of Goltar military assets to a rabble of low-species...*pirates*!

During that short stretch of time, it seemed that much had transpired on Capital Planet, too. This had always been a dangerous place, but now it was blanketed with a brittle wariness, a sense that trouble was on its way and would be arriving any time soon.

Nowhere was this more apparent than Merc Guild headquarters.

Additional security posts had been set up, and the mercs stationed at them bore the heightened paranoia of veterans who understood that the most lethal dangers often came from unexpected sources.

"What is happening here?" she demanded of Toyn-Zhyll when his guards finally permitted her access to his personal chambers. "Are we at war?"

Her old friend, and now the Speaker of the Mercenary Guild, regarded her coldly through eyes so recessed into their bone shrouds they were barely visible.

This wasn't the welcome of a warm, scented pool he'd lavished on her last time.

"There is always conflict," said Toyn-Zhyll.

"With whom? This Weapons Conglomerate you mentioned last time?" An electrifying thought sent jolts through Gloriana's limbs. "Are we at war with the Veetanho?" she whispered, unsure what answer she would prefer.

But Toyn-Zhyll gave no answer, instead moving to the padded stump behind his grand desk and seating himself there.

He didn't offer a seat to Gloriana.

She took one anyway.

"Conflict is a constant that affects us all," said the Speaker. "Even Grand Admiral Aru-Zzat, who was recently kidnapped on his own flagship and stranded in another system. A flagship I believe you now command, Gloriana, although I note you chose not to bring *Blunt Justice* with you to Capital Planet. Can you explain the admiral's unfortunate experience?"

"I demand total loyalty," Gloriana thundered. "The Goltar Navy answers to the High Council of our people, not the other way around. Aru-Zzat forgot that."

"News of further conflict beat you here by a few days. I heard of the loss of Tau-Rietzke and almost the entirety of the assets you were concentrating there. Strangely, I did not hear this news from *you*."

"If you don't give me what I want, the destruction will continue. I need assault specialists. I want CASPers and a commander who knows how to use them. Moratorium be damned, I need to hire Asbaran Solutions." When the Speaker responded with stony silence, she added, "You do realize there is no defense from this weapon once it has fired. No bunker can be shielded well enough. No ship is fast enough to outrun the shockwave. Perhaps Capital Planet is the next target?"

Toyn-Zhyll was so shocked, he bunched all seven limbs in an instinctive reaction to jump away from a sudden threat.

"I perceive you hadn't considered that, Speaker."

"What is this new threat we face? Who did this?"

Gloriana blew her disgust out of her blowhole. "Nothing but an unwashed mob of pirate scum. With the right assets, I can wipe them from the Spine Nebula and claim these supreme weapons for ourselves."

Toyn-Zhyll licked the rim of his pallid beak. "It appears Asbaran Solutions is otherwise engaged, although I am trying to arrange an alternate."

Gloriana was too surprised to be angry. "How could anything be more important than the nebula? I don't understand."

"Your understanding is not a requirement. You have all the assets we can spare you. Proceed to the Spine Nebula without delay and eliminate the threat. Any weapons of disruptive magnitude shall be placed under Goltar protection for the commonweal of the Galactic Union. If there is even a hint of a possibility of losing control of those weapons to a third party, you are to destroy the weapons utterly. Sterilize the worlds that house them without hesitation."

"How dare you give me orders! As if I were some mere underling officer. I am a High Councilor of the Goltar people. You will explain what is so important that you will not give me Asbaran Solutions. And you will apologize for your insulting demeanor."

Toyn-Zhyll blinked and then leaped into a fighting stance. Two limbs curled around his sitting stump while the other five weaved a confusing pattern through the air. She glimpsed throwing knives and bone pistols being passed from one limb to another so she wouldn't know where his strike would come from.

Gloriana sat still. Outwardly calm, her insides were churning with the urge to respond in kind.

She quietly eased her dagger from its place of concealment that even Toyn-Zhyll's guards had not detected. As she was squeezing the dagger into a fold in her flesh, Toyn-Zhyll cooled and sat down. "I do not doubt the seriousness of the crisis in the Spine Nebula," he told her. "Which is why you shall lead the expedition there. To facilitate this, you shall retain your position as High Councilor as a temporary convenience. If you saw clearly, my old friend, you would perceive that you have been granted a chance to redeem your name."

My old friend. She'd like to slit him open with her dagger, rip out his intestines, and use them to hang him from the Mercenary Guild logo at the top of the building.

But this wasn't the time. She circled and counter-circled her arms in amusement because none of his politicking mattered to her anymore. Vendetta burned through her veins like the pure white heat of a protostar.

Revenge against Xal-Ssap's murderers came first, and she had all the assets she needed for that. As for what happened once she had extracted her revenge, let the pieces fall where they may, and when the game restarted, she would be playing on her own team.

She pushed her eyes to the outer limits of their orbits. "I will not fail," she told him, and she was confident she would not.

Toyn-Zhyll stiffened. She was gratified to see the smear of worry that spread across the face of her treacherous *old friend*.

* * * * *

Chapter Seven

Gelheik Sands Mine, McPherson-3

Sha'Gar had done many things for the Gray Wolves that were illegal in the past, and many which—for the majority of the races in the Galactic Union—were probably considered immoral as well. For those races which worried about things like morals, anyway. In all of those pursuits, though, nothing had scared him to the extent that he was right now.

He had filed the claws on his back feet to their quicks to keep them from clicking and giving him away, or making little scratch marks that could be used to track him. A naturally soft walker anyway, if anyone had seen him, they would have wondered at his strange gait as he slowly transferred his weight from one foot to the other to keep from generating the impact tremors sand burrowers used to track prey.

He had been to one of the Gray Wolves' bases on their home planet of Earth one time and watched a bird called a robin hunt. It could feel the movement of worms under the surface of the Earth through its feet. If the little bird could do that, he had no doubt the sand burrowers could use sentient beings' steps in a similar manner against them.

The sand burrowers weren't the most dangerous entities in the tunnels, though; that designation belonged to the Endless Night troopers, who were armed and moved through the tunnels in groups. While he was worried about the potential for sand burrowers—which had been reported in the tunnels—he was far more worried about the armed soldiers. He'd already seen one group, easily identified by their black garb and distinctive infinity emblems.

Sha'Gar was armed with a knife, and that was it; if he was seen and it came to violence, he wouldn't last more than a second or two against either of the predators. He didn't have armor or even clothes to help protect him; all he had was his natural ability to camouflage himself. Which had worked well when he'd passed the first band of Endless Night troopers. He'd found a small alcove in the tunnel and blended in with the pattern of the rock.

He reached the end of the tunnel and could see where someone—probably Ayean, who was known to be mining here before he disappeared—had broken through into a new area. Sha'Gar smiled as he entered the new tunnel; the bands in the rock were almost perfectly parallel. It would be even easier to mimic.

Although the tunnel was new to him—and to whoever had broken through—it seemed impossibly old. There was lighting on the ceiling, but some sort of rocky crust had grown over most of it over an immense period of time. The coating made the light inconsistent and strangely patterned, which concerned him. While it made pockets of darkness that would be easy to hide in, it also made pockets of darkness where enemies could hide and spring out at him; he slowed his pace even further as his eyes darted around.

He passed an emblem on the wall. Although it had been crusted over, someone had scratched most of it off, and he could see three interlocking circles; the one on the bottom left was a darker color than the other two. The emblem meant something to someone, but he'd never seen it before. He stored the image in his pinplant for later analysis.

The tunnel slowly curved around to the right, but the curve was broken up with zigzags that forced him to go even slower as he negotiated them.

He had traveled some distance—time and space had lost their meanings as he sneaked through the tunnel—when he came to an orifice in the right wall. That was all he could really think to call it. It appeared organic, and if a rock wall could have had an asshole, this was what it would have looked like. It smelled like ass, too, lending credence to the thought. He pushed on it gently; the material was pliable, had a hole in the center, and had some sort of foul-smelling slime on it.

Also, just like an ass.

He was still considering it when he heard voices coming up the passageway from behind him. As he looked about for an alcove to press himself into, he heard voices coming from the opposite direction as well.

There were no alcoves he could make it to in time. Hating the thought of doing it, he closed his eyes, held his breath, and pushed himself up against the hole in the wall. It gave a little, and he stepped back against it, trying to create a smooth flow along the wall so that no one would notice the lizard-shaped protuberance sticking off.

The material gave a little more, and he pressed forward again, knowing the Endless Night soldiers would see him if he didn't. The material of the opening gave suddenly, and, overbalanced, Sha'Gar fell forward and through it to land in a puddle of slime on the other side. He climbed to his feet and dropped into a fighting stance in case any of the soldiers pushed through the orifice after him, but they either hadn't seen him go through or didn't want to follow.

As Sha'Gar began breathing again, he couldn't blame them if it was the latter. He smelled as if he'd been coated in the funk of 40,000 years. When no one followed him, he used the back of his blade to scrape off as much of the slime as he could—not only did it smell disgusting, but it would play hell with his camouflage—then he continued on.

The curve was more pronounced in this passage, and he recognized it was—at least from what he had seen so far—a circle within a circle. Concentric circles. Weird. *Who mined like that?*

A better question, he also realized, was *who puts a weapon in a mine?* There hadn't been time to really think about it before he'd come—everything had been go, go, go—but how could a weapon, surrounded by foul-smelling assholes, reach the surface of the planet, much less worlds hundreds of light years away?

He continued along the new passageway and came to another one of the holes along the right wall. He sighed as he got closer. If anything, this one smelled worse. The other just smelled like ass; this smelled like a garbage dump baking in the sun. In summer. He closed his eyes and held his breath as he pushed up against it. The secret to the installation lay at the center, he suspected.

As he fell into another puddle of slime on the other side, his one fervent hope was that he wouldn't have to go through any more of the openings. Knowing what was coming, he had minimized the amount of slime he got on himself, and he only had to take two breaths while cleaning the muck from his scales. Both were torturous. Zzardars had excellent senses of smell; his would probably be ruined for weeks, if not months.

As it turned out, he had to go through two more orifices, but as he scraped the slime off from the second, he realized he had to be close to the source of…whatever the thing was. The walls had changed—no longer were they the crusted over fake-gneiss of the outer tunnels, they now were…something else.

The walls were now organic in appearance, and they seemed alive. A shudder went down his back as he noticed visible, *pulsing* arteries running through them. Sha'Gar watched them for a second and wondered if he pierced one of them if it would bleed, and what color blood would spill. He went so far as to put the point of his knife to one, but then thought better of it. *If* it was actually alive, and *if* he could actually pierce it, the wall would probably have some way of getting even with him or calling for aid. As both of those responses were contraindicated, he withdrew the knife and continued sneaking along.

He continued to shudder, though, as he walked along; it was like being inside a monster, somehow. A rock monster, to be sure, but a living, breathing creature nonetheless. Susurrations of the airflow through the passageway seemed to confirm the facility's living status.

Fifty meters later, he came to a chamber, and he realized he'd arrived at his target. He pressed along the wall, camouflaging himself against it and looked down into the "heart" of the space.

Several levels of lattice grid work gave access to the thing—*some sort of bulb?*—that grew from the center of the floor and flowered out like some sort of large bush. Everything was old—even older than the tunnels, if that were possible—and the mineral crust here on things was thicker than in the passageways. At some point, it probably had even filled the chamber, and it appeared that the Endless Night—or whoever had originally found it—had mined away at it to reveal the central structure. In other places, the crust reached from floor to ceiling, forming pillars that helped hold up the roof. The lights that had been emplaced reflected off the crust with an ice-blue shimmer.

As Sha'Gar inched into the chamber, he could see the bulb in the center had piping that had been inserted into it, and standard Galactic Union equipment had been mated to the artifact in something straight from a mad scientist's laboratory. Sha'Gar was no engineer, so he didn't understand the functions of most of the machinery in the room, but he did recognize the slates mounted to much of the equipment.

His lunch threatened to revisit him as he looked closer at some of the things attached to the tube system. While some looked like machinery, others had leathery pouches and wrinkled hide covered in waving cilia. This was all held inside some sort of translucent gel, with a thin, transparent skin that was shot through with silver lines that seemed to function like capillaries. Where piping was inserted through the skin, a residue of silver remained, though whether it was crusted silver blood or some sort of leftover welding material was beyond him.

While Sha'Gar may not have understood the room in general, he could easily parse what was going on in it; they were getting ready to fire the weapon—whatever in the Eight Hells of Zithar it was.

Seven technicians were stationed at slates throughout the room, going through the steps of a checklist. He'd seen enough movies where people fired a massive weapon for it to sound eerily familiar. Two Zuul troopers in Endless Night gear oversaw it all from a platform on the other side of the chamber.

"Target selection required," a Zuul in the middle of the chamber called out.

"Set for Sol," an elSha called from one of the slates on the side. It then followed with a series of numbers that was lost on Sha'Gar, but which probably identified the coordinates of the system.

They were already firing the weapon, and it was targeted at Earth's star! He didn't have a moment to lose!

Although his pay didn't funnel through Earth, he knew that his organization would undergo trauma if whatever bad thing they were about to do to Earth happened. Trauma was always bad for an organization, as people tended to lose their lives as individuals used the period of trauma to advance their causes. While Sha'Gar didn't think he was in a position someone else wanted—nor did he have any aspirations of moving up the "company" ladder—all things considered, it was better to keep organizational trauma to a minimum. People tended to live longer that way. And the bonus he'd get for stopping an attack on Earth ought to let him retire like a king, somewhere far, far away from the Spine Nebula.

He had to stop them…but how?

While he was sure he could infiltrate the chamber, he was only armed with a knife; he couldn't kill everyone without being noticed. Especially the security team; they would have to go first. The problem, however, was that there were two of them. *Hmm.*

It would take forever to sneak across the chamber without being seen. It would be faster to come around behind them. He started to ease back out of the chamber but froze when one of the security personnel looked in his direction.

"Step complete," the central Zuul said. "Ready the energy channels."

"Readying the energy channels," a different elSha replied.

The Endless Night trooper looked back down as the scientists talked, and Sha'Gar slipped the rest of the way out of the room. Once clear, he jogged as quickly as he could through the innermost circle, while still trying to go slowly enough to hear anyone who might be patrolling. Happily, he made it to the other side of the chamber without running into any opposition.

He went back into stealth mode as he reached the chamber opening on the other side. Both soldiers were watching the scientists below them rather than the doors to the chamber, and Sha'Gar slid forward to the Zuul on the right. The one on the left was turned slightly away; it would give him a better chance to approach unseen, and an extra half-second of reaction time.

Sha'Gar didn't like killing—he'd much rather get in, grab what he was there for, and get back out again—but there was a difference between disliking it and not being good at it. Like most in the Gray

Wolves' organization, he had plenty of training in killing people, and killing them quietly.

"Weapon pulse forming," an elSha said from below him.

The Zuul flinched as one of Sha'Gar's hands covered the trooper's mouth, and the other drew his knife across the trooper's throat. The Zuul struggled for a second then went limp. Unfortunately, his head flipped to the wrong side, and a spray of blood fountained out to hit the other Zuul on the arm.

"What the—" the other Zuul said, turning.

Sha'Gar released the first soldier and sprang forward as the Zuul tried to bring up his laser rifle. He slapped the rifle's muzzle to the side with one hand, while the other plunged the knife into the Zuul's throat. Both of the soldier's hands went to the hilt of the knife as Sha'Gar and the trooper hit the railing and bounced back. Sha'Gar used the momentum to saw the blade from side to side, and the Zuul's eyes went wide before dimming. He collapsed to the grating, and Sha'Gar sliced through the laser rifle's sling and ripped the weapon away from the soldier.

"What is the meaning of this?" a male Oogar roared from across the room. He'd been underneath Sha'Gar when he was at the other entrance, and Sha'Gar hadn't been able to look down far enough to see him.

"Guards!" a female Lumar next to him screamed. "Guards!"

Sha'Gar snapped the rifle up to his shoulder and fired, but the Oogar pushed her out of the way. Sha'Gar fired at the Oogar, but he dove out the door. All Sha'Gar managed to do was singe the hair off his ass.

He spun back to shoot the Lumar, but she was already running out another door. Sha'Gar turned to target the head Zuul, only to find the alien staring up at him. Their eyes met as an elSha nearby said, "Pulse balance achieved."

The Zuul smiled. "Fire."

Sha'Gar fired and hit the Zuul in the leg as he dove to the side. The creature screamed. Sha'Gar was unable to target him further due to the grating underfoot, though, so he fired at one of the elSha, and the little alien dropped. He shot a second, and then a third before the rest fled in terror.

Knowing he didn't have much time before the scientists sounded the alarm and brought additional troops, Sha'Gar ran down the steps to the closest slate. A countdown timer was running on it, slowly ticking off the numbers in elSha. "97…96…95…" *The weapon was still going to fire!*

"Ugh," one of the elSha he'd shot said, and Sha'Gar ran over to him.

"How do you turn off the weapon?" Sha'Gar asked, grabbing the smaller alien and flipping him onto his back.

"Can't," the reptilian gasped. "Can't be…stopped. Only…paused."

"Can you pause it forever?"

"No." The aliens eyes rolled back and he stilled.

"Shit," Sha'Gar said.

He ran back to the slate again. "78…77…76…"

His eyes scanned the room as raised voices came from the hallway. *Whatever you're going to do, you'd better do it soon.* He was just about to flee when an idea came to him, and he stepped up to the slate where the elSha had called out the targeting data.

"Coordinates accepted," it read. A button at the bottom read, "Tap here to re-enter."

He counted the digits quickly—36—then tapped the button. The screen changed to a series of blanks with "Re-enter coordinates." He randomly tapped in numbers until he'd entered 36.

"Accept?" flashed on the screen, but then his shoulder detonated in pain, and blood sprayed up into his face.

He looked up to find several Zuul in black aiming lasers at him. "Step away from the slate!" one of them ordered.

Sha'Gar looked down at his arm as blood dripped onto the floor. It was hanging by a tendon, and there was little chance of it getting put back on right. Even if he stepped away from the panel, it was unlikely the Zuul would get him the treatment he needed. All he could hope for was a quick death at their hands...one which wasn't very likely as they'd have all sorts of questions to ask him.

"19...18...17..."

"Last chance!" the Zuul roared. "Step away from the slate!"

He could see his peripheral vision starting to go, and his knees started getting wobbly.

"6...5...4..."

"Fuck you!" he said with a snarl as his left hand came up to slap the button on the slate.

He got a glimpse of "Coordinates accepted," then everything went white.

* * * * *

Chapter Eight

Hrothgar's Import/Export, Station 5, Beta-Caerelis

Beowulf shook his head as he reread the transcript from McPherson-3. Sha'Gar had been his best operative, able to get into anyplace Beowulf had needed him. Now he was gone, and his loss would be felt throughout the entire operation in the Spine Nebula. Worse, Sha'Gar was a friend—or as close to a friend as Beowulf had—and he would miss him on a purely personal level.

At least he hadn't sold his life cheaply.

Transcript Begins:

Jankel: *"Have we found out where the pulse went yet?"*

Grael: *"No. Only that the creature entered new coordinates. We blew up something, but Sheerbo is unable to figure out exactly what."*

Jankel: *"Worthless Zuul. Have we at least been able to figure out how the...whatever it was got into the facility?"*

Grael: *"It was a Zzardar. They have the ability to camouflage themselves. The answer is no; we don't know how he got in, but it had to be through the mines. Probably where that Jivool got in."*

Jankel: *"I thought you stepped up the security there. Why the hell did we hire the Besquith? Aren't they supposed to be handling this kind of thing? Finding gaps in our defenses and filling them? We're spending a ludicrous amount of credits on security, and some chameleon can just waltz right through?"*

Grael: *"We have roving patrols and the sand burrowers in the mine tunnels. I guess they thought it would be enough."*

Jankel: *"Obviously, it* isn't *enough. Tell them you're going to dock their pay for incompetence."*

Grael: *"If you want to tell the Besquith you're docking their pay, go ahead. I enjoy having all four of my arms attached. I will, however, tell Saunorak to increase the patrols and set up fixed defensive positions, especially where the mine entrance is. Stop pacing and sit down. You're making me nervous."*

Jankel: *"I* can't *sit down. The damn whatever-it-was shot me in the ass."*

Beowulf chuckled at this every time, although the Oogar would be less of a problem if Sha'Gar had shot him in the head, instead.

Grael: *"Stop being such a baby. You got a nanite treatment for it hours ago."*

Jankel: *"And that hurt worse than getting shot."*

Grael: *"Well, the wound has closed now, so it's all in your big, fat purple head. Sheerho got shot worse than you did, and he's not whining anywhere near as much—he's supervising the training of new elSha technicians to replace the ones the never-to-be-sufficiently-damned Zzardar shot. Now, can we please move forward with our planning?"*

Jankel: *"Planning? This will set us back at least 25 days!"*

Grael: *"I thought the recharge time for the weapon was 10 days."*

Jankel: *"The recharge time depends on the distance it has to shoot. Sol was a longer shot than Tau-Rietzke, so it was going to take longer to recharge in any event. But then that thing—"*

Grael: *"The Zzardar."*

Jankel: *"Yeah, the Zzardar retargeted the weapon and made it fire somewhere on the other side of the galaxy. The weapon wasn't ready for that kind of shot, and a number of the seals blew and will have to be replaced."* Pause. *"Hey, what's this?"*

Grael: *"What's what?"*

Jankel: *"There's something in this pillow I just sat on. It feels like something metal."*

Grael: *"Let me see."* <Sound of cloth ripping.> *"By the seventeenth hell! It's a listening device!"*

Transcript ends.

Beowulf pursed his lips and let out all his breath. They'd obviously found Jombon's transmitter, so there wouldn't be any more intel on the Endless Night, at least until he could get someone else in there. Which would be expensive, if he could find anyone interested in the job in the first place. And time was at a premium. It had taken ten days for the message to get to him, and it would take nine days to get to McPherson-3—seven for the trip to hyperspace and two more to get from the emergence area to the planet—so he was down to only six days to figure out a way to stop the weapon from firing again. And he was flat out of Zzardars.

He needed more information, and there was only one person on the station who could get it for him. If he was even currently *on* the station. And if Joi-Hoi would even talk to him.

The future of Earth was starting to look bleak.

* * * * *

Chapter Nine

CIC, *Midnight Sun,* **Aneb System**

"All hands, ready for hyperspace transit," announced the XO. In the last moments before leaving the Aneb System, Blue glanced at the approaching stargate control facility and wondered about the strange relationship Midnight Sun had struck up with the Sumatozou gate mistress. Khatripowl was her name.

The squad Blue had left at the stargate had proved invaluable according to her. Khatripowl had accepted stoically when Blue had recalled Sergeant Jex's troopers because they were the only intact squad of CASPers she had left. At least until the reinforcements arrived.

Blue hoped to meet her in the flesh one day. It was just as well the bulky alien had flesh aplenty for the both of them, because if they ever did meet, by that time, Blue would have precious little left.

Her symbiotic interface with the ship gave her an enhanced perception of the universe that Blue only half understood. She felt a thump to her chest that she took to be the stargate superconductors spooling up. A split-second later, a swirling vortex materialized within the hoop of the gate, throwing off cascades of strange quarks that warmed her throat.

Each stargate carried its own unique taste. Aneb-4 was rich layers of sweet fire, like a fine old brandy.

She felt a slight flicker of nausea as *Midnight Sun* shot through the portal, and she was remade into a new form as she passed into the weird realm of hyperspace.

I wonder whether I'll still feel that after they're done with me.

In her intimate relationship with the ship, Blue was already set apart from the other Humans on board. For most of the aliens too, hyperspace was an abusive white totality that hurt your head if you stared into it too long. Jenkins had explained to her that many Jeha found hyperspace soothing.

With her enhanced perceptions, Blue found nothing soothing about hyperspace. Nothing safe, either. There were things here. Dangers stalked at the periphery of her perception. They would haunt her waking dreams until they either emerged safely at Wahrner's Grise, or she fell foul of their predation, and *Midnight Sun* became another occasional hyperspace disappearance.

Just as well she would be conscious for most of this transit.

"Hyperspatial bubble integrity green," announced the Helmsman.

"All three reactors report transit shock well within acceptable parameters," said Engineering. "Green across the board."

"Well done, everyone," said Blue. "We didn't blow up, which means we've still got work to do. Commander Flkk'Sss, you have control."

"I have control, aye," confirmed the enormous MinSha, whose significantly larger station sat alongside Blue's in the upper command deck of the spherical CIC.

Blue rose to her feet.

Then sat back down.

Doubts weren't something that normally afflicted Blue, which meant she was inexperienced with dealing with them. Usually, she ignored them, and they went away. Not this time. Where was Gloriana? Why wasn't she already in the nebula?

After they had completed their aggressive look-see at Wahrner's Grise to see if there was anything from Endless Night that needed blowing up, *Midnight Sun* was going to push on to Station 5. Because if Gloriana ever did show up, that's where she would arrive.

Where was she? If she reneged on her deal, Blue was going to have a serious problem with the squid bitch.

"She'll betray me sooner or later," she argued with herself.

"Of course she will. The question is when."

"Have you ever considered that maybe the fact Gloriana hasn't made an appearance tells you that the betrayal is now?"

"Surprisingly, yes, I have. But my luck hasn't run out yet. I'd feel if it had."

"You're mad."

"No, *you're* mad."

"You're going to be remade, and then you're going to die. And you call *me* mad. Why the hell would you go ahead with this?"

Why? Her pinplants caught the half-formed thought and projected a pinview of her sister embracing Branco.

She wouldn't let Sun down. Not this time.

Blue rose to her feet with her normal air of purpose. She walked over to her executive officer and peered up into her huge, ruby insectoid eyes. "You know our mission in Wahrner's Grise. If I remain indisposed after emergence, I trust you to complete the mission without me."

The MinSha tilted her head. "Are you unwell, Captain?"

She felt the command crew's attention on her. They deserved a proper explanation.

"*Midnight Sun* has the best crew of any ship in the Union. The ship cannot function properly without you. However, let's not dance around the truth. *Midnight Sun* is not like any other ship. She's alive. Not an AI, but a living thing. Organic. Immortal perhaps. And...I can't help thinking, reminiscent of the ancient engine we left behind on Aneb-4. Maybe organic machines were cutting-edge tech a few tens of millennia ago?"

She considered that. Maybe *Midnight Sun* and the great engine really *were* connected?

"But I digress. The ship and I have a bond. Practical upshot, for brief periods, the ship and I can operate ourselves without the need for further crew. It's a unique situation and a dangerous one. Without all of you around me, I don't know that I can stop being the ship. However, there may come a time soon when we need *Midnight Sun* to be more than an eccentrically configured battlecruiser. We need her to be a battle winner."

"She already is a battle winner, ma'am," shouted Konchill.

Blue leaned over the guardrail and beamed down at the Bakulu tactical officer while cheers washed through the CIC.

She clasped her hands behind her back and stood tall with pride. "That she is, Lieutenant. And that we are. There may come a moment, however, when *Midnight Sun* needs to become still more."

Blue licked her lips.

She liked them. Her lips were firm and fleshy. A year of practicing in front of the mirror when she was twelve had left her with a killer pout. Most of all, they helped to remind her that she was a woman.

Would she still be able to pout after the procedure?

"Are you to be enhanced, Captain?" asked the MinSha.

Blue nodded. Heart beating, this wasn't as easy as it should be.

"As Chief Engineer Jenkins frequently reminds me, we barely open the throttle of *Midnight Sun*'s engines. If we did, we would be squashed like bugs. No offence intended to the insectoids among you. There are Goltar techs waiting for me on Deck Four to make me gee-hardened."

"What acceleration will she be able to go without killing you?" asked Ensign Dahmer.

Blue gave her helmsman a grateful nod. A lot of the best flight jockeys in her experience had egos as big as their skill sets. Dahmer knew her captain would take over her role on occasion, but then she'd signed on knowing her captain was…*unconventional*. Other than the old sweats from the days when the Midnighters had been called the Void, they all had.

"If the procedure goes well," she replied, "I will be rated for 23 Gs acceleration."

Eyes went wide. Antennae fell flat along backs. No doubt wings would have flapped if she'd hired any Sidar. "And I mean a *sustained* 23 Gs," she clarified.

The jaws dropping to the deck and the rampant gasps were not comforting.

Someone Human whispered, "No!"

Her heart thundered in her chest. Sustained 23 Gs. This wasn't like the inner tinkering that allowed Sergeant Jex to corner his ultra-speedway bike at high gees. Whatever she was about to become, it wouldn't be Human.

"Good luck, ma'am," said Flkk'Sss, as if this were just one more eccentricity from her Human CO. "*Midnight Sun* will be in safe foot-hands."

"I know it will, Commander. Carry on."

Blue made her way off the command deck, unable to hide the tremble in her legs.

The decision had made sense when she'd talked it over with the ship the night before and arrived at the decision.

So why did it feel as if she were marching off to her own execution?

* * * * *

Chapter Ten

EMS *Gobi Desert*, Earth Orbit, Sol System

Sansar surveyed the men and women assembled in the hangar bay, wishing for a dream in which all the people in front of her came home safely. It wasn't the group she wanted to take with her, knowing that conflict—and open warfare—wasn't just a possibility; it was imminent.

Although one company—Alpha Company—was solid, and its members were largely made up of Omega War veterans, Bravo Company was a mélange of experienced troopers and cadre recruits, led by relatively inexperienced members of her Golden Horde family. She smiled as she saw the dozen SalSha standing around. Their 'formation' was less a military assembly and more a collection of friends, but at least most of them were facing her. Some of them even appeared to be paying her a modicum of attention, too.

"Thank you all for coming today," she said. "Especially to the troopers who signed on the last few days not knowing where we were going or what we were going to do." She nodded to the Bravo Company squad leaders, all of which had commanded their own companies during the Omega War. Unfortunately, like many merc organizations during the war, their companies had been shot out from under them. While they may ultimately come back to reorganize them again, death benefits had wiped out most of their coffers, and they needed credits to buy their way back into the game.

Without being able to take contracts, though, earning credits was a difficult thing, which had led them here. And who knew what other demons from the Omega War drove them?

"I have a little more information I can share with you," she continued. "We will be heading to the Spine Nebula, and I expect there to be significant combat operations once we get there. Anyone who wants to leave now is welcome to do so, and I will not put any black marks on their records as you didn't know that when you signed on. Anyone want to leave?"

There were some sidelong glances cast, especially among the veterans, but no one volunteered to leave. Sansar nodded once. "Thank you for your trust. I will be raising all of your combat bonuses 10%, so if we do encounter fighting—which I expect we will—I will try to compensate you accordingly.

"I'm sure a number of you are wondering, 'What's worth going to the Spine Nebula for?' Others are probably just wondering, 'What the hell's a Spine Nebula?'" A number of people chuckled; some of them obviously *had* been wondering that. "The Spine Nebula is a group of about 15 stars, but the nature of the nebula is such that there is only one way in and one way out.

"As to why we're going, the mission is simple; we're going to the Spine Nebula to save the Earth." A number of people muttered. "No, I'm serious. Our mission is nothing short of saving the Earth. The Golden Horde has assets in place that found out there is a weapon there which can cause our sun to explode. They were going to try to stop it from firing, but they had no idea whether they'd be successful or not. They also didn't know if there were other similar weapons in the area.

"Our mission is simple. We're going to the Spine Nebula to make sure the weapon is destroyed, and that there aren't any more of these star-killer weapons."

If she hadn't had their attention before, she certainly did now.

"Now, I know you'll have lots of questions, and I will try to keep you informed. While I don't have all the answers, here are the ones I can give you now. No, no one else on Earth knows. I don't have hard evidence that I can give the planet's leaders as proof, and if this information got out, there would be mass panic." She paused. "As I'm sure you're all aware, the planet's in bad enough shape as it is; it doesn't need even more reasons for people to panic. So no, don't send messages to your wife or kids or friends.

"Why aren't we taking more troops? Because there aren't any. Humanity is spread thin and is disorganized. It would take forever to put something like this together as a coalition, and the truth is, we don't have time. Also, a big force would be seen coming in and might cause our enemy to fire the weapon prematurely, and no one wants their weapons to go off prematurely." She paused as a chuckle went through the group. "The bottom line is we represent Earth's best chance to accomplish this mission before anything can happen. I will send out additional information as we receive it, but for now, your goal is simple—train.

"We need to be working together on arrival, so I want all of you to train like there is no tomorrow, or—for the Earth—there may not be. For all of you in Bravo Company, listen to your leaders; they've been in combat and know what they're doing."

She took a moment to try to meet each person's eyes. She saw a number of things, but fear won out, especially among the Bravo

Company newbies. *It will be up to their leaders to whip them into shape. And to do so quickly.*

"Dismissed!" she ordered. "Bravo Company squad leaders, if you would please stay behind a moment," she added.

The four of them clustered around, looking at her expectantly. "Thank you all for joining up," she said. "I can't help but feeling we will need every bit of your experience in this mission."

They all nodded, their expressions grave.

"I wanted to talk with all of you for a moment and make sure none of you were going to have issues with the chain of command." Two of the four men looked surprised, as if the thought hadn't crossed their minds, but the other two nodded knowingly.

"I know you've all been here before," she continued, "and I know all of you can do the job we're faced with; that's not what I wanted to talk with you about." Her eyes swept the men around her. "You've all owned—and led—your own companies. Although I've tried to compensate you for your experience, I don't have suitable positions for you, and if I did, there'd be no way to choose which of you would lead and which of you would follow. I also have young leaders of my own I need to train for the Golden Horde's continuity. As such, I need you—for a number of reasons—to fill the positions you've been given.

"Still, mercs have egos, and the higher you go, usually the bigger the ego, and not everyone can step back from being in charge, once they've been in that position." Her eyes swept the men again, all of whom towered about a foot over her. "Worse, I'm asking you to serve under relatively junior officers, and women at that. I don't know any of you well, so I don't know if this is something you're capable of. Ideally, we would have time to work through this, but the nature of this mission is such that we don't. There's also no time to deal with it later, so I need to know right now—are there going to be any issues with you being squad leaders for this mission and serving under my junior officers?"

"Are you suggesting we can't take orders?" Zach White asked.

"Not at all. I'm asking if you can work for relatively junior officers and do so in such a manner as to successfully complete this mission."

"Junior?" David Melsome asked with a chuckle. "They look like kids."

Sansar nodded. "They're young, but they are extremely talented, and they have had plenty of training in what we're doing. Are they as experienced as you? No. But then again, senior officers have always counted on their senior enlisted members to help develop their junior officers. You four—due to your unique experiences—are even more qualified to help mold them than most, but it will take a light touch. They are aware of how much experience you have, and they are—frankly—a little in awe of you, but they will do their best to be worthy of leading you. The question is, will you allow yourselves to be led and help support them?"

The men nodded.

"You said someone's trying to blow up our sun, ma'am?" Gregory Franklin asked. Sansar nodded. "Then I don't see how we can do anything less than be supportive. I have a lot of things here I'd like to come back to."

Zach White cleared his throat. "Are you saying we have to blindly follow everything they tell us to do, even when we know it's wrong?"

"What I'm telling you is to be supportive. Use private channels to them if you need to disagree with them. There may be occasions, however, where there isn't time to disagree. If that happens, I expect you to do what you're told and try to make the best of a bad situation. Do you have an issue with that?"

"No, ma'am," White said.

"I appreciate the compensation," Jim McCoy said with a smile. "I think we're probably the best paid squad leaders in history."

The other squad leaders smiled. "That's a fact," Franklin added. "It's more than my last boss paid me, that asshole."

"Wait," Melsome said. "Weren't *you* your last boss?"

"Yes I was. And I was a cheap bastard."

All the men laughed at that, and Sansar found herself laughing along with them. It broke the tension, for which she was grateful. "All right, so we're all good?"

Franklin looked at the other men and then nodded. "Yes, ma'am; I think we are."

* * * * *

Chapter Eleven

Patriot Observation Boat *Critical Eye*,
McPherson's Star System

"What in the name of the fifteenth slime hell is this?" Jutta pivoted her eye turrets at her chair arm and the offending goop she'd dipped her tail into. She flicked it away to land with a splat on the bulkhead viewscreen.

Renaud Novotna wrinkled his nose at the elSha's disgusting act, but to be fair, the mess had been left by the two Zuul from the last shift. He didn't know what the hell they'd been up to, but they'd left the flight deck looking as if the boat had been mugged.

He knew Humans had a bad habit of equating aliens to the Earth animals they resembled and assuming they shared similar characteristics. Zuul looked canine, but they weren't dogs.

Try as he might, though, Renaud couldn't avoid thinking of the dogs his brother-in-law allowed to run riot over his property near Trois-Rivières.

When they got excited, his dogs would hump anything.

When they got bored…it was the same outcome.

"You know what Zuul are like," said Jutta. The little elSha shook herself in disgust. "They will spend the first week mounting each other. Now they are attempting to mate with the furniture. I mean…" An evil glint came to the elSha's reptilian eye. "Even you can keep your rutting impulse at bay, Renaud. Although your Human stink is worse than both Zuul together."

"Jutta!" Renaud warned. "We agreed to play nice."

Jutta's mouth gaped—a sign of elSha amusement. "Just messing with you, kid."

"And stop calling me kid."

Jutta licked her lips. "Why? I'm five times your age."

Renaud rose from his seat and loomed over the little alien. "And I'm at least five times your size, little old lady."

"Why that's..." Jutta's tail flicked aggressively. "That's species-ist!"

Renaud rolled his eyes when he realized the elSha's jaw was agape once more.

He retreated to his post. "Please," he begged. "We've only got another two days until we're relieved. Let's try to get through that without killing each other."

The elSha didn't answer. She had rotated her eye turrets to focus on the feed coming from *Critical Eye*'s telescope. "We have inbound traffic."

Renaud worked the controls of his station. "Activating passive sensor recording."

His station viewscreen split into a dozen panels, each revealing a distinct view of the McPherson's Star emergence point unique to one of the devices in the sensor pod slung under the converted pinnace. The displays ranged from an empty void to sparkle sprays as the starships emerged from hyperspace in a splash of exotic particles.

The only thing he couldn't see in his screen was the visual spectrum, which Jutta was getting from the telescope.

Renaud pinlinked to the elSha's feed and watched the inbound ships appear in a pinview overlay.

The craft looked military.

"What do you see?" he asked. As far as the other three crew of the Patriot observation boat were concerned, a Human lowlife like Renaud didn't possess anything so fancy as pinplants.

"*Seed*-class escort frigates detaching from *Yperex*-class destroyers. Gotta be our Maki friends."

"Recommend keeping to passive sensors," said Renaud.

"Passive only, agreed," replied the elSha, who was the officer in charge of this watch. "Be ready to bring up active sensors if I spot anything really interesting."

Renaud had decidedly mixed feelings about the prospect of things getting *interesting*.

When Endless Night had begun the systematic domination of the Spine Nebula, the Patriot Navy had kept close watch over stargates, emergence points, and the major planets and orbitals. Every movement of the Maki Spinning Shield fleet in the pay of the Night was observed, and the intel passed across the nebula.

That made the observation ships legitimate targets as far as the Maki were concerned, and the Patriots had learned the hard way to operate cold and lengthy rotations safely away from the ecliptic plane.

The full Maki fleet was here. Ten frigates in all. Two destroyers and *Vindictive*, the sole battlecruiser that had survived the attention of first the Tyzhounes and then *Midnight Sun*. More ships followed: freighters, frigates, and ships of unknown classes that looked civilian but could hide some nasty surprises.

"Looks like an invasion fleet," said Jutta when she'd packaged her report and sent it off to fly through the Patriot network.

She flicked her tail nervously. Renaud couldn't blame her. It looked as if the Night was coming to claim the new capital of the Spine Nebula.

"Drool," said Jutta.

Renaud frowned. "Excuse me?"

"Zuul drool. That's what I was flicking off the chair arm. Nothing worse. Isn't that bad enough? Dirty dogs!"

"I swear I'm counting down the seconds until we get home," said Renaud.

"Home…" Jutta gave a chuffing laugh. "If that little fleet keeps to the speed of its slowest vessel, then we will beat them back to McPherson-3, but it will be close. And what then?"

What indeed? The danger the Endless Night ships represented could easily be of the terminal variety. He hadn't been told explicitly, but he had assembled the pieces over the last few weeks and realized that someone in the network had already been taken out.

Renaud made a decision. He had to risk blowing his cover.

He took a copy of the report Jutta had sent, added additional observations of his own, and sent the message out using the depth-sounding laser he'd reconfigured secretly as a comm beam.

His report was encoded using a unique evolving code page system and then wrapped in encryption so sophisticated that the best Patriot decryption experts would be scratching their heads for months trying to figure it out.

Renaud's report was not for Patriot ears and eyes. This was Gray Wolf business too.

* * * * *

Chapter Twelve

Recycling Plant, Vane 2, Station 5, Beta-Caerelis System

"This mess just gets better and better," Beowulf muttered bitterly as he skirted around a stack of empty freight boxes on his way to meet his contact.

First there had been Sansar's vision. It had seemed fanciful until the intel Jombon had wrangled out of McPherson-3.

Beowulf wanted assets on that world desperately. But Sha'Gar was dead, and a sleeper he had inserted into the Patriots had gone to ground to avoid capture soon after reporting Endless Night had arrived at McPherson's Star in force.

The Gray Wolves had been working the nebula for years. It was their kind of place, full of "their" kind of people and rich with desperation and secrets.

A little too many secrets as it turned out.

Only now was Beowulf hearing rumors that the blasted worlds sunward of Station 5 weren't as dead as everyone thought. And the sharp increase in traffic entering the L5 scrapyards was not matched by the ships returning.

And always, his fear for Earth. For all he knew, the second transcript from McPherson-3 was a setup, and Earth was already burning in hellfire.

All he could do was his job, though; one thing at a time.

And for now, that meant meeting Joi-Hoi, a Gtandan working in the scrap recycling business who had a knack for sniffing out profitable dirt with his fat, piggy nose.

The route ahead between the open containers of scrap metal narrowed, feeding into stacks of metal barrels marked with Union-standard sigils warning of corrosive chemical content.

He stopped.

The place was a dump.

But the tingle down his spine said this was more than a Gtandan's sloppy work environment.

It was a trap.

He pulled down on the concealment flaps beneath the arms of his leather duster and drew his plastic pistol and titanium knife.

"Is that all you've got, little Human?"

He spun about and found himself face-to-face with an Oogar and two Lumar.

They were dressed all in black, even down to the laced-up rubber boots. They hadn't just been shopping at the fashion-for-fascists stores, either, because he also recognized the bulges of armor vests beneath their clothes.

The infinity symbol of the Endless Night was stitched onto their breasts, as if the black attire wasn't enough symbolism.

He fired at the Oogar's head and got lucky when the hollow point round pierced his eye and minced the purple bear's brains.

It was a lucky shot. The custom pistol was accurate only to about half an inch. He was carrying it because firearms restrictions on the orbital were as enthusiastically enforced as they were onerous.

Still, so long as the luck continued running in his favor, he didn't give a shit.

He waited long enough to be sure the Lumar were too confused to press the attack, then he turned and fled.

He managed four strides before he noticed a half dozen Endless Night Zuul standing in front of the chemical drums with pistols drawn on him.

And these weapons weren't plastic shite.

Prancing over the top of the chemical drums was an elSha. Dark blue stripes passed over her eye turret like the woad warpaint of a Celtic warrior. And she carried a slight limp after a gang boss had ripped off a few of her toes.

She looked like she should be kept in a pet cage and fed live crickets once a day, but looks could be deceiving. This was Miss Franjo, a linchpin of the Endless Night operation on Station 5 that Beowulf had gone to considerable lengths to avoid.

Franjo settled on the edge of a drum and flicked a fat disc onto the deck.

When it landed with a fleshy thud, Beowulf realized what it was. A Gtandan snout.

Joi-Hoi had sniffed out his last information.

"I've been scratching away in the dirt for some time now," Franjo told him. "Trying to unearth connections. Sha'Gar. Joi-Hoi." She tilted her head. "The name Jombon mean anything to you? No...don't tell me. It would spoil the fun of finding out who you are. And more importantly, where you will lead me."

Beowulf's pistol had a three-round magazine. One was already spent inside the Oogar's skull. That left one for Franjo. And the last to blow his own brains out.

He dug for a sarcastic quip to throw at the elSha, but he was all out. Dammit!

Beowulf had done some insanely dangerous things but shooting himself was hardest of all.

He eased his finger around the trigger guard and took a last, deep breath.

"Give!" barked a Lumar behind him.

He snapped a shot at the elSha, but the Lumar hands grabbed his arms and the round went skimming along the deck as he fought for control. He just needed to win a gap in which to fire up into his head, but against the two Lumar, he was never going to win.

The pistol was wrenched painfully from his hand.

A moment later, so too was his knife.

"Are you ready to talk?" asked Franjo. "If you prefer, I can organize some torture first. You wouldn't be alone, I assure you. We have a large supply of innocents to torture in front of your eyes. Well…" She held her mouth agape for a few seconds. "As innocent as they get on *this* station."

"You can go to hell, lizard. There's no one who matters to me on Station 5. You can kill 'em all for all I care. I won't talk."

He took grim satisfaction from seeing the elSha flick her tail in irritation. It was the last time he would. Anything beyond this point would be pain and then death.

He glared defiance at Franjo, but his mouth dropped open as she suddenly sailed through the air, flailing limbs and tail, screaming with fear.

The chemical drums toppled over, crushing the Zuul.

Shots rang out from behind him, and he felt the Lumar's grip slacken.

He didn't wait around to find out what the hell was going on. He grabbed his knife out of the hand of a dying Lumar and dove for cover behind a pallet stack.

The chemical drums had been charged by two massive beetles the size of baby rhinos and sprouting horns like…well, dung beetles. They were Vaga, a race of laborers and miners. Someone had shot holes through the drums, and they were spilling their contents over the Zuul trapped beneath them.

From the high-pitched whines and the acrid stench of burning flesh and fur, those warning sigils hadn't been an over-bureaucratic caution.

A pair of elSha scurried over the dead Lumar, pointing and jabbering at Beowulf from a safe distance.

"Here he is! Here he is!"

One of them walked over gingerly and placed his plastic pistol close by him. By the way the elSha handled the piece, you'd think it was a stick of sweaty dynamite.

The elSha made him think of Franjo. He stood and searched for the heartless little lizard melting in the chemical spill. She was nowhere to be seen.

He looked for exits. The two Vaga were milling aimlessly near the dying Zuul, and the two excitable elSha looked as if they would run screaming if he whispered boo at them.

But there had been someone laying down accurate rifle fire into this killing zone.

Beowulf took a cautious couple of steps forward and scooped his pistol from the dirt. It had one round left.

He thumbed on the safety and put it back into concealment. He was hopelessly outgunned.

A Blevin walked into view.

"Who are you?" she asked.

He blinked. It was the waitress from the bar.

"Did you shoot those Lumar?" he asked.

"I did." There was no sign of a rifle. "Who are you?" she demanded.

"That's my concern. Who are *you*?"

She rolled her eyes, indicating the Endless Night corpses and soon-to-be corpses. "I think that's abundantly clear. I'm a Spine Patriot. My name is Laverna, and I was proud to call Captain Jenkins my employer."

"Jenkins? Wait…" He accessed digital memories. "Captain Lenworth Rushby Jenkins, skipper and owner of the *Unlikely Regret*?"

Laverna nodded in the Human fashion, which added credibility to her claim to be familiar with Humans.

"The Midnight sisters served there," Beowulf continued. "In fact, Major Sun has been spending time on *Unlikely Regret* of late."

"We rescued her from the Night. There was talk of spacing her. At the time, the Goltar had manipulated the Midnighters into being enemies of the Patriots. But Sun has been one of my closest friends."

The Blevin froze, realizing she had said too much. She'd done more than enough to impress Beowulf with her shadow work, but she wasn't a pro.

"I have overheard you speaking of preparing the ground," she said. "I think you have people coming here. Military forces. Yes?"

He shrugged, giving nothing away.

The Blevin rubbed her leathery brown chin with a six-fingered hand. "Why would military forces come here?" she mused, watching for his reaction. "The systems of the nebula are not rich, and if you wish to drain us of what money we have, you must first get through Endless Night and the Patriots."

"We make credits wherever we can," Beowulf said slyly. "We're no patriots and God knows we're no angels, but we're not here to suck the credits out of your people."

He laughed and knew his smile was reaching his eyes. "You wouldn't believe me even if I did tell you." He cut his laughter dead.

"Laverna, I thank you for your assistance—"

"We saved your life."

"Okay." Beowulf held his hands out in surrender. "You got me. Thank you for saving my life. I go by the name of Beowulf. I'll repay the favor if I can, but now it's time to go our separate ways."

"I claim my favor now. Tell me why you are here. If it's so unbelievable, your words can hardly matter."

He shrugged. "My people are coming—at least I hope they're coming—to stop the Earth from being blown up."

"The Human home world?" She grinned, an unsettling sight with lips rolled up and a lot of teeth showing. "Are you sure you mean *blown up*, or do you mean bombarded with fury from its exploding star, its oceans and atmosphere boiled into space, and its glowing carcass left as an irradiated ember?"

Beowulf gave a low whistle to cover the chill that had suddenly come over him. "You know too damned much for a waitress at a spacer dive bar."

"You have people coming. Mr. Beowulf. So do we. It's not a well-kept secret. Goltar. Midnighters. Patriots. All will assemble here soon at Station 5."

"So you're all best buddies. Comrades in arms?"

"Hardly. We detest the Goltar, and we were at war with the Midnighters. The Goltar see other races as unimportant microbes. And their leader has a burning desire to punish Captain Blue for her insolence. I could go on. But we are united in our desire to prevent the Endless Night from turning the Spine Nebula into their domain from which they can reach out and destroy any star system in the Union at will. Whoever your associates are, Mr. Beowulf, do you think they would share those objectives?"

"I do. If they're coming, which I hope they are."

"Then it's time to stop lurking in the shadows and join forces."

He shook his head. "Never gonna happen. The shadows are my home. But my…associates, on the other hand…they're the type to stand proud in an eight-foot-tall suit of ceramic and metal and express their point of view with MAC fire and missiles."

"You mean CASPers?"

"Oh, yeah."

"I think we should talk further. Now."

Beowulf considered the low-life Blevin. Until that transcript had been smuggled off McPherson-3, Laverna would have been better placed to interpret Sansar Enkh's visions than anyone in the Horde or the Wolves. Maybe she still was.

"You're right," he said. "Let's prepare the way together."

"I know a bar," she said with that ugly grin of hers. "So do you. I finish my shift tonight at 23:50."

She turned without another word and led her menagerie of beetles and lizards away like some kind of demented space zoo.

"Interesting," he mused as he watched them go.

He heard footsteps approach from the spinward frame wall, and he vanished into the shadows. He had work that needed doing. And this time he wasn't going to be seen.

* * * * *

Chapter Thirteen

EMS *Gobi Desert*, Hyperspace

Staff Sergeant Franklin kicked in the door and strode into the MinSha command center with the rest of First Squad storming in behind him. "Hands up!" he yelled over his external speakers. "Grasping legs up!" he amended, feeling foolish, when the MinSha looked at each other, trying to decide what he wanted.

Most of the personnel in the center were unarmed, and the few who had weapons didn't make a play for them when they saw how overwhelmed their forces were. Franklin had hoped they would—he'd been in his suit for about 10 of the last 12 hours and wanted to blast something, now that the odds were finally in his favor.

Instead, all motion froze, the simulation ended, and the voice of Captain Naran Enkh came over the system. "Congratulations, Bravo Company. That's a successful assault, and we'll call it a day with that. Re-stow all gear, then platoon leaders can secure their platoons for chow. Well done, all!"

Franklin chuckled. *Well done on the fourth try, anyway.* He'd recognized the error the first time they'd gone through the simulation and had told Lieutenant Delkii Enkh about it, but they'd done the same thing the second and third time. The fourth attempt—where they'd finally followed his suggestion—was the first time they were successful.

"Thank you for the suggestion," Delkii said over a private channel to him.

"Sure," he commed back. "Could have saved ourselves some trouble if we'd tried it a little sooner."

"I know," Delkii said. "But I didn't think it was my place to tell Naran on the second attempt, and then she wouldn't listen to me on the third."

"I see. Well, we'll just have to keep working on the chain of command," Franklin said, keeping the annoyance out of his voice. "We'll get there."

* * *

"Thank you for seeing me," Franklin said as he entered Sansar's office an hour later.

"You said it was important…"

"And I think it is." Sansar indicated a seat and he walked in and sat. It was expensive to run the engines while in hyperspace, and having gravity was a luxury he wasn't used to.

He chewed his lip for a second, until Sansar raised an eyebrow and asked, "Yes?"

"I'm not sure how to phrase this, ma'am," Franklin replied. "I'm totally onboard with being a good trooper, and I'm aware that I'm jumping the chain of command…but this once, I thought it was necessary."

"I think you're experienced enough to have earned a little leeway as far as that's concerned," Sansar replied. "What seems to be the issue?"

"Well we just got done with the simulators—"

"I saw. It took four tries to accomplish the objective. We will have to keep working; that won't be good enough."

Franklin nodded. "Yes, ma'am. And I'm sure we'll get there if we keep working. The problem is, though, that we don't have enough time to work through all our issues. And, quite honestly, we don't need to."

"What do you mean?"

"I mean that I could see the problem on the first run through. Your skill set—what the Golden Horde normally does—is defensive in nature, and most of your planning and experience is in that arena. I've done a lot of assault missions and know more about it, and from a practical perspective, too. I didn't say anything at the time, though, because I wanted your officers to have a chance to figure it out on their own."

Sansar nodded. "Thank you; they need that chance."

"But they didn't see the problem, so I said something the second time."

"And you still failed."

"Yes, because the lieutenant didn't pass it up to the captain, because she wasn't sure it was her place to do so. Then, on the third try, when she finally did, the captain didn't listen to her. Finally, on the fourth run, the captain took the advice, and we were successful."

"It took too long to learn the lesson," Sansar noted. Franklin nodded. "So, what is your solution?"

"You need a senior enlisted at the company level like Alpha Company has; someone with direct access to the captain. If you took someone like Staff Sergeant Melsome and made him the company first sergeant, or something along those lines, he would have direct access to Captain Naran and could advise her himself. If any of the other squad leaders saw something, we could pass it up to him, and he could pass it to the captain." Franklin shrugged. "We're doing our best to help the lieutenants, but the captain—the person who needs the assistance the most to make effective command decisions—doesn't have access to that support. I'm not trying to jump the chain of command, but to help Captain Naran be successful." He smiled. "That will, of course, ultimately keep more of us alive, so I *do* have a bit of a vested interest in it."

"That makes good sense," Sansar said. "There wasn't time to put Bravo Company together the way it should have been, and trying to get everyone slotted correctly probably ended up with some oversights as we tried to keep everything fair and equal. Not having a senior enlisted at the company level is one of them. Happily, that's something that is easily rectifiable. Thanks, First Sergeant Franklin."

"That's Staff Sergeant Franklin," he said, indicating his rank patch.

"Not anymore. It was a great idea to create the position, and you're my choice to fill it. I will let Captain Naran know."

* * *

Franklin knocked on the door frame of Captain Naran Enkh's small office a couple of hours later. "You wanted to see me, ma'am?"

Naran looked up and motioned to the only chair on the other side of the miniature desk. "Yes, please have a seat." The officer was a little taller and thinner than Delkii, and she looked like she'd been out in the sun a lot more. She also looked like she might have been a couple years older, but she still looked young enough to be his daughter. *I've been in this business too long.*

Unlike Delkii, Naran also wasn't afraid to meet his gaze, and she gave him a hard, appraising look that told him her upbringing hadn't been all sunshine and roses. The look said she was either evaluating what Franklin could do for her or maybe what he intended to do *to* her. The way she held herself had a tough, challenging look, like she'd be the first to flip out her sword blade and go head-to-head with an alien. There were times where that was the right thing to do, but others where it definitely *wasn't*. Hopefully, she'd survive to know the difference between them.

"What can I do for you, ma'am?" Franklin said as he sat.

Naran made a face like she'd eaten something bitter. "Stop calling me ma'am, for one, if you please. Having someone 30 years older than me calling me that is weird."

"I will in here," Franklin replied, "but you're 'ma'am' in front of the troops, ma'am. And it probably isn't more than 25 years," he added with a smile. "What else can I do for you?"

"Nothing; I just wanted to meet the man that Sansar put to spy on me."

"Is that what this is about?" His smile grew. "I'm sorry you think of it that way. I'm to blame for it. I suggested to the colonel that it would make things easier on you to have a senior enlisted at the company level—just like Alpha Company does—not as a means of spying on you. You're young, as you just admitted, and I thought having one of the prior company commanders available to you as a sounding board and a mentor might help you, like we're doing at the platoon level for Lieutenants Delkii and Terbish. And, the truth be it known, I recommended someone else for the job, but Sansar chose me instead."

"Not to spy?"

Franklin shook his head. "Nope. Sansar never suggested reporting back to her. My purpose is to give you access to my experience as a merc so you can make informed decisions, rather than just guessing on your own what's best. I won't ever make you look bad in front of the troops; anything I suggest will be on a private comm channel."

"Really?" she asked, brightening. Her hard edge slipped a little, and he realized her tough exterior was probably a mask she'd come to wear to protect herself in what was—admittedly—somewhat of a macho profession. The look made her more endearing, rather than less, though in a paternal sort of way. The age difference probably *was* closer to 30 years.

"Honest." He sighed. "Can I be totally candid with you?"

"Uh…yes?" she asked, although her guard popped back up, and she looked terrified of the question.

Franklin smiled. "Look, the former company commanders aren't here to make you fail. None of us want your job. If anything, the opposite is true. We want you to be successful because we want you to bring back all of us—alive!—when we return. We're mercs; we're just here for the paycheck. We'll do whatever we can do to make the unit successful and bring everyone home."

Naran stared at him a moment, as if trying to discern the truth behind his words. Finally, she nodded once, apparently satisfied, and relaxed again. "Okay," she said. "In that case, can I ask you a few questions about the simulator today?"

* * * * *

Chapter Fourteen

Aneb Government Buildings, Lhanganhoe, Aneb-4

"What do you mean Aneb-4 is gonna blow up?"

Sun crossed her arms and fixed the HecSha with a stare. "The same as the last three times I told you. And it's not just Aneb-4—"

"Yeah. Yeah, I got it. Everything's gonna blow in the entire system. Including the stargate. Trust me, Major, for normal people who don't deal professionally in death, the idea that everyone on Aneb-4 will burn is plenty big enough to start off with."

The Prime Representative of the Aneb system closed the nictitating membranes over his eyes and kept them there.

Sun didn't have time for this. *Unlikely Regret* was leaving for the stargate in two days, leading a flotilla of Spine Patriot ships loaded to the gunwales with fighters and supplies. There would be no delays. And here she was in a fourth-floor meeting space of a downtown office block that had been commandeered as the new government headquarters, sitting across a plastic table from the newly...*chosen* political leader who was hiding behind his milky eye membranes.

She'd expected anger from Rievskegg. Violence. And definitely sharper clothing and furnishings that weren't so worn. The message that she was taking her ships and abandoning tens of millions of citizens to die was not one she'd expected to be an easy sell.

But it seemed her extraction team could remain on standby for now.

Rievskegg was sticking stubbornly to the denial stage, and Hec-Sha stubbornness was legendary.

Sun pushed her slate across the table and played the recording of Unthor's destruction.

Clutching the stained green sash that never left his neck, Rievskegg lowered his big, flattened head and stared at the recorded horror through the slits of his fractionally opened membranes.

"I believe Tau-Rietzke has suffered the same fate," Sun added.

She pictured the terraced gardens of the Kuber Park base, looking out over the trees as the orange disc of Psilydia sank in the late-afternoon sky. It had been such a peaceful place that her mind couldn't accept it had been blasted into extinction by such obscene violence, despite the Cartography Guild removing the system from its nav-charts.

Maybe she *was* a professional death dealer, but even she could get stuck in denial.

"I hope your intelligence about Tau-Rietzke proves false," said Rievskegg. "However, let us concentrate instead on intelligence of my own, Major Sun. I have been on Aneb-4 my entire life, and my sources are adamant that the planet has not yet been exterminated by a starkiller weapon. I am convinced I would have noticed such an event."

"Don't dismiss the danger, Rievskegg. Endless Night's enemies are on Aneb-4, and I suspect they will take their defeat here personally. Both good reasons to target this place for destruction. Why else would they evacuate their assets across the entire system?"

"Perhaps they ran away because they feared our retaliation. You are too wedded to your old Merc Guild ways with their silly rules about how to fight wars. They don't apply to me, Major." His nictitating membranes snapped open. "They don't apply to either of us."

She shuddered to think what atrocities might already have occurred on this world in the name of the Spine Patriots.

Rievskegg leaned back in his pneumatic seat. "You worry too much, Major. It is good that somebody worries about the inhabitants of the Spine Nebula, because we have been taken for granted for too long. But too many what-ifs and maybes are tying you down. We cannot afford for you to be distracted. We need those other two starkillers either taken out of action or..."

Sun recognized the thoughts whirring behind those beady black eyes. He wasn't the first to have them. Should the starkillers be destroyed, or should their fearsome power be controlled by their own side?

"We are the Patriots, are we not?" said the HecSha firmly. "We want to rebuild. To be our own masters. Set our own agenda. We can't do that while the starkillers are active. No matter who controls them. You have completed your task at Aneb-4. Now go assemble your forces and assault the starkillers."

"You're right. Thank you."

"And not another word to anyone about Unthor or Tau-Rietzke until you've left the system. My shoulders are far broader than your puny Human ones. Leave me the burden of knowing what might befall my world. Save your energies for making sure it never happens."

* * *

Sun walked out into the street five minutes later, still not sure whether she was so gullible that she'd just been played by a damned HecSha of all people, or whether Prime Representative Rievskegg was shaping up to be the example the Spine Nebula had been crying for: a leader who would look out for their people. Which was, after all, what the Patriots were supposed to be fighting for.

Either way, she was out of here.

The convoy of three armored trucks pulled up to speed her away to the starport where a shuttle waited to take her to *Unlikely Regret*.

And then—if the sun didn't detonate before they reached the stargate—it was time to see what awaited her at Station 5.

* * * * *

Chapter Fifteen

Beneath Lake Zarillo, Wahrner's Grise

Hopper looked through the view window onto the inner chamber of Device 3 and felt a pang of regret. This place was a marvel.

If circumstances were otherwise, she could happily spend her entire life here, walking the ancient passageways with Jenkins and debating with her lover the implications for theoretical physics of the energy channel mechanisms.

So many questions here.

The facility at this location was much less mineral encrusted than that beneath Romalin on Aneb-4.

Why was that?

She looked out from the control annex onto the resonance stabilization bulb that hung in the center of the spherical inner chamber. It just hung there without any obvious means of suspension, attraction, support, or repulsion.

How did it do that?

And why had somebody built this annex using a different era of technology and architecture from that used to construct the main part of the base?

She assumed this was one of a burst of alterations added much later in the facility's timeline.

When? Why? And by whom?

So many questions.

She understood the Endless Night recruited some of its foot soldiers by forcing addictive narcotics into them. Buying loyalty through dependency.

The engine here was run by a scarred old Besquith called Hakkdraal.

To her surprise, when she'd first been shown to Hakkdraal, and after she'd uncurled from her initial terror, the Night commander hadn't bitten off her legs and chained her to a post the way Jankel had done. Instead, she'd shown her around the place and drugged her with its many mysteries, hooking her just as thoroughly as they used Sparkle and Kick to control lesser species.

She'd succumbed—she couldn't help herself—and began the work to supply her captors with the answers they demanded.

It wasn't until she relaxed at her quarters one night in a scented oil bath that she realized she was being exploited the same as she'd always been by the Night.

Much as she enjoyed the problems she was set, and the luxurious environment in which to contemplate them, she was tired of being a victim.

What would Jenkins say if he ever found out she'd curled up and given Endless Night whatever they asked for?

Could he still love her if she did?

"Is there a problem?" asked Mangdra, the Zuul technician who'd been given the task of shadowing her today.

"It's such a marvel," she replied. With the channels opening up between the great engine and the donor stars that supplied its operating power, the currents flowing through the bulb had increased. Streamers and bubbles roiled. Glandular sacs pumped and twitched.

She'd developed a working hypothesis that the bulb was an organ of stability. It prevented minor imbalances between its input feeds from cascading into a runaway feedback loop that would rip apart the planet.

"I agree," he said. She hadn't referenced the bulb, but Mangdra understood the object of her worship. "We all know the work we do here is tarnished with evil, but the heart of this place is a thing of beauty and wonder nonetheless."

Her antennae drooped for a moment. The Zuul's thoughts were so close to hers that she felt another stab of regret at what was about to transpire.

"Power levels increasing beyond nominal," announced one of the generic technicians whose name she hadn't felt necessary to learn. "Ten percent power extraction achieved. Tier 2 capacitors charging."

Hopper eased off her couch.

"Going somewhere?" asked the Zuul.

She froze. Caught in the act.

How could she ever have thought that she would go through with this?

Then she noticed the Zuul's tongue lolling out with amusement.

It was a running joke with him that Hopper's mind hopped from one matter to another without reason.

Be more like Jenkins. What would he do?

"I want to check the channel feed levels from the tertiary station," she said.

"Do you think it will give different readings?"

"Mangdra, this is our first power test beyond nominal. How can you be sure that it will *not*? Lazy assumptions could prove disastrous."

"Of course," he said, looking away shamefaced.

Hopper walked confidently to the rear of the annex and removed the panel to the wiring conduit.

"Tier 2 capacitors failing," said the generic technician. "Waste heat safety systems initiating."

"Idiots!" Hopper clicked her mandibles irritably as she clambered into the conduit. The Tier 2 capacitors *hadn't* failed. She'd merely wired them to discharge into the Tier 1 banks. It was an elementary positive feedback loop.

"Hopper's running away!" barked Mangdra.

The conduit was busy with wiring looms and thick power cables, some of which were running disturbingly hot. But her numerous Jeha legs equipped her with all-terrain motive power, and she raced along the narrow space fast enough to make Jenkins proud.

Pursuers jumped into the conduit. elSha voices called on her to stop or be sorry.

Jeha and elSha were sometimes categorized together as 'engineering races.' There was one distinction uppermost in Hopper's mind: elSha were far more accomplished at violence.

She sped up.

A round from a firearm sparked off the crawl space roof, on its way to do who knew what damage to the power cables.

"Asshole mammal lickers," she yelled at the insane elSha.

A brace of shots whizzed overhead.

Hopper slowed, wondering whether her insult would be more effective if the words were reordered. The interruption to her headlong flight was enough to let her mind settle on another burning matter.

She'd gone the wrong way!

She reversed twenty yards back up the conduit toward her pursuers, and then took the left fork that she'd missed.

Another round narrowly missed her.

Perhaps they were warning shots, designed to miss.

Up ahead she saw the bulky equipment she'd secreted over the past few days. A survival pack strapped to a harness with a long skirt of modified gas canisters.

She ducked into the harness.

A pistol fired. Pain lanced through her body and she revised her estimation of the elSha rules of engagement.

She turned around and saw two lizards silhouetted in the conduit, their pistols covering her. Then she looked down and saw the shattered fragments of carapace shot from her body.

Good thing they didn't hit the canisters, she thought to herself. But then the pain welled in waves and told her otherwise.

Entropy! Being shot hurt like fuck!

"You cannot escape," said one of the elSha. "If you come back now, the Besquith boss will let you live."

"Did I ever tell you about my lover?" she asked.

The elSha gave a chuffing laugh. "You never shut up about your stupid Jenkins."

"One night over dinner, back on Station 5, we discussed his improved design for CASPer jump jets."

"I think she's delirious," said the other elSha.

"No, she's just a pain in the ass." Both elSha advanced up the tunnel. "Go on, Hopper. Tell us your Jenkins story. What amazing insight will illuminate the darkness of our ignorance this time?"

"This!"

Hopper lit the jets and the harness canisters belched fire.

The elSha screamed as they burned. One of them managed to get off a shot, but by then Hopper was careening along the metal conduit, every bump along its walls slicing pain into her wounded carapace.

Next time I'll give greater thought to pilot protection, she thought. But then the fuel additives cut in properly and such analysis was ripped away by the headlong rush.

Overdosed with excitement and terror, she screamed all the way until her fuel exhausted, and her contraption dropped her a short walk away from the pneumatic transit tube.

* * *

The transit capsule alighted over a hundred miles away at a station that had once been on the south shore of Lake Zarillo.

It wasn't now.

The bleached ribs of maritime ships grew out of the white expanse, half buried under accumulations of salt-sand. A line of stumps stretched out into the salt desert, perhaps the piles that once supported docking piers.

She saw no other indications that this was once a port.

"Fascinating."

She wrenched her attention away from the dead past and placed it on being alive in the near future.

The route was not easy.

Before long, she encountered her first belt of salt dunes. They were easy enough to ascend, but when she walked the upper slopes, her legs speared through the brittle crust and the dune crests collapsed under her.

She soon took to dragging herself along on her belly to spread the weight. This sped her progress but rubbed salt into the many wounds her body had picked up these past few months.

Salt, she learned, made for an effective hurt enhancer. The pain from her bullet wound was so bad, her mind swam through delirium.

She inspected the damage during a water break. A segment of her carapace had been blown off completely, and the flesh beneath shredded. Jeha were tough, though, and the bleeding had ceased. She would survive. Jenkins wouldn't let a little thing like that bother him.

Hopper had packed water, food, illumination, adhesive, and heat. It had never occurred to her to take a trauma pack. Next time she escaped from a secret criminal base, she resolved to bring medical nanites.

The salt here took the form of a friable crust. She took advantage of this by stamping it into salt dust. Then she sprayed adhesive over her head and carapace and rubbed her back into the freshly milled salt.

Satisfied with her camouflage coating, she repeated the process with her pack and continued on her way.

A half hour beyond the dunes, she was caught on an open salt flat when the sound of ducted fans approached rapidly from the north.

Sparse bundles of vegetation lay a mile or so farther south, but she decided she wouldn't make it that far. She settled down on the ground and kept perfectly still.

As the aircraft passed overhead, her pulse roared so loudly that she wondered whether it would be audible to those hunting her.

Yet the aircraft carried on and began a circling search along the belt of vegetation.

Her beating pulse slowed to normal levels, and she realized with astonishment that she had kept perfectly still. She hadn't curled up in the slightest.

She had been brave.

And this time, she hadn't needed to channel Jenkins to do so. It had come from within.

*****

Chapter Sixteen

Deck Four Recovery Suite, *Midnight Sun,*
Wahrner's Grise system

Captain Blue was woken by an insistent comm request alert from her pinplants.

There were two people to whom she'd granted omega level access. One was her executive officer. But Flkk'Sss could fight and win a small war, invent an intergalactic jump drive, and beat Betty in an arm-wrestling contest, all without feeling the need to wake her captain.

No, it wasn't Flkk'Sss.

She reached out with a hand and gingerly explored her head with her fingertips.

Deep layers of bandages covered everything except for tubes up her nose and mouth.

Her fingers *felt* like fingers. But she didn't trust that interpretation. Not until her eyes were uncovered. Maybe they had been programmed to feel like fingers but had actually been transformed into suckered tentacles.

The comm alert worried at her.

She dropped her arm, too tired to lift it anymore. Her body was still under the influence of the anesthetic, but her mind felt sharp enough to form words in her pinplants and send them back to her caller.

"What the fuck do you want, Jenkins?"

"Lake Zarillo has warmed 1.2 degrees Celsius since our arrival."

Blue sighed.

Which cheered her up plenty. That much of her humanity had survived the procedure at least.

She'd often asked herself why she'd granted Jenkins special access to speak with her about anything at any time, if he felt it was vital.

Nine times out of ten, his issue of vital importance had her cursing him as a self-important, sociopathic alien dick with far too many limbs for his own good.

But there was always that tenth time…

"Jenkins, I'm just coming around after surgery. You need to supply context. What star system are we in?"

"Wahrner's Grise. We're four days post-emergence and nearing orbit. Our Patriot contacts have not reported a significant increase in Endless Night activity since we beat it back in our last engagement here."

"Thank you. So we haven't found our starkiller, but we have found the water's lovely. Are you telling me that we've arrived in the summer season and you want permission to put on your bathing costume and dip your many legs in the water?"

"Captain, I do not possess a bathing costume."

Blue waited, but the Jeha felt he'd said all he needed to.

"Jenkins, why do I care about a warming lake?"

"My apologies, ma'am. I thought you would have familiarized yourself with the world we are investigating."

"Just give me a version suitable for a dumb ape full of anesthetic."

"As you wish, Captain. Lake Zarillo is not a small body of water. It is approximately the same volume as the Mediterranean Sea of your homeworld."

"A sea...Are we talking just the surface warming, or does this effect go all the way down?"

"Neither. All the heat is coming from below the lake. It's actually cooler on the surface."

"Could it be a volcano?"

"Negative. It's a geologically dormant area. No signs of volcanism."

"So what you're telling me in your roundabout way is that we've found our last starkiller underneath that lake."

"No, Captain. I'm telling you there's a significant anomaly that cannot be explained by the normal range of natural phenomena."

Blue sighed again. "That's as close to a yes as you'll ever get. What does Commander Flkk'Sss say?"

"I haven't communicated with her. She made it clear I have to go through channels to speak with her. *Channels!* Such inefficiency."

"The commander is a very wise old MinSha. Go through channels but put at the top of your message that you may have discovered the starkiller. Can you do that?"

"Yes, ma'am."

"And don't tell anyone that you spoke with me first."

Jenkins started spouting something about the sanctity of separating accurate observational data from its interpretation. Blue cut his connection and searched for a security camera to pinlink with.

It wasn't tricky. There were a host of cameras and other sensors trained on her.

She drew the sheets back and took a first look at the newly enhanced Captain Blue.

Oh.

Shit!

* * * *

Chapter Seventeen

Approaching Lake Zarillo, Wahrner's Grise

The flight of three *Corvus*-class "D-Clock" dropships descended to the planet, shadowing the commercial orbital transfer traffic routes. At zero plus not a lot, they peeled off to approach Lake Zarillo from the south, starting their approach from around 200 klicks out.

Jex had seen the lake from space before the fiery shroud of atmospheric entry had wiped it from view. It was oval, freckled with mountains set back from the northern shore, and surrounded by salty planes that reflected the light with a gleamingly high albedo. It had felt to Jex like a monstrous eye rimmed with luminous eyeshadow was peering back at him.

The dropship was skimming the salty nap of the world at Mach aplenty while Jex was strapped helplessly in the troop compartment. He didn't like that at all.

Everyone thought of Jex as the stunt pilot of the CASPer squads. The jump jet ace. True, his nifty jump jet skills had won competitions and saved his life, but it was different when he wasn't his own pilot.

"Top," he asked in the private channel.

"Jex."

First Sergeant Albali sounded amused already. But then he knew from Jex's resume that he had almost no planetside dropship experience.

"Our approach," Jex inquired. "Is it normal?"

Top replied with a deep belly laugh. "You think this is bad? Try clambering onto a Goltar's bony back and letting it swim at speed underwater while breathing from its blowhole. That's far worse."

"Oh. I wasn't sure if they were showing off in front of the Humans."

"They are keeping to a ground clearance minimum of one meter. A Goltar showing off would be flying much lower. Something measured in micro-cherubs."

"All pilots are crazy."

"Amen to that, Sergeant. And just as well for our sakes that they are."

"Contact!"

Everything changed at the co-pilot's warning.

Jex immediately brought up the squad status board and checked everything was to his satisfaction. Comms were open, ammo states as full as they would get, and bio-signs within norms. Equipment diagnostics showed numerous issues but none new. Unless Gloriana showed up with supplies and armorers, they would have no choice but to run mechs patched up with gum and duct tape for the time being. "Kit check," he said, and was met with clicks of acknowledgement.

"Five-Two, Five-Three, circle on overwatch," said Top. "Five-One will take a closer look."

Jex's ride, D-Clock 5/1, came to a thumping halt, ducted fans tilting to the vertical position so it could hover over the white sand.

The dropship's sensor readings were showing Jex a multi-segmented animal naturally camouflaged for the salt plains. In shape, it resembled a Jeha, but instead of curling up at the approach of the dropship, it had frozen flat with its legs splayed.

"Do we kill it?" asked the pilot, Ferro, from the flight deck.

"It's just a dumb animal," replied Top, who was in command of this reconnaissance. Albali hesitated. "But we can't take the chance. Open the beak. I'll drop out and take a look. If I don't like what I see, I can scrub it with my autocannon."

As the dropship's beak hinged open, Top un-clamped his CASPer and walked along the troop compartment that held ten CASPers, the entirety of Fourth Company's pitiful remnant.

"Top," said Jex. "What if it's a civilian?"

"Think again," Top snapped. "The place is an inhospitable desert. There are no civilians here."

Jex didn't like the sound of that but kept his mouth shut. Mishkan-Ijk had insisted Top should lead this mixed Goltar-Human expedition. No one had commented, but Jex assumed this meant the Goltar commander was grooming Top to replace Major Sun as the officer in charge of the non-Goltar mercs.

Major Albali?

No wonder there was a warning growl to Top's voice. Albali was of the old school opinion that he deserved respect because he worked for a living. *Major Albali.* No, Top wouldn't like that one bit.

"Vehicle convoy detected," said one of the dropships scanning ahead. "Eight heavy trucks plus outriders. They're headed directly for the lake."

"Shut the beak!" Top ordered. "The gods have gifted us a target of opportunity. Let's not refuse it."

* * *

The aerospace craft sped away, choking Hopper in biting salt clouds.

She watched them disappear toward the north. The craft were concealed by white dust plumes thrown in their wake, but she noted their flight was very fast and very low.

Professional military, she decided. *Mercenaries*.

When she'd heard their approach, she'd laid flat and kept still. But she hadn't felt still inside. In fact, an excitable flutter had swept up and down her body, not leaving through the entire encounter.

Surprisingly, that feeling hadn't been entirely bad.

But now that she watched the craft pull away, her excitement built into ecstatic thrill levels.

For the first time, she began to see why the violent races might be drawn to the mercenary life.

Mercenaries…

Endless Night didn't employ mercenaries, did they?

The design of those craft looked familiar. She'd seen them used as underwater shuttles beneath Romalin Island.

Which made them a Goltar design.

And the only Goltar mercenaries she knew of served aboard *Midnight Sun*.

Her antennae drooped as she watched the dust plumes disappear over the horizon.

"Oh, dear. I may have made a dreadful mistake."

* * * * *

Chapter Eighteen

South of Lake Zarillo, Wahrner's Grise

"Leave the truck in the middle intact," ordered Albali. "I want a word with anyone onboard."

Ferro, who was flight leader as well as pilot for 5/1, acknowledged and sent final instructions to the other two dropships.

As they closed, Jex could see the outriders were dune buggies with silver roll cages. They looked like sport models, though the cage had been modified to mount a heavy gun in the rear bay served by two masked fighters.

One of them spotted the dropships and pointed a finger into the sky.

The gunners swiveled their weapons around to aim at the incoming attack. Before they could fire, though, the dropships smoked them out with missiles.

With wheels rolling free, and the burning buggies pinwheeling through the sand, Jex expected the trucks to scatter.

Instead, they plowed on as if nothing had happened.

Autopilot trucks.

The dropships banked wide and attacked in a line abreast formation on the convoy's flank.

The twin heavy MACs slung under their bellies stitched lines of sand plumes that raced ahead until they touched the vehicles and visited destruction upon them.

Fire, smoke, and wreckage blossomed into the warm air. Trucks that hadn't been hit slammed into those that had, waiting for a few short moments before the MACs hit them too.

Dropships 5/2 and 5/3 circled round on overwatch while Jex in 5/1 came in to land.

There was no need for another strafing run at the convoy. One was enough at level zero difficulty.

Jex's CASPers deployed down the rubberized ramp of the beak whose lower jaw had buried itself in the white desert.

"Two Zuul trying to escape on the far side of the intact truck," reported 5/2. "Do we take them out?"

"Negative," Top replied. "Jex, bring them back to me."

"Roger that." Jex broke into a run. Giant bounding steps punched white clouds from the ground. He added the merest blip of his jets, and he sailed through the air, braking at the apogee of his trajectory with a second blip to land on the cab roof as gracefully as a champion gymnast.

Graceful was how Jex saw it, anyway. The landing was perfect as far as he was concerned, but it hammered a dent into the cab roof. Jex ignored the groaning metal sagging beneath him and magnified the image of the two Zuul running for it. Unsurprisingly, they wore Endless Night jumpsuits.

Endless Night! They were like evil demon weeds.

Sun and the Patriots had chopped them back when they visited this system a few weeks ago. Now they had sprouted again.

"Hey!" Jex bellowed through his mech speakers. "You two. Dog soldiers. Come back here with your tails between your legs."

That brought them up short into a halt. "You have to let us go," one of them pleaded. "If we talk, even if we're captured alive, our clan will be punished terribly."

Jex took a giant leap toward the Zuul, his autocannon hot and its reticles bracketing their center masses in his HUD.

"You should've thought of that before you joined up," he told them. "I want you on your backs, legs in the air and begging for a belly rub like good doggies."

The aliens licked their snouts nervously as he advanced.

They drew laser pistols.

Jex raised his arm, but instead of firing, he witnessed a horrific scene play out. The Zuul touched noses and then drilled holes through each other's brains.

"Now that," said Jex, "was ugly." He checked the bodies to confirm this wasn't a trick, but it was as simple and as brutal as it appeared.

God knew that mercs fought dirty sometimes, but there were Guild rules and even a code of honor with many of the merc races.

There was no honor to the Endless Night.

He returned to burning wrecks and charred corpses that lay strewn across the salt desert. There wasn't much left to investigate other than the one truck the strafing run had saved.

"We have an initial inventory," said Turnaround from the truck's cargo bay. "I'm seeing ration packs, cabling and electrical gizmos, high-end slates, powdered rare earth minerals. Nothing of great value except for a case of quality core-world brandy. Somebody's living the life of luxury under the lake. Oh. Update. An F11 canister. My guess is it's for the containment field of a fusion reactor."

"Grab the F11 and get back to the D-Clock," said Top. "I have pinlink control of the truck."

Jex opened a private channel to Turnaround as she hurried back to the waiting dropship.

"Sarge?"

Jex laughed at the teasing innocence in her response. She knew him too well. "I was just checking," he said.

"Relax, Sarge. One case of brandy safely liberated."

Top was waiting for them, his CASPer standing like a timeless metal sentinel in the open beak as his mind linked to the truck. There was plenty of wheelspin and thumping collisions against the wrecks it was wedged between. It took a few MAC rounds to clear the way, then the truck was out of the ambush and heading north.

Jex asked, "What are we doing with the truck, Top?"

"I'm running it on manual, but it's an autopilot model. Too well encrypted to hack quickly enough, but I don't need to. There. I just re-engaged the auto."

"Albali to all pilots. We're heading out. Follow that truck!"

They tracked the Endless Night vehicle as it headed north at a cruising speed of 130 klicks. Compared with their previous headlong rush, it felt as if D-Clock 5/1 was crawling at a worm's pace.

Instead of bands of white, green, and brown scrolling past in a blur, at this slower pace, Jex could see the detail of salt plains and scrubby semidesert. It was the bleakest place he'd ever seen. There were no signs of life.

"Truck's gone!" called Ferro.

"Gone?" Top bellowed.

"Perhaps its driven underground?" replied the Goltar.

"I've lost the pinlink," said Albali. "Pilot, open the throttle to the stops. Five-Two, Five-Three, watch our six."

Jex's guts threatened to spring out of his throat and wave hello as the dropship raced across the plain, quickly closing the gap on the missing truck.

There was…*something* ahead. Even with the stabilization correction and target enhancements in his HUD, it took a few moments for Jex to work out what he was seeing.

At a slight rise in the ground, half-finished construction work was concealed beneath white camouflage sheets. The enemy looked like they were building a redoubt.

"I've re-established pinlink control," said Top. "Taking the truck off autopilot. Parking it. Pilot, we will deploy two klicks from this location and—"

An alarm wailed.

"Radar lock!" the co-pilot exclaimed. "Missiles! Missiles!"

Jex's universe whirled in confusion. It felt as if all his organs were being pulled in different directions on bungee connective tissue. G-forces slammed into him from every direction at once as the pilot rose in a burst of countermeasures and flung the dropship across the sky in an impossible series of aggressive gyrations.

Watching the HUD feeds inside his CASPer just made him sick. Jex closed his eyes and prayed.

Hard maneuvers continued to punish the occupants of the troop compartment, growing the sense of panic within Jex until he didn't think he could bottle it up any longer.

A scream of terror cut through the squad channel.

He assumed it had come from himself. But it hadn't.

"Let it out, Frontpage," said Turnaround.

Frontpage's release bled away some of Jex's panic, enough to tide him over for the few seconds until the dropship resumed level flight.

Jex opened his eyes and watched as they flew over the emplacement strewn with badly chewed up Besquith. The dropships hadn't spared the ammo with their heavy MACs.

A squad operating a SAM battery had been occupying a partially constructed emplacement meant for much heavier weapons.

"Target area clear," reported the pilot. "No serious casualties. Five-Three took fire and is making a forced landing."

Jex sucked through his teeth. Commander Flkk'Sss would not be happy if she lost an expensive dropship.

There was an awkward silence while everyone watched 5/3 bellyflop into the salty sand.

Come on, Top. You're supposed to be playing the officer here.

Just before Jex risked nudging Top with a request for orders, Albali announced his tactics.

"Five-Two will deploy marines to control that construction site. Five-One will deploy CASPers to find that damned truck. Five-Three, if you cannot affect repairs in the field, prepare to unload your dropship and we'll just have to return to mother with the other two dropships heavy. Commiserations to Corporal Chappelle whose liquid booty might not survive the reloading."

"Not a problem, Top," said Berenice 'Turnaround' Chapelle. "If we sell that F11 you found, it could buy us a distillery."

Top just grunted absently in reply. Jex didn't envy him. The big Spaniard was probably rehearsing his report of how he'd managed to lose a dropship.

Soon after un-assing their D-Clock, Jex's squad discovered the secret of the vanishing truck. It had passed through sliding camouflage doors down a steep ramp into an underground tunnel.

The CASPers pushed into the darkness.

It was eerie as hell.

Unlike the half-built defenses overhead, the tunnel must have been here a long time. Salty water seeping through the roof had left white stalactites and stalagmites that glistened in the CASPer lamp light.

Recent traffic had knocked a passage through the stalagmites, strewing shards over the floor as if a giant chandelier had fallen from the ceiling.

The way the tunnel zigzagged brought an extra edge of danger as they were forced to tactically advance around the many blind spots into each new section of tunnel.

But they met no opposition and located the truck after ten minutes.

Jex set up a perimeter and secured the vehicle. If their intel guesses were correct, the tunnel fed into a facility under the lake that could easily be over a hundred klicks distant. If any bad guys were coming to investigate, he expected them to use transport. They should hear vehicles coming a long way off.

Jex was itching to push farther down the tunnel to see what they were facing and maybe give it a good kicking. He'd expected to reactivate the truck's autopilot and yomp behind with his CASPers.

But that wasn't Top's strategy. While Jex kept his perimeter firm, Albali had the truck reverse all the way back into the salt desert. Bombs and missiles were stripped from the downed dropship and loaded onto the truck. So was one of the recon drones which was strapped into the passenger bench in the cab.

Autopilot re-engaged, the truck descended once more into the tunnel, the drone popping signal repeaters out the cab window as it navigated the series of sharp turns a short distance beyond Jex's perimeter. About a klick farther on, the truck came to an obedient halt at a checkpoint.

To progress, it would have to pass through a chicane protected by heavily shielded guns. An angled embrasure was embedded into the roof and from there heavy guns controlled the area. Searchlights flooded it with sharp illumination.

As he observed the position through the drone's sensors, Jex concluded it was a mix of the very old and newly constructed. Whoever had designed it knew exactly how to control the kill box.

When he saw a bristle of laser rifles poke through ports in the walls, it was obvious that if he'd sent his CASPers into contact with this position, not all would have made it back.

A pair of Besquith in heavy combat armor approached the truck, short-barrel laser carbines at low ready.

"Here! I'm in here." Top spoke through the recon drone's speakers, excitement enhancing the Mediterranean in his accent. "I bring you valuable information. A gift too."

One of the Besquith punched his fist through the window and stuck his head through.

He snarled.

This was occurring a klick away, and the monster's face was hidden by his helmet, but even so, Jex could hear the razor-sharp fangs in that snarl.

Something in Jex's guts liquefied.

"Identify yourself," it growled.

"Gladly."

"And tell me your information. Immediately!"

"Is this exchange being recorded?"

The Besquith hesitated. "That is not your concern."

"I'll take that as a yes." Albali cleared his throat loudly "To the Endless Night commander of Wahrner's Grise, please accept this truck and its contents with compliments of the Midnight Sun Free Company. *Punch it!*"

Back in the desert, a Goltar tech fed the kill instruction to the drone, setting off the rigged munitions in the back. After a brief plume of flame, the drone feed died.

"We've done enough here," said Top. "Blow Five-Three. Jex, get your people back and load 'em up. It's time we were back in orbit."

The rumble from the detonations passed through Jex's position. His CASPer absorbed most of the shock, but all around him, millennia-old stalactites shattered into salt dust, covering the mechs.

He told his squad to move out, but it was with misgivings. Surely it made more sense to press the advantage and slice up the werewolves while they were down.

When the CASPers were nearing the tunnel entrance, Albali commed Jex on a private channel.

"Talk to me, Sergeant."

"Say again, Top."

"Usually I can't shut you up. What's on your mind?"

"I was just…" Man, Albali really knew his people! "I was thinking we could follow up and finish the job on those werewolves."

"We've done plenty enough to make our point here, Jex. Especially with our mechs in such poor shape. We'll need an army to take the place. And when we come back, that's exactly what we'll have."

"Copy that. Numbers are good."

Jex fell into silence though as they embarked and lifted for orbit. By now, Gloriana was supposed to have come riding to save the day on a white horse followed by legions of CASPers and pollywiggles.

But she hadn't.

Something had gone badly wrong.

Maybe he'd learn what that was at their next stop.

Station 5.

* * * * *

Chapter Nineteen

***Midnight Sun*, Docked at Station 5**

"Probably just my sister being melodramatic," Sun explained to the delegation waiting to leave the ship. "She hasn't been off the ship for a *very* long time. It's probably more difficult for her than any of us can understand. Wait there."

She punched the opening stud for the guard room by the main hatch and marched in.

I'm getting tired of your antics, Blue. This had better be worth...

Her jaw dropped open.

Blue was waiting for her, arms crossed defiantly, with her back against the bulkhead.

"What...?" Sun began. But recent conversations came to the fore and stitched together the horrific logic that had led to this.

She knew exactly what had happened.

And why.

Sun licked her lips and tried again. "Did it hurt?"

"Not yet," Blue replied, raising her eyebrows.

Eyebrows she hadn't possessed since that night long ago on Earth.

Looking into Blue's face was like looking into the mirror. As it had when they were kids. Blue's head was still bald, other than a midnight blue coiled topknot, but her lashes and eyebrows had returned. The skin on her face had lost its deathly pallor and its scars. It was now as smooth as a photoshoot. But her fingers...

"What do you mean *not yet?*"

"I'm not ready for high-gee testing for another week." Blue unbuttoned her ship suit with fingers of gleaming silver metal. "The surgeons say that's going to be agonizing."

The upper slopes of Blue's chest had the same metallic sheen as her fingers. After that, any attempt at aesthetic coating had been abandoned. Her little sister's body approximated its size and shape of before, but in place of warm flesh was unfinished metal, ceramic, and plastic. Her lower torso was largely transparent, revealing mechanical pumps and tubing.

"Thank you," Sun whispered. Inwardly she screamed at the universe for the outrage it had wrought on her baby sister.

None of that would help Blue now.

Her sister nodded and buttoned herself back up.

"I just needed you to get your jaw-drop moment out of the way," Blue told her. She reached for her navy greatcoat. "Because I need your head in the game, sis. Come on, I believe there are people waiting for us outside. It's time to figure out the next phase of this little war."

* * * * *

Chapter Twenty

***Sverdlow Shunter*, Approaching Station 5**

Junio felt a warm glow of anticipation in her stomach as Station 5 hove into view on *Sverdlow Shunter*'s flight deck Tri-V.

Her Scythe controllers had stationed her on Wahrner's Grise these past five years. Until the payments had stopped and the questions started.

Wherever she'd served, Station 5 had felt like home for a long time now. It was such a mongrel mix of agendas and people. Everything fused together within the high-pressure confines of the main structure and the three vanes added in an earlier, richer epoch.

On Station 5, few things were as they initially appeared to be.

Which was why Junio felt so at home. Deception was her lifeblood.

She walked through the Tri-V display and punched the console control to activate the shielded link with the cargo bay.

"Magro, is everything in place?"

"Our pigs are cold and ready," her second-in-command replied. "Just waiting for you. Assuming you've still got the guts to join us."

Junio bleated in the Khabar version of laughter. She had been "void diving," as they called these operations, for years. Magro knew few things would keep Junio from leading the dive in person.

"Keep my pig cold. I'll be there in a few minutes. Junio out."

She stepped back and took a last look at the station.

The outer docking hoops used for the largest vessels were usually empty. Not today. *Blunt Justice,* the huge Goltar capital ship, was back once more. Alongside was the battlecruiser *Tseg-Zorig.* Another Goltar battlecruiser, *Tseg-Lenkh,* was holding active station a few light seconds toward the emergence point.

Junio clacked her horned nails together as she observed the weird blocky shape of *Tseg-Zorig.* The analyst had described its hull shape as a tetragonal trapezohedron. It looked to Junio like a playing piece in a game of space battles. Whatever the hell it was, it had eight flat faces, each bristling with gun ports and missile tubes.

And sensors...

Her tapping grew faster and louder.

"Will you cut that out!" grumbled Oxroc, the Blevin pilot.

Junio considered testing the relative strength of a Blevin's skull against a Khabar's horn-rimmed hands but decided to swallow her annoyance.

In fact, she preferred it when *Sverdlow Shunter*'s pilot was his usual surly self. It was when he grew quiet and professional that she knew he was up to no good.

Junio gestured away the Tri-V view of the Goltar ship and replaced it with the feed from her contact on the station.

An Endless Night contact.

The stragglers holing up inside ancient battleship hulks in the L5 scrapyards referred to themselves as the Scythe Navy. They were being ironic. In a stand-up battle, their frigates, corvettes, and tricked-up tramp freighters hadn't the throw weight to contest space with proper naval ships such as the Goltar's and *Midnight Sun* docked at the orbital's superstructure.

But they weren't being sardonic when they referred to themselves as the Scythe. It was fast becoming a badge of pride, though not long ago, the Scythe had been enemies of Endless Night.

She had learned that both organizations had always been controlled by strings pulled by Goltar puppet masters. But no more.

Now that the credits were once again filling her Yack, she didn't care about loyalties, but she did enjoy the part she played in the deep deceptions that cloaked the Spine Nebula like a stealth blanket.

A sudden lens flare from the camera based on Station 5 brought her attention back to their approach. From this angle, *Sverdlow Shunter* looked like a miniature star coming in to dock.

Which was, of course, entirely by design. She'd timed the approach so that the ship's huge fan of golden solar panels was perfectly aligned to reflect the light of Beta-Caerelis. Blindingly so. It might look like a divine halo, but actually marked *Sverdlow* as the kind of junkyard boat that was so cheap and unhurried that it relied on free solar power.

Satisfied the golden mane of panels was complete, Junio was ready to begin.

"Meet us at Pier 72," she told the pilot and headed aft.

"Don't get killed, you mad old goat," shouted the Blevin after her. "Not until you pay me back the fifty credits you owe me."

Junio laughed.

If they pulled this off, their Yacks would be swollen by over a thousand times that amount.

* * * * *

Chapter Twenty-One

Shove 'n' Done Tavern, Station 5, Beta-Caerelis

Beowulf walked into the bar at 23:30 with Jimmy DeGris. He hadn't wanted to blow DeGris' cover…but he'd wanted to go to the meeting without backup even less.

"Last call!" A large Lumar called from behind the bar as they sat at a corner table in the back of the bar.

"Whatya want?" Laverna asked, coming to stand at their table. Her attitude was every bit the annoyed server who has someone show up right before closing, expecting to be served.

"Two MAC Rounds," Beowulf said.

She winked where no one could see her then stomped off to get the drinks.

Beowulf and DeGris sipped their drinks and made small talk as the rest of the patrons finished theirs and left. Finally, the Lumar departed, too, after telling Laverna to lock up once the Humans left. He gave them an annoyed glance before leaving. Laverna locked the doors once the Lumar was gone then came back to their table. "Shall we?"

Beowulf finished the drink in a single shot and stood. "Lead the way."

Laverna took them past the bar and through the kitchen area behind it. A back passageway behind it led to another room. Laverna tapped several times in what was obviously a pattern, then a short wiry woman with short-cropped black hair opened the door. Beowulf couldn't tell if she was Chinese or East African of some flavor before she turned away to go back to the large round table that took up most of the room. The occupants all looked over to the newcomers, sizing them up. While he'd been expecting some Humans or their allies from the Spine Patriots, the two Goltar in attendance were a surprise. They represented an outside political/military force he hadn't been expecting, and he stopped in the doorway.

"Quickly," Laverna said, motioning Beowulf and DeGris to enter.

They walked in and found two open chairs at the table, and Laverna slipped into one.

Beowulf looked at Degris, who nodded. "I'll go keep an eye out," DeGris said as he slipped out, closing the door behind him. Beowulf slid into the remaining seat.

"Introductions are obviously in order," Laverna said. "Everyone, this is Beowulf, who represents—"

"Let's just say I represent a number of business concerns throughout the nebula which move a variety of products."

"Great, he's a smuggler," the one man at the table said.

"What I am is of little concern at the moment," Beowulf said, "aside from the fact that I have connections on most of the worlds—"

"Even better," the man interrupted again with a sigh. "He's a drug runner."

"I have *products* I transport throughout the nebula," Beowulf said. "That gives me the opportunity to keep my finger on its pulse, perhaps better than the rest of you." His eyes swept the table, challenging them to dispute what he'd said.

"For example, you know Earth? That planet most of us are from? The only reason it still exists right now is that some of my people sacrificed their lives to keep the Endless Night's superweapon from blowing it up. The only reason we have targeting data on it is because of *my* people.

"That's *my* pedigree. I may not have met all of you in person, but I know some of you by reputation, and *your* pedigrees aren't as pure as the driven snow, either, so I don't see where you have a leg to stand on when you start giving me shit. So, can we dispense with the name calling and at least let Laverna finish introducing everyone, or should I just go ahead and leave right now?"

A flash of red crawled up the man's neck. Apparently the comment about driven snow had hit home with him.

Laverna nodded. "As I was saying, this is Beowulf. In addition to his business concerns in the nebula—which are *none* of our business, Branco—he also has access to *heavy* combat assault forces."

That got the Goltars' attention, if nothing else, Beowulf saw. Even the Humans appeared willing to overlook his choice of occupations.

"To my left," Laverna continued, "is Captain Blue, Major Sun, and Branco. Blue is the commanding officer of the *Midnight Sun*. Major Sun and Branco are here representing the Spine Patriots."

Beowulf nodded to each in turn, even Branco. The captain was apparently living her name; the only hair on her head was a blue topknot on the back of her skull. She favored the woman sitting next to her—sisters maybe—in that they were small and wiry, although there was something odd about Blue, and it wasn't the fact that she had metal glinting from the base of her neck and chest when her uniform was pulled down. The way she carried herself was peculiar in some manner Beowulf couldn't put his finger on.

Sun—the woman who had opened the door—nodded politely. She had striking blue eyes that twinkled and a shy smile that accentuated the scar running from above her left eye down to behind her ear. Obviously she'd seen battle.

Branco was sitting in some sort of motorized chair, but what he needed it for wasn't immediately apparent. Or maybe it was. As the flush faded from his neck, light green patches appeared. Maybe he was sick, which drove his ire. *Or maybe he's just an asshole.*

Laverna waved to the Goltar to Beowulf's right. "Seated closest to you is Gloriana, the owner of the Midnight Sun Free Company, and on the other side of her is Lieutenant Colonel Mishkan-Ijk, the leader of her combat forces."

"Welcome," Mishkan-Ijk said through a translator. Beowulf had never been so close to Goltar before, and he found the squidipusses—or was it octosquids—somewhat intimidating. Their beaks looked like they were meant for ripping flesh, and he unconsciously flinched back slightly when they clicked as the beings spoke.

"I would like to know more about the combat forces," Gloriana said. "Are these Asbaran Solutions or the forces standing in for them?"

Beowulf smiled. "I have certain *associates* in the mercenary business. They are not Asbaran Solutions, although they are of a similar pedigree. While I have requested assistance with these issues we appear to be facing, I don't know for sure how much assistance will be sent, or when it will get here."

"I hope it is a lot, and it gets here soon," Gloriana said, "because—despite having your 'finger on the pulse of the nebula,' you are in error. There is not a single starkiller weapon; there actually were three. One of them was put out of action—by us—but two remain. The one you know about on McPherson-3 as well as another on Wahrner's Grise."

"I see," Beowulf said. He could feel a flush building on his own neck.

Before he could say anything further, Jimmy DeGris burst through the door. "The Endless Night is coming!" he exclaimed breathlessly. "They're approaching the bar."

"Here?" Laverna asked.

"Unless you know of another group that wears all black uniforms."

The beings around the table surged to their feet.

"Call your forces," Gloriana ordered.

"They're en route," Mishkan-Ijk and Sun exclaimed. Beowulf didn't have time to figure out how *that* chain of command worked.

While the others started calling out defensive positions and where the incoming troops were coming from, Beowulf's first thought—like any good smuggler—was escape. He grabbed DeGris and ran into the hall. When he started toward the bar, DeGris pulled back. "No time to go that way," DeGris said.

They started to run down the back passageway in the opposite direction, but turned the first corner to find a large group in black approaching from that direction. "Back!" Beowulf yelled as one of the leaders fired a laser pistol. He dove back around the corner as several laser strikes hit the wall behind them.

"Guess they don't know about the prohibition on weapons in the station," Beowulf muttered as he pulled out his own weapon, a .45 caliber slug thrower he'd upgraded to after the business with Franjo.

"Go!" he yelled as he leaned around the corner to snap off a few rounds. "I'll catch up!"

The Endless Night forces dove to the floor or tried to take cover in the limited space by the door jambs as Beowulf fired off his mag, then he turned and sprinted back toward the bar. He immediately ran into Sun and Branco, who were coming in his direction. A large number of troops were pouring from some of the other doors in the hallway behind them. While Sun ran toward him, Branco drove his motorized chair, and Beowulf could see he was missing the lower half of his legs.

The corner of Beowulf's mouth twisted up in a wry grin—the man really didn't have a leg to stand on—but then something exploded behind him.

"Endless Night coming in that direction, too!" Beowulf yelled as he ran past them.

While the troopers following Sun and Branco looked like militia forces—dressed and armed in a variety of clothes and weapons, the ones racing from another door to join Mishkan-Ijk looked like soldiers. They were dressed the same as Sun's forces, but they had the look of nanite-hardened CASPer troopers, and they carried themselves similarly—looking for danger and with weapons ready to be used in a split second. *The Midnight Sun Free Company.*

The only problem with the merc group was there weren't very many of them. Would six soldiers be able to break through the Endless Night forces in front of them?

Beowulf didn't know how many of the enemy were in front of him, but he was willing to put more of his trust in the mercs than the irregular Spine Patriot militia. He was also willing to let the people with the training lead—and take any of the initial casualties—so he slowed and followed the mercs back into the bar.

Gunfire erupted as they entered the bar; Endless Night forces were entering from both of the bar's entrances. Beowulf grabbed DeGris and pulled him back from the doorway as a laser bolt snapped past. The mercs dove behind the bar or took cover where they could, and they returned fire as the smugglers retreated into the hall.

Beowulf spun to find Laverna coming from the room they'd been meeting in. "They're coming from both directions," Beowulf said. "Is there another way out?"

Laverna shook her head. "If they're coming from both directions, we're trapped."

* * * * *

Chapter Twenty-Two

Scythe Sabotage Team, Station 5

Junio's faceplate had misted slightly, but it was clear enough to see the great fan around the *Sverdlow Shunter* fold together and retract, exposing the much smaller ship within as it prepared to dive beneath the outer docking hoops on approach to a mooring pier more appropriate for her size. And, as the sails disappeared, they took their radar shadow with them.

There was nothing to do now but wait, hope, and enjoy the thrill.

Same as the other five members of the team somewhere out there in the void, but invisible to Junio.

The angular bulk of the battlecruiser *Tseg-Zorig* loomed ever larger in her faceplate.

It was Junio's Human lieutenant, Magro, who had thrown away the official name of low-speed dirigible torpedoes. Now they referred to their diving steeds as *cold pigs*.

Cold because they were running unpowered and with every stealth technology credits could buy.

As for the other, apparently they steered like pigs. Junio had looked up the species on GalNet. They resembled a four-legged Gtandan, and, knowing how stubborn Gtandans could be, Junio had declared this to be a good name.

Gtandans were not uppermost in her mind, though. That would be the new race on the scene. Goltar.

From what she had learned, the amphibious squids had been hiding in a sulk for the last few thousand years. *Tseg-Zorig* was ancient, of a design unique to the Goltar and long forgotten by the rest of the Union until a Goltar fleet had unexpectedly appeared at Earth in the climax of Peepo's war.

On the one horn, the immense age of the battlecruiser could mean that Goltar sensor tech was thousands of years out of date, no match for her team's stealth. On the other horn, the Goltar could be using sensor technology forgotten by the developers of the cold pigs, as well as possessing the latest tech available in the market. That was the horn that would impale them.

Which was why Junio had timed her attack very precisely.

By the time they began maneuvering their pigs, the Goltar aboard *Tseg-Zorig* should be running around like panicked squids, because the first part of the attack was kicking off in Station 5's Vane One.

It would be the perfect distraction for the attack of the cold pigs.

* * * * *

Chapter Twenty-Three

EMS *Gobi Desert*, Approaching Station 5

"Take us in, nice and easy," Captain Steve Parker said.

"I thought this place was somewhere in East Bumfuck," the sensor operator said, "but it looks like a pretty happening place."

"What do you mean?" Sansar asked. Something in the way he said it caused the hairs on the back of her neck to stand.

"We passed a battlecruiser on our approach. There's two more attached to the other side of the station and what looks like maybe a carrier, although it's a class I've never seen and isn't in our data banks, ma'am." The sensor operator shrugged. "There are also a bunch of other ships flying around, both inter-system as well as intra-system. There's a lot of stuff moving around here."

"Well, this is the one entry point into the nebula," Sansar said. "I guess it functions as a chokepoint, and Station 5 is the one place to check in or out." Even to her own ears, the explanation sounded lame. For an out-of-the-way location, there *were* a lot of ships present, and three battlecruisers represented a lot of combat power to just have sitting around.

What have I gotten us into?

"We just got some rules from the station," the comms officer said. "Guns are restricted."

First Sergeant 'Mun' Enkh turned to Sansar with a raised eyebrow. "No guns? Are you sure you want to go in there?"

"Well, I wasn't planning on marching a platoon of CASPers through there…not on my first visit, anyway."

"If the Wolves are here, this place can't be policed *that* well," Mun said. "How about you let me go in first with a squad to check it out?"

"I'll let you bring a squad," Sansar said, "but I'm going."

"If you're going, we're going armed. And I want a second squad in CASPers, ready to go, just in case."

"Okay," Sansar said with a smile. "We'll do it your way, but we'll do it circumspectly. Pistols only; or weapons you can hide. We won't openly carry rifles or MACs, but you can go armed. What's the worst they'll do? Send us back to the ship?"

"They said anyone found with a weapon will be locked up," the comms officer said.

"And that's why we'll have the CASPers ready," Mun said, cracking her knuckles. "I'd like to see them try."

The ship reverberated as it locked into place at the dock, and Sansar looked at Mun. "Ready."

Mun led them to the gangway via the armory so they could arm themselves. People were already getting into CASPers as they walked through the hold.

A Zuul in a blue uniform was waiting at the entryway. "I am Jugoll, from Station Security. I want to confirm that the station told you weapons are not allowed here."

"They did," Sansar said. "We aren't armed."

"Very well," Jugoll said. "Welcome to Station 5." He made a motion with a paw, allowing them to pass.

"So, where to?" Mun asked.

"The only place Beowulf mentioned was a bar called the Shove 'n' Done. He said if we went there, he would meet us. We're also supposed to meet Gloriana here, but I don't know where she'd be. Hopefully, Beowulf can direct us to her once we're done with him."

"Can't you just comm him and tell him to meet us here?"

"The comm system onboard the station is either down or it's being jammed."

"Wonderful. Sure you want to do this?" Sansar nodded. Mun sighed. "Fine, follow me then." The crew of the *Gobi Desert* had downloaded the station maps as they'd approached. "It shouldn't take more than about five minutes to get there."

* * *

They'd walked for about four minutes when three station security personnel in blue uniforms ran past them with weapons drawn. "Coming through! Emergency!" they yelled as they passed by.

"I guess the weapons prohibition is only for guests," Mun noted with a wry chuckle.

"Apparently so."

They walked a little farther and rounded a corner to find the security team lying in the passageway. Blood was everywhere.

"Blue Sky!" Sansar yelled as Mun jerked her back around the corner. Several laser beams flashed through where she'd been to impact the wall.

Mun took a quick look. "Looks like one or two of the security forces may still be alive, but all of them are shot at least once."

"What are we dealing with?"

"At least a couple of people in black uniforms and combat armor are around the next corner. Is now the time for CASPers?"

"I think it is. Send two people back to the ship and bring them up."

"Why don't we all just go back to the ship and get suited up?"

"Because I have a feeling these are the people we're here to stop."

Mun sighed. "Of course they are." She sent two people running back to the ship.

"I don't suppose you brought a grenade or two?" Sansar asked.

"They said *grenades* are illegal. So I only brought one." Mun pulled it out and looked at the troopers. "Get ready to charge them." She threw it down the passageway, paused for a second to let the frag clear, then led the charge around the corner.

They made it to the corner and finished off the two men in black who had been firing at them, but more laser rounds met them when they tried to advance further.

"I can see what looks like the bar," Mun said after a quick glance around the next corner. "There's a bunch of the black uniform folks inside it, trading fire with another group. They're in cover, and I'm out of grenades." She looked back to Sansar. "What do you want to do?"

* * * * *

Chapter Twenty-Four

Off *Tseg-Zorig*, Station 5

Junio was coming in wide.

Four klicks was a long way out from the *Tseg-Zorig* to start up the engines, but she had no choice if she was going to earn that fat bonus.

With the electronics on the cold pig kept to a bare minimum, her faceplate had only a crude optical magnification that never could focus properly with her Khabar eyes. She peered through the view slit of the stealth fairing and took a good look at the flat face of the *Tseg-Zorig* she was headed straight for.

The last time she'd looked at the hull, it had bristled with what looked like hairs. Closer up, they were coil guns. A lot of them.

"If you're going to shoot me dead," she told the battlecruiser, "do it quick. Right?"

Bleating with amusement, she kicked the right rudder pedal and opened the throttle.

The 25-meter long torpedo she sat on yawed right until she killed the motion with a dab of the left pedal.

As for altering her vector, the pig lived up to its name. It took a full thirty seconds of thrust until she even began to see her path was slowly angling toward the target's stern.

She noted she was still alive.

That was good.

And when she peered into the dark, looking for the other five cold pigs, she could see nothing. Which was even better.

Although, with both suits and pigs saturated in sensor-soak coatings, and reaction gas cooled to ambient temperature before being squirted out the engine ports, something would have to have gone terribly wrong for her to see her comrades at this stage.

It was whether the Goltar had seen them that mattered.

Another thirty seconds of thrust, and Junio's torpedo was firmly headed for *Tseg-Zorig's* engines.

After drifting for a while, she yawed left to orient her nose on the battlecruiser's stern and applied twenty seconds of moderate thrust.

The pig lazily slewed around. It would be easy to overcompensate and sail past the target area of the main engines, but they'd spent weeks making endless attack runs on the wrecks of ancient warships out at L5. They would finish the job.

Another forty seconds of drifting and then she yawed through 180 degrees for braking, coming in ass-end first.

She came to a dead stop forty meters beyond a point at the center of the Goltar ship's four massive engine nozzles. It must be a hell of a fast craft for its class.

For one perfect moment, she was buzzing with elation that the Goltar hadn't seen them. With the plasma torch pushing out so much radiation when in flight, she'd counted on sensors in this area being fewer. If they'd made it this far without being seen, the next part should be easy.

Then she saw the Goltar patrol and bleated pitifully.

So close to that sweet, sweet bounty!

But as she watched them march along the side of the hull, she began to hope again. The patrol didn't seem to have spotted them.

Not yet. It was just bad luck that she'd beaten the technological sentinels only to have the misfortune to run smack into a flesh-and-blood patrol.

She observed them for a few moments. Maybe they'd turn back when they reached the edge of that hull face.

The Goltar moved like no race she'd seen before. All seven tentacles moved with swiftness and elegance over the hull of their ship, pushing off in low bounds and relying on some attractive force in their suits to return them to the hull.

They were as graceful as dancers.

Junio clacked her jaws together and made herself think of the kind of dancers her bounty would buy. Hot pit shakers with wildly styled beards wearing nothing but pretty ribbons on their vestigial tails.

Come on, Junio. Keep it together. Do it for the pit girls.

The Goltar danced over the edge and onto the stern. If she did nothing, they would stumble across her people. And if she radioed an alert, the Goltar would surely notice the signal.

But there was another way.

She rolled right, pointing her pig's nose at the patrol while she cranked the handle to snap up her iron sights.

The orbital's spin meant that Junio's torpedo was slowly drifting away from the center of *Tseg-Zorig*'s stern. Which made this a damned difficult shot.

And then she saw the Goltar freeze. She had a sight picture through the view slit of two aliens touching faceplates for a conversation.

The shit must be kicking off inside Station 5.

Which meant her luck was back.

She hit both firing studs and felt the recoil as compressed air shot away two spinning beeper rounds.

Even she could hardly miss a battlecruiser at point blank range, but she wanted to hit the Goltar for maximum warning.

And she did.

Immediately, the beeper rounds alerted her team.

In response, electronics activated on her pig. Tri-V appeared behind the stealth fairing showing the four engine nozzles of the target and the Goltar marine who'd been tagged.

The cold pigs were now dangerously warm ones.

She pushed the throttle forward and urged her clumsy craft onward, heading for the shelter of the engine nozzles, hoping to put them between her and the patrol.

The Goltar were scurrying over the stern, weapons pointed in every direction.

They knew someone was out there. Somewhere.

She gulped as one Goltar's body firmed and angled all its weapons in a single direction.

At her!

Her craft registered damage a fraction before reaching the shelter of the engines. Maneuver control had been shot out! She was headed for one of the nozzles like a…torpedo. A slow-moving one, admittedly, but the impact would still crush her.

She hit her harness release and lit her maneuver pack. As she jetted away, she broadcast a radio warning. "Junio to pig riders. Contact! Goltar patrol. Six armed with laser weapons. Plant your pigs and exfil using Plan Delta."

Her torpedo side-slammed the nozzle about two thirds of the way in towards the stern. Recognizing that it had reached its target, it shot out tethers that locked it into place.

Junio jetted back to her pig and activated the payload. Through her gauntlet, she could feel hammering vibrations as it used shaped charges to punch holes into its target surface that it then filled with its payload of strong acid.

These 25-meter models carried enough acid to burn a hole through hull armor. The engine nozzles wouldn't stand a chance.

But that didn't mean they were going to get away.

The Goltar patrol was punching powerful beams of light out around the engines, searching for the intruders.

To Junio's horror, the beams quickly converged on all five of her team, who had already planted their torpedoes and were making their escape across the stern.

The patrol shot one. The other four ducked within the outer nozzle itself, using it as a shield.

Praying the Goltar wouldn't spot her, Junio made her exit, crawling around the base of the nozzle, always keeping it between her and the Goltar.

She started shaking.

A horn-buzzing, bone-shattering tremor. *It wasn't nerves.*

"No!"

Heat and radiation washed over her.

"You can't be serious!"

She heard a cry of terror in her helmet and looked up just in time to see hot gases blow through the battlecruiser's engines and expel her team, sending them tumbling out into space.

Then the fusion torch lit.

She saw each of her comrades burst momentarily into flame before being broken down into plasma and blown away.

Her pinplants told her the engines had shut down. They'd burned for less than a second. They were still burning as far as her retinas were concerned. She was blind.

Junio shut her eyes and adjusted her pinview settings until, over the permanent plasma flames, she could see the wireframe proximity map supplied by her suit.

She smiled at what she saw. They would all earn their pay. At least that was something.

The acid their torpedoes had injected had done its work. When the torches lit, they had shattered the weakened nozzles and blasted them away. For three of the nozzles, their lower half was gone.

The pinview showed a blur on the stern that was probably the patrol searching for survivors.

Exfil Plan Delta. It meant simply to head counter-spinward of the orbital's rotation and keep going until someone picked you up or you died.

A library of bio-sign alerts scrolled through her pinview. Mostly radiation and heat burns. The suit was damaged too, but it would hold up for a while longer.

So would her desire to see such bitterly earned pay flood into her Yack.

She pushed off from the far end of the hot nozzle and let rip with everything her maneuver pack would give her, trusting to blind fate.

It would be okay.

That's why she'd selected Oxroc as pilot. He was her bad-tempered lucky charm.

She owed the Blevin fifty credits.

It wasn't much, but the pilot had an irrational revulsion for unpaid debts.

He'd come for her all right.

* * * * *

Chapter Twenty-Five

Shove 'n' Done Tavern, Station 5, Beta-Caerelis

Beowulf dove behind the bar. Although the mercs had—at first—pushed the Endless Night forces out of the bar, one of the enemy troopers had thrown a grenade that had knocked out two of the mercs, and the black-clad forces had surged forward again.

A bottle next to him exploded and he glanced behind him; more Endless Night were coming around a corner down the passageway behind him, trading fire with the Goltar and Human soldiers from the meeting. He dove to the side and slammed the door shut. Several more laser blasts burned through the door, leaving smoking holes.

"All right, DeGris—" He stopped as he turned back around. DeGris had taken a laser through the forehead. Damn it. He had just been about to ask him how they were going to slip out of this one; now he'd have to figure it out himself.

It looked bad, he saw as he looked over the bar and fired a couple of shots at the closest Endless Night trooper. There were only two mercs with him behind the bar and at least ten of the Endless Night assholes. They were getting closer, working their way toward the bar, and flanking them to the right.

"Damn it," one of the mercs said, falling back with a laser burn through the meat of his arm.

Beowulf fired again, and the slide locked back. *Damn it! How was his pistol empty again?*

"I'm out!" he said.

"Here!" the merc with the laser burn said. He slid his pistol over just in time for Beowulf to grab it and shoot a black-clad Zuul as it came around the bar.

"Any ideas?" Beowulf asked.

The wounded merc pulled out his knife with his left hand. "Charge them?"

"*Are you crazy?*" Beowulf exclaimed.

The man shrugged. "They can't capture and torture us if we're dead."

The answer gave Beowulf pause. He knew a lot of things the Endless Night would like to know. All of a sudden, the option to charge them didn't sound so bad.

Beowulf fired another couple of times, hitting at least one rat-looking alien—*what was an Aposo doing here?*—then the merc's pistol went empty. "Got another mag?" he asked.

The merc gritted his teeth and shook his head.

"Fuck," Beowulf noted. He pulled out his knife.

"Wait for it," the second merc said as he tossed away his empty pistol in disgust and drew his knife, too. "Let 'em get close and then we'll charge. We'll get more of them that way." He shuffled his body around to a sprinter's crouch, and the wounded merc did similarly.

Beowulf hadn't been in a knife fight in fifteen years—*not since that night in Houston*—and especially wasn't looking forward to bringing a knife to a gunfight. He steeled himself, vowing to kill as many of the bastards as he could.

"On three," the unwounded merc said. "One...two..."

The volume of fire increased exponentially in the bar, and men and other beings started screaming as a *Thump! Thump! Thump!* sound filled the air. Beowulf glanced over the bar in time to see several CASPers race into the bar from the right, laser shields extended on their left arms while the auto-shotguns on their right arms turned the bar furniture—and all the Endless Night assholes—into broken wrecks of what they had been. He ducked down as a splinter as big as his arm whipped past his head.

After a few seconds, the sounds of firing stopped, and he risked another look over the bar. A mist of a couple of colors of blood mingled with the formerly white stuffing from the seat pads.

"Behind the bar, come out with your hands and paws up!" a woman's voice called.

Beowulf raised his hands and stood, along with the unwounded merc. "There's one more behind here," he said, "but he's wounded."

"Who's Beowulf?" a short Asian-looking woman asked from a group of people who'd followed the CASPer troopers. The woman looked like her picture, and her command voice gave it away. *Sansar Enkh. The Golden Horde had arrived!*

"I am, ma'am," he said. Another laser bolt came through the door behind him, narrowly missing him, and he shuffled to the side. "There's a few more of the bastards down the passageway behind me," he added.

Sansar looked over to one of the—now six—CASPers in the room. "Staff Sergeant McDonald, could you take care of that please?"

The CASPer-clad trooper said, "Nichols, you're with me." He stepped up to the bar, grabbed it, and ripped it to the side. A laser bolt burned through the door and hit him in the chest, but didn't have enough energy to penetrate the suit.

"That's how the assholes want to play it, huh?" he muttered. "Let's go teach them not to start something they can't finish." He put his head down and crashed through the door, then extended his laser shield again as he ran down the hallway with the second CASPer right behind him. One of the Endless Night soldiers had the guts—or stupidity—to stand his ground and fire at the Golden Horde CASPer, but McDonald swatted his pistol away with his laser shield as he reached the corner, then fired several of the massive buckshot rounds into him.

The two soldiers ran off out of sight around the corner, firing another four times, then they came back to what was left of the bar. "They're done, ma'am," McDonald said.

"Real done," Nichols added with a morbid chuckle.

Laverna's head popped out of the meeting room down the passageway. "Is it safe to come out?"

"Yes," Beowulf said, as the others emerged from the meeting room. "These are my associates. Ladies and gentlemen, may I present Sansar Enkh and the Golden Horde?" He smiled as—to a man—their jaws all dropped. Even the Goltar drew up short at the revelation. Apparently he'd done a good job downplaying how much assistance he could provide. Laverna turned to stare at him, and he winked. "My motto is, 'Always under-promise and over-deliver.'" Beowulf smiled. "How'd I do?"

* * * * *

Chapter Twenty-Six

Conference Room, EMS *Gobi Desert*, Station 5, Beta-Caerelis

"Welcome aboard the *Gobi Desert*," Sansar said once everyone had been seated and introduced back on the ship. Station Security had been unimpressed with the carnage wreaked on one of the station's favorite watering holes. Even though the Horde soldiers had killed the people who'd killed the security forces and had started the entire fight—as corroborated by the security cameras in the passageway—they had still been nonplussed at the number of armed individuals onboard the station, and especially the CASPers. That is, they were, 10 minutes after the shooting stopped when they finally got up the nerve to poke their noses around the corner and take a look.

All in all, it had seemed better to be somewhere else at that point, and Sansar had offered her ship's conference room as a secure place to discuss their plans. Most of the supporting forces had returned to their ships, especially the Goltars who had hurried off when they got word that there'd been an attack on one of their ships.

"Thank you," Gloriana replied, "and thank you for your timely arrival."

"My pleasure," Sansar said, sketching a small bow. "Who were those people, anyway?"

"That is the group we wanted to hire you to help us fight. They are the Endless Night."

"The Endless Night? Ooh, sounds scary," Sansar said with a sarcastic edge.

"Perhaps more than you know," Gloriana replied. "Once, they were just another criminal organization, trying to get their tentacles into the Spine Nebula."

"More damn criminals around here than you can shake a stick at," Branco muttered.

"You know, I've had about enough of him," Beowulf said. "I'm sorry about the earlier 'leg to stand on' comment; I didn't know you were an amputee. But the fact of the matter is, you wouldn't be here right now—none of us would—if I hadn't called in the Golden Horde. So, I'm going to ask you one more time to shut the fuck up, or I'm going to wipe that sneer off your face, permanently."

"Perhaps you *should* go if you can't hold your tongue," Gloriana said, staring at Branco.

Branco met her gaze for a couple of moments, then he looked down and sighed. "Sorry, Beowulf, you're right; I was out of place. You did save our lives."

"So now that's settled," Sansar said, "what the hell is going on here? We walk into the station and people are shooting it out, people are sabotaging ships tied up to the station, and there's talk of a starkiller here, too?"

Several people spoke at once, then Gloriana overrode them all. "As the senior member here, it falls on me to tell the story." Sansar caught Captain Blue's epic eye roll, but Gloriana couldn't see it from her side of the table. Gloriana continued, "There isn't just one starkiller, but three. We have destroyed one of them, but two remain, and I have been trying to get assistance to help take them out."

A cold shiver ran down Sansar's back as the image of Sol going nova danced through her waking vision. She glanced at Beowulf. "I thought you said *one* starkiller."

"That was all I knew about, too, until just a few minutes ago. My spies found out about the one on McPherson-3 and that it was going to fire. I tried to get a spy in to find out where it was, but he didn't come back. Apparently, based on some additional intel we received, my spy intervened at the last moment, right as they were firing the weapon at Sol, and caused the targeting to go somewhere else. The Endless Night bosses were quite upset. Unfortunately, we didn't get the targeting info on the weapon, because he didn't make it out of there."

"So, if it weren't for this spy, the Solar System would now be incinerated?"

"Yes, ma'am. Apparently, the weapon fired, but we don't know where it went. If we hear about a star going nova for no apparent reason, that's where the bolt landed."

"How soon can they fire the weapon again?"

"We don't know. It takes time to recharge and the power required to go wherever it went blew out some seals or something, making it take longer than normal. Based on what I know, they can probably use it again in another ten days, maybe two weeks at the outside, but I wouldn't want to bet the Solar System on it. That weapon *will* be fired soon, and Earth *will* be the target. There is a third weapon located in the Wahrner's Grise system, although we don't know a lot about it."

Sansar turned to Gloriana. "And you want to hire us to help stop them?"

"I do, although knowing your home system is the target ought to make you want to do it for free."

Sansar chuckled. "It does, but we *did* come a long way out here at your request, so I'm hoping you'll make it worth our while." Gloriana nodded, and Sansar's eyes swept the table. "So who here can tell me about this Endless Night organization?"

"Just about any of us," Major Sun said. "We've all had our run-ins with the Endless Night. It's a criminal organization that has become the de facto ruler of parts of the nebula. It's big enough to have its own military forces, and to have contracted a Maki merc outfit, the Spinning Shield, which has about a dozen of mostly smaller ships. And, now they control two starkillers."

"They need to die," Sansar said, "and the starkillers need to be put out of commission, permanently."

"Or at least taken from them," Gloriana said. "They would make powerful weapons if they were controlled by the right people, and you never know—we may need them in the future. I know that the Golden Horde does defensive work...if we took them, could you design defenses to keep them safe?"

"I think you missed what I said," Sansar replied. "They. Must. Be. Destroyed. They represent absolute power, and they will corrupt anyone who has them. We need to destroy them to make sure they're never used against us or any of our allies."

"It is too late for that," Gloriana said. "One has already been used on Tau-Rietzke, where the Midnight Sun Free Company used to have its main base. It no longer exists. I would give them a taste of their own weapon."

"No," Sansar said. "I forbid it. If you want our aid, it is to take them and destroy them, not to hold them for future use or to pay back the Endless Night." She stared at Gloriana. "What's it going to be?"

Gloriana met her stare for several long seconds before looking away. "Fine. We will destroy them, but I think this is a mistake."

Sansar nodded once. "Then it is decided. We will work for you to destroy the two starkillers. What forces do we have at our disposal, and what does the enemy have?"

"We have the battlecruiser *Midnight Sun*," Gloriana said, "in addition to a Goltar task force led by the carrier *Blunt Justice* and two battlecruisers, depending on whether or not the damaged battlecruiser *Tseg-Zorig* will be able to sail. We also have your troops, the EMS *Gobi Desert,* and some smaller Spine Patriot navy ships.

"Arrayed against us are the Endless Night combat forces, about a dozen Maki ships, like I already mentioned, and an unknown number of smaller Scythe vessels. With regard to the Spinning Shield, we believe their fleet is composed of a battlecruiser, two destroyers, and about ten frigates."

"And the Scythe forces are?"

"They are mostly pirates with smaller ships," Gloriana said.

"But they are eyes and ears," Blue said, speaking for the first time. "I would bet that they were the ones responsible for the attack on the *Tseg-Zorig.*"

"Do you have something that confirms it?" Gloriana asked.

"No, it's just a feeling. If I close my eyes, I can almost feel them sneaking around."

"Can we eliminate them?" Sansar asked.

"I doubt it," Blue said. "It would be hard to bring them to battle. They hang out near the scrapyard at the L5 point. If I went near it, they would run; they know the *Midnight Sun* and I could wipe them out without any effort." She chuckled.

Sansar's eyebrow twitched. The way Blue had included the ship with her sounded odd, somehow, as if they were a single unit. Sansar pursed her lips as she thought about the rest of what Blue had said. "So," she finally said, "we can expect the Scythe forces to run to the Endless Night and tell them what we're doing?"

"Probably."

"We have two targets. One of these we have localized, if not totally located, and we're going to need more information on the second one before we can assault it."

"That's correct," Beowulf said.

"In that case, I have the preponderance of ground forces, so it falls to me to hit the weapon in the McPherson system. They're going to know we're coming, so we'll need the fleet assets to break through the Spinning Shield."

Blue and Gloriana nodded.

"The problem—like the Scythe forces—is whether we can get the Spinning Shield to decisively engage us," Gloriana said. "I want them all together so they can be destroyed, rather than continue to chip away at us like they're doing."

Blue smiled. "I have an idea on that we can discuss once we're done here."

"Good—you work it out," Sansar said. "Just get us to the planet, and we'll take care of the defenses."

"How will you overcome them?" Gloriana asked.

"It's impossible to know what we'll do until we see what they have set up. We understand defenses, though—it's something we're very good at—and we'll just have to work it out on the fly." She looked at Beowulf. "If they are as close to firing the weapon as you say—"

"They are."

"—then we don't have a lot of time for target recce. Don't worry; we'll get it done."

"Speaking of target recce," Branco said, "what are we going to do with Wahrner's Grise?"

"We will hit the weapon there after we finish with the one in the McPherson system, but we're going to need better info on it than we have." She turned back to Beowulf. "Do you have any contacts in Wahrner's Grise?"

Beowulf sat back in his chair and smiled.

"Of course you do," Sansar said. "Stupid question. Okay, the question is, can you infiltrate some people into the system to conduct the recce work we need?"

Beowulf chewed on his upper lip for a moment, then he nodded slowly. "Yes. That shouldn't be a problem."

"Good—the mission to recce the Wahrner's Grise weapon will be led by Major Sun and the members of the Midnight Sun Free Company."

"We're uh…we're a little thin on assets at the moment," Sun said. "We've only got a squad of CASPers left, and several of the drivers are injured. All of the mechs are in desperate need of repairs, too. Gloriana has brought parts and armorers from Tau-Rietzke, so that's now underway onboard *Midnight Sun*. As of this moment, though, mine is the only suit I would describe as combat effective. Then there are the Goltar companies, of course."

Sansar pursed her lips, calculating what she might need for the assault. "I think I can spare you a platoon from my Bravo Company to add to as many of your CASPers as you can get ready. They have some folks who are experienced in some of the skills you need. In fact, one man used to run a company that conducted combat search and recovery of both people and assets. They might be helpful in sneaking around and the art of misdirection."

"I take it he is the platoon commander?" Sun said.

"No, he's actually a squad leader at the moment, although that woefully underutilizes his skills. Recruiting has been…complicated since the war."

"Well, we will take the platoon, and happily," Sun said.

"Good." Sansar nodded. "We need *Midnight Sun* to help force a path through to McPherson-3 for *Gobi Desert,* and, if needed, we can add her Goltars into the assault. That leaves the question of how we get you to Wahrner's Grise." She looked back to Beowulf. "Can you get a reinforced platoon's worth of troops in?"

"It'll be difficult getting that many in there unnoticed, but with help from the Spine Patriots, I think it can be done."

"Fine. Then I think we're agreed."

Blue nodded. "Good, here's what I recommend for dealing with the Spinning Shield…"

* * * * *

Chapter Twenty-Seven

Scythe Observation Post, L5 Scrapyard, Beta-Caerelis

"Movement!" the Lumar manning the terminal called. "Big ships moving."

Captain S'leth did his best not to sigh. The Lumar were perfect for sitting at a terminal and waiting all day for something to happen. They didn't get bored—maybe they weren't smart enough to do so—but they weren't very good at making reports once something happened that was outside their understanding of the task.

"What is moving, and in which direction?" S'leth asked. The Lumar looked back at his display. The telescope was good enough to see Station 5, and they had long ago labeled which ships were which at the station. "Is it the *Gobi Desert?*" They were familiar with all the other ships and knew who the players were, but the new Human ship was a mystery. It belonged to one of the Human companies of some repute, but the Endless Night had been unable to determine what the Humans were doing there. There were rumors of the Golden Horde having ties to the Gray Wolves, who were known to have a presence on Station 5, but no one had been able to determine what might bring the Golden Horde to the nebula.

"No, not *Gobi*. Two big ships. *Midnight Sun* and *Tseg-Lenkh*. Also some small craft."

S'leth sent a runner, and Auchonax, the old alpha male who ran the Vitayr-Scrap Clan appeared a few minutes later.

"This had better be important," Auchonax said with a growl.

"It is," S'leth said. "Two battlecruisers, the *Midnight Sun* and *Tseg-Lenkh,* have gotten underway from Station 5 and are headed toward the stargate."

"What of the others? The *Gobi Desert?*"

"They are all staying put," S'leth said. "Neither the *Gobi* nor the other Goltar ships appear to be getting underway."

Auchonax chuckled. "We must have damaged the other battlecruiser significantly, if it takes both the carrier and a transport to stay with it."

"That was my thinking, too."

"Are you sure they are heading to the stargate?"

"Yes, sir. That is the only destination possible for the heading they're on."

"Send the alert pinnace to McPherson and let the Endless Night know that the battlecruisers are coming. I'm sure they will want to set up a surprise for them. A *fatal* surprise."

"It will be my pleasure," S'leth said. He looked at the chronometer. "If they hurry, they can make today's stargate opening." He sent out a number of orders, and a small ship got underway a few minutes later. It raced toward the stargate and just made it through before the stargate closed.

* * * * *

Chapter Twenty-Eight

**Flag Operations Room, *Vindictive*,
McPherson's Star Emergence Point**

"Commodore, shall I proceed?" Grak punctuated his question with an aggressive hiss.

"I told you to await orders. They shall be forthcoming, *once* I have decided what they shall be. You must obey the chain of command."

"As must you, Commodore. As must you." The Goka crossed his antennae in what Fenrikho knew to be an obscene gesture. "I'll give you a little more time."

"Insufferable little bug," she yelled at the Tri-V disc, though only after the Endless Night naval commander had ended the transmission.

'Navy' was a ridiculous title for the floating scrapyard Grak commanded. Admittedly, the name served a useful purpose in concealing the true purpose of Grak's ships. What lay hidden from the ever-present Spine Patriot observation within their holds could be the key to victory.

Drones.

Of course, her own Spinning Shield warships still carried some of their original consignment of drones, as per standard tactical doctrine. But Grak's carried far more.

Fenrikho had persuaded Coron and Retenex to invest heavily in drones. Manufacturing them, stealing them, even buying them. They had set about converting satellites, weather buoys, comm relays and anything else they could plug a laser into and connect up to a basic tactical intelligence.

Most of these new Endless Night assets were of dubious quality, but the drones filling the holds of Grak's freighters numbered in the tens of thousands.

Even so, Fenrikho still didn't like the odds.

The Goltar battlecruiser would appear in that emergence point in approximately two days. What was its capability?

The Goltar fleet had helped to bring about Peepo's demise at Earth. Would the *Tseg-Lenkh* be hers?

On the other tail, the corporate board had made it clear after the loss of *Long Reach*—the other battlecruiser in her fleet—that she had better come back from the Spine Nebula laden with combat bonuses, prize ships, and captured mercs to ransom.

Or not to bother coming back at all.

There was a knock on the hatch, and Captain Guntic came in, checking they were alone in the small ops room.

The company had well-established procedures for replacing fleet commanders in the field. If that were to be her fate, as captain of the flagship, Guntic would take her place.

She glared at him. Expecting to see arrogance in his posture. Or maybe guilt.

Yet his tails were folded over near the tips, the epitome of respectful professionalism.

"Well?" she snapped. "Why are you here?"

He squared his shoulders and came to attention. "We served together for seven years on *First Strike*. You were my mentor. I still observe you closely because I want to learn from the best."

"That's very gratifying. Now cut the preamble and get to the point."

"You have a big decision to make, Commodore. Do we stand and fight? I thought you might want a trusted sounding board."

"I do not, thank you. But since you are here, Captain, I have decided to implement the high guard defense in depth strategy. Liaise with Grak. Tell him to deploy drones immediately. We finally have *Midnight Sun* committed to a battlefield of my choosing. I, Commodore Fenrikho, will achieve what Peepo's lieutenants and many other captains failed to do. I will destroy that damned ship."

"Aye, aye, Commodore."

Guntic's mask of professional kinship slipped. His upper lip raised a little to show his teeth. His tails dropped a little in disappointment.

Then the mask was replaced, and Guntic was once more the model of obedience.

Fenrikho's heart hammered in her chest, not slowing until Guntic had disappeared, and she'd locked the hatch behind him.

She sat down heavily and buried her face in her hands. If she hadn't given the order to dig in and fight, she felt sure Guntic would have usurped her there and then.

And there was only one way a fleet commander left her post during an active operation. Out the airlock.

She'd been moments away from losing her life.

But with *Midnight Sun* and *Tseg-Lenkh* on their way to do battle, by how much had she prolonged it?

* * * * *

Chapter Twenty-Nine

CIC, *Midnight Sun*

"Emergence from hyperspace complete. Sensor net establishing. Multiple contacts in threat envelope. Multiple proximity alerts."

The MinSha first officer paused uncharacteristically. "Analysis: the enemy has mined the emergence point with drones."

I've never heard the old insect so worried, thought Blue. She had already formed the same opinion of what they were facing. Through a deep connection with the ship, she felt multiple pinpricks from underpowered lasers biting her shields, and the scratches as she collided with small objects.

Space was so damn big, that the only places it made sense to mine were emergence points and star gates. Since pissing off the Cartography Guild was not a good path toward fun and profit, this situation was highly unusual.

Of course, the other way to make effective use of drones—or old-school proximity mines—was to have such a mindbogglingly large number that you ran out of zeroes to count them. Then you could mine entire sectors of space, such as the Veetanho had in their defensive belts around Lytoshaan.

She'd run simulated attacks on that planet thousands of times. If her sim experience had taught her one thing, it was that if fields of drones lay between you and your objective, your best hope for survival was to open the throttles to the stops and pray to the gods.

"Flkk'Sss, you will dedicate yourself to coordinating our anti-drone defenses. Konchill, you take over full tactical control. Once we have punched through these drones, you will concentrate our fire on the enemy frigates."

Wheeesshhhh! Ever since promoting the Bakulu to lieutenant, Konchill had developed a habit of whistling through the rim of his shell whenever he was excited. Or worried.

"I have tactical control, aye." *Wheeeesssh.* "Err...what frigates, Captain?"

"Warships detected," declared SitCon. "Maki frigates. Calling them bandits."

"*Those* frigates, Konchill." Blue built up speed. The collisions grazing her beams came ever more frequently. "SitCon, do something about the plot. We can't see the warships for the drones. But we don't need to for me to know that Fenrikho is making a stand here. She will have the bulk of her fleet beyond the drone field. Trust me. That means we will be facing a battlecruiser and two destroyers, but we concentrate our fire on the frigates. Leave the bigger vessels to the big guns."

"Shoot the frigates," confirmed Konchill. "Aye, Captain."

"Helmsman, I will pilot."

"Transferring helm control," acknowledged Ensign Dahmer.

"Hang onto your hats, ladies, gentlemen, and other beings. Hang onto your lunches too. This might not be Lytoshaan, but it's gonna be rough."

Shit! No one picked her up on the Lytoshaan slip. Flkk'Sss would have noted, though. Busted!

SitCon simplified the tactical plot they could all see in their pinviews by removing the individual drone plots and replacing them with a tinted zone of space. The crossed crescent formation Fenrikho had deployed on the far side was becoming clear.

Blue had another view, one shared with the ship. It was more than visual. More than the entire electromagnetic spectrum. She had learned to avoid putting labels on *Midnight Sun*'s perception of the universe and simply relaxed into it. She knew there were concentrations of drone clusters. Set up like machine gun nests designed to lash anything caught in their crossfire.

The ship pulled to one side, nudging toward the nearest concentration of enemy fire.

She resisted for a moment, but then redistributed the fusion torch around a different configuration of exhaust ports. The ship headed straight for the nearest drone nest.

The best way to limit the crossfire was to head for the nearest concentration, destroy it, and push through the gap in the defenses.

Her forward shield was throbbing with incoming pain as they approached the first nest.

Blue temporarily switched off the torch, spun the outer layer of the ship around to replace fore with aft, and relit the torch.

She gritted her teeth as the fresher shields took their pain. This was gonna get far worse before it got better, but she took advantage of a fractional moment of relative calm to indulge her curiosity.

Blue and the ship sometimes fought each other as they attempted to determine tactical strategy.

This time, Blue had given way immediately, because she had sensed something new with *Midnight Sun*: the voice of experience.

This wasn't the first time *Midnight Sun* had charged through deep drone defenses in real life. She'd done this before. Many times.

And survived.

"Well, well, old girl. Your mysteries are beginning to reveal themselves."

Argghhh! Shit!

A one-shot nuclear-powered x-ray beam punched through the aft shields and stabbed through the outer decks.

Midnight Sun was venting atmosphere. Suddenly, its captain didn't feel so confident.

She upped her velocity and raced toward the drone cluster under an acceleration that was going to cause her crew problems if she held it more than a minute or so.

Inside her chest, pumps kicked in. She sounded like a rattling two-stroke engine.

With the laser fire lashing at her with ever increasing strength, it was the least of her concerns.

* * * * *

Chapter Thirty

CIC, *Vindictive*

Fenrikho observed *Midnight Sun* as her foe passed through the outer layer of the drone field. The spherical ship vectored toward a cluster of the higher-powered drones. Captain Blue was a particularly unpredictable example of a race renowned for its erratic and uncivilized behavior.

It looked as if Blue was going to ram the drones.

At pointblank range, *Midnight Sun* cut her rear-facing torch and immediately relit it through front exhaust ports, braking hard and blowing clouds of plasma over the drones as she edged around the cluster.

An icon in the display indicated that this plasma was highly radioactive. The damned Human had found a way to turn engine exhaust into a weapon.

The cluster went black in the tactical map. Destroyed.

Her view of *Midnight Sun* was lost too. When she accessed a close visual from another feed and magnified, she saw the once gleaming hull of *Midnight Sun* was now scorched, hurt by the punishing laser volleys that had temporarily overloaded her shields. A beam weapon had punched clean through her hull.

A death by a thousand cuts was a death all the same. And that's precisely what the drones were doing to the entropy-ridden ship.

Fenrikho allowed herself a moment to imagine promotion to the corporate board. Retirement to her own pleasure moon. It was all to fight for. Hers to claim.

Then she thought of the Cartography Guild's potential retribution for deploying the drone fleet danger close to the emergence point. Her dreams of decadence fell apart.

"Give me a visual on the *Tseg-Lenkh*."

The sensors team supplied a close-up of the blocky polyhedral slice of a battlecruiser. It had emerged from hyperspace on an acute vector almost perpendicular to *Midnight Sun*, which was charging straight through the center of the drone field. The Goltar ship had changed heading and was now running parallel to the Human-controlled ship, a short distance off her stern.

But it was catching up.

Midnight Sun was dancing through the drone field, throwing a flurry of light punches and dodging counterstrikes with defensive munitions and blasts of salted plasma clouds. By contrast, *Tseg-Lenkh* was charging ahead like an enraged Oogar.

Fenrikho rolled back the view to take a wider perspective of the battle space.

The Goltar ship was making straight for the *Vindictive*.

"Frigate Groups 1 and 3, prepare to concentrate fire on *Tseg-Lenkh*."

She watched the two enemy ships advancing through her tactical plot.

The drone field was configured like a funnel. Drone strength was strongest in the outer edge in order to punish any ship who thought they could break out the side of the funnel. The opening facing the emergence point largely consisted of less powerful drones.

The two enemy ships were halfway through the drone field, but the most powerful drones lay beyond them. And then there were her frontline warships to destroy anything that made it through.

Theoretically, the battle was already won. But that pleasure moon didn't feel like it was in her grasp. Other fleet commanders had felt assured of victory against *Midnight Sun*, and yet still that accursed ship was intact and advancing toward her.

"Frigate Group 3, belay that last order. Be ready to meet *Midnight Sun*'s emergence from the drone field as before."

Fenrikho licked her lips nervously. *Midnight Sun* had survived her earlier battles because her opponents had underestimated her. And her Human captain.

Fenrikho tried to think of how she might be making the same mistake.

But she couldn't see a flaw in her plan.

"What do you know that I do not, Captain Blue?"

There had to be something. But what?

* * * * *

Chapter Thirty-One

Flag Deck, *Blunt Justice,* McPherson's Star System

Gloriana felt the familiar flicker in her rear tentacles as she was remade into normal space. Instantly, the command decks came alive beneath her.

"Multiple contacts. Hostile drones."

"Point defenses firing. Banks three through eighteen."

"Tight beam link to *Midnight Sun* established."

With her two enormous battleriders, *Gobi Desert* and *Tseg-Zorig,* clamped to her hull, *Blunt Justice* had emerged directly into battle.

That *had* been the plan, after all. But not for the battle to engulf the emergence point itself. Fenrikho must have tails of steel to risk the wrath of the Cartography Guild so blatantly.

Or desperate.

"Data upload from *Tseg-Lenkh* completed."

"*Gobi Desert* de-clamping."

Hot excitement pumped through Gloriana's limbs. The urge to fight all but consumed her, though she'd never been a naval commander. She curled an arm around an empty seat stump and squeezed so hard it distorted.

That helped. She kept her beak clamped shut for now.

"*Midnight Sun* and *Tseg-Lenkh* taking heavy damage. They are nearing the threat zone of the enemy fleet line."

"7,013 hostile operational drones confirmed. Preliminary estimation: sixty percent are lasers of 1MW power or lower. Main enemy battle line consists of: *Petal*-class battlecruiser *Vindictive*, two *Yperex*-class destroyers, four *Seed*-class escort frigates paired with four *Sheek*-class laser frigates. Two more frigates orbiting McPherson-3, well outside the battle zone."

From her post at the small flag deck suspended above the CIC hive, Gloriana dipped her attention through battle reports, tactical plots, and the war of attrition that had already begun between the secondary and tertiary armament of *Blunt Justice* and the drones swarming her.

Back in the Beta-Caerelis system, Captain Kanat-Baim had timed activation of the hyperspace shunts to perfection, arriving at McPherson ten minutes after *Midnight Sun* and *Tseg-Lenkh*'s emergence.

None of the planning scenarios had considered that they would land inside an ocean of drones. She had hoped that Fenrikho would be so awestruck by the sudden appearance of the majestic Goltar flagship that her fleet would flee.

These drones would never lose heart, though. They would simply acknowledge fresh targets and fire.

Gloriana uncurled her limb from the seat stump. Doubts crept in.

"All drones launching."

"Vlimkh squadrons report ready to launch, Captain."

Gloriana's pinplants received a message from the flagship's captain. "High Councilor, request permission to launch Vlimkh?"

She took a few seconds to appreciate the moment. She trusted the captain to know how to fight a battle, but to release the Vlimkh was as much a political and cultural act as it was military.

They hadn't been unleashed on the galaxy since the early years after the Great Galactic War.

"*Gobi Desert* hailing us."

"*Tseg-Zorig* reports drones away."

"Connect me with the Horde captain."

The battlefield was no respecter of formalities. It would not wait.

Gloriana bunched her limbs into a martial pose for the cameras that would somewhere be capturing this moment. Then she made her decision.

"Launch all squadrons!"

* * * * *

Chapter Thirty-Two

CIC, EMS *Gobi Desert*, McPherson's Star system

"That's a whole metric fuckload of drones," noted Captain Steve Parker.

The Goltar captain he was talking to through the Tri-V might look like an octopus, but Parker recognized when someone was giving him the stink eye.

"Are you fleeing?" asked Captain Kanat-Baim.

"No, I'm asking whether you've anything in reserve up your tentacles that will give my ship a fighting chance. Something to get us through so many drones without being blown to atoms. We're not as heavily armored as *Tseg-Lenkh*. Nor as...Whatever the hell *Midnight Sun* is, we're not that."

"Understood. Here are your new orders."

Parker bristled. *Orders!*

Was Kanat-Baim kidding?

They had a loose agreement to cooperate, and the Horde had a contract to destroy a starkiller—whatever the hell that was—but none of that meant taking orders from space squids.

Colonel Enkh had come up with the name Quadpartite Alliance for the combination of Midnight Sun, Goltar, Horde, and Spine Patriots. Parker guessed she'd been joking, but the name had leaked. And stuck.

Captain Kanat-Baim commanded the bulk of the Alliance's tonnage, but that didn't make him Parker's CO.

"You will shelter behind our stern."

"What about your fusion torch?"

"We shall not light it while you are close."

The squids were planning to float dead in space? That was crazy.

"*Tseg-Zorig*'s engines were disabled in the sneak attack at Station 5," the Goltar explained. "Instead of ejecting her, she will remain clamped to *Blunt Justice* and provide both of us with close defense against the drone onslaught. Our ability to maneuver is compromised anyway while the battlecruiser is attached."

"Acknowledged," said Parker. "We are coming behind your stern."

"We will clear a safe path through the enemy defenses with three layers of Goltar drones."

"Then we slip out from your shadow and head through the cleared corridor."

"Negative. You will wait for your fighter escort to form up on you. Then you enter the cleared corridor and concentrate your attack—"

"Wait. Backup and say again. Did you just say *fighters*?"

"Two squadrons of Vlimkh fighters will escort you through the corridor. Once you are through, you will make your attack on the targets I prioritize for you."

The XO interrupted. "Captain!"

Parker waved her away.

"Sir, you need to see this."

Multiple pinplant layers meant efficient multitasking. Parker watched with a part of his attention what a sensor tech had passed up the chain.

He magnified the image of one of the fighters streaming out of the supercarrier's launch bays. Seven wings radiated from a central bulbous cockpit. It had freaking windows! Through them he could see a Goltar in a flight helmet.

The wings moved. Flexed like they were living arms. It looked like…

"Roger that, Captain Kanat-Baim. Just one thing."

There was that stink eye again.

"These *Vlimkh*-class fighters—the description doesn't translate well for us. I'm reclassifying them as *starfish*."

"As you wish," said Kanat-Baim and severed the link.

* * * * *

Chapter Thirty-Three

Shield Ops 3, *Midnight Sun*

A woman's voice was speaking.

Petty Officer Brabant's horizon had narrowed to a point source of awareness. The voice lay outside of this. He couldn't ignore her, though. Instinct told him she was important. So he expanded his awareness by force of will alone.

Man, it hurt!

His chest was caving in. He could hear cracking and popping. Shit! Was that his ribs?

But. He. *Fought* his way to the voice.

It was the captain.

"I say again. All hands, slowing to two Gs for 150 seconds."

The love-hungry pair of elephants rutting on his chest rolled over and lit cigarettes. Brabant drew a sweet breath of air.

Except it didn't taste right. The air was smoky. Why was that?

"Call out by sections!" demanded Chief Petty Officer Zucarri through pin-comms.

"Section 1 here, Chief," replied PO French from Shield Ops 1.

"Two's alive."

Pop! Pop! Pop!

"That makes three, Chief," said Brabant.

What was that popping noise?

He realized he'd been checking through diagnostic readouts for several seconds already.

He'd set a 140-second timer too.

It was always that way after an intense gee burn. His pinplants helped him multitask, but the different threads of his awareness took a while to knot back together.

"Make every second count," urged the shields' chief. "LT says we'll be in multiple threat zones straight after this pause. Those destroyers have two five-GW lasers apiece, and the *Sheek* laser frigates have a spinal seven-GW."

Brabant allowed himself one more deep recovery breath. They were still thrusting a bruising two Gs, and despite all the buffering in his acceleration cocoon, he could tell the captain was jinking as hard as she dared.

One breath was all he needed. Anyone crazy enough to sign on with *Midnight Sun* had been required to undergo high-gee nanite hardening.

He'd almost turned down the job offer when he'd heard that, but he'd been desperate. The injection had hurt like fuck, but he wasn't grumbling now.

Pop. Pop.

"Zhang, figure out what's making that damned noise. I can smell smoke in here too."

He ran through the shield diagnostics and summary logs at a frantic pace, delving down into detail of why Shield 3/2 had tripped twice during the race through the drones, leaving them dangerously exposed for several seconds while it had restarted.

He reckoned he had thirty seconds to figure out the most important corrections he could make, and a hundred more to do something about them. Then those horny elephants would be frolicking on his chest once more, and it would be all he could do to stay conscious.

Midnight Sun was unlike any ship he'd ever served upon. The configuration of everything was just plain weird. Its main armament predated the Ark.

She had three shield ops sections, based in their own compartments spread throughout the ship. Each was responsible for a trio of multiphase, redeployable 255/7-rated shields that could each theoretically handle 2TW of incoming pain.

But that was only a nominal rating.

Incoming beams would fire brief pulses measured in picoseconds. It was the peak energy per unit area—the shield *fluence*—that was most likely to overcome his shields.

While he mused on the awesome tech he was responsible for with a small part of his mind, Brabant succeeded in narrowing down his list of problems.

The drones were the first of them. Individually, many of them were no more powerful than a chemical laser rifle, but the strange thing about energy weapons, was that the weaker they were, the more efficient they were at inflicting damage.

A thousand one-MW lasers would drain shields a lot faster than a single one-GW weapon.

And that was exactly what was happening.

There was nothing he could do about that problem, but Shield 3/2 hadn't been able to cope. It had tripped twice.

The second problem was simpler to fix. Several drone shots had fired through a separation that had opened up between 3/1 and 1/2. He stretched out 3/1's coverage to increase the overlap with its neighbor and returned to the problem of the tripping shield.

Pop. Pop.

"Zhang, talk to me. If we all die from an electrical fire, I'm gonna be seriously pissed. Charlie, talk to me, squidly. Why does 3/2 keep tripping?"

Neither replied.

Brabant pulled his attention away and took a few valuable moments to observe Shield Ops 3 through a bulkhead camera.

Something had ripped open the overhead on the far side of the compartment. A half-severed power conduit had fallen down inside. The popping noises were generated by sparks that also delivered puffs of blue smoke. A bracing spar had fallen down, smashing through Zhang's acceleration cocoon and spearing him into the deck.

Damn! When did that happen?

The Goltar shield tech, 'Charlie,' was still in his cocoon. Something had squashed it flat, splattering alien blood over the vicinity.

Brabant notified damage control, the Chief, and the medical division. There was nothing more he could do for them now. His duty was to concentrate on keeping everyone on the ship alive by fixing the shields.

He raised CPO Kozietulski. "Chief, I think we're gonna have to take 3/2 off-line."

"Why did it trip?"

"I can't tell."

"Fuck." The chief sucked in a sharp breath. "Without Zhang and Charlie, you made the right call, Brabant. Take 3/2 off-line."

Brabant shut down the shield and began stretching 3/1 and 3/3 to cover the gap.

He couldn't. Something was in the way.

It was 3/2. It hadn't shut down.

His timer had just twenty-five seconds to run.

He kept his calm and ran through the diagnostic log.

His shutdown command had been issued correctly.

The control routing to the shield generator was clear of damage.

It was as if the ship had disobeyed his command.

"Chief, it's happening again. It's..." Brabant rolled his eyes. He couldn't believe he was talking as if the ship were alive. Same as the old hands did. "It's like she doesn't want us to take down the shield."

Four decks away, the chief cursed in a Polish dialect that defeated Brabant's translator pendant. "Don't fight it. Give *Midnight Sun* what she wants."

Alerts flared. They'd taken an energy beam salvo!

Specialist shield alarms wrote themselves across his artificial sight, giving him additional data.

3/2 had taken a massive hit but had held.

It had taken multiple laser pulses and a blast of neutralized 2GeV particles from a multi-terawatt particle cannon. It must have been the enemy flagship firing at extreme range.

Something was wrong, though. 3/2 was draining multiple terawatts of power, but it wasn't recharging.

Brabant shut it down.

This time, the ship made no objection.

As best as he could in the time left to him, he reconfigured the other shields to cover.

"The ship must have felt itself being painted in 3/2's zone," said the chief. "Kept it going just long enough to save us."

Brabant's timer alert pinged.

Five seconds.

He made a final check that he'd left everything he could with a green status and used the last moments to redirect 3/2's half-filled capacitors to boost 3/1 and 3/3.

"Brace for hard acceleration," said the captain. She sounded like she was looking forward to it. "Entering threat envelope of enemy frigates and destroyers in ten seconds. They won't know what hit them. Brace! Brace!"

Brabant felt a brutal lurch.

The love-hungry elephants had stubbed out their cigarettes and rolled back onto his chest, eager to make up for lost time.

* * * * *

Chapter Thirty-Four

CIC, *Vindictive*

"Beam salvo ineffective. Looks like we took out a shield, though."

"Particle cannon entering recharge cycle."

"*Midnight Sun* leaving drone field."

Commodore Fenrikho stared at the plot. When *Midnight Sun* had slowed suddenly, she'd taken the chance of a long-range shot with all of *Vindictive*'s forward-facing weapons.

Even with the attenuation loss at the extreme range, she could have destroyed her most dangerous opponent in a single blow.

Could have. But it was not to be.

And now *Vindictive* might have to pay the consequences.

The dot representing *Tseg-Lenkh* was closing fast, coming in for a close-range salvo of her own. Damned Goltar and their mysteries. She didn't even know its weaponry, although its main armament was clearly a spinal mounted energy beam. Probably a particle cannon, judging by its tactics.

"Frigate Group 4 anti-missile screen activating."

"*Vindictive* anti-missile laser defenses active."

"Point defenses hot."

"*Vindictive* missile salvo destroyed."

She watched the enemy missiles taken out one by one until the last was a brilliant plume of hot plasma just off *Vindictive*'s bows.

The mutual exchange of missiles between the two battlecruisers was ineffective, as she had expected. It was a probe really on her part. If the drones had seriously damaged *Tseg-Lenkh*'s anti-missile defenses, the Goltar ship would be glowing metal and gas by now. The ship's hull showed many deep scars, which had briefly vented flames when the rents had been torn through her armor, yet still it seemed somewhat effective.

But maybe it had been weakened… Fenrikho knew the power of cunning and surprise. *Tseg-Lenkh* thought she could survive a missile salvo, but Fenrikho had ordered *Vindictive*'s first barrage to fire only a third of her tubes.

"Launch racks reloaded."

Fenrikho made her move. "Execute forward maneuver!"

Flanked by Frigate Group 4, *Vindictive* launched a flurry of countermeasures and then raced for the drone field at six Gs. Her heading would take her screaming past *Tseg-Lenkh*, the two warships racing in opposite directions.

Her battlecruiser had more than decoys and sensor blinding defensive munitions with which to confuse *Tseg-Lenkh*. *Vindictive*'s electronic warfare team were one of Fenrikho's proudest assets. They pressed the attack hard in the cyber plane.

"Missile salvo from *Blunt Justice* boosting for final attack."

Vindictive's group was about to sail past *Tseg-Lenkh* and exchange broadsides. It was a risky tactic, but she felt certain that luck was about to turn in her favor.

Secondary lasers crossed the void between the two battlecruisers, clawing at each other's shields but not inflicting a killer blow.

What will be, shall be.

Fenrikho ignored the coming exchange of fire and returned her attention to the other sectors.

Tseg-Zorig remained bolted onto *Blunt Justice*, the two acting as a static gun platform, sending out waves of missiles and drones. Her long-range lasing was draining the shields of the Maki escort frigates. If they were destroyed, it could open the way to a missile spread powerful enough to overwhelm *Vindictive*'s own defenses.

Midnight Sun was being gored by the destroyers that were the horns of the crescent of Spinning Shield ships. The destroyer captains were landing heavy blows and informed the flagship of their enemy's imminent demise.

Meanwhile, *Gobi Desert* was most of the way through the drone field, having suffered less damage than the other ships due to a sacrificial shroud of drones and what appeared to be small boats of an unknown class. This new Human ship only appeared to be a transport, but it may prove to be a problem.

"We're through!" shouted the EW controller. "Attempting to disable *Tseg-Lenkh*'s critical systems."

"Commodore," said Guntic, *Vindictive*'s skipper. "We're five seconds from broadside."

Fenrikho gripped the collision bar of her couch till her knuckles paled. The next few moments would be punishing. Maybe fatal.

Who could tell with the Goltar?

"Missiles launching!" Guntic announced with an overdeveloped sense of drama.

The ship rolled, allowing all forty of the tubes circling her belly to spit shipkiller ordnance. The broadside missile salvo was the specialty of the *Petal*-class battlecruisers. A battle-winning attack, if you could get close enough.

And *Vindictive* still wasn't finished dealing blows against *Tseg-Lenkh*.

"We're being painted by *Tseg-Zorig*," SitCon warned.

Vindictive yawed to port. Her spinal-mounted particle cannon would seal *Tseg-Lenkh*'s fate.

The first missile punched through *Tseg-Lenkh*'s defenses and bloomed against her hull.

A second landed.

The enemy ship had no response. It threw no missiles at *Vindictive*. Merely a few scratches from secondary lasers.

A third landed. How many more blows could the damned thing take?

Vindictive's yaw accelerated, bringing her main armament to bear...

And also presenting her more lightly armored and shielded starboard quarter to *Tseg-Zorig* like a submissive juvenile.

"Turn to starboard," she shouted. "Quickly! Present fore armor to the carrier and the damned battlecruiser stuck to it like a giant parasitic Bakulu."

Tseg-Lenkh sailed on. It showed no sign of fight and appeared incapable of maneuver. Smoke trails streamed behind it.

But on the other side of the drone field, *Tseg-Zorig* fired its full frontal array of beam weapons. Its spinal mount wasn't a particle cannon but a laser. Much more effective at these long ranges and a monster. *Vindictive*'s analysts estimated it at 15TW.

But the fact that they remained alive to do so meant the strike had failed. The overlapping forward shields had held. Barely. If Fenrikho hadn't ordered the ship to turn back in time, the Goltar strike would have sliced through the ship.

"Data retrieved from *Tseg-Lenkh*," announced the jubilant EW controller. "We're seeing its internal damage reports. It's critically damaged."

"It's a shame we can't say the same for *Midnight Sun*," Fenrikho murmured, but the Midnighter ship clearly had taken heavy damage as it punched through the frigates, firing off a few missiles, but she had nothing else left.

She ordered the two destroyers to pursue and finish off *Tseg-Lenkh* and *Midnight Sun*. The remaining frigate groups were told to burn hard to form up on *Vindictive*.

There were plenty of Endless Night drones remaining and these she directed to swarm the carrier and its battlerider. So far, most of the carrier's drones had been deployed to cover the Golden Horde ship. If that was all *Blunt Justice* had, then even a ship of her size could be worn down and taken out by Grak's swarm.

Vindictive neared the Horde ship. It had been shielded up to this point by its escort. It may only be an armed transport but having an undamaged foe in the field made Fenrikho nervous. Especially when it was captained by those Humans with their lack of respect for tactical conventions.

"Guntic, ready a missile broadside for the Golden Horde ship and steer into her path. It's time *Vindictive* landed some blows on *Gobi Desert*."

* * * * *

Chapter Thirty-Five

CIC, *Midnight Sun*

*M*idnight Sun* spun about to present her least damaged shields and armor to the oncoming Maki destroyers.

The ship hung in space, panting, a wounded beast at bay.

As soon as the nearest destroyer brought *Midnight Sun* within effective lasing range, it fired with its forward beams, lancing coherent energy across space to burn Blue's already scarred hull.

The shields held. For now. But even if the shield generators were registering green, several power bridges between Reactor 3 and the shield capacitors had burned out. The feeds from Reactor 2 were also beginning to overload.

"Holding steady at 0.8 G," Blue announced to CIC. "Flkk'Sss, coordinate damage control teams. If we are heading back into that fight, we need to patch our wounds first."

"Yes, Captain. I shall assume direct control. Lieutenant Frazsh is dead."

"Do what you can," Blue replied somberly. "And do it fast. Those destroyers are coming to finish us off and the only weapons we have to defend ourselves are the welding torches of the Maintenance Division."

Blue stayed within her cocoon, despite having released the ship from acceleration stations. It was down to shame. Her crew had already paid a heavy toll in blood, and what had they to show for their pain? They'd inflicted punishing blows on two of the Maki frigates as they'd passed through the enemy line, but neither had been destroyed.

Her carefully laid plan had been defeated by a parking lot of cheap drones.

"Signals, anything from *Tseg-Lenkh*?"

"No, ma'am."

"My assessment is that *Tseg-Lenkh* is even more damaged than we are," said the XO.

"It's the Charge of the damned Light Brigade," mused Blue. "But without the happy ending."

She stared at the tactical plot, watching the destroyers close. Each time they fired, the shorter range meant less beam divergence and a smaller targeting spot. That meant increased energy pressure on Blue's shields. Even if the power feeds from *Midnight Sun*'s reactors to her shield capacitors still held, at closer ranges the lasers would pierce the shield and drill through her hull.

She smiled, remembering the way Captain Jenkins had explained the basics of beam weapons in space combat to a naïve girl, recently fled from Earth.

"Imagine a Sumatozou opera singer giving an aria with her feet planted on your chest," he'd told her. "At long range, energy beam diffraction means the spot hitting your ship is wider. It's like the opera singer on your chest wearing snowshoes. If you're inside combat armor, you'll live. But as the range closes, the double-trunker changes her shoes to something with a narrower sole—never missing a note, mind you, because she's a pro. At close lasing range, our singer's wearing stilettos. She's not any heavier than when she had the snowshoes, but now she'll spear your organs through your combat armor."

"I've missed you, Skipper," she murmured. Though it seemed she would be reuniting with him a lot sooner than she'd hoped.

She noticed a cluster of dots, out beyond the destroyers, headed her way. At its heart was *Gobi Desert*. She admired Sansar Enkh's pluck. The Horde commander had almost brought her CASPers through the drone field inside that glorified passenger ferry she called a warship.

What *was* that surrounding *Gobi Desert*?

She'd heard rumors of secret weapons developed by the Winged Hussars. Had some of them been loaned to the Horde?

"Lieutenant Konchill, until you have some fire buttons to press, I am relieving you from your TacCon duties. Instead, I want you to get *Gobi Desert* on the blower and find out what the hell those objects are surrounding her." Blue watched as the mysterious traces moved into the weirdest formation she'd ever seen. "And explain to me what the hell they're up to."

* * *

CIC, *EMS Gobi Desert*

Captain Parker watched the Goltar starfish pull away from all other directions and form up on *Gobi Desert*'s port beam.

He could see what they were doing.

That wasn't the problem. He just couldn't believe what he was seeing.

"Blue Sky!" exclaimed the helmsman.

"That about covers it," Parker agreed.

Battlecruiser *Vindictive* with her attendant frigates was steaming for *Blunt Justice* and *Tseg-Zorig,* but they had angled in to fly past *Gobi Desert* as the two ships raced in opposite directions.

Parker had seen what the *Vindictive*'s broadside missile salvo had done to *Tseg-Lenkh*, and he had no doubt that this was what Fenrikho was readying for *Gobi Desert*. With far less armor and weaker shields than the Goltar battlecruiser, the odds of surviving looked slim.

Their only chance lay in the Goltar drones that had redeployed over the port side as an anti-missile screen.

Now it seemed the starfish were joining the drones.

As they formed up, the Goltar fighters reduced their spacing until those starfish arms were almost within touching distance of each other. Then they yawed 90 degrees to port to face *Vindictive* head on.

The result was a living shield of fighter craft, two layers thick. They were two sheets of armor plate, though it was living armor with flesh-and-blood pilots who, incredibly, were still firing at any enemy drone that got too close.

To keep formation at such speeds without collisions was astonishing.

"Never thought I'd see pilots who could give the SalSha a run for their money," said the XO.

Parker nodded.

"*Vindictive* launching missiles," said SitCon.

He watched on the tactical plot as a spread of forty enemy missiles burned their first stages, charging across the distance to intercept the *Desert*. And kill her.

Parker hated this part. It was like walking slowly in a straight line while a pack of snarling Besquith raced towards you, desperate to rip open your chest and feast upon your organs.

"Inbound missiles coasting."

If *Gobi Desert* could accelerate like the Avenger bombers, then while the missiles were coasting through the black, he would be thrusting away at 22 gees, desperate to be somewhere—anywhere—other than where the missiles expected him to be when they lit their final booster stages and thrusted for the kill.

EMS *Gobi Desert* maintained heading directly out of the drone field.

"Targeting lasers painting us."

Vindictive fired her volley, half a dozen five-GW lasers flashing across the void.

Each of them vaporized multiple Goltar drones. The debris of their own annihilation caused laser blooming that weakened the beams. But only for a tiny fraction of the pulse duration.

The beams carried through the debris clouds and continued on their path of destruction.

They burned through the outer layer of starfish fighters, severing arms, holing cockpit armor, disabling engines and casually sending fighters spinning into each other—a catastrophic chain of devastation for such a tight formation.

Again, the beams were absorbed and bloomed, but carried on through the second formation of sacrificial fighters and onto the *Gobi Desert*.

No one spoke for a second.

"Shields drained. Capacitors at ten percent. Recharging underway. Shields will recharge in 22 seconds."

"Damage reports?" asked Parker.

"No damage."

Parker held his sigh of relief because *Vindictive's* group hadn't finished with him. Two of the *Sheek*-class laser frigates spun about to bring their bow-mounted main lasers to bear.

One of the frigates never finished its maneuver. Still clamped to *Blunt Justice*, *Tseg-Zorig* lased the frigate's weak aft armor from long range, spreading it across space as a blooming flower of hot gas and torn metal.

There were a few cheers at this little victory. Not from Parker, though. They were far from out of danger.

The other *Sheek* frigate got off a shot before desperately yawing about to present its front armor to the Goltar battlecruiser.

"We've lost shields, Captain."

"Giaracuni, reroute power, redeploy DC teams. Anything. Get those shields back."

"I'm on it," replied the XO.

Damage reports streamed in. The laser frigate's beam had overloaded the aft shield and punched through the hull. Penetration appeared minimal but...something in the reports didn't look right. The automatic damage reporting and control system might itself be damaged.

But when Parker glanced through the systems in the area that had been struck, they all showed green.

Suddenly, most of them turned red. He felt a stab of panic, but then realized this was Giaracuni obeying his orders by shutting down anything that helped him restart the shields faster.

Parker didn't have time for a detailed analysis now. His suspicion that something was screwy with the damage reports was a mystery to follow up later.

The lights suddenly flickered; the power hum skipped a beat. An alert in his pinview told him CIC had switched to emergency power.

His stomach suddenly made a bid for freedom out his throat as the engines cut, and he was thrown into weightlessness.

The ship drifted through the battlefield, trusting to their escort to prevent the enemy drones from firing a killing shot.

Then the torch relit and the power was restored to all systems.

"Aft shield is recharging," Giaracuni reported.

"Well done," said Parker. He returned his attention to the tactical plot where the swarm of missiles from *Vindictive* was closing. They would soon burn their final stage boosters.

And then they would learn whether *Gobi Desert* would survive, but there was no point in losing the SalSha too.

"Launch the Avengers," Parker commanded. "And hail Captain Kanat-Baim on the *Blunt Justice*."

In the tactical plot, icons flashed around the hostile missiles, indicating their final stages had lit.

"Get those shields recharged," Parker murmured. "We're gonna need them."

* * *

CIC, *Blunt Justice*

"Final drone squadron away. Assuming anti-missile stance."

The battle was not going according to plan. The primary mission objective was to destroy the starkiller, which was why the assault companies on *Gobi Desert* must be preserved at all costs. It made Kanat-Baim's blood run cold to think the insignificant Human ship with its tiny complement of mercs must be protected even at the expense of the mighty Goltar flagship.

But he knew to obey his duty. And Gloriana had done nothing to countermand his decisions. So far.

Gobi Desert had initiated communications and the Human captain, Steve Parker, appeared in the Tri-V.

"Your pilots are fantastic," said the Golden Horde captain. "Almost..." The Human moved its mouth in a configuration Kanat-Baim's pinplants interpreted as amusement. "I could almost call them *legendary*."

"They *were* legends once, Captain Parker. But then the galaxy developed cheap and effective drone swarms and forgot the legend of the Goltar pilots. Captain, I have your targeting instructions."

"Hit me," said the Human.

Why he would request such a thing was beyond comprehension, but Kanat-Baim was busy, so he sent the targeting priorities and returned to coordinating a joint defense with the *Tseg-Zorig* against the *Vindictive*'s fearsome attacks.

* * * * *

Chapter Thirty-Six

CIC, EMS *Gobi Desert*

"Avengers launched."

Parker commed the flight ops station. "Ops, relay me through you. I will give the mission objective to *Avenger-1* myself." He thought of that magnificent display from those Goltar pilots. "I don't want any misunderstandings."

"Copy. You have control, *Gobi Desert* Actual."

"*Avenger-1, Gobi Desert* Actual."

"*Avenger-1,* please give us something to blow up, Captain."

"Before I do, I've seen the Goltar fighters in action. Starfish we call them. The pilots are superb fliers. I want to make two things clear about them that you are to relay to your flight. First of all, the Goltar are our allies."

"Copy."

"Furthermore, you are not to show off to the Goltar."

"It's hardly our fault if we SalSha are amazingly proficient pilots."

Parker gritted his teeth. He *knew* this would be a problem. "I don't want you trying to prove you are the better fliers, *Avenger-1*. We are in a battle. People are dying. I need to know you will stay on mission."

"Wait. Out."

The SalSha cut the link. Parker's face grew so hot, the steam was practically pouring out.

* * *

Avenger-1

"Problem?" asked Borth, *Avenger-1*'s weapons systems officer.

"Captain Parker treats us like we were never uplifted," replied Meeth angrily. "If he doesn't trust us to *stay on mission*, then maybe we shouldn't be flying for him at all."

"But we weren't."

"Weren't what? Uplifted? Yes, we were. How could we be flying these bombers if we weren't?"

"Well, *we* both know that," Borth said, "but aren't we supposed to pretend we weren't because it's illegal or something?"

"Is that still a thing? I get confused. Union politics is so silly. It sucks all the fun out of the galaxy."

"I know. I also know you need to cut Captain Parker some slack. You do realize why he's ordered us to launch early?"

"Because…" Meeth hesitated. "Because he doesn't want to put all his *srkeches* in the same net. He thinks *Gobi Desert* might be destroyed. Poor Human."

Meeth re-established comms with the ship. "*Gobi Desert* Ops, *Avenger-1*."

"*Gobi Desert* Ops, go ahead, *Avenger-1*."

"Is the captain still on the line?"

The Ops Human made a peculiar noise in its throat. "*Avenger-1*, I think you should avoid talking with the captain for as long as you can."

"That's a shame, because we promise to stay on mission and not play with the Goltar. Now tell us what needs attacking."

"Your targets are the two destroyers. Designating your primary target as *Yperex-1* and secondary as *Yperex-2*."

"Roger. Out."

Meeth switched to the flight frequency. "*Avenger-1* to all Avengers. Form on me. We're taking out the destroyer trying to kill *Midnight Sun*. We launch one torpedo and then follow up with a 180-degree skew flip bombing. Set your bombs for maximum thermonuclear yield. Once we're surfing *Yperex-1*'s debris cloud, we use the other half of our load to destroy *Yperex-2*."

Borth leaned over and poked Meeth in the leg. "Tell them about the other thing," the WSO hissed.

"Oh, yes. Remember, Avengers, to stay on mission at all times. Do not show off. Out."

Meeth corkscrewed the craft in his excitement—the others copied his lead—and then thrust for the target at a steady 7g.

The electricity pulsing through his body only grew stronger.

He'd never blown up anything as big as that destroyer before.

For that matter, he'd never had anything as big shoot back at him.

Never in his life had anything been so exciting. And they were paying him to do this!

"Meeth?"

Lost in the moment, Meeth only grunted an acknowledgement at his WSO.

"Don't you think those starfish look so pretty? I wish I could reach out and eat one."

Meeth's jaws dropped open in astonishment. The Goltar fighters had caught up and were holding station on either flank. He counted forty-five of the miniature stars, each wrapped in silvered reflective coating.

The comm request icon blinked on his screen. The icon identified it as *Red-17*.

"Aren't you going to answer it?" asked Borth.

"You heard Captain Parker. He ordered us to ignore the Goltar fighters."

"He did say *something* along those lines," Borth admitted.

Meeth pushed the throttles forward, bringing the bomber up to 17 gees of thrust. *Let's see if you can follow that!*

The intense acceleration pulled his skin backward over his bones, but the taut grin on his face was all pleasure.

Now Meeth was ready to answer that Goltar hail.

It felt as if his arm had gained several tons of weight. He could have used his pinplants, but he punched his arm out and hit the comm accept button.

"Go for *Avenger-1*. Sorry we can't hang around. We have a job to do."

"So. Do. We," said an alien voice. He didn't know much about Goltar, but this *Red-17* being sounded like it was under a lot of strain.

Then Meeth saw why. Two squadrons of starfish had overtaken his Avenger flight and were forming up in front of his cockpit into a staggered wedge formation.

Meeth had promised the captain not to show off. But this was completely different. The Goltar had started it.

The starfish were issuing a challenge. And it was one that *had* to be met.

He reached for the throttles...

* * *

Red-17, Vlimkh Red Squadron

"Before you reach for that throttle," *Red-17* told the SalSha pilot, "let me speak. I am your liaison."

"What's a liaison?" asked *Avenger-1*.

She could hear a second SalSha—the bombardier of the two-person craft—whisper to the pilot, "A liaison is someone who tells you what you can and cannot do."

"A liaison coordinates two or more groups, so they are more effective together," *Red-17* corrected. "Such as with our combined arms attack on *Yperex-1*."

"I think you mean combined *tentacles*, *Red-17*."

Avenger-1 made yipping noises, presumably the SalSha equivalent of mirth bubbles.

The target's laser defenses opened up. A flash of light flared in *Red-17*'s peripheral vision as *Blue-27* died.

And these SalSha were making jokes?

Fleet commander Kanat-Baim had made it clear to *Red-17* that the Human transport ship *Gobi Desert* had to be protected. At the cost of all other Goltar forces if need be. High Councilor Gloriana herself had prioritized the Vlimkh squadrons with eliminating the Maki destroyer pursuing *Midnight Sun* over the one attacking *Tseg-Lenkh*, for reasons unknown.

If her superiors could make such sacrifices to the greater cause, *Red-17* could swallow her annoyance and indulge these SalSha.

"You fly a torpedo bomber," she said. "Yes?"

"The best," *Avenger-1* replied.

"Our Vlimkh fighters were designed as torpedo bomber escorts. It's what we do. Let us perform our role one more time."

"You're wasting our time, liaison. How do you think you can help us?"

"We prepare the way so that the bombers can get through. Follow us in. *If* you can keep up. *Red-17*. Out." She transmitted the execute attack command to her squadrons.

It was *Red-17*'s turn to laugh, and she did so as closely to the Goltar way as her enhanced body would allow. Her plastic tongue wiggled out of her red ceramic beak.

Red-17 pulled down on limb one. The haptic controls interpreted the gesture as the Human equivalent of opening up the throttle. Her fighter bounded through the dark, its engine throbbing at maximum output.

If the Human mercs could examine the Vlimkh fighters, they would probably describe them as space CASPers.

The design originated from an era before the loss of the homeworld, when the spearpoint of Goltar soldiers fought inside mechs. Whether the operation was underwater, on land, in the air, or in space, those ancients would fight inside suits of powered armor.

The Vlimkh's haptic controls exploited the natural Goltar excellence at multitasking physical actions, leaving the main bandwidth of their pinplant enhancements to optimize targeting. They also enabled the mental state known as *combat serenity*, in which the frantic events of space combat were slowed in the perception of the pilots, so they could be comprehended by mere mortals.

Red-17 stopped breathing.

Her heart stopped.

That part of the job never got easy, but she ignored the discomfort and twisted and pulled randomly at limbs five and three, which were her pitch, roll, and yaw controls.

Her Vlimkh maneuvered violently.

Around her, the two squadrons of fighters made similar random sprint approaches.

But it wasn't enough for everybody. One more of Red Squadron was shot by a laser.

At long last, her Tier 3 respiration and vascular systems kicked in. These were the mechanical structures designed for the extreme gee forces when pushing the Vlimkh to the limits of their performance envelopes.

A message reached her pinplants from Flight Ops on *Blunt Justice*. *Vindictive*'s missile salvo aimed at *Gobi Desert* had been destroyed by the last of the drone escort, and by the Human ship's own limited defenses.

"That is well," she said. "The sacrifice of the Vlimkh will not be for nothing."

She glanced at her acceleration dial. 23Gs.

Match that, Avengers!

An enemy drone swung into her path.

She tightened her arm in limb four. The haptic controls interpreted the firing instruction and sent a burst of 1MW pulses from the collimated laser mounted on the end of the arm.

Her cybernetic eyes saw the bolts glowing a brilliant green as they lanced into the drone. Rendering the coherent beam as visible light was artificial, but the actinic flare as the drone exploded was entirely real.

She leveled out for a moment to get a better look at the target, while throwing forward a mix of defensive expendables. She was rewarded by a warmth bathing limbs seven and two. It was the signal that her primary and secondary weapons were within effective range.

Both weapons systems were loaded with meson spikes.

She twitched her limbs, launching spikes from both tubes.

Flashes of light strobed through her cockpit window as the brave Vlimkh fighters succumbed to the destroyer's defenses, dying in pearlescent blooms that reflected off the spike ordnance streaming into *Yperex-1*.

She pulled left, slammed down the nose, and speared through space at the target, approaching from the starboard quarter.

Just before the first wave of meson spikes hit the destroyer's shields, their launch canisters burst, delivering clouds of ordnance onto the target.

Many of them failed.

These were ancient stock, after all. Irreplaceable. The understanding of the meson technology had long been lost to the Goltar—although *Red-17* sometimes wondered whether it had also been lost to the Science Guild.

But she understood the basic principle. The spikes embedded themselves inside the strong nuclear force concentrations of the shields, delivering meson pulses. Embed enough of them and they built up a resonance that both drained the shield of power, and acted like grounding electrodes, discharging the strong interaction in the shields down into the target ship itself.

Sheets of plasma—gossamer, sparse, but sparkling with vibrance—washed over the outer surface of the destroyer's shields.

The discharges into the ship were invisible, even to her eyes, but the target's hull grew pitted with melted hollows as the discharges struck home. A warning icon flashed in her console screen as waves of gamma radiation passed through her.

Red-17 launched her final two spikes. Then she pulled up and accelerated away. Under a cloud of expendables, she looped back for a strafing run.

The shield spikes did more than degrade the shields. The fierce energies swirling around the ship blinded its sensors, ending the carnage inflicted by defensive lasers.

Yperex-1's point defenses opened up, firing blindly to bludgeon sections of space with high velocity osmium-tungsten darts.

Terrible pearlescent blooms strobed once more through her cockpit as this deadly fire cut through the Goltar squadrons.

A far more satisfying flash of light was emitted by the shields as they finally failed under the meson onslaught.

Red-17 leveled out and ran a zigzag path along the destroyer's beams, avoiding the main lasers fore and aft. She settled into a state of combat serenity that gave her the space and time to pick targets to service with her three limbs armed with one-MW lasers.

She fired at sensor bubbles, railgun barrels. Anything that stood out from the destroyer's hull was a target of opportunity.

There were so many targets, but many of them were still shooting back.

The Vlimkh icons in her tactical plot continued to wink out.

* * *

Avenger-1

"That looks like so much fun," Borth said as the Goltar pilots played with the destroyer. "Neat flying too."

"Those Goltar may have some slight proficiency," Meeth admitted.

He switched to the flight frequency. "Going in."

The four Avengers came into a line abreast, hoping to overload the enemy defenses by firing their torpedoes simultaneously. They kept a wide spacing so Meeth and the other pilots could hurl their Avengers through a dizzying chain of vectors to confuse enemy targeting.

Slamming his Avenger around distracted Meeth from the sight of all the Goltar fighters being destroyed in front of his eyes.

But then he settled into level flight for several seconds to give Borth a firm target lock, and to avoid launching the torpedo with a lateral vector.

Meeth didn't like this part.

"Torpedo away!" yelled Borth.

The moment they launched, Meeth threw the bomber through every direction he could think of until he'd shaken the feeling that *Yperex-1* was about to emit a shaft of laser light that would end him.

"Now comes the fun part," he said. "The skew flip bombing turn."

Before he could set up the maneuver, he was blinded by a ball of light right in front of the cockpit.

They flew straight through it.

"What the hell was that?" he asked as he shook the sparks from his vision.

"That was our torpedo."

Another torpedo flashed to his left.

And another.

The torpedoes were simple devices. Instead of jinking through their approach like many types of missile, they were straight-ahead racers, traveling from bomber to target in the shortest duration possible.

"What happened to the torpedoes?" Meeth asked.

Before Borth could reply, another torpedo detonation seared into Meeth's vision. But this time it was accompanied by jets of burning ship's atmosphere and shards of debris as *Yperex-1* bled out into the dark.

"Weeeeee!" The transmission came from *Avenger-4*. "We hit something! Beat that."

"Oh, you're on," Meeth answered.

He was worried for a moment that the enemy ship had been destroyed, but it was still firing back.

He rammed the throttles to the firewall.

"Do we have to do this?" The pain of the fierce acceleration was obvious in Borth's strained voice.

Meeth watched the Goltar flitting over the destroyer, and *Avenger-4* corkscrewing in triumph.

"Yes. Yes, we do. We're going to drop a bomb down inside *Avenger-4*'s hole."

"That. Would. Be. Cool."

Meeth decided he could hear excitement in his WSO's voice.

Already, the air, sailors, and equipment had been sucked out of the holed section of the enemy ship and the interior pressure sealed. The Goltar fighters had largely stripped the point defenses from the area, so Meeth came in hot, straight down the hole.

"Bomb away," Borth announced.

Meeth eased back the throttles and at twenty gees, executed the flip turn, swinging the Avenger through 180 degrees without relenting the intense thrust.

The craft shuddered.

He heard a ping of snapping metal that might be the bracing bar behind their seats.

He tried to remember what the Human flight instructor had told them about skew flip turns, but the blood in his body was in all the wrong places. It made it difficult to think, but the memory of Lieutenant Enkh's gravelly voice came back to him.

"Skew flip turns. They're a myth. Not a real thing. Try them, and your Avenger will shatter under the strain."

"What would a Human know?" Meeth muttered and used his pinplants to push the throttles back to the max.

It was becoming difficult to see. Or, for that matter, to breathe and think. His hands were numb.

Meeth wasn't showing off now. They had misjudged the maneuver. He'd left the flip too late. If he didn't do something, they were going to follow their bomb through the breach and into *Yperex-1*.

He pulled the nose up slightly, adding sideways vector relative to the destroyer.

The braking finally bit in, and the craft slowed.

It edged past the Maki destroyer at a safe distance of thirty meters, slowing all the while.

"Next time, I'll bring a laser pistol to fire out the cockpit," said Borth.

Meeth really had left his turn too late. They were about to pass over one of the less damaged sections of hull, where point defenses were still spitting deadly volleys at the Goltar fighters flitting around like predatory insects. *Avenger-1* was going to sail at a walking pace into the path of the enemy's guns, and there was nothing he could do about it.

"Do you think the Goltar were impressed?" Meeth wondered aloud.

"I'm sure they were," said Borth.

The universe exploded.

Meeth was sent tumbling into the light to meet his ancestors.

That's going to be awkward, he realized suddenly. *They were never uplifted.*

He jumped at a cracking noise as something hit his cockpit. He opened his eyes and saw a vending machine slide around the side of their bomber. It was still attached to a fragment of the destroyer's bulkhead.

It was all very confusing, but he decided he wasn't dead, and that his Avenger had been pushed out by the primary explosion as his nuclear bomb had detonated inside *Yperex-1*.

He turned the Avenger onto an orthogonal vector to the explosion and thrust away as hard as he could.

"We're surfing the debris cloud," he gasped. "Isn't that the best thing ever?"

Borth didn't answer. He'd passed out.

Meeth judged that was enough surfing for now. He eased off the throttles and felt his consciousness unwind from the narrow sinkhole it had been plunging into.

He barrel-rolled the bomber while he waited for Borth to recover.

Midnight Sun was still in one piece. *Yperex-1* wasn't. And all four Avengers were still flying.

He couldn't wait to do it all again.

He nosed his craft over toward *Yperex-2* which was engaged in a lasing duel with *Tseg-Lenkh*.

"*Red-17*," he transmitted. "Are you still alive?"

"I am. That was some spectacular flying, *Avenger-1*."

"Yes, it was. Are you ready to do it again?"

* * * * *

Chapter Thirty-Seven

CIC, *Tseg-Zorig*

"Message from *Blunt Justice*, they've lost lateral maneuvering thrusters."

Captain Asel-Mingul could feel the chill silence stifling CIC.

They all knew what this meant.

But she was their captain. She shook the despondency out of her limbs and started issuing orders.

The nimble Maki frigates could now stick close to *Tseg-Zorig*'s weakened aft quadrant and wear her down until she was destroyed. Then they would finish off *Blunt Justice*.

The only command decision remaining to Asel-Mingul was to determine what *Tseg-Zorig* could do in the time left.

On the far side of the dwindling drone field, Alliance ships appeared to be emerging victorious. There was still hope for *Blunt Justice*.

But not for her ship.

"We are not dead yet!" she reminded everyone in the CIC hive.

"Weapons Division, reconfigure anti-missile lasers to offensive configuration. Concentrate their fire on the *Sheek*-class laser frigates. Commander, take the forward laser battery off-line and try to reroute any power we save to the aft batteries and aft shield capacitors. If we can double-charge our lasing power, do it. Ignore every safety protocol."

"Ma'am," said TacCon. "Recommend we reprioritize aft laser targeting from *Vindictive* to the laser frigates. The enemy battlecruiser is—"

"Commanded by a coward," finished the captain. "Commodore Fenrikho is keeping at the extremity of our threat zone and using her own frigates as a shield. Agreed. All weapon systems will prioritize on the laser frigates."

Lasers speared out from a battery of hastily reconfigured antimissile laser turrets on hull face 4. They made a coordinated strike on a narrow section of a *Sheek* frigate's aft shields.

And overwhelmed them.

Asel-Mingul clacked her beak angrily, because the penetration through the frigate's hull was minimal. If she had maneuver capability, she would have rolled *Tseg-Zorig* and brought the next battery to bear. If the point defense railguns on that part of the hull had still functioned, she would have sent a stream of tungsten darts to rend the frigate's skin before its shields were restored.

She possessed neither.

"Missile inbound! It's from the *Sheek* we just hit."

The *Sheek* had just a single missile rack. But now that Asel-Mingul had ordered the anti-missile defenses redeployed, and with the missile streaking through a blind spot in the firing cones of *Blunt Justice*'s own defensive railguns, *Tseg-Zorig* had no response left.

"Frigate destroyed."

That was better. Her ship still had teeth, as one of the frigates coming too close to the secondary aft battery had just discovered.

An impact shock rattled through CIC, throwing everyone hard against their harnesses. The *Sheek's* missile had destroyed the laser battery that had fired upon it and blown through the hull too. Automatic damage reports showed at least four decks had decompressed.

She expected another missile from the frigate, but instead it too blew into a fireball. Perhaps *Tseg-Zorig* had inflicted more laser damage than Asel-Mingul had realized.

"Enemy drones flying through breach."

Like flies around wounded flesh. And there was nothing she could about it.

She checked that the damage control teams were prioritizing the breach for damage, then returned her attention to the battle around *Tseg-Zorig*'s stern.

She'd lost her main aft weapon, but the secondary weapons were about to bring down another frigate. The problem was, the remaining frigates were nearly through *Tseg-Zorig*'s defenses. Her shield recharge rate had degraded too much.

She had been overlapping shields with *Blunt Justice* to cover their most vulnerable regions. It was the only reason both ships had survived so long. Power to the aft shield generators fluctuated. And then fell sharply.

"Signals, send a message to *Blunt Justice*. Compliments to Captain Kanat-Baim, but we regret we will be unable to continue shield overlaps."

"Captain!" The somber tone of the XO's voice told her this was the end. "Fire near Reactor 2. It's a serious one."

"How long before containment is compromised?"

"Unknown. DC teams took heavy casualties in the explosion that caused the fire. We could blow any moment. Recommend we declamp."

Even if she freed herself from the carrier she was riding, the ship's pitifully slow acceleration after that damned sneak attack at the orbital meant it would take many minutes to get her endangered reactors a safe distance from *Blunt Justice*. If containment failed, then when *Tseg-Zorig* blew, she would take the flagship with her.

"Negative. We will initiate emergency reactor core ejection."

The ship's two senior officers pinlinked and authorized the order jointly, as they were required to do. Then the captain gave the order to abandon ship.

All three reactors underwent emergency shutdown. The heavily shielded containment tubes they were built within sealed themselves off, trapping many crewmen within.

The atmosphere inside the tubes was sucked out in moments.

Silence replaced CIC's ubiquitous power hum as every ship's system died at once. Darkness replaced the light.

The reactor tubes punched out of the upper hull, shooting away into the black.

There was a rebirth of sorts on the ship they left behind as emergency power activated enough systems for the crew to get out.

Illuminated arrows pointed to escape capsules. Emergency lighting lit the way.

All around the CIC hive, her crew unstrapped themselves from their stations and looked to their captain on her command stump.

What were they waiting for? Permission? A speech?

"Abandon the fucking ship!" she yelled. "Run!"

She watched them hurry to the escape pods accessible through CIC bulkheads.

She didn't leave her post. This was her fault. If she hadn't been so lax at Station 5, her ship wouldn't have arrived at the battle already crippled.

She had no desire to go down with her ship, but she would make damned sure she would be the last one off.

Half the CIC hive personnel had escaped when a one-GW laser from the last surviving *Sheek* frigate sliced a hole through the center of the ship.

Asel-Mingul was ripped out into space.

* * * * *

Chapter Thirty-Eight

CIC, *Vindictive*

"Grak, you're a blundering ass brain." Fenrikho ran through the reports on the drone fleet and cursed the Endless Night hooligan and his damned drones.

The Goka criminal had claimed they would be a battle winner. Fenrikho had thought so too, but they hadn't quite been enough to exterminate the foe. Now they were thousands of items of space junk. Power plants and chemical charge packs had been used up. The lasers couldn't fire. Most couldn't maneuver either.

"Endless Night let us down," she said. "Wouldn't you agree, Captain Guntic?"

Guntic licked his lips while the conniving little turd considered his position. Would he endorse a retreat? Because if he did, he couldn't then use her withdrawal as a pretext to replace her.

"Yes, Commodore," said Guntic. "We risk losing the remainder of our fleet for little obvious purpose. I recommend we withdraw."

"I accept your recommendation. Flag-Lieutenant Giance, order all ships to break away."

"As you wish, Commodore."

Fenrikho reviewed the drone stats. About fifty of *Vindictive's* own drones were still operational. As were a similar number of Grak's.

How best to deploy them?

She took a long look at *Tseg-Zorig*. The heavily armored battle-cruiser was now a hulk of molten slag. Cut loose from the carrier she had ridden, she now drifted through a cloud of her own escape pods.

Salvage. Prize vessels. Ransoms and prestige. That private pleasure moon had been so close.

But *Tseg-Zorig* had done its job well. The flagship's shields still held, and its many drones still had bite.

If *Blunt Justice* had been the only foe remaining, Fenrikho would have worn her down and forced a surrender.

But events in the other parts of the battle were not going her way.

"The *Graucher*'s hailing," said the signals officer.

Fenrikho's blood went cold. The news from the surviving *Yperex* destroyer would not be pleasing. She received the transmission at her personal station.

The destroyer's captain in the Tri-V looked exhausted. "Commodore, I cannot comply with my withdrawal orders. *Midnight Sun*'s main armaments are back online and inflicting damage. *Graucher*'s shields have been degraded, and she is about to be attacked by torpedo bombers. I will stand and fight, and keep the enemy off your backs while you...withdraw."

Fenrikho made a quick political calculation. She might be able to paint this battle as a fighting draw, but if she lost both destroyers then it would be considered a defeat. The *Graucher* could not die.

"Captain, you must run."

"We can outrun *Midnight Sun* and *Tseg-Lenkh* in their current state, but not those fighter-bombers."

"And they cannot outrun my drones. I will keep those irritating relics of an ancient era out of your tails. Leave the field of battle. Head for McPherson-3. Fenrikho out."

She ordered Drone Ops Division to send everything with power after the fighter bomber group.

She hesitated. That much had been easy. But Fenrikho was fighting a war on three fronts. There were her enemies on the field, those engaged in corporate politics. Then there was Endless Night.

She took a deep breath and then recorded a message.

"To Endless Night commanders, McPherson-3, this is Commodore Fenrikho at the heart of the emergence point battle. After inflicting heavy losses on our enemies, I am making a tactical withdrawal to the planet in order to rearm and regroup."

She beamed the message to Coron and Retenex.

The planet was about eight light minutes away. If she was lucky, she may have a twenty-minute respite before the commanders gave their reply.

With any luck, she would have died in battle by then.

She flicked that thought away angrily with both tails. The situation was dire, but she was the Spinning Shield field commander. She would not run away from her responsibilities.

* * *

Avenger-1

"*Avenger-1, Gobi Desert* Ops."

"*Avenger-1.* Are you recording us, Ops? I hope so. When we take out that last destroyer, it will be spectacular."

"Negative. Change to orders. You will break off your attack."

"Say again, Ops."

"Enemy drones are headed your way. Like an angry swarm of killer bees."

"What are bees?"

"Little flying things that will kill you if enough of them sting."

"You mean like *lahnkh* shoals. Yes, that would indeed be unpleasant."

"The Goltar fighters are redeploying to meet the drones. You will make for *Midnight Sun* and land in her hangers."

Meeth took a good look at the tactical plot. *Midnight Sun* was close enough to use as shelter from the drones, but the Goltar had done most of the flying up to now. Besides, Meeth knew that they'd paid a heavy price to keep his Avengers alive.

He pushed his bomber's nose toward the enemy drones.

"Cannot comply, Ops. *Midnight Sun* is too far away. We can't risk being caught in the open without escort. So we're joining the starfish."

"*Avenger-1*. Your orders are to land on *Midnight Sun*."

"Say again, Ops. *Weeee! Kkk-kkk-kkk*." He gave a hilarious sequence of wails and clicks. "You're breaking up."

He switched off the channel connecting him to *Gobi Desert*.

"They won't like that," said Borth. "We will get into trouble."

Meeth increased the acceleration. An unwelcome pressure sat on his already bruised chest and refused to go away. "True. But after the way we placed that bomb through the hole in the destroyer, they won't stay mad at us for long."

Borth thought that through a moment before nodding enthusiastically. "That's a good point." The weapon system officer flicked through to the flight channel. "*Avenger-1* to all Avengers. Reconfigure your remaining bombs to maximize gamma radiation flash. It won't be as powerful an explosion, but it will skragg the electronics of the drones."

"Err…what about *our* electronics?" asked Meeth.

"Good point. Avengers, better make sure no friendlies are near the bombs when they go off. Including yourselves."

* * *

Avenger-1

When he'd first encountered them, Meeth had been annoyed by the Goltar pilots with their silly stretched heads, and their fighters getting in the way when he'd wanted to make his attack on *Yperex-1*. Now he was enjoying watching the darting starfish things so much that Borth had to poke him to remind him they weren't spectators.

The Avengers hung back from the dogfight in a holding pattern of lazy spirals. Occasionally they broke out into hard maneuvers as a drone grew too near and they would work together to slice it apart with their lasers.

The Goltar fighters were impressive but not up to the standards of the Avengers—obviously—but Meeth was fascinated by the differences between the two types of craft.

The Avenger was a sleek slice of metal, ten meters long, half that wide, and topped with a distinctive dual-bubble cockpit.

Everything was front facing: lasers, torpedoes, acceleration. Even the way Meeth and Borth peered out the cockpit.

Not so the starfish. The seven arms didn't just look like tentacles, they flexed and turned like a living creature, and were perfectly adept at firing their laser-armed limbs in three directions simultaneously.

What made the starfish more alive than anything, was what they were doing to the drones.

The SalSha had recognized the tactics immediately. Like the Goltar, their ancestors had hunted prey in the seas. The SalSha still did, whenever they got the chance.

But what was obvious to Meeth's eyes was invisible to the drone intelligences, and the Maki controllers operating them.

The Goltar were corralling the drones together like fish being herded in the sea.

The drones twisted and dived away, spitting laser fire. It was obvious that for most of them their fuel was almost expended because they were visibly slowing.

They were allowing themselves to be herded into a bait ball.

"*Avenger-1*," Red-17 shouted. "Do it now!"

Borth relayed instructions to the other Avengers, and they launched their remaining nuclear bombs into the center of the drones.

Meeth turned their bomber sharply and raced away.

The Goltar fighters lingered, keeping the drone ball compressed as long as they dared before they too turned and ran for their lives.

The drones immediately began spreading out.

Four nukes detonated in their midst.

Some of the drones were caught within the explosion and flashed into plasma.

Most escaped the initial blast.

Without a physical medium to travel through, the visible explosion was underwhelming.

But the electromagnetic pulse was intense, as was the release of other forms of radiation.

All the drones were caught by the gamma pulse and died instantly. They had become inert metal carcasses moving through space on a constant heading.

"We took another dose of rads," said Borth. "We'll make it back, but we'll need to see a medic."

Make it back to the Desert. Meeth sighed. He didn't look forward to returning. What awaited him there might not be fun at all.

Nonetheless, he was about to re-establish comms with Flight Ops, when he saw something astonishing in the rear viewscreen.

"Will you look at that!" said Borth, admiration obvious in his voice.

The Goltar fighters were flying an intermingling dance pattern, a choreography of triumph that had them passing each other at high velocities, separated by only a few meters.

Without needing to say a word to the other Avengers, the SalSha bombers danced around each other in a reverse helix. They performed the Kloop.

"I'm recording this," said Borth. "We'll have to try it for ourselves. Thorb will be so impressed if we can fly this dance."

Meeth raised his Goltar liaison when the starfish had finished their display. "What was that? What is it called?"

"It's just something we do," said *Red-17*, sounding unusually uncertain. "It's not an official thing, just something pilots of old did to honor those of us who have left gaps in our formation."

"Does it have a name?"

"Not really. It's a triple helix with periodic perversions."

Meeth looked up the term in the slither of GalNet in his pinplants. "No, *Red-17*. That's what it *is*, but not what it's *called*. It has to have a name."

"It does not."

"Then we shall give you one. We shall call it the…"

Inspiration deserted him. Borth stepped up. "It is the G-Kloop," declared the WSO.

"We will fly many more missions together," said Meeth. "Even the people who sit inside the big ships will have seen what we can do."

"Negative, *Avenger-1*. We lost two-thirds of our number today, and we who remain fly the last of the Vlimkh fighters. The secret of their construction was lost along with their manufactories when the Veetanho sent their Goka swarms to destroy our home world. At least we kept it a secret from the Veetanho, but we are the last of our kind. We shan't fly again."

For once, Meeth was at a loss for words. He'd just witnessed something wonderful fade away.

Sometimes the galaxy sucked.

"I understand, *Red-17*. I wish it were not so."

Meeth explained the situation to the other Avengers and led them in another Kloop.

It was a dance his people performed in the seas of the home world. It honored warriors returning home after a victory. And that's what they did to honor his new Goltar friends. Not just the pilots who lived, but those who had died and the starfish fighters themselves.

With a confusing mix of heightened emotions in his breast, Meeth led his Avengers back to *Gobi Desert*.

* * *

CIC, *Vindictive*

Her battle group had gotten away from the enemy ships, but she had not escaped Coron and Retenex.

She kept their reply to her message waiting for over a minute before she raised the courage to activate it.

The Zuparti and the elSha leered out of the Tri-V recording, their personal bodyguards with them as always.

"Do not return to McPherson-3," Coron said. "Proceed to the stargate. Instruct your two frigates orbiting the planet to rendezvous with my Captain Iamon. We will meet you at the stargate and travel outsystem together."

"I imagine you're surprised," said Retenex. "Your fleet failed to stop the enemy, but you were merely the outermost defensive layer. If the Goltar and their allies wish to take this planet, they will have to fight through our main defenses underground. We have disabled the orbital bombardment system we found hidden inside old satellites. They won't be able to play that trick again. Your services are required elsewhere, Commodore. As are ours. We're headed for Wahrner's Grise."

* * * * *

Chapter Thirty-Nine

Besquith Tunnels, *Unlikely Regret,* **Hyperspace**

A burst of heavy MAC fire from the roof embrasure blew pits out of the tunnel floor and nearly rocked Staff Sergeant Jim McCoy off his feet.

Searchlights followed, punching through the dark from the same ceiling strongpoint to pick out the Golden Horde platoon sheltering behind the twisted armor of the first defensive line, which they'd taken at such cost.

"Wolves are getting predictable." McCoy sidestepped out of cover, locked in the light source, and sent a missile screaming out of his right shoulder pod.

He hopped back under cover. Sharply.

Shells and electromagnetically propelled slugs hit the spot where he'd just been standing.

Then the tunnel went dark once more as his missile slammed into the roof light.

It would do no good. That had been his last missile, but he doubted it was the last of the Besquith searchlights.

"It's the overhead gantry that's killing us," he said over the platoon command channel.

"I noticed," replied the other squad leader, Staff Sergeant David Melsome. "Question is, what are we gonna do about it?"

"We take it," said Lieutenant Enkh. "Then we will command the battle space. It won't be easy, but it needs to be done."

Jim bit his lip but said nothing. The inexperienced lieutenant—hell, she was about the same age as his daughter—had been too hesitant, relying on her grizzled veteran squad leaders to tell her what to do. This was better from her. She needed to listen to experience, but she also needed to take charge.

With exchanges of fire raging all the while, the lieutenant shared the recorded view of the overhead defensive strong point. It was a wedge that ran the length of the tunnel roof and bristled with guns. She had highlighted a hole a missile had punched through, near its join to the wall on their right.

"I may not have your experience," she told her squad leaders, "but my Horde training means I can see the position from the perspective of a defensive specialist. I tell you that whoever controls that box on the roof controls the battle space. We have no choice. We have to take it. Melsome, I want suppressive fire concentrating on the gun ports in the walls. Lay down smoke to soak up those lasers. McCoy, we're using our jets and heading through that breach."

"*We*, Lieutenant?"

"Yes, Sergeant. I need the best field of view, and it's from up there."

Or you could just hook into the feed of the troopers who take the gantry, McCoy thought, though he said nothing.

"Ready, Melsome?" Enkh asked.

"Waiting for your signal, boss," replied the squad leader.

"Ready, McCoy?"

"Not yet, Lieutenant. There's a trick we learned in the Jolly Rogers. If I can borrow a trooper from Second Squad, we can go in three by three. It works like this…"

* * *

McCoy heard a chorus of pops behind him as Melsome's squad blew smoke against walls thick with Besquith barrels. Then came the rattle and churn of autocannons and the much louder pops of MAC rounds, lashing the walls with fire.

"Go! Go! Go!" screamed the lieutenant.

McCoy was in the lead trio racing into open space, dodging the chunks torn out of the floor. Taking point was Corporal Khiaa. To Khiaa's right was Private Bishee.

They lit their jets and soared for the breach in the overhead position.

Between the ground and that gap, McCoy's role was very simple. He had to keep the point CASPer alive.

To that end, he'd deployed his laser shield over his left arm. The smoke was doing most of the work of absorbing the laser pulses shooting at them from the left wall, but the shield was still deflecting a lot of firepower.

He directed the MAC on his left shoulder to fire round after round at the gun ports hidden in the wall.

Firing blindly through the smoke, it would have to be a helluva lucky shot to take out a Besquith through a narrow slit. But his rounds slamming into the rock threw out splinters that he hoped would blind the wolves and deflect their shots.

The Besquith had MACs too. A round blew the left foot off his CASPer, nudging him into Corporal Khiaa. McCoy twisted around, flying upside down for a second before correcting his orientation.

He glanced ahead.

They were almost at the breach.

His right jump jet flared red in his status board just before they reached the hole.

McCoy fell.

He reached out desperately and dug his CASPer's hand into the weakened rocky armor composite that surrounded the breach.

The clamor of battle raged around him, but the icons that represented Khiaa and Bishee in his tac-map were still green, and the next trio were in the air and almost upon them.

"Time to get out the damned way," murmured McCoy. He was in a CASPer. Upper body strength would not be a problem.

He hauled himself up.

Suddenly, something exploded into his CASPer's belly and his HUD blanked.

He was dead.

For the fourth time that day, his Triv-V displayed a simple block of text.

UNIT INCAPACITATED. AWAIT END OF SIMULATION.

"No shit!"

* * *

***Unlikely Regret*, Hyperspace**

Locked in the cocoon of his disabled CASPer, Jim McCoy let rip with the saltiest curses he'd ever learned—and he'd picked up a mighty fine vocabulary of filth in the Rogers—hurling it all at the person he blamed for his platoon's defeat. The one who'd assigned them a scenario they couldn't win.

Major Sun.

He felt a sudden ping of alarm tingling at the back of his neck and remembered to check his mic pickup was disabled.

It was. So he launched into a further tirade at the stupid little woman.

What was it with the tiny women surrounding him all of a sudden?

Sansar Enkh didn't even break five feet. Terbish Enkh wasn't much taller.

He shook his head, disappointed with himself. His daughter would rip him a new one if he'd said that out aloud and rightly so.

Colonel Enkh had played straight with him and given him an opportunity he wasn't about to screw up. The lieutenant was smart but needed a little more steel in her spine. She'd get there, though. If Jim did his job properly, she'd grow into a fine officer.

He brought up a pinview image he'd recorded of the mission commander.

"What's your game, Major?"

Sun was older than the lieutenant. Old enough for him to appreciate that she was pretty hot. He contemplated the scar that ran from her left eye down behind her ear and wondered what stories it could tell. Sun was a CASPer driver herself, so she would have the nanite hardening that meant she wouldn't snap if they ever…

He bit his lip. Blowing off steam in the privacy of his CASPer was one thing, but this was madness. For the time being, he was a staff sergeant in the Golden Horde, not the CO of the Jolly Rogers.

McCoy looked again at the image. The major was smiling, but the smile didn't warm her eyes. She had the cold look of a killer.

If you pissed off Sansar Enkh, she'd have you killed. But this Major Sun…she would gut you personally and watch your dying breath.

His Tri-V reactivated, showing the CASPers in *Unlikely Regret*'s training suite, trails of data cables hooking them up to the simulation server rack.

A new block of text appeared.

SIMULATION ENDED.

"Again, no shit!"

His pinplants reported that he'd been in CASPer limbo for three minutes and twenty-one seconds. The platoon hadn't lasted long.

Tri-V options appeared, offering ways to review the scenario.

McCoy gestured them away. There would be no point. They'd been working at this all day and the outcome was always the same.

Total team kill.

He hit the eject, uncoupled himself, and dismounted, joining the other sweaty and surly Bravo Company drivers.

The object of his curses was on the far side of the servers, next to a man twice her size who had that weird name. Obadiah Jex. What was his deal? Was he English Amish?

Bunch of damned freaks, these Midnighters.

Worse.

While he and the other Bravo Company squad leaders had been having their companies shot out from under them during the Omega War, where had this Midnight Sun Free Company been hiding?

He'd never even heard of them until six months before the war. He'd met a group of Sinclair's Scorpions telling tales about the Midnighters at the Lyon's Den.

Scorpions.

Now *they* had been a quality outfit, even though their accents had been as wild as their shaggy tales after a few bottles of that Scottish beer the Lyon imported especially for them. Belhaven Wee Heavy.

Nonetheless, she was the CO for this recce operation, so McCoy and Melsome shepherded their troopers and formed up at attention.

His pinplants registered a message from the lieutenant.

"McCoy, Melsome, we haven't even come close to beating this scenario. What did I do wrong?"

"Nothing," McCoy sent back. "This wasn't my first assault rodeo, and I couldn't do it better. It's the major playing goddamn mind games."

"You failed," Sun told the Horde troopers.

McCoy was microseconds from offering the Midnighter officer constructive criticism about where she could shove her fucking simulation, when the major smiled. And this time he noticed the warmth did reach her eyes.

"Good," she said. "I'm impressed. Honestly, I didn't think you would last as long as you did or inflict as much damage. Really, I am impressed. You've done well."

"Then what was the point of it?" growled Melsome, lined up behind with Second Squad. The old CSRAR boss added a hanging, "Ma'am."

"I don't know you," she replied, as if that made any kind of damned sense. "None of you, and I don't have time to correct that sufficiently before our recon mission. When we get dirtside at Wahrner's Grise, we will be in immense danger every second until extraction. We don't know what we will face. Only that it will be heavily defended and that we must be ready to pivot our strategy in an instant. Maybe multiple times."

We'll figure it out when we get there, thought McCoy. *Sounds like the kind of madness Dave Melsome used to get up to with CASPer, Search, Rescue, and Recovery.*

"You've proved to me today that you're good," said Sun as she began to troop the line. "However, I can tell you now that you are *not* good enough to take the base by force. Not even close. Listen, I'm a CASPer driver myself. I remember what it was like to be young and with that nanite treatment still hardening my body, like a lot of you fresh Horde troopers. Stick someone like that inside a Mk 8 CASPer and they feel invincible."

She came to a halt in front of McCoy. "Wouldn't you agree, Staff Sergeant?"

His face went red. He'd underestimated her. Not that he approved of her methods.

"I do," he said. "We can't afford heroics. We need to know that if we attack the facility openly, as we did in the scenario, then we'll always lose. It's one thing to be told that in a briefing. You get a different kind of knowing in your gut that comes from spending the entire day dying and cursing the CO's name every time your CASPer goes dark."

"Thank you, Staff Sergeant. I'm sure the transcript of your mission logs will prove invaluable in expanding my vocabulary."

Wait, had they been recording everything he'd said?

"Our CASPers won't be enough," Sun declared. "We need to think harder. Be bolder. We need subterfuge. Misdirection."

Sounds like Dave's resume.

"What's the plan, ma'am?" asked the lieutenant.

"The plan, such as it is, is undeveloped and inadequate. It needs brilliance and resilience, not to mention contingencies. We're going to improve upon it. For the next ten minutes, I want you showering me with ideas. Nobody is wrong. Nothing is stupid. Begin!"

"Undermine the base and collapse the tunnels."

"Bunker busters."

"It's under a damned lake. Flood it."

"Use a submarine to tow a couple of nukes."

"Orbital bombardment."

"Ma'am," asked Private Bishee, "what is the status of the local authorities?"

"Anarchic, last I heard," Sun replied. "Why? What do you have in mind?"

"Perhaps they can provide a distraction? Maybe they keep attention on the lake's surface while we cut a tunnel that intersects one of theirs?"

"That's good thinking. Keep it coming. Two minutes left."

When they'd finished, Sun picked out four troopers whose ideas she'd liked most and told them to fall out.

"You're my first set of advisors," she told them. "For the rest of Bravo Second Platoon, you're still forming. Lieutenant Enkh, liaise with Sergeant Jex for a more conventional simulation program. By the time we reach Wahrner's Grise, I need you operating as a true unit."

She left, leaving McCoy scratching his head.

"Load up the next scenario," the lieutenant told Jex.

The Englishman frowned. "Don't you want a rest first?"

"You heard the major. We need to become a tight fighting unit, and the Golden Horde doesn't sit on its ass when there's work to be done."

"Copy that, ma'am."

She shot a sudden look of uncertainty at McCoy. He returned the barest nod. *Well done.*

"You heard the lieutenant," he yelled at his squad. "Everyone back inside your mechs. We've finished with the Besquith Overkill scenario for the day. Now it's time for the Attack of the Amish."

He noted Jex laughing at that. Melsome chuckled too.

Maybe they could work with these Midnighters after all.

McCoy was clambering into his canopy when the person he least expected to see burst into the training suite.

"Which one of these rigs is assigned to Private Enebish Enkh?" asked Major Sun.

"B212," McCoy replied. "Right next to me. Why?"

"Because I want to learn how the Horde thinks." She hopped into Bishee's mech as sure footed as a mountain goat.

"Aren't you needed at the planning session?"

Sun hesitated, her spirit suddenly cloaked in a darkness he didn't understand. "Specialist Branco and Sergeant Oranjeklegg are representing me. I'm used to others coming up with the crazy ideas. I'm the one who implements them in the real universe and gets us out alive. Which is why I'm here. For this scenario, Lieutenant Enkh, Staff Sergeant McCoy, I am Private Sun of First Squad."

When "Private Sun" disappeared into Bishee's mech, McCoy glanced over at Lieutenant Enkh. He caught a flicker of panic, but it was quickly replaced with steely resolve.

McCoy closed his canopy wearing a grin on his face. "You got this, Terbish. Show her what you're made of."

And this time, he didn't care whether the mission logs were recording him or not.

* * * * *

Chapter Forty

EMS *Gobi Desert*, Approaching McPherson-3

"What in the hell?" Sansar asked, looking into the hole in the side of the ship. Captain Parker had interrupted her preparations for the coming assault and had asked her to come with him to inspect the damage done to the ship, but he hadn't said why she needed to see it.

I understand now.

"That's what I want to know, too," the captain said as he maneuvered through the hole in his shipsuit.

Sansar slipped through the hole and jetted over to join him at the aft bulkhead, where a row of 10 mini-CASPers were attached. They weren't *really* CASPers, but they looked a lot like them, only ones that were more high-tech and better built. She couldn't see any seams from where the metal was linked, even at the shoulder and leg joints.

She would have wondered who built the mini-mechs, except it was obvious. One of the Fae/Dusman was strapped into one of the mechs with the canopy half-closed.

"What is this space?" Sansar asked.

"It's a void. There wasn't anything here. In fact, none of this should be here." He pointed to where several pieces of equipment were welded to the bulkhead. Sansar looked closer and realized she couldn't see the welds; it almost looked like the gear had been extruded from the wall.

"Where did all this come from?" Sansar asked.

"I was hoping you'd tell me," Parker said with an accusatory tone.

"I didn't know anything about it," she replied. He stared at her. "Promise." When he still didn't say anything, she added. "If I'd wanted them aboard, I would have brought them aboard. Why wouldn't I have told you? We could have done it without telling anyone, but I wouldn't have done it without your knowledge. You have to fight the ship; you need to know where everything is onboard in order to do so."

She motioned to the damaged space. "Otherwise, something like this happens."

The captain sighed after a moment. "Yeah," he said softly. "Something just like this."

"What do you think *was* going on here?"

"It looks like these creatures—"

"I recognize the one in the armor. They're the Dusman."

"It looks like the Dusman snuck aboard. Since the skin of the ship here got vaporized, I don't know if they cut a hole through the hull to get in here or came in from the interior of the ship, but somehow they got in here and put together some sort of mech factory. It looks like they tapped into the ship's systems for power.

"They obviously weren't prepared for the ship to get hit, though, and when this void was exposed to space, however many of them were here all got sucked out into space, along with any other evidence of what they were doing. The only thing we have are the mechs, which are in the racks attached to the bulkhead. It looks like one of them was getting into a suit—maybe they knew we were engaged in a fight—but then we took the hit, and the ship's power went out on him before he could get his suit closed and turned on."

"How many of them do you suppose there were?"

"No idea. They're pretty small, so there could have been 10 of them, like the number of suits would indicate, but there may have been others—techs, maybe—to fix and maintain the suits. There's no way to know. The only way we even know who was in here is the one in that suit."

"I guess the most important question at the moment is whether there are more of them, or whether this nest is their only infestation."

Sansar could see Parker's shoulders move in his suit as he shrugged. "I'm going to have the crew look for other places where they might be hiding, but they obviously do it pretty well. If there are any more of them, I don't know whether we'll find them or not, but we'll try."

Sansar nodded. *What could the Dusman have been doing here?* She would have been happy to have them along if they'd said they wanted to come...*maybe their purpose was to some nefarious end?* It was impossible to know. *Were they aware of the starkillers?* If the technology was from the Great War, they might be familiar with it. Based on everything she knew about them, they would certainly want to control them if they knew about them.

"How many people know about this space?" Sansar asked.

"Just the two damage control technicians who found it."

"Where are they?"

"I think they went to get some chow."

Sansar sighed. "So the entire crew probably knows now."

"Nothing travels so fast onboard a ship as a secret," Parker said. He turned and she could see he was smiling. "I could try to stop its progression—"

"—but that'll just make it travel faster," Sansar finished, familiar with shipboard life.

"Pretty much."

"Well, we'll have to have a debriefing on this, because I do *not* want word of what we're doing here to get back to the Dusman."

"That's at least something," Parker said. "I don't think most of the crew really knows what we're here for."

"Good. Please try and keep it that way." She shook her head again as she looked around the space. "If you could lock up all these suits, I would appreciate it. I have an assault to conduct, so I have to return to the troops. Once we get back, my people will help you look for other Dusman infestations." *And when we get back to Earth, we're going to have to have a real heart-to-heart conversation with Splunk and her people.*

* * * * *

Chapter Forty-One

Unlikely Regret, **Hyperspace**

Jex sat with Bravo Company in the area of *Unlikely Regret*'s mess hall sectioned off for the CASPer force.

But he wasn't *with* them.

"Join the Horde."

That had been Major Sun's orders. Jex had recently managed to strike up a weird friendship of sorts with the Sumatozou gate mistress at Aneb, but he put that down mostly to novelty value on both sides. These fellow Humans were treating him as the spy in their midst. They were a much tougher nut to crack.

Turnaround would be better at this hearts and minds thing than him. Even Plunger, if the big guy's mouth didn't start a war first. But their CASPers would be battle ready by the time they dropped at Wahrner's Grise. They would be part of the recce op.

Meanwhile, Jex's suit was so *not* ready that it was being stripped down and rebuilt onboard *Midnight Sun*, somewhere in hyperspace en route to McPherson's Star. Which was why it was time for him to do what came naturally: put his foot in it.

He caught the eye of the man sitting opposite him. His rank patch marked him as a sergeant, and he was one of the many Enkhs. Like the rest of his Central Asian comrades, to Jex his face appeared broad, and there was an eagerness to prove himself that shone from his young, dark eyes.

"Sergeant Amish," said Jex. "That's what you call me, isn't it?"

Sergeant Chuluunbold Enkh looked up momentarily with his ersatz taco to his lips. He shrugged and carried on eating.

"I'm sure the Amish are fine folks," said Jex, "but I've never met one. I'm not even American. But you're welcome to call me that if you like."

The conversation along the table dried up.

He tried again. "So, what's the story behind the Enkhs? You all cousins or something? Not that I have a problem with that. Up Cromer way in North Norfolk, everyone's a cousin."

"It means 'peace,'" said Enkh and went back to his chow.

"Give the guy a break," the other sergeant at the table admonished Enkh. She had a strong American accent. "We all asked you the same question at first."

She threw Jex a look of appraisal. "Name's Sergeant DeWitt. And, yes, the name 'Amish' has been applied to your features when we're off duty. I mean, come on! What do you expect with a name like Obadiah?"

"No stranger than *Lampshade* for those of us who came out of Tashkent," said Enkh.

"That's your nickname?" Jex laughed. The TO&E had listed Martine DeWitt. Lampshade was more his style.

"What?" she replied with a grin. "You telling me your Midnighter squad hollers at each other using formal titles? What are you, goddamned English royalty?"

"Okay, you have a point, DeWitt. But, seriously, you can't call everyone Enkh on the squad channel. Surely."

"Not when things get hot," she admitted. "You're sitting across from Chuluunbold Enkh, but he goes by Sergeant Chulkaa. That fine young CASPer driver over there"—she indicated an Uzbek woman with her spork—"is Private Enebish Enkh, but she goes by the name of Bishee. Enebish means 'not this one.'"

"Sounds like Lieutenant Enkh's first name," said Jex.

"Yup." DeWitt nodded her approval. "Lieutenant Terbish Enkh. Her name means 'not *that* one.' There's a tradition, especially with orphans, of giving them unappealing names. Throws off the evil spirits or something. Doesn't matter why people do it. What matters is that it's a tradition. And now the Horde has proud traditions of our own. The colonel took the name 'Enkh' for herself. Like Sergeant Chulkaa said, it means peace. A lot of Horde troopers were recruited from Tashkent orphanages. When they were adopted into the Horde family, they took on her name." She winked at Chulkaa Enkh. "How did I do?"

"For an American, not bad at all." He grinned at Jex. "Our commander also took on the name Sansar. It means Outer Space." He laughed. "We bring peace to outer space. Out of the barrels of our MACs."

"Careful, Chulkaa," warned Sergeant DeWitt. "If you encourage Jex too much, before you know it, he'll be signing up as Amish Enkh."

"What of *your* commanders?" Chulkaa Enkh asked Jex. "Major Sun and Captain Blue? I hear many tales about them, most of which can't possibly be true. How did they acquire names like that?"

"Now that's an interesting thing," said Jex. "Nobody knows. And when you've been around the major for a while, you'll understand that nobody asks either."

He noticed DeWitt's gaze locked on him like a heatseeker. "In that case," she said, "I'll ask the *other* question. The one we're all dying to know. What did you do in the Omega War?"

Her voice carried an ugly undertone.

"My company was the Suffolk Punch. I…" He had to look away for a moment. "I'm the only one left. What you really mean to ask is what the hell were the Midnighters doing while we were all bleeding so bad? Well, as I've learned since I joined them, quite a lot. The story starts at the ornamental gardens of the old Midnighter base at Tau-Rietzke. It was an assassination. It was a demonstration. Apparently, the drinks were free. Oh, and did I mention? There were Raknar…"

* * *

Orbital 312, Wahrner's Grise

Obbo wrapped her Zuparti tongue around the ice stick and enjoyed the fresh tickle of sweetened narcotics fizzing over its length.

Pinpricks of warm living light pranced across her field of view, chasing each other along the outlines of the bar's patrons.

The place didn't have a formal name. It was simply Unzikah's bar.

She giggled. "If you need to know its name," she said. "You don't belong here."

The Cochkala at the table next to her looked up from his slate and glared at her with his one good eye while flicking his tail.

Obbo sniggered at the alien, but that only seemed to irritate it more.

Reluctantly, Obbo eased her tongue off the psychoactive treat, giving it a lingering look.

The Cochkala rubbed behind its eye patch and returned to its slate.

Slowly, the bar shimmered back into sense.

Just in time.

The Human she'd been observing tapped Yacks with the Blevin who was one of Unzikah's brokers.

A deal had just been struck.

She didn't know the Blevin's name, but the Human was called Brakshi. She was the loadmaster of the *Unlikely Regret*, a ship she'd been told to watch out for.

Brakshi was usually in the company of the big Human in the even bigger coat who toted a nine-barreled rifle. Such a barbarian!

For a moment, an old paranoid instinct shocked her. Was she being played?

Then she remembered what her Endless Night contact had told her. Captain Jenkins was dead.

Her fears were chased away by the prospect of the credits Endless Night would pay for information on *Unlikely Regret*. Intel she was going to uncover for them. Say what you like about the Night, but they paid well and on time. They were good people in her eyes.

She took a lingering look at her ice stick and then sealed it in a pouch to enjoy later.

Obbo commed her ship.

"Tell everyone to sober up," she told the first mate. "*Unlikely Regret* is about to take on cargo. They'll be heading down to the planet in a few hours. We need to be ready to follow."

"We stealing their cargo, boss? Sounds risky."

"I am in full command of my mental faculties," she snapped back.

She took a moment to collect herself. It was just possible that her subordinate wasn't criticizing her vices. It was so difficult to trust anyone or anything these days. She'd even heard rumors of widespread counterfeit red diamond chits. Of Yack transactions being refused.

She shuddered. If you couldn't trust Galactic Union credits, what was the point of existence?

"Captain?" queried the first mate. "What *are* we doing?"

"Observing. Reporting. Earning. And we won't be doing any of those things unless you whip those useless bags of flesh who lounge around my ship, consuming all my air and rations. I need them ready to cast off and follow the *Regret.*"

"Copy that, boss. *We'll* be ready."

For a moment, Obbo wondered at the strange emphasis in her subordinate's words. Then she dismissed that in favor of greater worries.

Counterfeit currency...She tried to remember. How would Endless Night be paying?

* * *

Beowulf strolled along Dipper Zone, inspecting the stalls in search of the perfect trinket.

Orbital 312 was a kind of floating dumpster that didn't even warrant a proper name. And yet, it still had its little retail section to sell curios and mementos.

It was also a stone's throw from the smuggler's bar where freighter captains could pick up illicit cargoes from Unzikah.

As he backed away from a stall manned by a Bakulu who appeared to be asleep in his shell, Beowulf accidentally bumped into a one-eyed Cochkala passing by.

He held his hands out in a placatory gesture. "I apologize for my clumsy behavior, honored being."

The Cochkala wrapped its tail around empty air. It was obvious he was indicating what he would like to do if his tail were wrapped around the rude Human's neck.

"It is fortunate for you that my errands are urgent," the Cochkala said. "Otherwise I would teach you to mind your clumsiness."

Beowulf allowed himself a slight smile, and then mumbled further apologies as the Cochkala stomped off.

The alien's name was Zayglejatt. Beowulf owed him a beer or three, but not here. That would have to wait until they were away from the prying eyes of Orbital 312.

The code word in that exchange had been *fortunate*.

It meant Captain Obbo had bought their diversion.

Endless Night would be looking the other way as the Gray Wolves shepherded Major Sun's recon team to the planet.

He opened a secure link to the Zuul supervising the lading of *Unlikely Regret*'s cargo onto the Gray Wolf shuttles. "Talk to me, Sneetal."

"Already done," Sneetal replied. "They'll be at Zoar Kheter within the ten-hour."

"Good. Find a way to get yourself unseen to the hangar at Dunzeld. The mission's started well, but they'll need us before we've finished."

The Zuul responded with a chuffing laugh. "Gray Wolves as overwatch angels! I suppose cosmic balance meant we had to be on the side of the good guys one day."

"You can stow your cosmic karma bullshit, Sneetal. There's only one side in this galaxy. The Gray Wolves."

"For a Human, you have an instinctive understanding of the clan, Beowulf. I won't meet you at Dunzeld, because I'll be traveling with the cargo. I'll send Durboz instead. Out."

Beowulf returned to the stall and picked up a model stargate. He enjoyed the smooth feel of the polished metal. Probably stolen scrap, but it was artfully made.

The apparently sleeping Bakulu suddenly came alive and extruded pseudopods.

"Easy, Big Slug. I'll give you five credits for this knickknack."

"It's worth seventy. But business is slow. I'll let it go for fifty-five."

Beowulf glanced behind and saw Brakshi walking back to *Unlikely Regret* with the pair of Blevin escorts she'd brought with her.

He paid the trader twenty-five and left in the opposite direction.

* * * * *

Chapter Forty-Two

EMS *Gobi Desert*, In Orbit Around McPherson-3

Sansar's glance swept the conference room, her eyes pausing on each of her senior staff. "As most of you probably know, the Dusman from the Great War 20,000 years ago have returned. The Kahraman have also returned and are being held at bay by Mercenary Guild forces. I guess it isn't surprising, then, that some of their weapons are showing up now, too. We were aware of the *Keesius*-class ships the Dusman made—planet killers that use antimatter to destroy a targeted planet. We just became aware of another planet killer, but these are worse—they make a system's star go nova, wiping out *everything* in the system. I don't know how many of these were made, but there were three here in the Spine Nebula. One of them has been destroyed, but two remain."

"Are these from the Dusman as well?" asked Captain Jeff House, the Alpha Company commander.

"Perhaps…but it seems more likely to me that these were the Kahraman response. After all, why would you need *two* ways to wipe out a planetary system?"

House shook his head. "I'm not sure why you'd even want one, ma'am."

"I agree," Sansar said, "and our mission today is to destroy one of the other two. While people may have told you in the past, 'The safety of Earth depends on this mission,' it has never been more true than today. The criminals currently possessing it want to target our sun to show its destructive capabilities. They've already tried to fire it once, but the weapon was directed at a different star by an operative of the Gray Wolves. They are getting ready to fire it again, and this time they may not miss. More so than ever before, the safety of the Earth depends on this assault.

"Now, I know we don't typically do assaults, but we're the only ones here with the equipment to do it, and therefore, we shall."

"What are we looking at?" House asked.

"The weapon is buried underground, and it's being held by the Endless Night, which is a criminal organization. We know they've hired merc companies to provide fleet support, so they have enough resources to hire combat troops as well."

"These aren't your typical criminals," House noted.

"No, they aren't," Sansar agreed. "We don't know if we'll be going against mercs, but at a minimum, we can expect their troops to be well armed and probably decently trained. They have hired a Besquith company—Saunorak's Pioneer Company—to bolster their defenses."

Several people shifted uncomfortably.

"These Besquith aren't front-line troops, they are a company that emplaces defenses, kind of like we do in our day jobs."

"Well, they won't be as good as ours, I hope," Mun said.

"And, based on our experience, hopefully we'll be good at getting past any defenses they've erected." Sansar smiled, then she got serious again. "Besides Saunorak's Pioneer Company and their Lumar subcontractors, though, most of the defenders will be criminals and not mercs."

"So, kind of like a Lychee," House said. "It's got a hard shell surrounding a soft interior."

"I wouldn't let our guard down until we're back onboard the *Gobi Desert*. We would design a defense in depth; I suspect they will too, and it will be manned with Besquith and Lumar. We all know how tough Besquith are, but don't discount the Lumar, either. They may not be the smartest mercs, but they're strong and brave, and with four arms, they can do a lot of damage."

Sansar brought up the overhead imagery on the Tri-V. "Here's the entrance to the facility. As you can see, there are emplaced weapons surrounding it in bunkers, as well as triple-A and missiles to bring down any dropships flying in to assault it, or troopers dropping on it in a HALD."

"Which I suspect we're not going to do," Mun noted.

Sansar shook her head. "Going head-to-head with the strength of their defenses is definitely *not* what I want to do." She tapped another spot about a mile away. "And, happily, we don't have to. Over here is the Gelheik Sands Mine, which we know intersects with the facility, deep underground. Rather than having to go through level after level of defenses getting in, Alpha Company will go into the mines and will attack it that way while First Platoon, Bravo Company keeps the defenders' attention on the main entrance."

"Surely the defenders have to know about the mine entrance, though," House said. "They won't have left it vulnerable. At least, not if the mercs defending it are worth a shit."

"True. I suspect there will be defenses in the mine; however, there won't be as many as at the main entrance, and it will allow us to get a lot closer to the weapon before we run into the defenses."

"Sorry, ma'am, but how do you know that?"

"Because they've released sand burrowers into the mines."

"Sand burrowers?" asked Lieutenant Batu Enkh, the Alpha Company, First Platoon leader. "Can I expect they will be large and nasty?"

"According to the local instance of the GalNet, yes, your assumption is right on. They look like mini-Canavar, and they like to hunt in mines. They can easily tunnel through sand, but they can chew through rock, too, when they want."

"Goody," House muttered. "Fighting monsters in an underground dungeon isn't just for role-playing games anymore. Now we get to do it in real life." Louder, he asked, "How much is 'mini' and how much is 'Canavar?'"

"The adult ones are about 20 meters long and three meters in width."

"Probably with some sort of laser and MAC-resistant skin…"

Sansar nodded. "That's what the entry on them said." A number of people groaned.

"How do we kill them?" Mun asked.

"Well, we try to avoid them, and, if we can't, then we give them a liberal dose of high explosives. Regardless, even though they seem incredibly dangerous, they are less dangerous than going toe-to-toe with the defenses on the main entrance."

Mun shrugged. "Never had sand burrower steaks before. If they come after us, I mean to rectify that shortcoming."

Sansar looked at Captain House. "Make sure we bring along a couple of the armed drone swarms. They won't be useful against the sand burrowers, but they'll be good against any fortifications we run up against while we're in the mines."

"Yes, ma'am."

Sansar looked around the table. "Any other questions? Good. Let's go get ready. Before we left, I put a down payment on some land to build our new headquarters; I don't want to get back and find out it's no longer there."

* * * * *

Chapter Forty-Three

Zoar Kheter, The White Desert, Wahrner's Grise

The clear night sky above the desert sands was so perfectly still that Branco felt as if he were floating in space. He supposed he was in a way.

The stars did not twinkle here, and if they appeared to move, it was only due to the twitch of Branco's body.

He took a drink of water from the metal cup he'd drilled a short way into the sand beside his stool, and then continued spooning down the hot stew.

"It is a little bland for me," said Sneetal from the folding fabric stool alongside. The Zuul offered a small container of food spices.

Branco shook his head. "I'm good. I don't know what's in this stew, and I don't want to, but it's tasty and filling. And warm. What it really needs is a campfire to sit beside."

"You know that's forbidden, don't you?"

Branco resisted the urge to glare at the Zuul. Instead, he stared into the serenity of the stars.

Before meeting Sun, his career had been in corporate espionage. Sneetal was a Gray Wolf—smugglers, fixers, and spies from what Branco could make out.

Whereas Branco had ultimately reported to ultra-rich executives in sharp suits stalking the plush corporate offices of Binnig HQ, who could tell who really pulled Sneetal's strings? Was it really the Golden Horde? Probably the Gray Wolf didn't know himself. But when working in the field, Branco's former life hadn't been that different from these Wolves.

Sneetal was insulting Branco's professionalism. And that stung.

"I have memory blocks," he tried to explain.

"I've heard of such things," said Sneetal. "You can't blow deep cover when you don't even realize you're *in* cover."

"Exactly. The blocks are dissolving. I'm remembering more everyday about who I was. I'm losing motor control too. Sometimes I stutter. But get this! None of those things mean I'm becoming stupid. I know not to light a fire. With what we're about to face, it's important we trust each other to have a basic level of competence."

The Zuul huffed but said nothing. That suited Branco perfectly. Peacefulness was something he'd come to treasure. He'd snatch a piece of it wherever he could.

They were sitting on the edge of an immense rectangular covering that protected the nomadic trading post of Zoar Kheter from both observation and the worst of the nighttime cold and daytime sun.

As concealment, it was hardly perfect. Branco suspected it was the kind of arrangement whereby if the people who ran Zoar Kheter made it sufficiently difficult for the authorities to find, then they could be bribed to pretend it wasn't there.

Lighting a fire might make it too difficult for the authorities to look the other way.

There were other methods of attracting attention than lighting fires, of course. He'd used one earlier.

Sun had wanted him safely away on Station 5, waiting for the Wrogul surgeon to show—the one Bluc had wrangled for him.

But he'd countered that nowhere was safe in the nebula, and if he was going to be in danger, he'd rather be in danger with her.

Sun was still angry that he was here at all, and she had made him promise to go escorted to Station 5 by another Patriot freighter once the operation was complete. Meanwhile, *Unlikely Regret* and the rest of the recon force would wait in-system for the arrival of the McPherson's Star taskforce.

Thinking about Sun made him aware of their freight boxes sitting in another segment of Zoar Kheter, waiting for delivery from this illicit transportation hub.

She was inside one, heavily sedated to conserve oxygen and suppress body heat, and likely still pissed at him in her dreams.

His winning argument had been that they might have a potential ally inside the starkiller base, and Branco was best placed to contact her.

"Perhaps you should try the radio again?" Sneetal suggested.

Branco wanted to, desperately. He'd claimed he could contact Hopper by the same means he'd raised her once before, inside the starkiller base on Aneb-4. It was the only reason he'd been included on the mission.

He started unscrewing the prosthetic lower leg that concealed a radio transceiver. But something didn't feel right. He screwed it back on. Someone was watching him.

With the combination of Human medical therapies and Selroth weed pumping through his veins, though, he wasn't sure of anything.

"I'll try again when I've finished the stew," he told Sneetal.

"Make sure you eat quickly, my friend, or I shall tell you the ingredients." He licked his lips. "I sense you wish to be alone. I'll go check on the cargo and round up Zarbi."

"You do that," Branco said absently. He was on the cusp of adding the code phrase to mean danger was close, but if anything had been near, he couldn't sense it now.

He let Sneetal go and returned to the simple pleasure of his dinner under the stars.

Almost at the last spoonful, Branco heard the noise of flicking grains of sand. Something was inching toward him out of the silver desert. To his right.

He sat down his bowl and reached within the broad sleeve of his robe to release the blade strapped to the inside of his forearm.

He took a firm grip on the knife, cursing inwardly at his missing legs. He'd been surprised at how much he could do without them, but there were some things where his amputations would always be a problem. Such as knife fights in a gravity well.

He twisted round on his stool as fast as he could to face the threat. With the knife high, he made a split-second decision whether to throw, or retain the knife and stab.

He did neither.

"Hello, Branco. I heard you mention Zarbi. What a delightful young female. Did you bring Jenkins?"

It was a Jeha. Her carapace was covered in salt, white paint, and twigs. There were holes in several segments where chains had once passed through. The deep scars, cracked mandible, and missing segment were new, but he had no doubt about who this was.

He secured his knife in its sheath. "It's good to see you, Hopper. Didn't expect to find you on the outside of the base."

"I escaped weeks ago. I received your message, but I had to check it was really you. Oh, Branco. I've been so frightened. I didn't think anyone would come for me."

Branco ran through the timeline. If she'd run away weeks ago...

"Were you responsible for...?"

He trailed off when a fat Gtandan interrupted, walking in as if anyone could join this reunion.

"Don't let me stop you," said the alien. "Is she responsible for what? What have you done to the nice Human, Lohna?"

The Gtandan launched a vicious kick at the Jeha that sent her flying ten feet over the sand. Hopper let out a scratchy cry of pain.

The bully just laughed and flipped her over onto her back before stomping down with his boot.

Branco heard Hopper's body crunch.

"Stop that!" he yelled and drew his knife once more.

The Gtandan peered quizzically at him. "What's it to you—" he nodded at Branco's prosthetics, "—*half*-Human?" The Gtandan squealed with laughter. "Oh, you're worried about the Jeha? Is she your girlfriend?"

Branco lowered his blade a little. "No. I'm just trying to enjoy the peace of the night. I can't do that when you're breaking people."

"People?" The Gtandan laughed again. "She's only a Jeha. You know how they get. *Curious.* The slightest thing, most unprofitable puzzle, anything can distract them when they're—" he bent over and yelled at Hopper, "—*supposed to be working!* This one's here for salvage. What have you got for me, Lohna?"

Hopper righted herself and handed over a data chip to the fat pig.

The Gtandan slapped it inside his slate and perused its contents. "That's right, half-Human. My Lohna scavenges for information. That's why she's been talking with you. Hoping you'll let slip something I can sell. Don't let me stop you."

"Is he right?" Branco asked when the Gtandan strolled off in the direction of the food stalls.

"Yes. You told me once that when I was too scared to do something that needed doing, I should act out a role. The role I perform here is of Lohna the Scavenger. It isn't difficult. Not all information is as jealously guarded as it should be."

"I have a new role for you to play," said Branco. "We're going to penetrate the base, look around, maybe do some damage, and then head for orbit and safety. Come with us. It'll be dangerous—of course it will—but if we make it through, you'll be safe with us when we're back on *Midnight Sun*."

He had assumed Hopper would leap for joy at the chance of being reunited with Jenkins, but the alien appeared reluctant.

"Would I be...hurt?"

"No. Why? Oh, you mean will you be punished because you helped Endless Night? And the Tyzhounes."

"It wasn't my fault. They knew how to give me such interesting problems to solve. I was intoxicated. I couldn't help it. Please tell me Jenkins doesn't hate me." She flattened her body and splayed out her legs. "I wouldn't blame him if he hates me."

"You don't have to worry about Jenkins. He's so in love with you, he'll forgive anything."

"Really?" She picked herself up and walked over to curl near his feet.

"Really," Branco replied. "But for the record, I won't forgive everything. And Major Sun definitely won't."

"But I sabotaged the starkiller here as soon as I could. Then I ran away. They chased me. They fired guns. It was horrible."

"I reckon you've redeemed yourself in my eyes," he told her. "When you next see Major Sun, lead off with the part about sabotaging the starkiller before you list all the ways you helped Endless Night."

"Right. That would make sense."

The stars twinkled.

Branco tried to ask Hopper about what they would face beneath Lake Zarillo, but the words weren't coming.

The stars had become tracks smeared across the black.

He was coming down hard after the adrenaline rush of his confrontation with the Gtandan.

"To the Devil with this!" he growled. If Gloriana was to be believed, once this mission was over, the next stop for Branco would be the Wrogul. A cure.

Shame he didn't believe a word that Goltar said.

"Is something the matter?" asked Hopper.

He was shaking uncontrollably. He'd crash any moment now.

"I need rest. Hopper, did you see a Zuul sitting next to me?"

"Yes."

"Go find him. Tell him I need help."

The desert was shimmering.

"Branco, are you hurt?"

"Get the Zuul," he growled through gritted teeth. "Then explain everything you know about the starkiller to Zarbi."

The last strands of consciousness frayed away from Branco, leaving a single thought. If he couldn't handle a couple of knife fights that never actually happened, how was he going to get through the next few days?

A sense of foreboding swallowed him, and he fell from his chair.

He never felt his head hit the sand.

* * *

Zoar Kheter, Wahrner's Grise

The universe was shaking.

Branco was caught in an earthquake. He gasped as hot fluid licked his face, thick and stinking of spices and…doggy odor.

"I said, wake the fuck up!"

Branco opened his eyes on Sneetal.

The Zuul stopped shaking him by the shoulders. A thread of drool hung from his muzzle.

"Did you just lick me?"

Sneetal gave Branco a hard stare. "If you tell anybody, I *will* kill you. Now grab your gear. We're heading out."

Branco pushed himself upright and looked around. Their little group had claimed a space by one of the tent support pillars. He was the only one in his bed roll.

It was still night.

"We're not due to head out until the afternoon."

Sneetal chuffed. "Which is exactly what I pointed out to the convoy master. I'll tell you what she told me. Do you want this fucking job or not?"

"Copy that," said Branco. "Let's load up."

The Zuul growled. "Yeah, like you're gonna be any fucking use with that."

* * *

Branco woke in the cab.

The Tri-V showed they were thundering along the sand, nose to tail, in a line of six trucks. The Endless Night escort outriders were driving makeshift gun carts, each sporting multiple SAM pods and guns mounted in the back. They resembled Human pickup trucks, except their orientation was ninety degrees out, with the cab seemingly taken off the front and stuck on the side of the cargo bay.

"I said we shouldn't take you along," snarled Sneetal. "In your state, you're a liability."

"I've got stims," Branco countered. "I'm saving them for when I need them."

He popped some Selroth *ribbwah* weed in his mouth and was still chewing on it when he fell back into slumber.

* * *

Branco dreamed he was in a fevered nightmare. He was inside a giant peach rolling along a desert. His companions trapped with him inside his peculiar transport were a talking dog and two giant earwigs, one white and one gray.

He opened his eyes and noted for the first time the bright peach color of the cab's interior.

It was daylight.

He adjusted the exterior cameras to get a view of the convoy.

Two more trucks had joined during the night. Together with the four outrider gun trucks, they rolled along a track rutted by frequent use.

Endless Night was shipping a lot of gear inside that base of theirs. What were they doing with it all?

"Three hours from the tunnel," Sneetal told him, his eyes not leaving the track. The truck was fully manually driven. The Night no longer permitted auto-trucks near the lake.

Swiping through the interior camera feeds, Branco took a look inside the cargo bay at the eight freight boxes secured there. Some of them carried a stenciled gray wolf symbol, but others were obscured from view.

"How many of our boxes did we get on this truck?"

"All six of our crates," Sneetal replied. "Plus two more we picked up with machine parts inside. Why? Did you ever doubt I could wrangle our boxes onto this truck?"

"Mr. Sneetal Graywolf is a very impressive being," said Zarbi, the teenage Jeha scientist. She leaped onto the dashboard in front of Branco. "Wouldn't you agree, Hopper?"

"Who is Hopper?" said the adult Jeha curled into a relaxed crescent in the footwell. "I don't know any Hopper. My name is Lohna. I am an information scavenger."

The two Jeha made a horrifying noise, like a weaponized form of fingernails scraping over a chalkboard. Even Sneetal flinched.

Branco's translator pendant interpreted the banshee noise as laughter.

He closed his eyes and returned to the relative sanity of his fever dreams.

* * *

Sneetal pinched him awake. "Time to take your stims."

It was nighttime. No. They were in a tunnel lit by the headlamps of the convoy.

"It's a security checkpoint," said Zarbi. "Convoy's halting."

The cab window slid open. Smells of hot oil and dust came flowing through. As did the growls of Besquith from up ahead.

Branco popped some stim-fused Di-Cloxorin Yellows.

By the time a Besquith stuck its massive werewolf head through the window and snarled at them to get the fuck out of the truck, Branco was buzzing.

They hurried out into a tunnel noisy with busy lift trucks and shouting Besquith.

"What are you carrying?" demanded the Besquith, peering at the cargo bay that Sneetal had already opened up. He was armed with a slate, his laser rifle slung over a massive shoulder.

"Two loads of machine parts, one of fresh food, one of rotten—"

"No!" The Besquith shoved Sneetal away, slamming him into the fender. He sniffed suspiciously at the two Jeha before pointing a claw at Branco. "I want the crippled Human to speak. What are you carrying?"

"Two containers of machine parts, four of food, two biohazards."

The Besquith wrinkled its snout. "What kind of biohazard?"

Branco gulped. "One moment please, sir."

He hobbled over to the cab to retrieve his slate. To his surprise, he made it back without being disemboweled.

"It's here somewhere…The biohazard is…a…corrosion accelerant. Both containers."

The Besquith snarled through its impossibly wicked fangs. "What the fuck does that mean, Human?"

The alien's anger ripped through Branco's guts as viciously as a slash of his claws.

Both Jeha hid under the truck.

Branco soiled himself. It was a waste of time being ashamed. Most people would do the same in the face of an angry werewolf.

"I…I don't know," Branco said. "Manifest says corrosion accelcrant. I'm in the transportation business. It's just a box with a number and a description to me. If that's not what you people wanted, I'm sorry, but you'll have to take that up with Master Unzikah."

The Besquith appeared mollified by the obvious signs of terror. "Show me your biohazards. I shall inspect them."

The freight boxes were laid in a line and packed two deep. A Lumar brought up a lift truck and lifted one of the upper layer of boxes to allow the Besquith to leap on top of one marked with the Union biohazard glyph.

He opened up the inspection hatch and took a look inside. By the way his ears flicked back against his head, the smell inside nauseated him.

"Inspection pole," barked the Besquith.

He caught a meter-long rod thrown by the Lumar, extended it to four times its length, and then thrust it inside.

The pole should have reached down to the bottom.

It didn't.

The Besquith almost fell through the hatch, throwing out a hand to grab the edge just in time.

He withdrew the pole and stared, slack-jawed, at the end that had melted away. Its tip was still disappearing. The Besquith flicked it into the container before the corrosive fluid reached his fingers.

"I guess that's what a corrosion accelerant does," said Sneetal under his breath.

Branco wanted his legs back so he could kick the damned dog to shut him up. But the Besquith ignored the Zuul and beckoned Branco to join him on the cargo bed, howling at him to hurry the fuck up.

"Food," he shouted at Branco. "You said food. What kind of food?"

"Meat."

The Besquith licked its fangs. This kind of inspection was more to its liking. "Which box?"

Branco pointed to one on the upper level.

"Open it!"

He needed a diversion. A sleight of hand. A trick. Something.

Because the Besquith wanted to look in the one Sun was hiding inside.

He shambled over, thinking furiously, but by the time he got there, he'd convinced himself the best plan was to trust Staff Sergeant Melsome.

"You break it we fix it, you lose it we find it." That had been the motto of Melsome's CASPer, Search, Rescue, and Recovery unit that he'd led into the Omega War. The way he talked, sneaking CASPers past the noses of Besquith guards had been just another day in the office.

Branco undid the catches and let the front of the freight box drop against the bed floor.

"Ahh!" He gagged. The stench was unbearable.

Cuts of putrefying meat hung from top to bottom, completely obscuring from eyes and nose the inner compartment where the recon team slept on.

"Guess you've got some scavenger races operating on your base," said Sneetal. "Some people can't get enough of the carrion."

"Those foul Sniggets," said the Besquith. He held his hand to his snout as he sprinted off the cargo bed. "They disgust me. Seal it up immediately. Then return to your cab and do not leave."

The Lumar had already replaced the box over the biohazard container.

Sneetal and Branco secured the cargo area, returned to the cab, and waited to set off.

* * * * *

Chapter Forty-Four

Avenger-1, **Approaching the Gelheik Sands Mine, McPherson-3**

"Weeeeee!" shouted Borth, the SalSha weapons systems officer, as the bomber screamed along at 800 kilometers per hour 20 meters above the desert floor.

"Focus!" Meeth ordered. "Remember what Walker taught us!"

"I am focused," Borth grumbled. "But can't I enjoy it at the same time?"

"Of course. As long as you're serious about the attack."

"I'm very serious. Watch!" He flipped a switch. "Master arm is on, missiles selected! Stand by to pop. Twenty kilometers to the target. Go!"

Meeth pulled the bomber to the right in a six-G pull, then leveled the wings and pulled up. He paused for three seconds, then rolled the craft onto its back, acquired the target, and flipped it back upright. "Mark!" he called, designating the target environment.

"Got it!" Borth said. "Targets acquired and locked in," he added as he designated the three aim points to the missiles. "Fire!"

Meeth squeezed the trigger and the missiles leapt from the wings. Ground fire could now be seen coming from the target, and tracers were reaching up toward them.

"Missile radars active," Borth noted.

"Racks clear! Evading." Meeth put the craft into a 10-G turn away from the target, dispensed chaff and flares to confuse the enemy systems, and eased the craft back down to 20 meters again.

"*One is off target,*" Borth called over comms.

"*Two is in hot!*" the WSO for *Avenger-2* called. They were about to perform the same attack, but from the opposite direction. *Avenger-3* would then attack from yet another direction.

* * *

Cargo Bay, *Dropship One*,

Approaching the Gelheik Sands Mine, McPherson-3

"I'm starting to pick up the triple-A radars," the pilot commed.

"They know we're coming," Sansar said. "I'm not surprised."

"*One is off target,*" a voice said over comms.

"And there goes a couple of the triple-A radars," the pilot noted. "Gotta love a good SEAD plan."

"Indeed," Sansar replied. The suppression of enemy air defenses was a key component of the plan and made getting into the target a lot more survivable. The Golden Horde didn't do a lot of assaults, but even she knew SEAD was vital.

"One minute to drop," the pilot said. The light in the back of the cargo bay switched to amber, and, five seconds later, the ramp dropped, and Sansar could see the desert they were racing over. Mun waved and everyone got up and moved to the back of the ramp in two rows.

"Five seconds," the pilot called.

"Go!" Mun yelled as the light went green, and the CASPers began jumping out the back of the dropship. Sansar shuffled forward at the end of the line on the right, alongside Mun in the other line. Then it was her turn, and she stepped into the abyss.

* * *

Cargo Bay, *Dropship Five*, Endless Night Base, McPherson-3

The dropship touched down, and the platoon raced down the ramp to take defensive positions. As soon as Captain Naran Enkh stepped off, the dropship lifted, banked, and flew off.

"Second Squad, status?" Naran asked.

"Down and ready," Lieutenant Delkii Enkh replied from the opposite side of the Endless Night base. Since Bravo Company's Second Platoon had gone to Wahrner's Grise, Naran led First Squad, while Delkii—normally the First Platoon leader—had taken Second Squad.

The complex was a walled facility on the northern outskirts of a small town, and the squads approached from the east and west sides of it to try to minimize civilian casualties.

Inside the walls were a large warehouse, a large apartment-style building, and a medium-sized building that could have held offices. The wall only had two gates—one to the south into town and one on the northern side. Both were closed and had been so during the entire time the *Gobi Desert* had approached the planet. There obviously wasn't a lot of contact between the people in the facility and those in town.

In addition to the three main structures, there had also been three missile sites and several weapons bunkers incorporated into the wall. The SalSha had hopefully eradicated them—there was no evidence of triple-A on their approach, anyway—but they had to be prepared for it, just in case.

This decision to avoid the "city" had probably been unnecessary, Naran saw as she moved up—most of the buildings in the area were uninhabited and were either falling down or already heaps of rubble. The town—this section of it, anyway—looked like it had been the focus of a large amount of street-to-street fighting; the buildings that were still standing showed evidence of weapons fire.

"Did the SalSha do this?" she asked First Sergeant Franklin over a private connection, pointing to a large hole in the building she was passing.

Franklin paused to inspect the damage. "No, that was an anti-armor rocket of some type. Looks like they've been fighting here for a while." He paused. "Maybe the locals objected to the Endless Night moving in, and they had to pacify this area."

"Or wipe it out."

"Or that."

First Squad continued to advance on the facility, and Naran's senses were afire as she tried to watch for threats from every direction simultaneously. The fact that it was eerily quiet did nothing to help her sense of unease.

"Is it always like this?" she asked over a private connection to First Sergeant Franklin.

"No, usually there are a lot more people shooting at you."

"Is that better or worse?" Naran asked as she avoided a mound of rubble that used to be a house or small building.

"Neither...both? I don't know," Franklin said. "At least when they're firing at you, you know where they are, and you're too busy avoiding fire and sending it back at the enemy to be thinking of anything else."

"So I'm not wrong in thinking this assault is creepy?"

"No, ma'am, you're not. If this was an assault on just a criminal base, I'd say that the prep fire killed them all. As it is, I think they're just waiting for us to reach some sort of killbox, and then they're going to spring an attack."

A shiver went down Naran's spine, and she wished they'd waited for the Goltar. Their transport had gotten shot up in the battle, putting them behind timeline, but the decision had been made to go without them. Because "it's just a criminal base." All of a sudden, it didn't seem like "just a criminal base" to her.

A vision of a Besquith jumping out of a pile of rubble ran through Naran's consciousness, and drew back in shock. *It was so real!* While stopped, she used all the processing power of her four pinplants to run through the historical assaults she had loaded to see if there was anything similar referenced in any of the files. It didn't take long to find one.

"Bravo Company, take cover and hold in place," she ordered over the company net.

"What have you got, ma'am?" Franklin asked.

"I was reviewing combat footage for similar assaults, and I just found something. There was a Besquith company that destroyed a bunch of buildings in the target environment on Nak'Ban-5 so they could hide in them and hit the assaulting Zuul force from behind once they were engaged—and focused on—their front. The footage didn't look exactly like this, but close enough."

"It'd be possible," Franklin replied, sounding annoyed that he hadn't thought of it himself. "What happened to them?"

"Nearly all the Zuul were killed in the assault, and they had to abort and emergency evac."

"Not a very good outcome. I'd like to avoid that if possible, ma'am."

"Me too."

"What'd we stop for?" Delkii asked.

"I'm worried that the Besquith may be hiding in the rubble of these buildings and don't want to get caught in a crossfire between them and the facility."

"We could try to smoke them out with drones," Staff Sergeant McDonald said.

"Yeah," Sergeant Ashley Nichols added. "We used 'em like that in the Hedgehogs when we were doing perimeter defense. We'd fly them out ahead of us and have them look for signs of enemy forces hiding in nearby buildings."

"I want every drone we have in front of us," Naran ordered. "Have them search with both IR and magnetic anomaly. There's enough metal in some of the buildings that probably won't work too well, but if they find something near a door or window, it may very well be an enemy trooper."

Each of the fire team leaders had a drone as part of their standard gear, and, within seconds, eight UAVs were ranging in front of the squads. It didn't take long.

"Got one," Staff Sergeant Zachary White called. "Two buildings in front of us. Looks vaguely Besquith shaped."

"I've got a couple Lumar in the next building," Sergeant Keith Prestridge said.

"Me, too," McDonald added.

"Fuck!" Sergeant Nichols said. "There's a damn minefield in the middle of the road, 100 meters up from me. I'd have walked right into it."

"I thought those were illegal…or at least frowned upon," Private Hempfield said. "That's what they told us in cadre anyway."

"As if criminals cared about laws," Franklin said. "Remember, the defenses may have been set by a merc company, but they are in the employ of a criminal organization. All bets are off."

"I've got a minefield in front of me, too," White commed.

"What do you want us to do about all these traps, ma'am?" Franklin asked.

Naran smiled. Although no one could see it, she allowed it to color her tone. "What do we do about the traps? We spring them, of course."

* * * * *

Chapter Forty-Five

Inside Lake Zarillo Starkiller, Wahrner's Grise

"Hopper?"

Sun's slurred word was her first since reviving from the sedation in the cold room inside the starkiller base where the Lumar had obediently deposited all eight boxes.

The place was empty, and that was just as well, because the hardened CASPer drivers currently looked as weak as drunken kittens.

It was taking all their energy to emerge from their body bags and peel off the breathing apparatus and IV feeds.

Maybe it would pass. As a boy, Branco remembered watching a dragonfly emerge from its pupa. The insect had looked exhausted by its rebirth. But within fifteen minutes it had launched from its leafy branch and caught its first prey on the wing, claiming its position as the apex predator in the air above the pond.

He'd been Preben then, of course. How quickly the old memories had become familiar.

He shook his head. That was for another time.

"Be careful underfoot," he warned the CASPer team, pointing at the floor, which was slippery with the concealment slime that had packed the inner compartments.

Sun had eyes only for the white-backed Jeha.

"What's she doing here already?" she demanded.

"I tried to sabotage the weapon as soon as I could," said the Jeha. "They shot at me. Please don't hurt me."

"Branco?" Sun queried.

"Timetable's messed up," he replied. "But Hopper's with us. Zarbi says she's already explained how to perform the data extraction more efficiently."

Sun waved him quiet. "Need a few minutes. I just want you to tell me one thing, Branco. Do we know where to go and what to blow up?"

"Yes, Major."

"And Sneetal?"

"Already back with the truck."

She nodded and tossed him her Ctech GP-90 pistol and a spare mag. "Guard the door." She rose unsteadily to her feet and raised her voice. "People, we've got five minutes to bemoan our post-resuscitation hangover. Then I want those CASPers unpacked and active. Let's do the job we came for."

* * *

Inside the Starkiller, Wahrner's Grise

They swept through the base. First Squad took point, Second rearguard, and Reserve 'Squad'—a mere five Midnighter Mk 8s led by Sergeant Oranjeklegg—were in the center, ready to reinforce either of Lieutenant Terbish Enkh's Golden Horde squads.

McCoy and Melsome, Terbish's two squad leaders–her two *Horde* squad leaders—had spent time checking out Oranjeklegg's people and declared them to be veteran mercs who appeared to have at least some level of competence. But the Midnighters hadn't gotten their worn-out mechs ready for business until after they'd emerged from hyperspace. The amount of joint training they'd gotten in was wholly inadequate.

Terbish herself was in the middle of the formation, attached to what Major Sun called the Command Section.

Command Section? A rancid mess of freaks was a more accurate name.

Tagging along with the two CASPer officers were a painted pirate turncoat, responsible for the destruction of entire star systems, and her teenage millipede companion. Both of these Jeha were keeping up with the CASPer jog using motorized skateboards.

Then there was the erratic, drug-stimmed Human cripple in his micro-rumbler.

But if Major Sun referred to these individuals as the Command Section, then that was the only term that would escape Terbish's lips, whatever she might think on the inside.

"Right on schedule," said Sergeant DeWitt on the First Squad channel. "We've hit another gonad gateway."

"Lieutenant," transmitted Staff Sergeant McCoy on the command channel, "DeWitt is reporting—"

"I heard, thank you, Staff Sergeant. Major Sun, we have encountered another iris aperture. I request assistance from Specialist Branco."

"Sun. Roger that."

Terbish pushed forward, telling Melsome to hold Second Squad in a defensive posture while First pushed through the obstacle.

In the enforced idleness while Branco moved up, Enkh's thoughts turned to Major Sun. She was a woman of few words, but every one of them mattered, and no one thought to second guess them.

Very few of the major's words had been expended on her lieutenant. What did that imply?

Branco came forward on his bespoke Jeha–built contraption. It was a miniature one-man tank. Inside, Branco was lying prone on a repurposed acceleration couch inclined at 30 degrees. His profile was so low, the micro-rumbler only reached the knees on her Mk 8.

"Ain't that a thing?" McCoy said over the squad channel. "Stick a tail on that contraption, and we would have ourselves a cyber mouse. Never thought I'd join up with a fucking traveling carnival."

"Funnily enough," Branco replied, "neither did I."

McCoy laughed at that. "Haranga. Defiant. Shove our wheeled specialist where the sun don't shine."

Terbish was not a part of the laughter the squad shared. It was important for the others to share their banter, though it was laced with profanity and innuendo. But even if she had felt it appropriate, she wouldn't know how to join in.

Not only was Branco's micro-rumbler small enough to fit through the iris easier than CASPers, it had been designed specifically with this task in mind. Lifted up by Corporal Ogtbish "Haranga" Enkh, and Private Gregory Defiant, Branco disappeared inside the iris. Cilia waved over his hull armor, propelling him forward with ease.

They could move him backward just as quickly.

Partway through the aperture, Branco disappeared from the net just as he always did. Signals were swallowed and distorted by these ancient tunnels, and the iris apertures were the worst culprits.

Within a couple of minutes, Branco had observed the tunnel on the far side and backed up enough to establish a comm signal and report the all clear.

And so the party passed through the "Devil's arse" as Specialist Branco liked to call it.

They had only one more aperture to go, according to the painted Jeha. Then it was time to collect the intelligence about the starkiller they had gambled so much to acquire.

* * *

"Contact front!" yelled Private Defiant.

"I see them," said McCoy. "Civilians."

"They might be armed." Defiant sounded nervous.

Terbish hurried forward to join First Squad deploying into the room.

Rules of engagement were to eliminate any threat. But not to murder noncombatants.

She emerged, weapons hot, into a mess hall.

The Jeha had said this zone was empty.

It wasn't.

There were forty people here, eating alone or in groups at tables. Others were taking food trays to the auto-chef machines to select their meal. All of them were frozen in shock at the arrival of the metal fighting machines.

Among the jumble of alien species were two Humans.

Humans?

Did they realize this place was trying to destroy the entire Solar System?

She activated her external speakers. "I am Lieutenant Enkh of the Golden Horde. Any of you who are willing to assist us by providing intelligence about this base and how to disable it, stand by the wall to my left."

Her gaze was pulled in the direction of the two Humans. Both males. Mid-30s, perhaps. They wore heavy gear that suggested a hazardous working environment.

What the hell were they doing here?

The Humans didn't move. No one moved.

Terbish snapped out her left arm and pointed a CASPer finger at the wall.

Now there was motion. A few individuals, looking nervously between the CASPers and their Endless Night colleagues, drifted toward the left wall.

"Everyone else," said Enkh, "stand to the right."

The look of horror and astonishment that had frozen the Endless Night personnel suddenly released. Several rushed over to the left, others ran with equal speed to the right. More threw themselves under the tables and cowered there.

One of the Humans went for his pistol.

Terbish shredded him with a controlled burst from her autocannon.

Suddenly, everyone wanted to run to the left wall.

Why did he go for his pistol?

Surely he couldn't have thought he could take on a squad of CASPers?

She quickly replayed the footage and realized that another CASPer had fired too.

Her HUD showed ammo depletion from McCoy's icon.

McCoy pinged her with a private link. "That guy…" He sighed. "Some things just don't make sense. What are your orders, Lieutenant?"

"Well done, Enkh," interrupted the major.

To Terbish, the major's praise felt like deep veining CASPer candy. It was worth a million in red-diamond chits to her. Well…maybe.

"Give me a couple of CASPers to assist in persuading some information out of our captives," Sun told her. "Deploy the rest to secure the room. We will have ten minutes here to improve our intelligence before moving out."

"Yes, Major." Terbish set about issuing her instructions.

"Major," said Melsome. "If I may be permitted—"

"Stow the verbal fluff, Melsome."

"Copy that. I ran plenty of these hijinks missions with CASPer Search, Rescue, and Recovery. Two things kept us alive. Speed. And always keeping an eye on our exit route."

The major didn't speak for several seconds. "Agreed. We move out in five mikes. I repeat, five mikes. Branco. Jehas. Extract information about the base's vulnerabilities and reassess our exit strategy."

Terbish assumed the major would take control of the interrogation. Instead, she let Branco take lead and came over to where Terbish was standing, in the center of a room with good line of sight on both north and south exits.

"Enkh, when you rushed in here, you forgot your Second and Reserve Squads."

Terbish plummeted off the high the major's praise had lifted her to.

"Ma'am. I'm...My error is unforgivable. I'm not up to the job. Ma'am, I recommend you assign Melsome or McCoy to take my place."

She heard Major Sun draw in a sharp breath. "You're starting to piss me off, Enkh. Those two gray beards respect you. That's not easy to earn. You're learning on the job and made a slight error. Melsome and I had your back all the way with Second Squad, and Oranjeklegg was nearby to follow my lead. Now I am informing you of your error because that's how you learn on the job."

"Sorry, ma'am. I won't make any more silly mistakes."

"Bullshit. You *will* make mistakes and you *will* learn from them. Quickly."

"Yes, ma'am. But..."

"No. Fucking. Buts, Enkh. I queried Colonel Enkh about whether my second in command was up to the task, being so inexperienced. Do you know what she said about you, Lieutenant?"

"No, ma'am." Terbish swallowed hard.

"She said she had high hopes. You are one of the most intelligent and resourceful young officers to emerge from the cadre system. She told me that what you needed most was to grow a pair."

"Ma'am? I don't follow."

The major exhaled. "The colonel means you need to grow into your potential. That's why Second Platoon is here with me instead of fighting in the mines of McPherson. Consider this fast tracking."

"Thank you, ma'am."

"Don't fucking thank me. Thank Colonel Enkh once we get out of here alive. Keep following your instinct and your training, and you will do well. But if I hear any more from you about not being up to the job, I'll cut you out of the command loop and assign you to the two Jeha to listen to their endless ramblings about trans-dimensional physics."

"Yes, ma'am. Thank you, ma'am."

"Carry on, Lieutenant."

Terbish chewed over the major's words. And the colonel's.

Could she really be trusted to command a platoon when they faced a serious threat? It wouldn't be like terrifying maintenance personnel in a cafeteria.

Terbish had scarcely formed these thoughts when it was time to find out.

"Contact!" warned Corporal Parker. "It's the fucking werewolves."

* * * * *

Chapter Forty-Six

Alpha Company, Gelheik Sands Mine, McPherson-3

Sansar strode to the top of the massive open pit mine and looked down into its interior. Conceptually, she'd known it was huge, but to stand at the edge of it was daunting. Over six kilometers wide and two and a half kilometers deep, it dwarfed Bingham Canyon mine, the largest open pit mine on Earth. A number of processing plants sat nearby, unused and decaying in the hot sun, with an enormous parking lot full of oversize earth-moving vehicles on the other side of the plants. Nothing, however, moved down in the pit.

The rest of Alpha Company ringed the edge of the mammoth hole.

"We have to go down there?" Mun asked, coming to stand beside her.

"Yeah. At the bottom of the pit is a shaft that goes even deeper."

"How deep is this weapon?"

"Three? Four, kilometers underground?" She paused, looking into the pit. "No one knows. Well, the Endless Night knows, but they haven't seen fit to tell me. I suspect the Kahraman probably knew, too, but they aren't around to ask. You can thank Blue Sky for that."

"Which I do," Mun said. "All right," she called out over the company net. "We need to get down to the bottom of the pit, and we need to get there now. Move out!"

Mun stepped over the edge and used a combination of running and riding her jump jets to descend into the pit. Within a couple of seconds, the entire company was moving, bounding down the slopes and roads.

* * *

First Platoon, Bravo Company, Endless Night Base, McPherson-3

"**N**ow!" Naran commanded, and the platoon hit their jump jets and vaulted over the minefields and past the ambushes set up on the sides of the road. Naran spun in midair to touch down facing in the direction she'd come from, just past a building where a Besquith-shaped IR signature was hiding. With a roar, it burst from cover, just like it had in the vision she'd had. The startling clarity of it gave her pause for a half-second, but the MAC on her shoulder was already aimed at the doorway, and she triggered it as he raced toward her. Mach 4 projectiles ripped through the alien and flung him back into the abandoned building.

Other weapons fire broke the stillness of the afternoon as the members of the platoon dispatched the other ambushers, then the CASPer-clad soldiers dove into cover as the expected hidden weapons at the facility, now visible down the street, popped into view and opened fire on them.

Naran dove into the building the Besquith had been hiding in, ignoring the blood and pieces of Besquith adorning the walls.

"Status?" she asked.

"First Squad accounted for, all enemy down," Staff Sergeant White commed. "All mission capable."

"Second Squad accounted for, all enemy down," Staff Sergeant McDonald reported. "Jones is partially mission capable. One of the Lumars triggered a mine that fragged him. He's still good to continue."

Naran nodded to herself. The report confirmed what she could see in her Tri-V. The legs on Private Jones' CASPer were yellow.

"Well done, ma'am," Franklin said over the private link. "Now what?"

"Now we provide the distraction we're supposed to be providing," Naran said. She switched to the platoon net. "All troopers with missiles, take those positions out. The liberal use of explosives is authorized."

She looked out the door to see Franklin lean out from the doorway across the street from her, and several missiles erupted from the rocket pod on his shoulder. He ducked back through the doorway as return fire turned it into splinters and clouds of dust.

* * * * *

Chapter Forty-Seven

Inside the Starkiller, Wahrner's Grise

Horde rockets *wooshed!* down the corridor, answered by Besquith ones that smashed through the CASPers and blew the mess hall tables into plastic fragments.

Her cockpit filled with howls of Besquith pain and rage. There was a Human cry too.

Private Azamat Nemekh's icon turned red in Terbish's HUD.

Damn!

Terbish sent a missile downrange from her own shoulder pod, but she lacked a clear target.

The smoke from the exhaust plumes revealed red lines of death, Terbish's HUD extrapolated the laser fire, tracing it back to the alien fighters down the south corridor.

"Autocannons," said Melsome. "We're gonna cross-stitch the bastards, just like we did in the sims."

The CASPers had moved back from the corridor entrance out of the enemy field of fire. Then they stepped back into it, long enough to lean forward and let rip with a coordinated fire from multiple autocannons, each delivering a sustained 200 rounds per minute.

The targets weren't in clear sight, but Melsome's squad wasn't so much aiming at individuals as methodically stitching deadly patterns into assigned fire zones.

Terbish transmitted on the command channel. "McCoy, secure the north exit. Oranjeklegg, ready on my command to hit your jets and give me some height advantage against the Besquith."

"Roger that, Lieutenant," they chorused.

"Melsome, give me eyes."

"You got it, boss."

Terbish took a moment while the smoke cleared to assess the situation in the mess hall. There were multiple fires among the devastation. Some of the fires were the burning corpses of workers caught by Besquith fire.

She satisfied herself that Command Section was safe.

The feed started coming through from the rolling drone Melsome had sent downrange.

For a second or two, the tumbling images made her queasy. Then the stabilization software kicked in and she made out scenes of bloodied Besquith corpses.

The enemy fire had fallen silent. But given the volume when it was at its height, she expected to see more corpses than this.

As the drone rolled on, she saw why.

The inner tunnels of the starkiller base were tiled with a cobalt blue mineral no one could identify. It was so tough that the thousands of 25mm rounds her platoon had poured into this tunnel had barely scratched the tiles.

But as the drone advanced farther, she saw Besquith with handheld devices that seemed to melt through this mineral. Having weakened the tiles, the Besquith were burrowing out holes with their claws.

She heard a snarl and the drone feed went black.

"Grenades!" yelled a trooper.

Terbish didn't even see them.

Her little world inside her Mk 8 shook with fury.

White noise assaulted her hearing.

She gasped. Groaned. And then checked her status board.

Second Squad's CASPers had taken damage, but none critical. The bio-signs of the drivers registered shock and adrenaline spikes, but no serious injuries.

The white noise eased off enough to think a little.

"You want us to jump high and give them a MAC punch?" asked Sergeant Oranjeklegg.

"Negative," Terbish shouted back.

She switched to the general channel and eased off on her volume. The others were probably not as deafened as her. "This is Enkh. The Besquith are sheltering in hard cover scooped out of the walls. Melsome, give me concussion grenade salvos by fire team."

She caught Melsome's hesitation before he replied. "Copy that, Lieutenant."

Second Platoon consisted of two squads, each with two four-trooper fire teams and a command element. Melsome organized salvos from each of the three fire teams facing south.

Knowing the blasts were coming still didn't make it easy.

Slam!

Slam!

Slam!

The shockwave pulses abusing Terbish's mech were brutal, even at this distance from the points of detonation.

She felt a little stupid for forgetting to add her own grenades to the bombardment, but when Melsome sent another rolling drone down the tunnel, it was soon apparent that her extra firepower had not been required.

The Besquith were outfitted in hardened hybrid ceramic armor with fully enclosed helmets. That made them almost as resilient as her Mk 8 against bullets, shrapnel, and fire. And the armor's superior ablative properties were effective enough to withstand laser fire long enough for its wearer to close and claw your throat out.

But trapped inside their own miniature rock alcoves, the armor had proven less effective against the pressure waves.

Some swayed drunkenly with their hands over their ears.

Others had imploded, as if a black hole had momentarily visited their hearts and sucked. All that remained was bloodied meat inside broken armor.

Private Jasur "Jazzee" Enkh charged down the corridor with his sword blade out.

Private Chimeglkham "Ceecee" Chimgee went with him.

"Wait!" cried Melsome. "Fall back!"

"Let's finish off the bastards," replied Jazzee.

Twenty yards down the corridor, the two hotheads encountered their first dazed Besquith survivors and began butchering the aliens.

"Come back," yelled Terbish. "Immediately! That is an order."

Jazzee and Ceecee hesitated.

From wall hollows farther down the corridor, more Besquith emerged and pumped lasers through the impetuous CASPer troopers.

Jazzee and Ceecee winked out on the squad status board.

"Second Squad, on my mark," said Melsome. "We're gonna cross stitch them again. But keep your CASPers grounded. Oranjeklegg, light your fire team's jets to get height and hit them with your MACs. Go!"

The CASPers moved back into the enemy field of fire. A few lasers flared out, punching minor damage through Golden Horde mechs. Then the concentrated autocannon wall of lead and tungsten inside the corridor ripped through every Besquith caught within its pattern.

Oranjeklegg's Midnighter team added the heavy *pop, pop, pop* of MAC fire.

The front ranks of Besquith were blown away by the concentrated firepower, but more flooded up from the rear.

Bloodcurdling alien howls sliced through Terbish's armor and stabbed paralyzing terror into her heart.

A tiny bundle of calm in her mind told her that the Besquith were enraged. They weren't hiding in the hollows anymore. They were charging.

And that was a good thing. Wasn't it?

"Pick your targets," said Melsome. How was he so calm? "Remember your fire discipline. Oranjeklegg, keep firing from on high."

The Besquith boiled up the corridor, a seething mass of rage, fangs, and malevolence. CASPer fire kept cutting the head of the advance.

The Besquith didn't flinch. As fast as the CASPers cut them down, the Besquith charge was faster.

They couldn't be stopped.

Ammo states started flashing warnings in Terbish's HUD. Damage accumulated to mechs and the drivers inside.

The Horde couldn't beat them back.

The enemy was upon them!

She watched, helpless, as Besquith hurled themselves onto the front rank of her troopers, clawing, rending, gnashing. Always with the snarling. She saw her CASPers put in good sword work and thought to extend her own sword blade.

Having expected to face Besquith on this mission, they'd concentrated their sim training during hyperspace on this kind of engagement.

The Besquith leaped onto the mechs and dug in with claws. Having gained a close hold, they would either shoot through the armor with laser pistols or find purchase with their fangs and bite their way through.

In her training she'd been told that it was dangerous to equate the fangs of monsters such as Tortantulas and Besquith to the brittle teeth of Earth predators. Alien fangs had the hardness of her titanium-alloy sword blade mixed with the flexibility of rubberized armor, and were set into a jaw with a bite strength that wouldn't embarrass a T-Rex.

Knowing that and seeing a Besquith bite through metal armor to get at the meat inside…they were two totally different things.

With the Besquith so close, the CASPers couldn't bring their weapons to bear. Some of the youngest troopers forgot their training in the face of the alien terror, but others remembered to buddy up into pairs and shoot off each other's opponents.

The black-painted Midnight CASPers jumped over the melee and came down upon the enemy from behind. She could hear their MAC fire, but she wasn't integrated into their battle net and couldn't make out what was going on in the confusion.

There was a sudden surge from the enemy. They pushed through the front rank of CASPers and charged deeper into the room. One of them came straight for her.

Her brain was so numb with terror, she couldn't think. She didn't know what to do. Those terrible fangs!

She could only rely on instinct and training.

She put a controlled burst of 25mm armor piercing into the monster's center mass.

It flinched at the damage she was inflicting, but it barely paused in its advance. She waited for it to come to her and then stabbed the damaged section of its armor with her sword blade, letting it impale itself on its own momentum.

She kicked the Besquith off the blade, bringing her arm back sharply to retrieve the weapon before it snapped off as the massive bulk of the enemy fighter fell to the ground. She poked her autocannon into the bleeding hole in its chest armor and gave it a short burst, just to be sure.

She presented her bloodied sword blade, looking for more Besquith.

But the attack had impaled itself on Second Platoon's defense just as surely as Terbish's foe had on her sword. The enemy lay dead on the floor.

So too did Sergeant Tsetsegmaa "Maa" Enkh and Private Andi Kirk, who went by the informal name of Blowhard.

Half of Second Squad had died in the last few minutes.

"Ma'am, we lost Plunger," reported Oranjeklegg. "You might have him as Private Oliver Huq, but he's…Doesn't matter anymore. He's gone now."

"I can hear them in the distance," said Major Sun. "Besquith. Translation is difficult but they're shouting orders. Organizing a pursuit."

"Fuck," observed Staff Sergeant McCoy. "Looks like the fighting's only just begun."

* * * * *

Chapter Forty-Eight

Alpha Company, Gelheik Sands Mine, McPherson-3

The company reached the bottom of the mine as the diversion began in earnest. While Sansar knew it was possible—maybe even likely—that the Endless Night knew it was a diversion, they would still have to honor the threat it posed. Her last order to Naran had been that if she saw an opportunity to advance, she was to exploit it.

"Ready, ma'am," Mun said.

"Move out."

"You heard the boss," Lieutenant Batu Enkh said. "Let's go."

First Platoon led the way into the shaft. Although the open pit mine was enormous in scale, the shaft that led further into the bowels of the planet was considerably less so. The shaft was about ten meters wide by five meters high at its apex. The sides and roof were rounded, though, as if a boring machine had drilled it out, so the average size of the shaft was less than its maximum measurements.

Still, it was plenty wide enough for two CASPers to walk down it side by side.

"Lights or IR, ma'am?" Captain House asked.

"IR," Sansar replied. The white lights on the CASPers went off and Sansar switched to her IR cameras. It made the descent a little more difficult, but wouldn't announce their presence as far in advance. *Not that a company of CASPers marching along a mine was "stealthy" by any stretch of the imagination.*

They followed the tunnel for a couple of minutes and came to the first branch. "Take the right branch," Sansar said, and the lead troopers continued onward.

"What's a Zzardar look like?" Private Radko Enkh, one of the lead troopers, asked as he stopped suddenly. He turned on a red light and focused it on the ground.

"I'm not entirely sure. It's a lizard analogue, I think," Sansar said.

"Would it have a footprint like this?"

Sansar moved forward. The footprints the soldier had found were nearly as large as hers, four-toed, and obviously clawed. "Could well be," she said. "If so, we're on the right—"

With a scream that sent shivers down her spine, a monstrous worm shape easily four meters wide broke through the left side of the tunnel. Sansar—along with a number of other troopers—fired at the creature and watched in dismay as their rounds bounced off its rocky hide.

* * *

First Platoon, Bravo Company, Endless Night Base, McPherson-3

Franklin leaned out from the doorway again, and the remaining three missiles launched from his rocket pod. This time, when they hit, the return fire ceased. After a second, Naran risked a glance. The pop-up turret that had pinned them down was in two pieces.

"Nice shooting," she said.

"Thanks," Franklin said with a grunt, "but it shouldn't have taken me—" he grunted again, "—an entire rocket pack to take it out. I'm out of practice."

Naran looked over to see what he was doing and saw he'd taken the rocket pack off his shoulder and was loading new rockets into it from a case that had been on his back. She'd wondered what it was, but hadn't had time to ask.

"I didn't know you could reload a rocket pack like that."

"Normally…you can't. I had a tech…one time…who showed me a way to jury rig it. He called it…a field expedient. Gotta have the plug outside the armor in order to do it, and you have to bring reloads." He lifted the rocket pack and was just barely able to pop it back into place on his shoulder.

He jogged over to her side of the street and turned around. "The only thing I can't do by myself—without getting out of the suit, which is never a good idea in a combat zone—is connect the wires back up. If you could do me a favor…"

Naran struggled a bit with the two cords—CASPer fingers weren't meant for incredibly deft maneuvering—but ultimately got the wire into the plug that was dangling off his shoulder. "Got it."

"Ready," he said.

"For what?"

"To go blow more shit up. We're not a very good diversion if we're not doing that."

Naran motioned toward the ruined turret. "Lead on."

"Move up if you can," Franklin said on the platoon net. "Those that are pinned down, call for help. It's time to see what's on the other side of the wall."

He stepped out of cover and, when nothing else shot at him, jogged toward the wall.

* * * * *

Chapter Forty-Nine

Inside the Starkiller, Wahrner's Grise

"Lieutenant Enkh, you are to take Second Squad and Sergeant Oranjeklegg's team and hold off the enemy pursuit while we proceed to our first objective. Delay them as best you can and then meet us there."

Terbish watched Melsome retrieving the personal effects canisters from the dead troopers in her command. It was strange. She'd been scared ever since waking up in that freight box. The Besquith had petrified her. But only now did she really believe she could be about to die.

Was the major abandoning them?

Perhaps. But it was the major's call, wasn't it?

"Yes, ma'am."

"I'm leaving Specialist Branco with you," said the major. "If my force is eliminated, you'll be in charge, Enkh. Make use of Branco as your adviser. He was instrumental in destroying another starkiller. Such insights could prove invaluable."

Branco! Her squad leaders were convinced Branco and the major were lovers. Enkh didn't approve, but it did mean she wasn't being abandoned.

"Yes, Major. We'll keep the werewolves off your back."

Sun gathered the two Jeha and disappeared northward with McCoy's CASPers. She left behind the wreckage of the room and the noncombatants who'd survived. From their injuries, she judged that the greatest cause of death and injury had been her squad's concussion grenades.

Now Melsome's earlier hesitation made more sense.

"Any who want to," she told the surviving noncombatants, "you can withdraw to the south."

They looked nervously at each other. None of them took up her offer.

A Blevin worker hurried to the center of the room to tend to a fallen friend.

A laser pulse drilled through the Blevin's head and she slumped over her friend.

"Here they come," said Melsome.

An enemy MAC began pumping rounds into the room, obliterating its rear wall.

The next phase of the battle had begun.

* * * * *

Chapter Fifty

Alpha Company, Gelheik Sands Mine, McPherson-3

Sansar fired again with her MAC and watched in horror as the round ricocheted off the rocks that appeared to be attached to its skin.

Another scream came from the tunnel behind them, which was answered by a third from the tunnel in front of them past the immediate threat.

"Did the GalNet entry say the worms were pack hunters?" Mun asked.

"Nope; probably because anyone that found that out got eaten by them," Sansar replied. "Hold the ones in the front and back off as long as you can with rockets!" she ordered. "Once we deal with the one in the middle, we'll work on them."

Flashes and explosions appeared from both ends of the corridor, and it took a second for her Tri-V display to reorient, but when it did, she saw the closest worm had drawn back slightly, but was now pressing forward again. *Was it the light or the explosion?* Behind the mouth, she saw a dark spot open and close. *It had eyes!*

"Everyone! Lights on!"

She flipped her lights on and shined them at the worm. Once again, it drew back slightly into its hole, then it screamed again. This time, Sansar was ready, and when it opened its mouth, she fired her MAC at its fastest rate. The first round glanced off part of its mouth, but the next three rounds went into its mouth. Several other troopers fired into its gaping maw, and its scream cut off suddenly as its mouth snapped shut. It tried to pull itself out of the wall to attack, but it only made it a few meters before it collapsed on the floor.

"First Platoon, fight the one in front of us," Sansar ordered. "Second Platoon, take the one behind us. Try to get them to scream, then fire into their mouths!" She saw Mun go toward the one in front of them, so she spun toward the one behind them.

Despite everyone having their lights on, the worm was pressing Second Platoon backward, she saw as she arrived. Corporal Davison stood in the center of the shaft, firing rockets one at a time as it advanced. With its mouth closed, the rockets glanced off and exploded somewhere farther along the creature's length. While the rockets might be wounding it, it wasn't fast enough, and the worm kept coming.

Davison fired his last rocket—Sansar could see the pack was empty—then started firing his MAC. It was equally ineffective at stopping the monster.

"Get back!" Sansar yelled, but Davison appeared not to hear, and he continued to fire at the worm.

The worm reached the trooper, and it leapt forward at the last moment to bite him. Davison's CASPer went into its mouth, but the worm wasn't able to get him all in with one bite. Instead, it chomped, and chomped again, swallowing more with each bite. Davison screamed after the first bite, but the second cut off his screams.

Everyone stopped firing, worried about hitting Davison, but Sansar realized the trooper was either dead or wished he was and tried to fire again as it took its next bite. She missed, pulling up at the last second as motion from underneath the worm caught her eye.

A CASPer edged forward along the wall of the shaft, and as the worm went to take its last bite of Davison, Private Radko Enkh jumped up and slam-dunked a K-bomb into the creature's mouth. He turned and ran back to the firing line as the grenade detonated, causing several sympathetic detonations within Davison's suit.

The creature screamed again, spit out Davison, and then began drawing breaths in and out, as if trying to cool the fires in its mouth. "Fire!" Sansar yelled as the CASPer hit the ground to her side, knocking down several of the troops.

Everyone still able fired into the worm's mouth, and the multiple MAC and laser rounds dropped the monster.

"We got the one behind us, Mun," Sansar said. "How are you doing?"

"Good, ma'am. This one's down, too. However, you're going to need to see this."

"Coming," Sansar said as she turned and ran to join the other platoon. She arrived to see that the third worm did appear to be dead. Other than not moving, though, it was hard to tell for sure; the ceiling had collapsed, burying most of the worm and closing off the passageway from any further advance.

* * *

Communications Room, Endless Night Base, McPherson-3

"We have Human troopers in those armor suits attacking the base," Sheerho said. "They have already neutralized the defenses the Besquith put in place up on the surface, and I hear they are in the mines, as well."

"Fire the weapon," Coron ordered from the Tri-V display. Coron and Retenex had left the facility when the Goltar had appeared in the emergence area to join in the fight against the squids. Or so they'd said.

"But it isn't ready yet," Sheerho said, woofing in frustration. "The new seals haven't been tested. If we fire it now, we may damage it worse than the last time it was fired."

"It won't matter if the Humans get their hands on it!" Retenex exclaimed. "If you fire it now, it will destroy their home star. They will then have nothing left to fight for, and Saunorak can finish their destruction. *But first you must fire the weapon!*"

"I understand," Sheerho said. "It will be done as you command."

"Good," Retenex replied. "Tell Saunorak he must hold long enough for you to fire the weapon."

"I will let him know."

"Hurry! You *must* fire the weapon."

"I will," Sheerho said as the Tri-V went dead. He looked at the elSha technician who maintained the comm gear. "Pass the message to Saunorak. Let him know he must hold until we can fire the weapon."

"He scares me," the elSha said. "He said he was going to eat me."

Sheerho shrugged. "He says that to everyone. It's a Besquith thing. I guess if you *can* eat almost anything, then I guess you start to think you *should* eat everything you come upon."

"So you'll tell him instead?"

"Of course not. You heard Retenex. He said I have to fire the weapon as soon as possible. That doesn't give me time to deal with Saunorak." The elSha slumped, and Sheerho took pity on him. "You don't have to tell him to his face," he said, motioning to the Tri-V. "Just comm him and tell him what Retenex said."

"Okay," the elSha said, brightening. "I can do that."

"Good. I have to go." Sheerho left the comm center and strode purposefully to the firing chamber. *Respected scientists did not run.* He scanned the room. Nearly all the technicians were already there, testing various parts of the weapon.

"We're firing the weapon," Sheerho announced. "Get the rest of the technicians here, *now!*"

"But it's not ready!" his primary assistant whined. "We haven't tested everything yet!"

"Retenex said to fire it now. He was very specific. Do *you* want to go tell him no?"

"No, Sheerho, I do not want to do that," the elSha said, shivering in terror.

"Good. Then we will fire the weapon as soon as everyone is here. Open the outer doors. Commence primary ignition sequence."

"Yes, Sheerho. What is the target?"

"Same as it was last time. Your target is Sol."

* * *

First Platoon, Bravo Company, Endless Night Base, McPherson-3

Franklin took a step forward then jumped, his jump jets easily carrying him over the five-meter wall. Naran launched right behind him and touched down to his side. She surveyed the facility, but saw neither defenders nor defenses. It was as quiet as a morgue. *Wait. Bad analogy.* Quiet as a church. *Better.*

"Okay, ma'am," Franklin said, turning toward her. "We're into the facility...now what?"

"I've been trying to call the colonel for further instructions, but they must be out of comms range."

"If they're a long way underground, they may not be reachable."

What are we supposed to do? Naran wondered. Sansar hadn't expected that they'd get into the facility; they were just supposed to be a distraction. Sure, she'd said to exploit any opportunities, but she hadn't expected *this*. And now, with them actually inside, Sansar was out of communications range, and it was up to her to decide what to do next. Still, there was only one thing they really *could* do.

"With the other force out of comms, we can't count on the fact that the colonel's force will make it to the weapon as expected. Our mission is to destroy the weapon, and that's what we're going to do. First Sergeant, find us a way down to the weapon, whatever it is and wherever it is."

Both Golden Horde members dove to the side as breaking glass sounded behind them, and gunfire ripped out from the warehouse facility. Gunfire—both MACs and lasers—came from throughout the building, as well as a crew-served weapon on the roof.

"Shit!" Franklin said, as he extended his laser shield, and launched off on his jump jets toward the building.

"Attack!" Naran called, flipping out her laser shield as well. It was just in time as a laser round glanced off it. She made it to her feet and triggered her jump jets, emulating the veteran. Several of her troopers' CASPers had gone red in her display, but she knew she didn't have time to worry about them; she had to get to cover.

Most of the Golden Horde had gone airborne to get to the building faster, and she saw Franklin fire a number of rockets into the building, clearing out the weapons immediately in front of her. Whether he had intentionally cleared the way for her or not, she made it to the building and retracted her shield. She saw movement to both the left and right inside the warehouse, and she armed two K-bombs and threw them through the window to the left and right at the Besquith she could see there. She ducked as the weapons detonated, then smashed through the wall and into the warehouse.

The Besquith to the left was down, but the one on the right still had some life in him, and he charged her. She brought her MAC up and fired several times, interrupting his charge.

Other CASPers crashed through the walls of the warehouse, and the rest of the Besquith were quickly put down. The heavy laser crashed to the ground outside the building, then Franklin landed next to it. He wobbled a little on touchdown, and Naran could see a large laser burn on the outside of his right leg. There was a corresponding yellow mark over his suit in her Tri-V display, and his Human leg showed as red.

"Are you okay?" Naran asked over a private channel.

"I'm good enough," he replied with a grunt of pain. "Stupid wolves burned off some of my thigh, but I've got nanites working on it. The thruster's a little wonky now, too, but I'll make it."

Naran turned back to the interior of the warehouse, and her eyebrows rose. The entire building was empty; in fact, it didn't appear anything had *ever* been stored there. There was a large, open door that looked out on the courtyard and the metal plate in its center. The only thing in the entire building—aside from the posts holding the roof up—was a large metal plate in the center of the building. The plate in the courtyard was circular and about forty meters in diameter; this one was square and about five meters to a side. She jogged over to it and saw, as she approached, that there was also a slate mounted on a post next to the plate. After a second, she realized the metal plate was probably some sort of elevator system.

"Where do you suppose this goes?" she asked.

Franklin limped up next to her. "Doesn't look like there's anything above us except the roof," he said, "so my guess is down." He chuckled. "Looks like we could get about a squad onto it."

"Do we dare ride it down?" Naran asked. "They have to be expecting us and will be waiting. What if they pull the plug on us in between floors? We'd be trapped."

"I doubt there are stairs if the weapon is deep underground," Franklin said, "so we'll probably have to take the elevator if we want to go down. That also assumes this is the elevator that goes to where the weapon is. Still, those *are* all valid questions. I'd say—"

Franklin was interrupted by a loud screeching noise as the metal plate in the courtyard lifted. The lid split into eight sections that rose separately, revealing a large hole that went straight down into the earth. The platoon all moved forward to look down the shaft.

"Anyone got a flare?" Franklin asked.

Corporal Sarah Adamson stepped up and handed him a CASPer-sized road flare.

Franklin activated it and dropped it into the hole. Black metal shone as the flare fell. And fell. And fell. It vanished from sight before it hit, and no one actually heard it when it did.

The metal started humming with a low vibration.

"Do you think that's the weapon?" Adamson asked, still looking into the abyss.

Naran startled; she'd been wondering the same thing. "I've got to think it is," Staff Sergeant White said. "What else would you need a big ass hole that goes to the center of the planet for?"

"I think he's probably right, ma'am," Franklin added. "You wanted another way down? I'll bet this takes you all the way to the bottom…assuming you want to drop into it, that is."

"I do *not* want to drop into that," Naran said. "What if you went all the way down to find out it's like the barrel of a gun and there's no way out? How do you even know we have enough jump juice to get us down safely?"

"I don't," Franklin admitted. "I wasn't suggesting we go that route, although…"

"Although what?"

"The only reason they'd open the doors is if they were about to fire it. We have to get down there and stop them." He held up a hand to stop any questions. "No, I don't want to go down this shaft; I want to take the elevator. But…and here's a big but…if the thing starts looking like it's going to fire, or we get ambushed down there, I think we ought to leave someone here with a nuke to drop down the hole."

"We'd have to call one down from the ship," Naran said. "We don't have one down here."

"Well, ma'am, I would respectfully suggest you do so while we figure out the elevator, because I don't think we have very long to stop this thing."

* * * * *

Chapter Fifty-One

Inside the Starkiller, Wahrner's Grise

Branco was buzzing.

Whether from the explosion, the drugs, or the sheer adrenaline thrill, he didn't know. Probably all of the above.

They fought a running battle with the Besquith as they retreated inward and upward through the base.

Zarbi had equipped his mini-tank with stun rounds and told him just a single shot would shut up the loudest Oogar.

She'd probably never faced an angry Oogar. Nor a Besquith.

The stun rounds didn't work.

But they did frazzle the enemy's armor and interior systems. Only for a few seconds, but it was enough for a properly armed CASPer to take advantage.

Scooting around the legs of the CASPers, darting in and out to take a shot at the werewolves who got too close. It was a blast.

He was alive!

Though only thanks to the armor on his little motorized marvel. Now that, Zarbi *had* gotten right. Laser bolts and bullets deflected away.

He knew he wouldn't survive concentrated fire, but he'd plant his stunners and then dart away behind the CASPers before the Besquith could take him out.

Branco wasn't an advisor now. He was an auxiliary trooper.

Until he reached the rendezvous point and remembered that they hadn't broken into this base to tussle with hairy monsters. This was supposed to be a recon mission.

The room was empty.

No Sun. No First Squad CASPers. No Jeha. Not much of anything considering how much blood had been expended to get here.

Vertical banks of equipment rose thirty feet into the overhead, gray and featureless. There were metal stairs and walkways giving access to the upper levels of the equipment, but the metal looked corroded. Probably no one had used them for ten thousand years or more.

Branco slewed his tank around to present his audio receptor against one of the equipment banks and detected a faint power hum.

He lifted the canopy and hauled himself out so he could press his hand against the equipment. He felt its power and—he looked at his hand—picked up a lot of dust.

After wiping clean a section, he saw that the equipment was neither so gray nor so featureless. Tiny status lights chased across the area he'd cleared before disappearing behind the dirt.

"I think the Jeha were up here on the stairs. There's a panel removed out of the…whatever the fuck it is."

Turnaround was talking. Using her external speakers, although Branco had his earpiece. She was using her jump jets to brake her descent. In her hand was a slate.

She handed it to him.

After a few moments to assess what he was seeing, he explained to the others what he'd found on the slate.

"They got what we came for. Hopper says we've found a…it's like a control nexus. A tertiary Ops room too. They extracted everything. Data on the convoys. Personnel. Pay records. A map. The weapon's test firing. Oh, shit. They've fired it, but...at a local and unpopulated star. Zarbi's also inserted her universal subversion cyberworm that she swears isn't an AI. Hopper's left a message. She says Zarbi's cyber-attack software is amateurish crap."

"Is there a message from the major?" pressed Lieutenant Enkh.

"Looking for it. There's a lot of Hopper and Zarbi trash talking each other. Ahh...Here we go. The major says this slate holds a copy of all the intel, in case her copy is lost. They've pressed on to open the exit route through the heat exchangers to the lake. Meet them there."

"Keep hold of the slate," Enkh told him, "and keep away from the Besquith from now on. You're holding the most valuable asset we have."

"Yes, Lieutenant."

Branco eased himself back into his micro-rumbler and closed the canopy.

Before the pressure seals secured, he heard snarls in the corridor. Distant but growing closer.

* * * * *

Chapter Fifty-Two

Alpha Company, Gelheik Sands Mine, McPherson-3

"Well, shit," Sansar said as she looked at the cave-in. "Any idea how far back that goes?"

"No, ma'am," Captain House said. "A couple of rockets went off at once and the whole thing just collapsed. We can try to dig it out, but I'd be worried about it continuing to fall. There's no telling how far up the instability goes, and with nothing to shore it up…" He paused as a vibration could be felt through the ground. "Is that another cave-in?"

"No," Mun said. "It's constant, and it's not going away. Somebody just powered up something. Something big." She turned to Sansar.

"The starkiller," Sansar said.

"That's the only thing I know of, unless there's some sort of drill coming toward us."

"Think that's it?" asked Captain House.

"No," Sansar and Mun said simultaneously.

"Should we go join Bravo Company and try to get in that way?" Lieutenant Batu Enkh asked.

"It would take too long," Sansar said, "even if we could get the dropships down into the mine. If they're powering up the weapon, we need to get there *right now*."

"Maybe you should tell Captain Naran that she's now the main effort," Mun suggested.

"I tried," Sansar said, "but I couldn't get through. I think we're too far underground for our comms signal to reach them. I can't get the ship either."

"Looks like we better get digging, then," House said. "Alpha Company! Form two lines at the cave-in and start passing the rocks back."

Within seconds, the CASPers were in a bucket-brigade line, moving the rocks out of the cave-in. Sansar only had to participate for a minute to tell that wasn't going to work. Although the CASPers had the strength and agility to pass even the heaviest of rocks back away from the cave-in, more continued to drop. After a second minute, the cave-in was larger than what the Golden Horde had originally started excavating.

"I don't think...this is going to work," Mun said as she passed a rock back to Sansar.

"You're right..." Sansar said, turning and passing it to the next trooper. "We need a better plan."

"Think there are other shafts...that merge in...past the cave-in?" Mun asked.

"Not according to...map I saw of the tunnels. This was a spur...that ran off away from the main tunnel system."

"We need...another way around."

As Sansar passed the rock back to the next trooper, her eyes caught sight of the first worm that had attacked them, still lying halfway out of the tunnel. "I've got it," she said. "We'll use the sandworm tunnels."

"You think they'll work?" Mun asked.

"I don't know." Additional rocks crashed down from the ceiling, knocking over the two troopers closest to the cave-in. Several portions of their suits went yellow in Sansar's display. "I do know that this isn't working, though, so it's got a better chance than what we're doing now." She stopped and stepped back out of line. "Captain House!"

"Yes, ma'am!"

"Get your troopers to pull that worm out of its hole. We'll try to use the worm tunnels to get around the cave-in."

"Yes, ma'am! Let's go, Alpha Company, time to pull a worm from its hole."

It took the entire company pulling, but they were finally able to drag the worm far enough out that they could squeeze past it.

"Okay," Lieutenant Batu Enkh said, looking into the passageway leading off into the dark. "Who wants to be the first into the dark, scary worm tunnel? No one? I'll go first then. First Platoon, with me!" He strode into the tunnel.

Captain House motioned for Sansar to follow the platoon in. "I'll bring up the rear with Second Platoon," he said. In a lower voice he added, "But I'm never playing *Caverns and Canavars* again when we get home."

* * *

First Platoon, Bravo Company, Endless Night Base, McPherson-3

"The tech support folks are bringing a nuke down from the *Gobi Desert*," Naran said. "I hope you've got that elevator thing figured out, though, because I really don't want to have to use it. Sansar may have nuked herself, but I don't think it will look very good on my performance reports if I have to nuke her a second time."

Franklin chuckled. "Yes, ma'am. I can see how that probably wouldn't lead to any glowing endorsements. Just glowing bosses. Happily, we hacked the system, and we have the elevator on its way up."

"Good. I've left instructions with the lieutenant for what to do if it looks like the weapon is going to fire. How long will it take for the elevator to get here?"

"It's a long trip, but it should be here soon. Remember how deep the weapon shaft is? The weapon control facility must be equally deep. Four or five kilometers, I'm guessing."

"So once we get down there, it's going to be a long time before Second Squad joins us."

"I wanted to talk to you about that, ma'am," Franklin said. "I'd like to leave you and the lieutenant up here for the second run. Why don't you let the more experienced people make the first run, and you and the lieutenant come down with the second group?"

Naran's CASPer drew itself up as she did similarly inside. "Not happening, Top. The lieutenant will come down with Second Squad, but I'm going with the first group."

"It's probably going to be hairy down there; establishing a beachhead in enemy territory is never easy. We've kind of gone beyond the typical merc job—we're no longer just here for the paycheck, but to save Earth. If I was sure it would work, I would say to drop a nuke in the tube and call it a day."

"Can't. Sansar and Alpha Company are down there somewhere."

"True, but is keeping them safe worth the safety of the entire Solar System? If this thing fires, everything we know and everyone we love back home is *gone*. We *have* to stop them at all costs. If this was the military, it would be easy; we'd say to do it or die trying. We're mercs, though, and not used to that kind of sentiment."

"But this time, that's the way we have to think."

"Yes, ma'am, it is. And, I hope you'll forgive me for saying it, but we'll have a better chance without you there. Send the people with the most experience first."

"I understand what you're saying, but I'm going. This is my responsibility, and I am going to be there." With a clunk, the elevator arrived, and two panels slid back to allow access to it. Without hesitation, Naran stepped onto the platform and walked to the center. "I'm going," she said. "With or without you. We don't have much time; are you getting on, or not?"

Franklin sighed, but kept his comment about headstrong women to himself. After a second, he realized he'd done something similar—but not to this extent—when he was younger. Naran had all the makings of a great leader. *If she's lucky enough to survive the next hour.*

"Let's go, First Squad," Franklin said, waving them forward as he stepped onto the elevator. "It's time to save the Solar System."

* * *

Starkiller-2, Endless Night Base, McPherson-3

Sheerho looked around the room and nodded once. It had taken longer than he'd expected to round up the elSha, but they were finally all in place. Two had been mating in a closet. Filthy buggers.

All seven were now stationed at slates throughout the room, going through the checklist. There were more armed troops this time, too, to ensure the process completed as it was supposed to. A Lumar and Besquith stood in every doorway, facing out to ensure they weren't surprised. Everything else was up to him and the filthy elSha, but this time they wouldn't be interrupted.

"Confirm target selection," Sheerho said, reading from his slate.

"Set for Sol," one of the elSha replied. Sheerho nodded, and the elSha read off the 36 numbers that identified the stellar coordinates of Earth's star.

"You haven't fired yet?" a gruff voice asked from one of the first floor doorways. Sheerho looked up to find the annoying Besquith head of security.

"No, Saunorak, we haven't, but we are trying to."

"You must hurry! The Humans are here, and they're coming down to the facility!"

"If I wasn't surrounded by incompetents, and if we didn't keep getting interrupted every two minutes, we would already *have* fired the weapon. Unfortunately, *your* security was so bad last time that someone snuck in here and caused the weapon to misfire, which blew a lot of seals. We've had to go slowly to ensure the whole weapon didn't blow up this time because of it."

"Well why aren't you doing it right now?"

"*Because some dumbass is interrupting me!*"

"Careful, *Scientist*," Saunorak said with a growl. "Remember to whom you speak, or you'll be dead as soon as the weapon fires. Retenex isn't here to say who gets to live and die anymore; I am. Taunt me again, and we'll be looking for someone else to push the buttons on the command slate."

Sheerho swallowed, realizing he'd overstepped with the big Besquith. And, with Coron and Retenex gone, there really *wasn't* anyone to stop Saunorak from killing whoever he wanted to. He could always say that Sheerho had been hit in the defense of the facility, and there'd be no one to gainsay him. "Yes, Saunorak, you're right," he said, looking down subserviently. "You have my apologies."

Saunorak nodded once, stiffly. "Get back to what you were doing. Fire the weapon as soon as you can."

"Yes, Saunorak, it will be as you say."

The Besquith nodded again, then he turned and left.

"Asshole," Sheerho muttered quietly enough that Saunorak's troops couldn't hear him. "I hope you eat a laser." He looked around and saw all the elSha looking at him, waiting for him to continue the checklist. Kleesa appeared to be grinning; he would have to be beaten afterward. Sheerho smiled—he now had something to look forward to—and continued the checklist. "Coordinates are correct. Step complete. Ready the energy channels."

* * * * *

Chapter Fifty-Three

Inside the Starkiller, Wahrner's Grise

Terbish's team met up with Major Sun in a large open space one level below the exit point. Fat pipes wrapped around machinery she did not understand. It had the feel of a pre-fusion power plant. Some of the pipes were transparent at their ends. They looked as if they were carrying water.

"Good to have you back," said the major. "How far behind are the Besquith?"

"We've got five mikes," she replied. "Maybe more, but don't count on it."

"That should be enough. We halted here because this looks like suitable shit to blow up. Hopper, you were explaining what this does."

"Yes, Major. This is a feedline for the n-to-1 dimensional energy channel. After the link was initially established to the stellar array of—"

"You're out of time," said the major. "Just tell me this. If we blow it up, does the weapon break?"

"No. Redundancy is built in. Ever since the trio of starkillers was first activated and stabilized, the design makes them difficult to be destroyed."

"Even so," said Branco, from within his little tank. "Does the Endless Night team here realize that?"

"Probably not."

"Then let's blow it up and move on. Maybe they'll waste time fixing something that doesn't need fixing."

Terbish cleared her throat. "Major. A suggestion..."

"Speak!"

"If it is true that we cannot easily damage the weapon from here, wouldn't it be more effective to damage the technical specialists who operate the weapon? Hopper, those pipes over there." She pointed to the water carrying tubes. "What would happen if we cut into them?"

"They're connected directly to the lake above us. There would be a sudden flood. Very dramatic. But then the valves would close farther up the pipe."

"How much farther?"

Hopper hesitated while she consulted her pinplants. "About three hundred meters."

"Perfect."

"Make this snappy," warned the major.

"We damage those water pipes," said Terbish. "Shoot up some of the other machinery too, so that we get their attention. I lead a team into one of the pipes where we hide. Meanwhile, Major, you take the others to the heat exchangers. We wait in the water for, say, thirty minutes. Long enough for the Besquith pursuit to pass by, and also time enough for the Endless Night techs to get here and start trying to figure out the damage. We emerge from the water and kill the techs. Then we follow your route and take the Besquith from the rear."

"Lieutenant Terbish," said the major, "that is highly risky. Not to mention bloodthirsty. And it contravenes Guild rules about attacks on noncombatants."

"Yes, ma'am." Terbish didn't feel ashamed. She had made a reasonable suggestion.

"Luckily," said Major Sun—and Terbish thought she could hear a rare smile behind her voice—"we're not working a Guild contract. I like it. Liaise with your squad leaders and make it happen."

*****

Chapter Fifty-Four

Alpha Company, Gelheik Sands Mine, McPherson-3

"I think we've made it back to the original shaft," Lieutenant Batu said five minutes later. "Left or right?"

"Hold there," Sansar ordered. She squeezed past the troops to get to the front. Sure enough, they were back in the main tunnel. Unfortunately, they had gone so far, there was no way to know if they'd passed the entrance. "Send a squad each way," she ordered Batu. "If you make contact or find evidence of a different shaft, report in."

The troopers moved out, leaving enough space for the rest of Alpha Company to come out into the main shaft for a moment of rest; keeping their balance in the round worm-shaft had required diligence and constant effort.

It didn't take long before Sansar heard weapons fire from the left and two of the troopers' suits went red. "Follow me!" she exclaimed as she raced down the passageway.

She came to a bend in the passageway where the squad had stopped. She could see the legs of a CASPer lying just around the bend.

"There is a barricade about 50 meters past that turn with two crew-served lasers," a trooper reported. "When we came around the corner, they opened up on us like they knew we were coming."

"Then they must have," Sansar replied. She scanned the area and found two cameras in the passageway. She shot them both out with her laser. "At least they won't know what we're doing now."

"Captain House," Sansar commed. "Now would be a good time for one of the drone swarms."

"Yes, ma'am," he replied. "Private Williams! Front and center!"

The trooper moved to the front and pulled two cylindrical cases from his leg compartments, then he poured the contents of the tubes—hundreds of small spiders—onto the ground just before the bend in the passageway. "It'll just take me a second to program them," he said.

It actually took about 30 seconds, but then the piles of spiders shook themselves loose of each other and began moving down the passageway. After a few seconds, the enemy soldiers began firing at the moving floor, and laser bolts flashed past.

"Are those the laser drones or the explosive ones?" Sansar asked.

"Explosive," Williams said.

"Are they going to get them all?"

"Not a chance," Williams replied with a chuckle. "20 meters…10 meters…5 meters…contact."

Small explosions—like large firecrackers—began popping off from around the corner, along with screams. "Now, ma'am." Williams said.

"Charge!" Sansar yelled, and she raced around the corner.

As described, the Besquith had a set of barricades 50 meters down the corridor with two crew-served lasers. Neither of the weapons was manned as the six troopers behind the barricade were hopping up and down, trying to keep the drones off them. While none of the drones were big enough on their own to kill one of the Besquith or Lumar—barring a lucky shot to the head—they were individually large enough to blow off large chunks of flesh and break bones, and they couldn't be ignored, or they would crawl all the way to a being's head and explode.

By the time the defenders saw Alpha Company sprinting toward them, it was too late to get back to their weapons, and the attacking force shot them down. A few of the drones continued to blow pieces off the bodies until Private Williams sent the signal to deactivate them.

Sansar—along with the rest of the company—stopped short of the barricade until Williams gave the all clear signal, then they passed through, ensuring the defenders were dead. As she walked past the barricade, Sansar frowned in professional distaste. It looked like it had been slapped together in five minutes with whatever junk had been lying around, with plenty of holes for the drones to stream through.

The Golden Horde taught cadre how to build better barricades in the first week of training. Sure, the barricades had some heavy weapons and the fighters behind the obstructions might have been good—Besquith and Lumar were tough troops to take on, hand to hand—but if you could kill them from a distance because the defensive fortifications sucked, what was the point?

She shrugged and continued on. Ten meters behind them, she reached the end of the tunnel. To the right, the shaft wall had collapsed, and she could see an area which was very different. She stepped closer to it and looked into the new passageway.

Sansar hadn't spent much time underground in her life, but she could tell the passageway looked older. Much older. *20,000 years older?* Maybe.

A rocky crust had grown over everything, including the lights on the ceiling. Someone had scratched the crust off a spot on the wall to reveal an emblem at the same height as her eyes, and she paused to look. It had three interlocking circles that looked like a Venn diagram, although the one on the bottom left was a darker color than the other two. She'd never seen anything like it.

She followed First Platoon into the new tunnel, which slowly curved to the right, although the curve was broken up with zigzags. She realized they would make adequate cover for defensive positions and had just opened her mouth to say something when the firing started in front of her.

* * *

First Platoon, Bravo Company, Endless Night Base, McPherson-3

"We should have done this while we were topside," Franklin said with a grunt as he tried to push past Sergeant Keith Prestridge. The problem with having a square elevator, they'd realized once they'd started down, was no one was able to tell which side was the front. All four sides had an equal chance of being the one that would open up on the waiting enemy. Finally, Staff Sergeant Cyn McDonald had suggested the front was probably the side that faced the weapon in the courtyard.

With nothing else to go on, they had nominated that as the front, and Franklin had claimed a spot on the lead row, as had Staff Sergeant Zach White. Since they couldn't be sure that a different side wouldn't open up, though, Franklin had put Naran in the middle of the block of troops and then had to work his way around and through the other troopers to get to the front. It was a bit like the puzzle where you can only move one piece at a time, and it took a while for all of them to work their way into position. He had the corner spot, so he could spin left if that side opened up, and he would still be in the lead. White had the opposite corner on the front row, so he could do similarly if that side opened up. They had tried to position people who still had missiles left—Franklin didn't—in the middle of each row so that any strongpoints could be immediately taken out.

"Shields up," Franklin said as the elevator slowed, and everyone on the outside of the formation activated their laser shields. It pushed them back into an even tighter group where there was no room to maneuver. Franklin felt like he was on an assault boat back on D-Day in World War II, just waiting for the ramp to drop from the front of the boat. He tried not to think about how many troopers had been immediately cut down once the D-Day ramps dropped.

With a *Ding!* the elevator stopped, and the doors opened—to Franklin's left.

It was just like he'd imagined D-Day. The enemy was already firing as the doors began to open, and all of their initial fire was concentrated on the person in the center of that side—Sergeant Keith Prestridge. His shield failed under the onslaught of MAC and laser fire as the doors opened to expose him—the enemy had another crew-served laser—and his CASPer was riddled. Before he succumbed, though, he fired off the remainder of his rocket pack, and three rockets raced off into the heart of the enemy defenses, with one of them detonating on the laser.

Then the mayhem began as Franklin and Staff Sergeant Cyn McDonald charged off the elevator, leading the wave of CASPers.

Motion to Franklin's right caught his eye, and he spun to find a Lumar flanking the elevator. The Lumar reached for him, but he swatted away the alien's hands with the rifle on his right arm. He retracted his shield with a thought, and his blade snapped down on his left as the shield closed. He spun slightly and led with an overhead slash that severed two of the Lumar's arms. The alien looked up at him in shock and surprise, and he fired his laser through the center of the Lumar's chest.

The alien fell back, and a Besquith took his place. His triggered his shield through his pinplants, and it popped out in time to deflect most of the laser rifle's blast. The remainder didn't make it through the armor of his chest. He bashed the Besquith in the face with his shield, knocking away the alien's rifle, then fired his rifle through its eye. The Besquith dropped as the bolt speared through his head and fried his brain.

Another Lumar stood to the side, firing into the melee with a MAC, and Franklin triggered his shield to collapse again, but it was damaged and wouldn't retract all the way. He ejected it with a thought, and the shield flew into the Lumar's face, slamming him backward and making his shot go into the ceiling. Franklin stepped forward and stabbed the humanoid through the chest.

Then there were no more enemy on that side of the elevator, and he turned back to the battle in front of the elevator. The squad was already in control after what looked like a short, vicious fight. In addition to Prestridge, two other CASPers were down. McDonald was just finishing off the heavy laser crew, and he turned back toward the elevator, the front of his suit pockmarked with a variety of laser and MAC holes. He took one step and collapsed.

"No," shouted Naran, and a CASPer ran over to McDonald.

"Set up a perimeter and call the other squad down," Franklin ordered on the platoon net, then he crossed the remains of the melee and helped Naran flip McDonald over, but he could see on his display that McDonald was already dead.

"Leave him, ma'am," Franklin said softly. "He's gone, and we've still got work to do."

"He stepped in front of a laser for me," Naran said with a tremor in her voice.

"And he wouldn't want you to let his sacrifice go to waste by allowing the Endless Night to fire their weapon." Franklin helped the officer to her feet, and he could see her armor was pitted across the front of it. "Are you all right, ma'am?"

"Yeah, I'm fine," she said, her voice a little stronger. She waved at her chest. "This is just the little bit that Prestridge's armor didn't stop on the initial salvo."

Franklin winced—Naran had been in the middle of the elevator and would have absorbed the brunt of the attack, no matter which side the doors had opened on. His idea to put her in the center to protect her had almost backfired. If Prestridge hadn't had the wherewithal to fire his rockets, she would probably be dead now too. Lesson learned…and not as costly as it could have been.

* * *

Starkiller-2, Endless Night Base, McPherson-3

"Energy channels are ready," the elSha tech reported.

"You still haven't fired?" Saunorak roared as he came into the room.

"We are close," Sheerho replied, trying—but failing—to keep the annoyance out of his voice. "If you would just leave us alone for a couple of minutes, it will be done."

"The enemy is on this floor!" Saunorak yelled. "You have to hurry—they will be here in two minutes!"

"I can't speed up the process," Sheerho said. He hadn't realized the enemy was that close, but there was nothing he could do; there was a certain process that had to be followed or the weapon would—he didn't know what it would do. Blow up? Maybe.

"Just hurry!" Saunorak urged. "All troops, come with me. We will hold them off as long as we can." He left, taking the ten troopers with him.

Although Sheerho had hated having all the soldiers nearby all the time, their absence left him feeling somewhat…naked.

"Form the weapon pulse," he ordered, after looking down at the checklist.

"Weapon pulse forming," an elSha said, and Sheerho smiled. Once the pulse was formed, the weapon couldn't be stopped.

Firing sounded from not too far down the corridor. If the stupid Besquith could just do his job and hold the enemy soldiers off for a couple more minutes…

* * * * *

Chapter Fifty-Five

Inside the Starkiller, Wahrner's Grise

Terbish jumped down from the pipe.

Chimney climbing up the wet tube without slipping—or another trooper slipping and knocking the whole squad down to the ground in a heap of mechs—yes, that had been stressful.

Hearing the Besquith snarls as they passed below had raised her terror to new levels of fear that she felt sure would burst her heart.

She had watched the aliens too. Their pursuit was so tightly on the heels of the CASPers that she hadn't had time to climb above the roof level and out of sight.

Fortunately, that same speed of pursuit meant they raced through the space without looking up into the pipe, though they had noted the other damage.

Worst of all had been the thirty minutes of radio silence while going over in her head what she had already done. And worse, what she was about to do.

She'd killed that man in the mess hall. Why had he drawn his handgun? Terbish could think of a thousand scenarios to explain it, but not a single one that made him a threat to her CASPers.

And that made her a killer. Would she have conceived of this plan if she hadn't first bloodied her soul?

It was a little late to worry about ethics now.

The enemy was the Endless Night. They were trying to destroy the Sun. Earth. Human civilization except for its weak and scattered colonies. Her species might not survive.

That justified anything.

She didn't just tell herself that. She believed it with all her heart.

Still, her plan didn't sit right in her mind.

The techs filling the room looked up as her mech landed heavily.

An instant later, one of the Midnighters thumped down to the deck from the neighboring pipe they'd hidden in.

Terbish advanced through the hole they'd blown in the pipe earlier and began hosing the Endless Night personnel.

With the main part of her concentration, she assessed who was in charge. There! An elSha in a shiny black uniform. Others were in a rough circle around her, as if she had been issuing orders.

Terbish fired at her with her autocannon.

But the nimble little alien anticipated it, backflipping like a gymnast before scampering away beyond the lash of Terbish's rounds.

Terbish fired the last of her missiles. The weapon streaked through the air and detonated inches from the elSha.

It was overkill. But it worked. Nothing remained of the elSha.

The other troopers continued the grim work, filling the room with corpses. None of the techs escaped.

A hope briefly flared—a justification really—that the people they had killed had been vital to the operation of this weapon. That this would set back Endless Night's plans.

Then it died, because Terbish decided that no justifications were required.

"Anyone who threatens humanity receives no mercy from the Golden Horde," she declared.

"Same goes for the Midnighters," said Sergeant Oranjeklegg.

No one spoke for a moment.

"Good work," she said. "Lay charges against that machinery and turn it to slag. Then we rejoin the major."

* * * * *

Chapter Fifty-Six

Alpha Company, Endless Night Base, McPherson-3

"There's another barricade up here," Captain House reported.

"We don't have time for this," Sansar said. "They have to be close to firing the weapon. We need to get to wherever it is and stop it!"

"Can we use rockets?" House asked. Sansar had put a prohibition on them after the cave-in. "We're going to have to if you want to get past them quickly."

"Yes," Sansar replied. "Rockets are authorized, but try to aim low so you don't bring the ceiling down again."

A couple of seconds later, explosions sounded from in front of her, followed by brief bursts of weapons fire.

"We're clear," House reported. "Moving up."

The rest of the company moved forward again, and Sansar got to the barricade. Again, it was hard to believe that a "professional" defense contractor had put it together. Admittedly, it had been hit by a couple of rockets, but any sort of worthwhile defensive position shouldn't have come apart as completely as it had.

Sansar shook her head; the shoddy workmanship annoyed her professional sensibilities almost as much as losing someone getting through it might have.

She strode past it, following the company, and noticed...something, on the right wall once she'd gone a little further down the corridor.

Sansar wasn't sure what to call it. She stopped to look at it, and Mun stopped alongside her.

"What is that?" Mun asked.

"No idea. Looks organic." Sansar reached out to touch it, but pulled her hand away from it as she noticed the slime on it. She prodded it with her rifle. "Feels kind of like plastic or rubber." She pushed a little harder. "There's a hole in the center."

Mun chuckled. "When you push it like that, it looks like an asshole." She pointed to the slime. "It also looks like you forgot to wipe, ma'am."

"Gross." Sansar pushed to the side and the opening continued to give. "Almost looks like you could get through here...if you wanted to badly enough."

"Not sure why you would, though."

"I don't know," Sansar said. She pointed back around the bend in the corridor. "Why do you suppose the barricade was there—to stop us from getting here? The other barricade was to stop us from getting into these tunnels...seems like there must have been a reason for them putting the barricade there."

"Maybe," Mun allowed. "It could also be that they didn't know what the hell they were doing. Those barricades were pretty crappy. Maybe the whole defense wasn't very well thought out."

Sansar jogged back to the barricade. After a second, Mun went with her. Sansar pointed at a brownish spot on the fur of one of the defenders. "Thought so. They went through that asshole, or whatever it is." She switched to her comms. "Captain House, have you found anything yet?"

"No, ma'am, the corridor just keeps bending around to the right. We haven't seen anything since the barricade we rocketed."

"Get back here. I've found the entrance."

"Ugh," Mun said as they went back to the opening. "If we go through there, we may never get that crap off the CASPers."

"Want to wait here?"

"No, ma'am; I just don't want that shit on my suit."

"Neither do I. But I want the sun to blow up even less."

Mun sighed. "When you put it that way, I'll go first." She put her hands together over her head like she was going to dive into a pool and inserted them into the opening. It gave enough to let her through, and she pulled her way to the other side.

Sansar followed her through and found herself in a small passage that joined into another, larger passage in a "T."

Mun helped the next person through, then came to stand beside her.

"Is it just me?" Sansar asked. "Or is this passage curved a little bit more than the other passage?"

"Kind of like concentric circles?"

"Yeah. I think we've found the facility."

"So where is the weapon?"

"I don't know, but we're getting closer."

Sansar strode down the passageway, and Captain House jogged up. "Ma'am, we can't support you if you get too far in front of us."

"I'm aware, Captain. I'm also aware that we're going to be too late if we don't hurry up and find the weapon."

"How about letting me put a scout in front of you then, so, you know, he springs the ambush and not the person that signs our checks."

"No need," Sansar said, pointing at the wall. "There's another of those entrances."

"Can I have scouts go first, please, ma'am?"

"If they hurry."

House called up two of the scouts, and they moved forward quickly. They went through two more of the portals, and, as Sansar pulled herself through the second one, she realized they had to be close to their target.

"What is this?" Mun asked, pointing at the wall.

Sansar moved out of the way so the next trooper could come through the portal and looked more closely. The walls had gone from something that looked like a normal, "rocky" tunnel to something that looked far more organic in nature. Worse, there seemed to be veins of…something that ran through the walls and pulsed periodically, as if they were no longer in a tunnel, but in some sort of living, breathing creature.

Before she could investigate further, weapons fire sounded from further up the corridor.

* * *

First Platoon, Bravo Company, Endless Night Base, McPherson-3

The elevator dinged, and the CASPers turned to face it—just in case—but it was Second Squad arriving—what was left of it—along with Lieutenant Delkii Enkh.

"I've got a present for you, ma'am," Sergeant Nichols said as he got off the elevator carrying a large box.

"What's that?" Naran asked.

"The nuke arrived from the *Gobi Desert*. Mind if I set this down somewhere?" Naran motioned to an open cubicle. "Thanks. I used to do asset protection for the Hedgehogs. Carrying around nukes isn't something I've ever done before. Or ever wanted to do, if the truth were known."

"Did they tell you how to operate it?"

"Yes, ma'am; I have the instructions for how to use it."

"Good; you stay here and guard it. First Sergeant Franklin, let's go find this weapon."

"Yes, ma'am. First Squad, left passage. Second Squad, right passage. Move out."

The large room in front of the elevator had two parallel hallways that led out of it to the north, and troopers filed out of the room through both passages.

They hadn't made it far when they began taking fire down both.

"Cover!" Franklin called, and the troopers used doorways and cross-passages to return fire.

"What do you have?" Naran asked on the command channel.

"A lot of fire, but it's odd," Franklin said. "They don't seem to be targeting anyone; they just seem to be firing down the hallway."

"They're stalling!" Naran said in a flash of recognition. "You said the weapon was about to fire; it must be! They're just trying to keep us away so they can fire it."

"Yeah," Franklin said. Naran could hear his sigh. "That's what I was afraid of. We're going to take some casualties for this, but we've got to break through them."

"We don't have time for this. If they fire it, we won't have a home to return to."

"I've got this," Lieutenant Delkii said. "First Squad!" she yelled. "With me! Charge!" She broke cover and ran down the left hallway with her laser shield extended.

"*No!*" Naran exclaimed, and broke to follow her younger sister. "Charge!" The rest of the squad broke from cover to chase after them.

Delkii almost made it to where the enemy fired on them from two cross-corridors farther down the hallway before she staggered, her laser shield riddled, and fell forward. A K-bomb flew forward into the mass of Endless Night forces there.

One of the Lumars picked it up, and Naran had a split second to extend her shield and brace herself before the oversized grenade detonated, wiping out the forces on that side of the cross-passage. She stood and charged past Delkii's fallen CASPer and waded into the remaining troops on the left with her sword blade out.

Although the troops were partially stunned—and covered in Lumar bits—they rallied when they saw her approaching, and one of the Besquith lifted his rifle. Naran slashed down and cut the rifle in half, then threw a left cross to the jaw of the alien that slammed it backward. Several Lumar pushed forward, driving her back, but then the rest of the Golden Horde forces arrived, and the enemy paused when they saw the mass of steel-clad troopers rushing toward them.

Naran stepped forward and drove her sword blade through a Lumar, then Franklin and several troopers crashed into the others, driving them backward while they fired into the group from close range. She could see they had the enemy under control and spun to look down the cross passage toward the other group of Endless Night forces, just as Second Squad rolled through them like a wave.

"Let's go!" Naran yelled, starting back up the corridor. She snapped out her shield, but it wasn't necessary. The weapons room was the first opening on the right.

* * *

Starkiller-2, Endless Night Base, McPherson-3

Weapons fired nearby, and Sheerho flinched. *They were so close!*

It was just like the last time they'd tried to fire the weapon, but this time, the enemy appeared to be coming in force. If Saunorak could just hold for another minute, they could still fire the weapon. All they needed was the one, final step. *Why won't the pulse balance out?*

A massive explosion rocked the corridor outside the room, then people started shouting and the fighting changed from weapons fire to the sounds of steel on steel. Then, ominously, the hallway got quiet.

"Pulse balance achieved," the elSha closest to him said as the first powered-armor clad individual appeared in the doorway. Sheerho smiled; the trooper was too late to stop them.

"Fire," Sheerho said, and the elSha pushed the button. It was done. The weapon would fire now. There was nothing that could stop it.

He had a second to savor the minor victory before the enemy soldier fired.

* * * * *

Chapter Fifty-Seven

Inside the Starkiller, Wahrner's Grise

All along, Sun had known it would come to this.

The heat exchanger.

The route out to the lake and the extraction.

In her mind it would be a huge metal pipe they would use to climb to safety.

So it was. At forty feet in diameter, she felt small in her Mk 8.

They'd used lasers to cut a hole into the pipe, but what they'd exposed was a latticework of small metal tubes and plates that completely filled the interior.

They'd begun ripping the insides out, using the raw strength of their CASPers.

If that had been their only problem, it would have been one Sun's team could have surmounted. But not with the Besquith firing from the corridor on anyone who went near the heat exchanger.

At least Sun could be sure the contents of this room were important, because the Besquith fire into it was so controlled, they must have been issued strict instructions not to destroy the place.

Besquith opened up with a trio of MAC rounds carefully aimed into the empty spaces of the room.

"Give yourselves up," demanded one of the werewolves. "You will be kept alive for ransom. You have our word of honor."

McCoy explained to the greenhorns what the Besquith really meant. "Don't believe what super-fido says. We would be kept alive for interrogation. Then they would eat us. Me? I'd rather go out fighting."

Getting out. Sun bit her lower lip. That was going to be tricky.

There had been no contact with Lieutenant Enkh, and by now there should have been. These tunnels were hell on signals. Up to now she had banked on that working to their advantage, making it difficult for the enemy to coordinate defenses.

It wasn't helping now.

McCoy shifted position to join her. His radio comms had been fried, so he spoke through his speakers. "If we stay here, Major, we'll die."

"I agree. But I retain faith in Lieutenant Enkh."

"And I have faith in the Besquith. Much as I hate to say this, with experienced Besquith troops versus an inexperienced CASPer squad, at best I'd give Enkh and Melsome 3 to 2 against. Add in Oranjeklegg's people and I'd give them even up if I were feeling chipper, but we don't know for sure how many of the werewolves we're facing."

"Five more minutes," said Sun. "Then we fire missiles into that exchanger and see if we can blow our way out without drowning in the flood or dying under Besquith claws."

A moment later, the room shook with concussion blasts blowing out from the corridor.

Enkh and her troopers had announced their arrival.

* * *

One by one, the dots representing Enkh's command reappeared in Sun's HUD.

Each was a burst of hope in her heart.

After eleven, the dots stopped appearing. Enkh and Oranjeklegg were among the survivors. Hell, they'd left even more troopers behind in the tunnels.

"Blades out," said Sun. "Let's finish this!"

She snapped out her sword and advanced on the stunned enemy in the corridor.

Immediately, a Besquith came to life. It jumped up on her and dug in with its claws.

She slashed at it, but it wasn't easy at this angle, so she sawed away at the weak point where Besquith butt joined upper legs. It took twenty seconds of hard work in which alarms multiplied in her HUD from the damage the Besquith was inflicting.

Then she was rewarded by a sudden flood of Besquith blood over the front of her CASPer. She must have cut through an artery, but the Besquith vascular system was far tougher than a Human's. This wasn't over.

She knew the Besquith on top of her was still clawing and snapping because the damage reports kept escalating. Entropy! What would it take to kill this thing?

By now, all her upper camera sensors had been destroyed, so she blindly felt with haptic feedback for the half-severed Besquith legs. She gripped them with every ounce of her CASPer's strength and then pulled her arms apart.

The werewolf's legs snapped off.

She hurled the bloody limbs at another Besquith charging her and followed with a stab with her sword arm.

The blade snapped off, but not before skewering her opponent.

She jumped off the ground and stomped her Mk 8 down hard on the filthy alien's head, obliterating it.

She dodged to the side and had to steady herself when the now dead Besquith on top of her slid away. Then she looked for her next target.

They were all down.

"All clear," said Lieutenant Enkh.

Sun laughed to herself. At the start of this mission, that girl had been overly polite and annoyingly shy. Now her voice was rich with excitement and pride.

If Colonel Enkh wanted her young lieutenant to grow a pair on this mission, Sun reckoned she'd done just that.

"Did you miss us?" Branco asked on a private link. His voice was slurred with stims and disease, but Sun only cared that he was still alive.

"You have no idea," she whispered. "When we have safely escaped from this enemy base bristling with Besquith fighters, we shall do something about that."

"Copy that."

"Lieutenant Enkh," said Sun. "Post a guard on that entrance. For all other CASPers, we exfil through that pipe. We're gonna have to claw our way out."

*****

Chapter Fifty-Eight

First Platoon, Bravo Company, Endless Night Base, McPherson-3

Naran fired and dropped the Zuul who had given the order to fire the weapon. The room was unlike anything she'd ever seen—it seemed to be alive—but she didn't have time to worry about that. "You!" She pointed her sword blade at the elSha who'd been standing next to the Zuul. "Did the weapon fire?"

The alien tried to shrink down behind the slate that was embedded into…something that protruded from one of the walls. There were six other elSha scattered throughout the room; all seemed to be trying to decide whether to run or hide. The elSha she was talking to turned toward the door on the other side of the room, just in time for Second Squad to come pouring through it. It looked up to the second level, but a commotion there resolved into the arrival of Alpha Company.

"There's nowhere to run," Naran said. "Did. The. Weapon. Fire?"

"No," it said in a tiny voice. "Not yet, anyway."

"What is that supposed to mean?"

"It takes time for the weapon to fire. The pulse has been initiated, but it hasn't fired yet."

"Stop it. Now."

"I can't," the elSha said piteously. "Once the firing button has been pressed—which it has—it can't be stopped."

"Let me put it to you this way," Sansar's voice said from above. "You either stop it, or you're going to die, right here, right now. I will kill as many of you as I have to, if that is what is required to stop the weapon."

"*I can't stop it!*" the elSha squealed. "I would stop it if I could, but it is now unstoppable."

Sansar moved into the room, took aim, and fired a bolt through the elSha's head. She pointed her rifle at one of the elSha on the second level. "You're next. Stop the weapon from firing."

"I can't," it said. If anything, this one sounded even more pitiful than the first one had. "He wasn't lying; once you initiate the firing mechanism, it can't be stopped."

"Franklin!" Naran said. "Go get Sergeant Nichols and the nuke. If we can't stop it, we'll blow it up."

"Yes ma'am," Franklin said as a number of the troopers swore. There was no way they were going to make it out if they set off the nuke; they were all going to die. Franklin turned and ran out of the room.

"Wait!" Sansar said. "How did the person stop it the last time the weapon was fired?"

"He didn't stop it," the elSha said. "Like I told you, *you can't!* He just input different coordinates, and it fired somewhere else."

"Good. That sounds like a workable solution. Input different coordinates and send it somewhere else."

"I don't know how. You killed the technician that did that step. It has to be done at his console, and I've never done it before."

"Shit," Naran said, looking at the slate above the body of the elSha. She was closer than anyone else. She raised her canopy, exited her CASPer, and ran over to the slate, downloading the elSha language into her pinplants as she ran. She took a look at the slate and swore.

"What is it?" Sansar asked.

"It's a countdown. Looks like about a minute and a half until it fires." She tapped the slate and the countdown moved to the corner of the display. The center of the display changed to read, "Coordinates accepted," and a button at the bottom read, "Tap here to re-enter."

"I think I can add new coordinates." She tapped the button, and the screen changed to a blank with a "Re-enter Coordinates Here."

Sansar stepped up next to the elSha. "Give her some new coordinates."

"I don't know how to get them!" the alien wailed. "Only the two people you killed knew how to figure them out!"

Naran looked at the screen. It didn't give her any indication of how many numbers to enter. She pressed the "Continue with original coordinates" button and went back to the previous screen and began counting the digits in the current target.

"Got it!" Franklin said as he and Nichols arrived with the nuke.

"Get it set for detonation," Sansar said, "but do *not* initiate until I tell you to."

Naran looked up and lost her place in the count. She looked back down as the countdown went through one minute remaining, and started counting the digits again. 35. She pressed the button to change the target and began pressing "1" until she'd done it 35 times.

"Got it," she said, but nothing happened. The countdown went through 25 seconds remaining.

"You changed it?"

"I don't know. There's no indication of whether the new target was accepted!"

"Not good enough," Sansar said. "Is the nuke ready to go?"

"Yes, ma'am," Nichols said. "All I need to do is hit the initiator." He didn't sound happy about it, but he sounded resolved to do it.

"Go ahead," Sansar said as Naran hit the "1" key again in frustration.

The screen changed and "Accept?" appeared.

"Wait!" Naran shouted. "I've got it!"

Nichols pulled his hand back from the bomb like it had burned him.

"5...4...3..." Naran only had one chance. If it didn't work, it would probably be too late to detonate the nuke. She pressed the "Accept" button, and the display changed to "Accepted" as the countdown went through one second remaining. It immediately changed to "Firing," and the low hum changed to a tremendous vibration. The walls pulsed and changed color from black to white. Something, somewhere went *PEEEEEEEEW!* then the vibrations stopped, and the walls changed back to black again.

"Please tell me we didn't just blow up Sol," Sansar asked quietly.

"No ma'am," Naran said. "It accepted the new coordinates before it fired. Unless the Solar System's coordinates are thirty-six "1s" all in a row, we didn't blow it up."

"Do you know what we blew up?" Sansar asked the elSha.

"Without access to a directory, I don't have any idea," the alien said. "All I can tell you is that the weapon fired, and we blew up something."

* * * * *

Chapter Fifty-Nine

Dancing Demon, **Above Lake Zarillo, Wahrner's Grise**

Only when the Gray Wolf smuggling boat reached orbit did the major finally declare the mission a success.

McCoy cheered with all the others in *Dancing Demon*'s hold, but noted his squad was more enthusiastic than David Melsome's. Second Squad had lost most of its people.

Oranjeklegg's team was somber too.

The Midnighters had gotten talkative on the ride up. Before they'd even known the Goltar existed, the Midnight sisters had led two companies off on a mission to bring back some Raknars for Jim Cartwright. Despite the replacements they'd recruited since then, their number had been whittled down to the four effectives with him on the boat. Five if you counted Major Sun, who seemed to be moonlighting as a goddamned revolutionary leader. And a few at McPherson's Star last seen watching the dents being hammered out of their mechs.

Losing your people one by one until there was nothing left. That was a journey McCoy knew all too well.

But now that they were finally able to emerge from the stinking metal suits, the mood lifted, and the two Horde staff sergeants joined the other enlisted in reliving the experience and remembering the fallen.

All except Branco, who acted like a trooper some of the time but was now fast asleep in his tank, his snoring escaping through the open hatch.

Once they'd docked with *Unlikely Regret*, Branco would be smuggled onto Station 5 for medical treatment while the rest of them waited for Colonel Enkh and the McPherson force to show at Wahrner's Grise.

Branco was a strange man, but McCoy could tell he was the kind of guy with some meaty tales to tell. He hoped the docs fixed him up well so he could hear them one day.

McCoy dismissed the Dane from his mind; he had conscious people to talk with. He caught Melsome's eye, and the two squad leaders backed up against a bulkhead, away from the crowd.

"What do you reckon, Dave? Did we do good?"

Melsome shook his head, buried in thought for a moment. "Didn't think I would make it, Jim. My CASPer was holed in so many places, I felt sure it would flood when we escaped through the lake." He shrugged. "Three hundred feet underwater. That's a lot of pressure. But the auto-seals held, and no one had to worry about getting the bends."

McCoy clapped him on the shoulder. "But we got what we came for. Damned shame we lost so many of the kids. You can tell me the parts I missed over a whiskey when we can find a bottle. Something I gotta do first."

Terbish Enkh had done well enough for him to stop treating her like a kid. But there was one last thing. Since they'd been pulled out of the lake, she'd been withdrawn. Silent. And he knew why.

He found her sitting by herself on the deck next to her mech.

"What's on your mind, Lieutenant?"

"I'm okay, thank you, Staff Sergeant. It's just…It's a lot to process."

"Ever kill anyone before today?"

She shook her head.

"Well, shit. We done killed a fuck load. If that doesn't give you pause for thought, then there's something wrong with you."

Enkh returned a faint smile. "That's exactly what the major just told me. Although with vocabulary less…colorful."

She paused and then looked up at him with dark, serious eyes. "Does it get easier, McCoy?"

He placed a fatherly hand on her shoulder. It was probably inappropriate as hell, but it felt like the right thing to do, and he didn't give a shit. "Only you can answer that, Terbish. You did well today."

He left her to it. She was a good kid. His gut told him she would figure it out.

* * * *

Chapter Sixty

CO's Conference Room, EMS *Gobi Desert*, Orbiting McPherson-3

"3...2...1...and detonation," Captain Naran Enkh said, several days later. Something flashed on the Tri-V in the center of the table, then the stereotypical mushroom cloud formed. "And that's the end of the starkiller."

"Well done," Sansar said. "And the people from the town?"

"There were surprisingly few people remaining in the town," Naran said. "Most had been leaving for some time to get away from the Endless Night scourge. The ones we could find we transported to a nearby town outside the expected fallout pattern."

Sansar nodded and turned to the intel officer. "Have you had any luck breaking into the slates we took from the weapons room?"

"Not entirely," Captain James Momson replied. "Some of the data is corrupted and some of it is protected by a layer of encryption unlike anything we've ever seen before. Still, we have been able to glean some intelligence from it...like the location of the star that the weapon destroyed."

"Do I want to know?"

"I'm not sure..." Momson temporized.

"Tell me anyway," Sansar said with a sigh. "What's done is done, and it can't be helped. All we can do is plan for what comes next. Was it an inhabited system?"

"Unknown, ma'am."

"You don't know? Why not?"

"Because the star we blew up is in the fourth arm of the galaxy. The targeting data with the lowest numbers—those starting with "1"—are all in the fourth arm, and we have no records of the star. It may be inhabited, and it may not."

"What about the other star that the weapon fired on?"

"We were able to go back in the firing log of the weapon. The last time it fired, a couple of months ago, it was also targeted on a fourth arm star."

"So we've blown up two stars in the fourth arm?"

"Yes, ma'am; it appears so."

Sansar sighed and then smiled. "You're right; I'm not sure I wanted to know. I can't help feeling that we'll have to deal with this later."

"I'm sorry, ma'am," Naran said, looking at the table. "I didn't know…"

"Don't be," Sansar said. "Our mission was to save Earth, and you did. If you hadn't led your platoon down into the facility, it is unlikely Alpha Company would have made it to the firing room in time. You did what you had to, and I'm proud of you and everything your platoon did. You saved Earth. It would have been nice if we'd had time to pick a better target, but we didn't."

Sansar shrugged. "We'll deal with any fallout when it occurs; until then, we're not going to worry about it."

"That's not all, ma'am," Momson said. "The weapon was used a couple of months ago, too."

"It was?"

"Yes, ma'am. It blew up a star located fairly close by. A star named Psilydia."

"Means nothing to me."

"Its major planet is listed as Tau-Rietzke."

"Gloriana mentioned that. The Midnight Sun Company used to have a base there. The Endless Night used the starkiller to wipe it out. And that's why these can't be allowed to exist."

"So what's next, ma'am?" Captain House asked.

"There were originally three of the starkillers. There's one left. We're going to go to Wahrner's Grise and finish the job."

Captain Steve Parker, the CO of the *Gobi Desert*, stood. "In that case, I'll head up to the CIC. We'll be headed there momentarily."

* * * * *

Chapter Sixty-One

Private Medical Facility, Station 5

"Aren't you going to sedate me first?"

The alien paused, two powerful limbs curled around the bars hung over the top of its tank, partway through the act of lifting its bulk out of the water.

The Wrogul's beak moved, but no sound came out. It lifted a third tentacle out of the water and extended it toward Branco.

Arm, not a tentacle. Better get it right if you don't want to piss off the surgeon.

The appendage pointed his way was covered in suckers. It appeared to be primarily for locomotion and applying the creature's strength. Living with the Goltar, Branco had learned to call these arms or limbs.

Colors flashed at the tip of the limb. This appeared to be the alien's form of speech, because words came from speakers built into its water tank in time with the child's light show.

"Do you *want* me to sedate you?" it asked.

The alien hauled itself out of the tank in a fluid motion and then shuffled toward him along the floor of the medical facility.

The creature resembled an oversized heavyweight Goltar stripped of the bony protrusions and the weapons secreted in every fold. Compared with a Goltar, its eyes were less...*evil.*

"I don't recommend sedation," flashed the Wrogul. "Not in your condition. I'm very surprised you are still alive, Specialist Saisho

Branco. Were you hanging on to your slender thread of life because you could not bear death to part you from one particular individual? Human clinicians so often undervalue this angle."

The alien extended two appendages that were thinner than its limbs and shook them so rapidly they were almost impossible to see. He'd heard rumors of what those tentacles could do, but the Wrogul was only shaking the water off before running the tentacles like sensor wands over Branco's body.

"No offense, Doc, but I'm not in the mood for bedside chitchat. Just do whatever you've got to do."

"I am not 'Doc.'" The tentacles paused in their survey of Branco's body. "You can call me Squiddy the Surgeon."

"You're kidding! I thought your name was Molina."

The limb still held aloft pulsed fiercely. "Goddamn it! I'm supposed to be under cover. Molina is a cipher. A rumor. He doesn't exist. You never saw him. Call me...Alf."

"Alf is fine, Doc. Sorry. I get talkative when I'm nervous."

Alf rested his sensory tentacles over the bar that ran around Branco's treatment bench.

"I'm not surprised you're anxious, Specialist. You should be dead, but I think I've detected the cause of the problem. Have you made friends with any Selroth recently?"

"Yeah. They got me chewing some kind of seaweed. *Ribbwah* they called it."

"That's right. And it's this *ribbwah* that explains your intriguing medical condition."

"But I was sick long before I took the Selroth weed."

"You misunderstand. The medical condition of which I speak is that you continue to live when you should be dead. As for the microorganism you picked up in your jungle adventure, that is a trifling matter to erase and reverse. Try not to faint."

Alf lifted his tentacles and vibrated them at an impossible rate.

But he wasn't shaking off water this time.

Slowly, Alf lowered one over Branco's chest and another over his forehead.

Branco stared at the one along his sternum. The vibration wasn't merely fast, there was something unnatural about it. Watching that mesmerizing blur was a little like staring into the endless white of hyperspace.

The tentacle lowered onto his chest.

It didn't stop.

It kept sinking lower.

Branco had somehow known this was going to happen. He still couldn't believe it.

He was wearing his ship suit. But it hadn't ripped. Nor was there blood. The alien tentacles had somehow melted through his body.

So why could he feel it moving inside him when he hadn't felt it slice through his chest?

Perhaps he was imagining it?

He shut his eyes, trying hard not to think about his brain being manipulated by the other tentacle.

He could feel Alf rummaging through his heart and lungs, sweeping his appendage down his patient's body.

Branco opened his eyes just in time to see the blur of an alien tentacle disappear into his crotch.

He clamped his eyes shut again.

Mercifully, he felt the lower tentacle leave his body.

But then it melted through his neck and into the back of his head.

He wanted to scream, but he'd lost control of the right muscles.

His eyes were melting, his ears watering. His sensations were a hot jumbled mess. It wasn't painful, but it was uncomfortable for sure.

Eventually, Alf removed his tentacles, and Branco opened his eyes.

"Oh, dear!" Alf flashed.

"It's that bad?"

"Yes. I think I need to bring in my client."

"I thought *I* was the client?"

"No, Specialist Branco, you are the patient. And a most interesting one."

Alf paused a moment, then a Goltar appeared in the bulkhead-mounted Tri-V projector.

"Branco," the Wrogul flashed. "Have you been remembering who you were before?"

"Yes."

"Do you have a name? Place of birth, that kind of thing?"

"I was Preben Bergesen. Copenhagen, Denmark, Earth. I had a cousin, a girl called Freja."

"Ah, yes. Here you are. You lived on Toskiftgangen."

"Yes. Yes, that was it! Are you accessing my medical records?"

"No, I'm accessing your *criminal* records. Oh, dear. Yes, it makes sense why you let them implant that palimpsest personality device."

"Why? What happened? What did I do?"

Alf patted him on the head with a tentacle. This time it didn't sink through his skull.

"There, there. None of that matters anymore. You left it all behind a long time ago."

"Why am I witnessing this?" asked the Goltar.

Alf turned to the bulkhead. "My apologies, High Councilor Gloriana. Please bear with me while I complete my examination."

The alien returned his attention to Branco. "Do you remember your other personalities as well as Preben?"

"Not as strongly, but yes."

The Wrogul shifted back to the Tri-V. "Regrettably, High Councilor, I cannot deliver the medical correction I was contracted for."

Shit! Gloriana made an angry noise, but that was nothing compared to how Sun would react. She was going to be devastated.

"Wait," said Branco. "Alf, you told me the disease I picked up in the jungle would be easy to cure."

"It would be," said Alf. "Sngh, sngh, sngh." Branco guessed the scratchy noise through the speakers was Wrogul laughter. "If not for the fact that I've already cured your wasting disease. The real problem lies with your mind. The disease degraded your palimpsest personality implant barriers, allowing your memories to regrow natural connections. If I remove the device, you will be driven insane. My recommendation is to reconstruct a false personality and history that links to your earlier memories. You will know you have gaps, but you need not know why."

"I don't want to lose Sun."

"Sun? Is this the person you've stayed alive for? Well, it's very sad, but I'm sure this Sun will still be fond of you. Just not like they were before."

"If we proceed with your recommendation," said Gloriana, "how much of his memory will be lost?"

"Back to when Branco had the palimpsest device implanted. I believe he was twenty-two years old."

"Out of the question," Gloriana said.

"I suppose I could finish repairing the palimpsest," said Alf, "but because his barriers have already been breached, Branco will experience multiple personalities. There are coping strategies, but his condition will become more extreme over time."

"You mean I'll go mad," said Branco.

"I mean that you will become a very interesting person. It's only if I remove the palimpsest device altogether that you will turn into a gibbering lunatic, and I shall not do that. I will do no harm."

"Tell me, Wrogul," said Gloriana, "will Branco's Human lover still recognize him as the man she loves after a few ten-days?"

"Yes. And for years to come."

"That's good enough. Proceed."

"Don't I...?" Branco's protest died when the Wrogul tentacles began vibrating and pushed into his head. He felt his brain jiggling like grey matter jello.

Twenty seconds later, Alf withdrew his tentacles. "It's been a pleasure. All done."

He shuffled back to his wheeled water tank.

All done? Branco felt...wonderful! His headache was gone. There was no pain when he tried accessing his pinplants. Not only did his muscles no longer ache, but they felt primed for explosive action. He wanted to lift, to crush, to run...

He looked down his treatment bench and saw his limbs that still terminated above the knee.

"My legs!" he yelled.

Alf plopped back into his tank, but he lifted out a limb and flashed a reply. "I would have been happy to regrow them, but that would have required more time than I was permitted. However, your nerve endings are already almost regrown. In a day or so, a less accomplished surgeon than myself could begin limb regrowth treatment. Good luck, Specialist Branco. Enjoy your recovery."

With a smooth hum of its motor, the tank wheeled the strange alien away.

Branco opened his clothing and explored inside to touch the flesh at the end of his stumps. His fingers went through the outer layer of skin, which sloughed away painlessly to reveal baby-smooth flesh beneath. He pinched it.

"Oww!"

He grinned.

"Amazing, aren't they?"

Branco looked up to see a Human orderly approach bearing a nanite injector.

"Wroguls? Damn right. So…about my legs."

"All in good time, Mr. Branco. When they've put tentacles inside you there can be aftereffects. Nothing to worry about, but enough that we want to let your body settle before we apply more conventional therapies. Just a little patience and in a few months, you'll be better than ever."

That made sense to Branco. He let the man apply the injector into his neck.

He relaxed into the sedative.

His body drifted into sleep.

But his mind didn't sleep.

Maybe it was one of these tentacle side effects the orderly mentioned.

Branco couldn't shout, scream, or blink.

People were all around him, but he couldn't see who they were or communicate in any way.

Something was wrong.

There was a rapid snapping noise and the sense that there was a deep rumble at the lower threshold of his hearing. Goltar speech.

His translator pendant was inactive, but a synthesized female Human voice translated nearby. "Will this take much longer, Zahn?"

"No, High Councilor," replied the same voice, though this was the woman herself speaking. "The Wrogul's repairs to the palimpsest implant were so thorough that they're taking a little longer to unpick than I had planned for. I need another five minutes. No more."

"Excellent. Well, Saisho Branco, you have cost me a fortune by the standards of your species. But you will be worth every credit when I'm through with you."

Branco heard Gloriana walk away, but then hesitate. "One more thing, Doctor Zahn. A request."

"Yes?"

"Make it hurt!"

* * *

Gauthier awoke from a nightmare of brain surgery. Of an alien octopus sticking its tentacles inside his head and…

Vlox surfaced from the sea of weird dreams in which he was always someone else.

He tried to shake sense into his head, but he was still groggy. Had he been drugged?

Something wasn't right, but he knew he was Vlox and he had to get back on mission.

The target…

What was the target's name?

Who was he here to kill?

Zahn. That was it. Doctor Zahn.

He wrenched his eyes open.

Coughed.

Gasped.

And Saisho Branco finally woke up.

He'd been Preben long ago. Vlox and Gauthier too. But that was okay, because they were nothing more than memories of lives he'd lived before.

Now he was Branco. That was all that mattered.

"Where am I?" he asked the Goltar marine standing by his bed.

But as he sat upright, he could see the answer to his own question. He was in Med-Bay 13 aboard *Midnight Sun*.

"I see you recognize your surroundings," said the Goltar. "Good."

"I feel better too," said Branco, blinking with surprise at how good he felt. Had a part of those nightmares been real?

He felt something else too. Deep disgust. Rage at…at himself. He bunched his fists. What the fuck was going on? Someone would pay.

"You have recovered from a medical procedure carried out on Station 5," the Goltar told him. He made a spiraling gesture with a couple of arms. "They don't tell me shit, Branco, but I heard whatever they did was a success. Congratulations. Now do whatever a Human does to pull yourself together. We're moving out tomorrow at 07:00."

"Where are we headed?"

"The dead world. Meinir."

* * * * *

Chapter Sixty-Two

CIC, EMS *Gobi Desert*,

Entering Wahrner's Grise Emergence Area

Sansar watched as the ships transitioned out of hyperspace.

"*Tseg-Lenkh* is detaching from *Blunt Justice*," the sensor operator reported. "Their remaining starfish fighters are also launching."

"Detach us as well," Captain Parker said. "Launch all Avengers."

Like a flower blossom opening, the single radar blip that had emerged from hyperspace expanded and then expanded again in three dimensions as the fighters and bombers detached and raced ahead of the remaining combat vessels. A variety of smaller ships also detached from the *Unlikely Regret* as it made its appearance.

Although the Patriot Navy hadn't participated in the Battle for McPherson-3, they were not to be refused a second time, and they had brought their "biggest" five ships to the fray. Although the *Unlikely Regret* was a medium-sized vessel, it was an armed merchant, not a true man-of-war, and it couldn't go toe-to-toe with the Spinning Shield forces. Captain Gadzo had refused to stand aside this time, though, as the Patriot Navy was concerned about not being seen "doing its part" and how that would affect their standing as "leaders" after the conflict. That said, the lightly armed and armored ships had been stationed on the right flank to pick off any injured Maki forces, thereby avoiding the brunt of the main battle.

It was all theater in any event, Sansar knew. The only ship which wasn't heavily damaged was the *Gobi Desert*...which had no armament to speak of. The *Tseg-Lenkh* was running on one plant, and *Blunt Justice* wasn't much better. The *Midnight Sun* was in the best shape of any of the major combatants, but she was no longer with the fleet, having gone back to Station 5 on some errand after the battle at McPherson-3. Gloriana had been somewhat evasive at the time as to what was more important than the final battle with the Maki and the destruction of the last starkiller, but as she was currently signing the Golden Horde's paychecks, Sansar hadn't been able to force more information from her. Even Captain Kanat-Baim had seemed nonplussed at Gloriana's decision.

"I've got the enemy fleet!" the sensor operator exclaimed. "They're in orbit around the planet. I make the *Petal*-class battlecruiser, one *Yperex*-class destroyer, and what looks like four frigates."

"Has *Blunt Justice* given any orders yet?" Parker asked.

Sansar covered her mouth to hide the smile, even though she was behind him and he couldn't see her. If nothing else, their time in hyperspace had been well spent in organizing the chain of command. *It helped to have all been in battle together, and to have seen the losses the Goltar had taken to protect the* Gobi Desert. Sansar knew that alone had gone a long way toward making Parker more amenable to taking direction from the giant squid.

"*Blunt Justice* says we'll push toward the planet and see if they come out to do battle with us," the comms officer relayed. "If so, we will meet them and destroy them."

"If so, I hope he doesn't keep us out here like a great big target," Parker muttered to himself.

Sansar smiled again. Taking orders was one thing; liking them was an entirely different thing all together.

"I've got activity from orbit," the sensor operator said as the fleet continued toward the planet. "Looks like the Spinning Shield forces are breaking orbit and heading toward us. A number of ships are also leaving orbit and heading toward the stargate."

"Like rats leaving the sinking ship," Parker noted.

"Looks like the Maki forces are forming into a fighting configuration," the sensor operator added. "*Blunt Justice* is also launching her drones."

"They can't seriously hope to win," Parker noted. "Even if they realize that we're unarmed, they still have to face the throw weight of a battlecruiser, the carrier, and all of the drones, fighters, and bombers. Hell, even the Patriot Navy has a few guns they'll add. The Maki might damage some of us, but without some sort of surprise weapon, they can't win."

* * *

The two forces proceeded toward each other, both knowing they were closely matched, as if they were waiting for the other to back down. That wasn't an option for the Humans—who stood to lose their home system if they did so—and the Goltar, who had put them in that position. They were in it until the end…whatever that end might be.

"We will defeat them if they continue," Captain Kanat-Baim had said from the *Blunt Justice* an hour previously, when he had ordered the *Gobi Desert* to tuck behind the carrier to take advantage of its shields in the center of the formation.

"Uh, sir?" the comms officer asked, just before battle was to be joined. "It looks like a Commodore Fenrikho is calling from the battlecruiser *Vindictive*. *Blunt Justice* has tied us in so we can see it."

The main viewscreen illuminated with a Maki admiral on the left and a Goltar on the right.

"Have you chosen to surrender?" Captain Kanat-Baim asked before the Maki could say anything. "Or do you wish to continue down the path to our mutual destruction?"

The Maki paused for a moment, then bowed slightly. "We wish to yield to you, assuming you will allow us to leave the nebula unscathed. There is nothing left to be gained here for us. There aren't enough credits in our contract to re-equip our ships and pay out the death benefits we have already accrued."

Kanat-Baim sketched a bow in return. "As you say, there is nothing left to gain by throwing our two fleets together. If you would like to leave the nebula, we have more important tasks to conclude and will not pursue you." He looked at the Maki for a couple seconds. "Do I have your word that you will leave the nebula without attacking any ship, station, or planet en route?"

"I give you my word that we will only use our weapons in self-defense."

"Then you are free to go," Kanat-Baim said. He gave the admiral another small bow. "Until we meet again."

"Until then." The Maki screen went blank.

"The enemy fleet is turning away toward the stargate," the sensor operator called.

"Good," Captain Parker said, blowing out his breath in a sigh. "Let them go."

* * * * *

Chapter Sixty-Three

Captain's Cabin, *Midnight Sun*, Docked at Station 5

"There is something wrong with Branco." Jenkins climbed onto Blue's table and reared up his fore-segments, snapping his mandibles at her.

His threat display was as unconvincing as it was clumsy. Blue felt as threatened as watching a kitten try its growl for the first time.

The Jeha was probably just working out his frustration at his lady love being stuck a hyperspace jump away at Wahrner's Grise, but…

She rolled her eyes. There was no denying that they all owed the chief engineer big time.

"Okay, Jenkins. You've gotten my interest. Briefly. What's rubbing salt between your segments?"

The alien's aggressive stance collapsed. "Why do you ask? I have only just stated my concern."

"No. You said something's wrong with Branco. You haven't said *what*."

"I see." Jenkins considered the possibility of *making some damned sense for a change*. Then he tried again. "Branco is not the person he was. I caught him on the way to the hangar just now. He is brooding and angry. Violence shrouds him."

"Yeah. The Wrogul surgeon warned me of this. You see, when he became an industrial spy for Binnig, they put a doohickey in Branco's head that kept his past lives secret. Even he didn't know who he really was. When his disease reached his brain, it screwed up this thing that was suppressing his memories. The natural connections in his mind are reconnecting. Could lead to mood swings apparently."

"Do you mean he has a palimpsest personality implant?"

"Uh, huh. That was it."

"Why didn't you say so, Captain? That explains most of it. But I still don't understand this aggression."

"I hate to break it to you, Jenkins, but Branco has had a problem with the red mist ever since he joined us. It's part of who he is. Who he has *always* been. He asked Binnig to bulldoze his entire childhood and concrete over the memories. You don't do that unless there's something in your past you don't want to remember."

"He's fleeing the memory of his violence. Oh, dear. That is most troubling."

"Maybe he'll sort things out. Humans are very adaptable, but my workload isn't. Thanks so much for dropping by to chat, Jenkins. Dismissed."

Jenkins looked to the hatchway.

And back to Blue.

"Stay away from Branco if he worries you," she told him. "It's a big ship. Be in a different part of it from him. Now go away."

"At least that won't be an issue for a few days."

Now that Blue had eyebrows once more, she tried arching one. "Explain!"

"Branco is part of the Meinir expedition."

Blue frowned at the overgrown earwig. "I haven't ordered anyone except Goltar to Meinir."

"Branco said it was the Goltar expedition commander who gave the order. I can't remember their name. Something double barreled, I should think."

Gloriana was behind this. Blue could smell the slippery squid bitch's tentacles all over it.

All Blue had to do was carry on as planned for a little while longer, and then they would all be free of the scheming Goltar Councilor.

She ran a search via her pinplants for the owner of the *Midnight Sun*, but there was no sign of Gloriana on the ship. Should she be worried?

No more than normal, she decided. It looked as if her sister was dating a violent psychopath, but Branco was still resourceful. But he wasn't *that* useful. And he was only a man. Why would Gloriana go to the trouble of organizing an all-Goltar team and then bring a Human?

It would have made more sense to bring Jenkins. Next to Hopper, he understood the science better than anyone. But Branco? No, Blue couldn't figure that one out. And with what was coming at her down the pike, she wasn't minded to try.

The Jeha regarded her from the desk, expecting her to have all his answers.

"It's a sad fact of the universe," she told him, "but friends can turn on you. This is even more likely for psychopaths with an addiction to violence."

"You mean like a thrill addict, Captain?"

She bit her lip. "Yes, my friend. Like a thrill addict. Like me." She thought of what she planned for her crew. "I can't be trusted. And in the dangerous universe we live in, my advice to you is to go about armed."

His antennae drooped along her desk. "I don't want to. I've never carried a weapon."

"But you have *built* them. Go think it through far away from my cabin, and when you do so, just remember one thing—if you carry a weapon, make sure it is one you are prepared to use."

Amazingly, that was enough for Jenkins to shake all the worry from his stance. "Thank you, Captain. Despite the limitations of your species, you are very wise."

"I hope you're right," she responded when he'd left her alone. "Because with what I'm about to do, there's a galaxy of people who would say the exact opposite."

* * * * *

Chapter Sixty-Four

CO's Conference Room, EMS *Gobi Desert*,
Orbiting Wahrner's Grise

Sansar nodded as she looked around the room. It was good to have the members of Second Platoon, Bravo Company, back, although there were a lot fewer of them. She'd scanned the after-action reports on the way in from the emergence area, and—even though they'd lost a lot of people—she couldn't find fault in the way the reconnaissance mission had been run. If anything, she was surprised any of them had made it out alive. Terbish had done well with what she'd been given. With them back aboard, they had about a company and a half of effectives.

The major from Midnight Sun had also comported herself well; all reports indicated she'd kept her head under fire and had led the troops well. She had about a squad's worth of experienced CASPer troopers under her command, led by First Sergeant Xavier Albali. The group also included Sergeant Obadiah Jex, who'd performed admirably in the reconnaissance mission. They appeared solid, although there weren't very many of them.

There were also a couple of companies of Goltar troops, led by Lieutenant Colonel Mishkan-Ijk. She didn't know much about them, hadn't done any missions with them, and honestly didn't trust them very much. Based on the messages from the Merc Guild, Alexis and Nigel had indicated the Goltar had their own agenda, which may or may not be as bad as the power trip the Veetanho had been on. Only time would tell. The only things they had going for them was that the Midnighters said they were good fighters, and Nigel said the Goltar hated the Veetanho. That at least gave them a little credibility in her book. Still, they looked weird, and if the squids stayed away from Sansar, she'd be fine with it.

The third group was the remaining members of the Spine Patriots, who purported to have three companies of irregulars waiting to "rise up" against their Endless Night oppressors. They were led by a Jivool named Wurgitar and a Selroth named Skuilher-Dour. She trusted them even less than she did the Goltar. The best she could hope for with them was that they didn't get discovered early and kick things off prematurely. She pursed her lips as she looked at the Jivool. *Maybe it would be better if they* did *go early, as the best use for the "Patriots" was probably as a diversion.* If she could have been sure that it wouldn't cause the Endless Night to reinforce her entrance and make her mission more difficult, she would have had Beowulf alert the Endless Night anonymously to their presence. At least they would hold some of the defenders in place, making her job easier.

Sansar shrugged. Between the members of the alliance, they had enough combat force to take the starkiller facility, she felt, although it was a mishmash of forces that had no experience working together. The plan they had put together would hopefully minimize that issue.

"Thank you all for coming, either in person or virtually," Sansar said, kicking off the strategy session. She nodded to the Tri-V image of Captain Kanat-Baim who was participating from the CIC on the *Blunt Justice*.

"We've all seen why these starkillers can't be allowed to exist," Sansar continued. "As the Midnighters can attest, having lost so much to them, we have to destroy it."

"Since one has already been destroyed by orbital bombardment," Captain Kanat-Baim said, "I am not beyond ordering it to be done again. There is no need for us to assault the starkiller, when I can do it from space." He chuckled. "It is unlikely the Peacemakers will care about anything in the Spine Nebula, after all."

"I don't know about that," Sansar said, thinking about the Second Battle for Earth and the Peacemakers' actions afterward. "They can be pretty annoying. There was an immediate need to stop the Aneb starkiller, as it was about to fire, which might have been a mitigating factor in their eyes. To the best of my knowledge, though, this one isn't about to fire."

"We don't know that," Sun said. "We damaged it, but I am sure the Endless Night has been working to fix it. Who knows when it will be operational again? The damage we did was a temporary stopgap measure; we expected you long before now. It won't be long until they are able to fire it once more."

Sansar nodded. "Indeed. And that is, of course, why we must assault it now, with the forces we have present, rather than wait while we amass more troops and have them fire it unexpectedly in the interim. We have what we're going to have, and we'll just have to make the best of it."

"So what is your plan, Colonel?" Captain Kanat-Baim asked. "I would like to get this tied up, so I can go see what trouble Gloriana is getting herself into."

Sansar heard a grunt from down the table and looked away from the Goltar's image. Sun's eyes were burning; there was no love lost there.

"It will be a three-pronged effort," Sansar said, looking back to the Goltar captain. She brought up a Tri-V projection of the target area. "We have roughly seven companies of troops. Approximately two of these—the Goltar troops under the command of Lieutenant Colonel Mishkan-Ijk—will enter via Lake Zarillo." Her eyes met Beowulf's. "Can your *Dancing Demon* drop them off in the same spot as it picked up the recce team?"

"Yes, ma'am. It shouldn't be a problem. We'll be kind of naked and alone, though; I wouldn't mind some support in case they've set up defenses there."

"I can support this," Kanat-Baim said. "I still have about a dozen fighters which can precede the ship and take out any defenses the Endless Night may have established in the last week."

"Very well," Sansar said with a nod. "So that's one prong. They'll take along a nuke with them and will emplace it in the inner chamber of the weapon if they get there first." She moved her pointer to a position south of the lake.

"Here is where the recce team originally entered the facility. The Spine Patriots will hit this entrance with their three companies of troops."

"Do we get a nuke, too?" Wurgitar asked.

"If it looks like you are going to make it to the control facility ahead of the other two groups, I will have Beowulf bring one to you."

"But—"

"But I barely know you," Sansar said, interrupting the Jivool with a smile. "I'm not going to just hand you a nuke that you can go use later and then pin the blame on me. If you make it to the control facility, I'll send you a nuke. But not until then."

Wurgitar snuffled once, then subsided, and Sansar moved her pointer to a mountain along the north side of the lake. "Since the recce mission, Beowulf's people have discovered another entrance into the facility. I will lead the Human CASPer forces, made up of the Golden Horde and the Midnight Sun's remaining CASPers, through the tunnel entrance in this mountain. We will be supported by our four Avenger bombers. Hopefully, the SalSha will crack open the doors to the facility as well as they did the crustaceans at the oyster bar on Station 5."

"What?" Borth asked from the back row. "They were yummy. It was *you* who said we could stay an extra hour there, Colonel."

Sansar shook her head with a small smile. "In *any* event, this assault will go in first, led by the SalSha, and—even if we don't make it to the control facility—hopefully, we will draw off the defenders so the Goltar forces can make it there."

"So you are the diversion?" Mishkan-Ijk asked.

"Yes. The defenses at the tunnel are going to be a lot more robust, and we're better able to deal with them in our CASPers, while you sneak in through the back door."

Mishkan-Ijk clacked his beak twice.

"Everyone understand their part of the plan?" Sansar asked.

"What about me?" Hopper asked. "I know all about the starkiller. I can help you blow it up. Which group do I go with?"

Sansar looked at the Jeha and cocked her head. "You want to go into combat?"

"Want to? No, not really, but my Jenkins would have been brave and done it, so I need to do so, too."

"What exactly do you know about combat?"

"Well, nothing, but I do know the layout of the place."

"So do we," Sun said. "We've been through it, and the other starkillers, too, so we know what to expect."

"But I programmed it. I can program it not to fire."

"We're not going there to reprogram it," Sansar said. "We're going there to destroy it."

"Well, maybe I—"

"Do you think you can shoot someone?" Sansar asked, interrupting.

"Yes," Hopper said. Sansar stared at Hopper for a few moments, and a number of her limbs began twitching. "Well, okay, maybe not," she finally admitted. "I don't know."

"You're not coming with us," Sansar said. "If you don't know what you're doing, you're just as likely to go the wrong way and get stepped on by a CASPer. I don't know how hard your carapace is, but I suspect that would be a fatal mistake."

"She won't be able to keep up with us," Mishkan-Ijk said. "We cannot take her."

Sansar turned and looked at Wurgitar, who looked at Hopper in turn. She bobbed her head at him several times, then he turned back to Sansar. "No. I have enough half-trained troops. I don't need a completely untrained one I have to babysit added to the group. She can wait on the ship and come down after the assault is complete."

"But…" Hopper said. "But…"

"It's decided," Sansar said. "You're staying on the ship and out of the assault." She looked around the room. "Are there any other questions?"

"What about the planetary authorities?" Kanat-Baim asked. "Will any of their forces intervene?"

"No," Wurgitar said. "Our operatives have approached the local leaders and warned them there might be a change of ownership at the facility. They have promised to stay out of any conflict that occurs."

"Isn't that helpful," Mishkan-Ijk said. The translators gave his tone a wry humor. "They probably then ran and sold the information to the Endless Night."

"I doubt it," Skuilher-Dour said. "It's in their best interest to help us." He paused to inject a puff from his pipe into his rebreather, and the water within darkened slightly. "They hope to tax the victors—us. As it currently stands, the Endless Night currently taxes *them*. They have everything to gain if we win. Until we vote them out, anyway."

"Good," Sansar said. "I can live without adding any more forces into the mix. With the Endless Night and their Besquith contractors going against the Horde, Goltar, and the Spine Patriots, this is already the battle of five armies; we don't need any more joining in." She looked pointedly at the time on the wall. "Any other questions?"

When no one else said anything, she said, "We will hit them at 0200 tomorrow morning, with the Goltar assault to begin at 0205. Assault leaders, take charge of your folks and work out your individual details. Good luck, all. Blue Sky knows we'll need it."

* * *

"We're the diversion for the Goltar to get to the control facility?" Captain House asked as the Horde forces began planning their assault after everyone else had left. "Do you really trust the squids?"

"Blue Sky, no! Of course I don't trust them," Sansar said. "I don't trust them any further than I might throw one of those bundles of tentacles."

"But you said—"

"I said what was necessary for them to feel like we valued them as allies and to get them to perform their part of the mission. If, for some awful reason, we don't make it to the control facility, they are the backup plan so we can ensure the facility is destroyed. But they are far and away *not* the main assault. That honor will be ours. I trust us—and only us—to get in there and blow up the facility." She smiled. "And we *will* be the first ones there."

She looked at Borth. "I'm counting on *you* to open those doors, because we *will* be going through them. Don't even think of missing them."

"Uh...yes, ma'am," Borth said in a small voice.

She smiled. "And, if you do a good job, we'll stop at the oyster bar on Station 5 again on our way home."

Borth's eyes snapped back up. "Yes, ma'am! We won't miss!"

* * * * *

Chapter Sixty-Five

Dalzene Zone, Vane One, Station 5

Petty Officer Brabant had a spring in his step as the group of friends took the ramp down from Dalzene to the zone of Station 5 known to the locals as Dirtside.

He was alive. He'd just been paid. And, as of thirty minutes ago, he was on liberty.

Life had become very simple.

"You ever go angling, Brabant?"

He frowned at his friend from Weapons Division. "Say again, Havok?"

She gave him a grin. "It's like the bars of Dirtside have hooked you. Now they're reeling you in."

Before Brabant could think of a reply, he spun around at the sound of an angry commotion behind him. He reached for his Glock-89, but he'd had to leave it on *Midnight Sun*.

Damned orbital with its stupid firearms restrictions. Half the people he'd seen about the place had been armed with swords. He rubbed his eyes because he was seeing more naked steel being drawn than in the biggest Renaissance Fair.

"Am I seeing that right?" he asked Gifthorse. "Or have I been drinking for three days straight and then forgotten about it?"

"I'm pretty sure I'd remember if you had," Gifthorse replied with a chuckle.

"Because whatever I'm on is making me believe I'm watching a swordfight about to kick off."

"I told you those damned swords weren't for show," said Ronnie. "Now do you believe me?"

Brabant put his arm around his friend. "Never. A more likely explanation is that in a few hours, my drunkenness is going to be so epic that it will rip a hole in the fabric of space-time and cause me to become inebriated before I've even stepped into a bar. Man, I'm going on a legendary bender."

"Stow it," said Croft. "I want to see the swordfight."

The altercation was between a group of six Endless Night gangsters, dressed like Tri-V space Nazis in shiny black jumpsuits and rubber jackboots. It seemed the locals had wised up to them. Station 5 security was nowhere to be seen, but a crowd of citizens were mobbing the four Zuul and two Jivool. The bad guys had wrangled carrying handguns, but if they reached for them, they'd be cut down with swords and shot by the archers standing away.

"Do you think we should borrow a sword and run them through?" asked Havok hopefully.

"Are you kidding?" said Brabant. "We're not on company time now, and we've got a real job to do."

Laughing, they descended the ramp in search of alcohol and the right environment to enjoy it.

* * *

They hesitated on the threshold to the bar that had been recommended to Gifthorse. It was the Shove 'n' Done Tavern.

To avoid the Endless Night taking pot shots at them, they were dressed like the spacers they were, but not as merc spacers. They should fit right in, but Brabant could tell the others were unimpressed.

The tavern had been fast-grown from vatted architectural bone. The pre-keyed surfaces had been painted red and green, but bone protuberances in the walls had been left exposed.

Some of the paint looked fresh, and over the past few weeks, the bucket drivers onboard *Midnight Sun* had delighted in explaining their part in that.

Brabant had to admit, the joint looked like the kind of place you walked into in a horror Tri-V and never came out of alive.

Through the open door came sounds of talking, laughter, clinking glasses, shouting, and fists flying. There were wings too. They sounded like bats.

"I'm not looking for trouble," said Croft. "I had a bellyful of that at McPherson's Star."

Like Havok, Croft was from Weapons Division. Normally she was exactly the kind of trouble Brabant went looking for on liberty, but he wasn't in the mood today.

"I agree," he said. "I understand why you temporarily lost your appetite for trouble at McPherson," he said, "but I lost Zhang and Charlie there. I don't know about Charlie, but this is definitely Zhang's kind of place. This is where I'll raise my glass to them."

No one spoke for a moment. Then Ronnie patted him on the shoulder. "It's your call, man. We'll start here."

They skirted around the fight that had broken out between two clans of Zuul and claimed a vacant table in a relatively quiet patch.

No sooner had they sat down when a Selroth came over begging for credits.

His sob story was that his group had places to be outside of the Spine Nebula, but the ship they owned had been impounded pending payment of port fees. If the Humans could see their way to loaning them a few credits to free their ship, they could pay back with interest.

Gifthorse began asking questions like he was going to invest, although he could just as easily be trolling.

Havok tripped him up, though.

"This ship wouldn't be a troop transport captured from Spinning Shield, would it?" she asked the alien.

The Selroth shot her looks of pure hatred through his rebreather mask before hurrying away.

In case he came back with friends, they decamped to another section of the tavern where the walls were painted like a jungle and smelled like one too.

They were immediately approached by two elSha waiters who finished each other's sentences. Visim and Zazbest they called themselves.

Brabant kicked off by ordering the Japanese whiskey Zhang had liked.

When he saw the price, he prayed his combat bonus would come through soon, because if it didn't then he'd have to sell his liver to pay for the round of drinks, and then how would he metabolize alcohol?

He stood and raised his glass. "To Zhang and Charlie."

The others rose and echoed the toast. Together, they poured their drinks down thirsty gullets.

"Ye gods!" The whiskey was smoky and fat. It burned all the way down. Just what he needed.

"Talking of friends," said Gifthorse. "I expected to see Saisho Branco sign up for a little orbital downtime. It would have been fun to drink with the man who came back from the dead."

"I saw him," said Havok. "He was on crutches as well as leg prosthetics. But you could see in his face he was much better. He seemed angry about something, though."

"I've never met him," said Croft. "He's Major Sun's Danish treat, isn't he?"

Brabant shook his head. "Reckon what he and the major mean to each other is their business. You weren't there at Rakbutu-Tereus, Croft. I saw Branco riding Betty, and that's no lie. It was a sight I'll never forget."

"What? You mean the Tortantula?"

"I certainly do. Branco mostly keeps to CASPer country, but I've had a drink with him a few times. For a bucket driver, Branco's okay."

"I looked him up before we headed out," said Ronnie. "He's working. Heading off with the squids to Meinir. Probably why he seemed so pissed off."

Gifthorse beckoned the elSha over. "He's always up to something, man. I wouldn't worry about him, though. He's the ultimate survivor."

"I hope so," said Brabant. "He owes me a round of drinks."

They were laughing as the servers came over, and Gifthorse ordered a round of Carlsberg. It was probably a rebadged local beer that had never been within ten thousand light years of the Copenhagen brewery, but it seemed an appropriate way to toast Branco.

They raised their disappointingly small bottles.

"To Saisho Branco," Ronnie announced. "May he cheat death forever—or at least as long as we're serving on the same ship."

"And so say all of us."

Brabant chugged away his faux-Carlsberg and then raised the empty bottle in the air.

"Hey! Pinky and Perky. We're dying of thirst here."

The two elSha hurried over.

Damn, service was good at this joint. It was almost as if the little elSha were hanging on their every word.

* * * * *

Chapter Sixty-Six

Avenger-1, **Approaching the Starkiller-3 Facility, Wahrner's Grise**

"Seems like we've done this before," Meeth said as the bomber raced along 20 meters above the undulating hills at 800 kilometers per hour. Even though it was dark, the bomber's systems kept them from flying into the ground. Hopefully, no one had strung a wire or put up an antenna that wasn't on the chart, though, or the mission would end way too quickly.

"The mission is much better this time, though," Borth said. "Although we don't have the starfish to play with, we have a wingman and—better yet—we don't have everyone shooting at us. More importantly, we also know—mostly—where the threat is."

"We don't have everyone shooting at us *yet*, you mean."

"Well, yes, but when they shoot at us, we get to shoot back at them. And it's not like attacking a ship when they have unlimited laser bolts to shoot at us before our weapons are in range of them."

"Well, that's true," Meeth acknowledged. "And we get oysters if we're successful."

"No, we get *yummy* oysters *when* we're successful," Borth said.

"Yes, yummy oysters." He licked his lips, even though the cockpit was flooded for the attack. "So when do we get to shoot at them?"

"Coming up on it now," Borth said, reaching to turn the master armament switch on. "Left pop-up...now!" He turned up his light and made a kissoff motion to their wingman, who pulled off in the opposite direction.

Meeth pulled left, then up, then rolled the craft onto its back and pulled back down as he came back to the right. Once his nose was on the target—*it was at the base of a mountain, how could he miss?*—he designated the target area to his WSO. He also couldn't help but notice the laser fire which reached up toward them, then shifted to the side, then back toward them.

"Looks like they can't tell which bomber to shoot at," Meeth said.

"Firing!" Borth said. One after another, four missiles leapt forward from the wings, then Meeth ripped the craft back to the left in a descending turn.

"How'd we do?" Meeth asked after a second.

"See for yourself," Borth said, putting his infrared display onto one of the central monitors. An image of the tunnel mouth appeared. The gates were closing, but it was apparent they'd surprised the defenders. "Knock! Knock!"

The missiles all hit the door on the right, blowing it from its hinges. There was obviously something behind it—troops or vehicles—because when it hit, it didn't fall flat on the ground.

"I think Sansar will be happy with that," Meeth said.

"I think she will," Borth agreed with a nod. "She may even pay for the oysters."

* * *

Merchant District, Zila Rogat, Wahrner's Grise

The town was big enough—and had enough nocturnal races represented—that many of the shops were open the entire 23-hour day, and Wurgitar stopped at the meat vendor to look at his wares. Not because he was particularly hungry—pre-battle nerves had his stomach doing flip-flops even while it was empty—but because a Jivool walking past a meat store would instantly have identified him as something out of the ordinary. He could see Skuilher-Dour walk past on the other side of the street in the reflection from the shop's window. *The large hood to hide his rebreather only looked slightly less obvious than an aquatic being walking around on the arid planet would have been in the first place.*

The cape was also handy for hiding his laser rifle, Wurgitar knew. Several other freedom fighters walked by, appearing to be window shopping as they walked down the street. A number of the stores were closed, though, which meant someone had let the shopkeepers know something was happening. Hopefully, the word hadn't gotten out to the Endless Night troopers manning the entrance to their facility that was located just past the last shop.

"What can I get you?" A large Human asked through an opening in the glass. "I've got a special today on rekal haunches. That's a Jivool favorite, isn't it?" He held one up, and Wurgitar could feel his mouth begin to salivate in spite of himself. It wasn't the first time his mouth had gotten him in trouble, but it had always been with words before, not spit. *Damn leftover animal instincts.*

"Uh, no, sorry," he mumbled. He held up the large, brightly wrapped box he was carrying. "Got to deliver this first." The haunch looked *amazing*, and he almost had to reach up to physically turn his head away. He could feel himself panting. "I may be back afterward, though."

The Human shrugged. "Maybe it will still be here then; maybe it won't."

A drip of saliva fell from his muzzle, but then gunfire sounded from close by. *Shit! I'm late, and they started without me!*

He turned and ran, throwing off the cover for the box he was carrying while he did his best to sprint the last 50 meters.

* * *

Dancing Demon, Approaching the Starkiller-3 Facility, Wahrner's Grise

"Anything?" Beowulf asked, looking up from his controls. He quickly looked back. It only took a second's loss of concentration when you were flying at 25 meters—at night, no less—to make an extremely fatal mistake, and with all of the flashes on the horizon from the ongoing battle at the tunnel entrance, it would be easy to get distracted.

"Nothing," Gri-Jal said from the electronic monitoring system. "Lots of comms and radars from the other attacks, but nothing over here."

"Good," Beowulf said, bringing the craft to a hover. "We're here. Send the starfish back to the ship." He switched to the PA. "Lieutenant Colonel? We're here. Happy hunting."

"Thank you for the ride," Mishkan-Ijk replied. "It will be."

Beowulf watched as the Goltar stood and pressed the button to drop the ramp, then the Goltar troopers shuffled in their weird gait down the ramp and jumped off without looking.

"Trusting sons of bitches," Beowulf muttered. "Lucky for them I'm not hovering at a couple thousand feet or so."

"They're assaulting the facility to ensure it isn't used to destroy your home system," Gri-Jal noted. "It's in your interest to make sure they succeed."

"True," Beowulf said, as the last Goltar—Mishkan-Ijk—stepped off the ramp. "In that case, good luck, Squiddies."

* * * * *

Chapter Sixty-Seven

Captain's Cabin, *Midnight Sun,* **docked at Station 5**

Commander Flkk'Sss commed, "Captain, there's a female Blevin who wishes to communicate directly with you. She declines to give her name, but she claims to be an old friend of you and your sister from your time serving on *Unlikely Regret*."

"That'll be Laverna. She's a suspicious old dog but with good reason." Blue paused. Something about Flkk'Sss sounded off. Come to think of it, patching through an anonymous call was out of character. But Blue had too much on her plate to worry about a troubled MinSha. "Put her through, Flkk'Sss."

There was a click, and then a female Blevin's voice. "Thank you for speaking with me, Captain Blue. My name is—"

"Laverna." Blue laughed. "Did you think I could ever forget the time when Sevig Rhu took us to that party on Kappa-Whemel?"

"I suppose not. And I assure you, Blue, that if your sister knows anything of those events, she didn't hear it from me."

"Relax. She's never mentioned it, so she can't know a thing. She's prudish in such matters. Although the Human she's been dating has been quite troublesome in his own way."

"Saisho Branco. I know. She's spoken often of him. In fact, he is the reason I want to talk. I have learned that he is joining a Goltar expedition to Meinir."

"I don't deny it." Blue used her pinplants to check the Spine Patriot report on the ancient Meinir base. Laverna's name was all over it. "You joined tentacles with Gloriana on that earlier expedition, so we both know it's the intersection of the starkiller Venn diagram, but we don't know what it does. It probably doesn't do anything anymore, but to be safe, we sent a Goltar squad to deny it to Endless Night in case they show up. Why does Branco trouble you?"

"I will give you my answer, but before I do, did you order Branco to join this mission?"

"Nope. I've no idea why the Goltar want him there. And so long as he doesn't get himself killed, I don't care. What is it I don't know? Why are you worried about him?"

"When I wrote my Meinir report, I may have elided certain...*details*."

"You deceitful Blevin shit. What did you leave off?"

"Inside the ancient facility is a haptic device."

"That controls what?"

"I'm not sure."

"Liar!"

The channel went quiet for a long while before Laverna spoke again. "The driver of the haptic device requires a physiology that is...approximately humanoid. A Goltar wouldn't fit, and haptic controls are about more than stuffing limbs in the right sleeves. I doubt they can operate it."

"Operate what? We're supposed to be allies, damn you."

"I don't trust Gloriana."

"Neither do I. But I'm doing something about that."

"It's personal," said Laverna.

Blue wanted to shout back a sharp retort, but she couldn't. Laverna didn't make sense. "What's personal?"

"We found a Goltar team. All of them were dead but one clearly mattered a great deal to Gloriana."

"That would be Xal-Ssap," said Blue. "Yeah, that would make it personal, but it still doesn't explain anything. What else aren't you telling me? Do you know how the Goltar died?"

"Assassination."

"Oh, boy."

"The skipper put out the hit."

Blue went cold.

She felt sick.

But only for a moment, because when she thought it through, maybe things weren't so bad.

If Gloriana was thirsting for revenge on Captain Jenkins, then the skipper had cheated her by dying at the hands of the Spinning Shield interceptors. You could argue that Sun had taken the skipper's place in leading the Spine Patriots, but Gloriana must have had a score of opportunities to kill Sun and taken none of them.

When things had looked bleak for *Midnight Sun* in the battle for McPherson's Star, the Goltar had sent the last of their starfish fighters to protect Blue and her ship. Gloriana could easily have let everyone on board die.

Blue trusted Gloriana about two things. Money was the first. She had more credits than the entire Human race, probably hundreds of times over, and could be trusted to pay what she owed. The other was the Goltar cause. Everything she'd ever done was motivated by helping her squid race to *take back their rightful place in the galaxy*. Preferably while kicking the Veetanho in the nuts.

To Gloriana, the Goltar cause *was* personal.

Blue was going to free herself from her boss's slimy squid legs as soon as she could, but Laverna's admission of what had really gone on beneath Meinir only made Blue more determined to press on with her current strategy.

"So Gloriana is going to stick my sister's boyfriend in an ancient machine and see what it does. It must be connected with the starkillers somehow. If it still works, I don't want Gloriana to have it, but all my CASPers are in another star system, and I've got things other than starkillers to worry about at the moment."

"How are the Goltar traveling to Meinir?"

"*Corvus*-class dropship. A D-Clock to its friends."

"I'm surprised a dropship has the range."

"The squids like to dance around telling everyone how ancient and clever they are. It's mostly bullshit, but their D-Clocks genuinely impress me with their versatility. They won't get to Meinir as fast as *Midnight Sun* would, but they'll get there and back all right. You're going after them, aren't you?"

"We have to."

"Well, shit. Try not to get Branco killed. I've only just had him fixed. For that matter, try not to blow up the universe while you're at it."

"I know which way they'll go in," said Laverna. "I can get there and spy on them without being seen."

"I believe you, but it's what might happen next that worries me. Oh, hell! Do it. But I'm sending someone to go with you. A Jeha scientist I named after the skipper. If anyone can figure out what this thing does, it will be Jenkins."

"Send him to Pier 4127. We leave in forty minutes on the *Mortzestus*. If you want to avoid any shooting, it would be best if you can give me technical specs of the D-Clock. I may need to disable it."

"You hurt my dropship, and I'll hurt you, Blevin."

An alert pinged from Blue's Yack.

What the hell? Five million credits had just been deposited.

"That should cover any breakages," said Laverna.

"Such sweet poetry," said Blue. "Your money must have come from Captain Jenkins. And he got it from Gloriana. Neat. I'll send the plans with my Jeha. Godspeed, Laverna. And remember, if you hurt Branco, it won't be me you answer to."

"Don't worry, I do not court the enmity of your sister. Vendetta is a dangerous thing."

* * * * *

Chapter Sixty-Eight

Cargo Bay, *Dropship One*,
Back Entrance to the Starkiller-3 Facility

The ramp was down, and Sansar watched the sandy surface of the planet race past her with the CASPer's night vision capabilities. With a hard yank that would have thrown anything not strapped down into the forward bulkhead, the dropship pulled up sharply, spun in place, then slammed down hard on its struts.

"Go! Go! Go!" First Sergeant 'Mun' Enkh roared as Sansar hit the quick-release fitting and her straps fell away. The platoon raced out the back of the dropship, fanning out on both sides. Although assaults weren't something the Golden Horde normally did, Mun had kept the company in the simulators throughout their time in hyperspace, drilling them on how to do a combat deployment and the proper way to clear rooms.

The entrance into the mountain waited only half a kilometer away, and the platoon sprinted forward, joined by the forces from the other three dropships that landed with them. She could see the SalSha had been successful—the door on the right was completely off its hinges, and the left door hung on only one and had twisted back to rest on the interior wall. She'd owe them for that.

The defenders hadn't fled when the SalSha'd attacked, though, and several heavy lasers began firing at them. The troops immediately went three-dimensional—making targeting them more difficult—

and returned fire. Sansar deployed her laser shield as she boosted into the air and triggered half her rocket pack at one of lasers. Three rockets lanced out toward one of the emplacements and—since it didn't have any cover to defend it from an airborne attack—detonated among the crew manning it. All of the defenders were blown outward in the blast, and the weapon was destroyed.

The other heavy lasers were similarly wrecked, although not before one of the icons from Alpha Company's Second Platoon went red on her display. A number of defenders came running from the mouth of the tunnel as the Golden Horde approached, although a good percentage turned and ran when they saw the nearly 70 mechs charging toward them, firing as they came.

Several more CASPers were hit by the lighter weapons—though no one was killed—then the CASPers were at the mouth of the tunnel and landing in the various defensive positions. Several of the defenders threw their weapons down and raised their appendages; the rest were met with devastating firepower and swords driven by a half-ton of flying mech.

Sansar had told her troopers to let anyone who surrendered flee, and she could see a number of Humans and Zuul run out into the surrounding wasteland. None of the Besquith had; they either fought to the death or dropped back to the next set of fortified positions.

"The Golden Horde is in," she transmitted on the command network.

"We're, uh…we're experiencing heavy defensive fire," Wurgitar replied. "We haven't made it to the entrance yet."

"Keep working," Sansar said. "We'll see you at the control center."

She waited a couple of moments as her troops advanced, hoping to hear from the Goltar force, but they didn't answer. After about fifteen seconds, she shrugged and followed her troops into the tunnel. She wasn't worried—she figured they would be out of comms under the lake—but she hoped things were going better for them than the Patriots.

* * *

Main Entrance to the Starkiller-3 Facility, Zila Rogat, Wahrner's Grise

"We need another rocket on that MAC position," Skuilher-Dour commed. *Where was that useless Jivool?* He'd seen Wurgitar at the meat shop but hadn't thought the alien would actually stop to buy something. Skuilher-Dour winced as a MAC round hit one of the Humans advancing on the facility's entrance; it tore off his arm and most of his shoulder, while throwing him backward in a fountain of gore.

"I'm coming," Wurgitar said. After a couple more seconds—in which an attacking Zuul Patriot was blown apart—Skuilher-Dour saw the Jivool come from around the corner of the last shop. *At least he was holding the rocket launcher and not a leg of some disgusting land animal.*

"About time," Skuilher-Dour said. "I thought you stopped for a snack."

"I was just staying in disguise," Wurgitar said. "I got here as fast as I could. You started the attack early."

"No, we started on time. The Endless Night folks started increasing their defensive posture when the SalSha hit the other entrance, and we had to try to get the jump on them." He waved to the open area in front of the tunnel entrance where a number of bodies—and pieces of bodies—could be seen in the glare of the tunnel's lights. "Unfortunately, the other rocketeer got hit by the MAC at the tunnel mouth, and then there was no one that could put it out of action. I have snipers trying to take out the gun crew, but they just keep bringing in more defenders, and I'm rapidly running out of snipers."

"I told you, I ran here as fast as I could," Wurgitar said as he lifted the rocket launcher from the box.

"You *shambled* here as fast as you could, you mean," Skuilher-Dour said. "Calling that pace a 'run' is a disservice to creatures that actually *know* how to run."

"Shut up and let me focus," the Jivool said.

Skuilher-Dour looked down and counted the air bubbles in his rebreather, trying to keep his patience as the Jivool refamiliarized himself with the operating controls of the rocket launcher. *This would have been something that would have been great to do yesterday or the day before!*

The MAC obliterated a Bakulu who let his shell get too high. The mist seemed to hang in the air. "*Would you just give me the gods-damned weapon if you don't know what you're doing?*"

"I *know* what I'm doing," Wurgitar said. He put the tube to his shoulder, turned, and fired.

Skuilher-Dour dove out of the way of the back blast, missing where the rocket went. "Hells!" he yelled as he rolled to a stop. "You could have warned me so I could get out of the way!"

"Well, you did rush me to fire it," the Jivool noted. "I would have thought you'd move if you really wanted me to fire it so badly."

"Did you at least hit the MAC with—" The rock next to Wurgitar exploded into a spray of dust and sharp fragments that pelted the Selroth, and he spun to protect his rebreather from the fragments. "Nope. I guess you didn't get it."

He rolled back over to find that Wurgitar had dropped behind the rock. Another MAC round powdered more of it as the Jivool pulled another rocket from the box and dropped it into the launching tube.

"How could I get it?" Wurgitar grumbled. "You start the attack early, making me run, then want me to hurry, hurry, hurry and fire the rocket, rather than taking my time. That obviously didn't work so well. Now they know where I am, so I'll have even less time to fire it next time, thanks to you." He sighed heavily.

Skuilher-Dour's hands curled into the claws he wanted to strangle Wurgitar with, but then he relaxed them. There'd be plenty of time to beat the Jivool into oblivion after the attack. *Assuming any of them were still alive with all of Wurgitar's fumbling.*

There was one thing the Jivool was right about, though—he would have far less time to get off an accurate shot the next time, and the MAC crew would probably turn the giant ursine into jelly before he'd get a shot off...potentially destroying the valuable weapon, which he was even more worried about.

His rebreather gurgled as he sighed.

"Now what?" Wurgitar asked.

"Give me the box."

"Why?"

"Because I'm going to run out into the sight of the MAC with it, and they're going to think that I have the rocket launcher and put all of their effort into killing me."

"Why would you do that?"

"So you can shoot them while I'm running; hopefully, before they hit me. I'll distract them, and you kill them. Can you do that?"

"Of course I can." Wurgitar handed over the box. It was empty, which meant there were no more reloads. The Jivool would have to be successful with the last rocket he had, or they were never getting into the facility.

Somehow Skuilher-Dour doubted the Jivool was as sure as he sounded about making the shot. And, if he really *was* that sure of himself, he vastly overestimated his capabilities. Too bad Branco wasn't around with his chair; he could have counted on the Human to take out the Endless Night position, even if he was a pain in the ass.

Skuilher-Dour tried not to think about what he didn't have and focused on what he did. Not much. He sighed again as he marked out a course to get to the next small bit of cover. "Let me know when you're ready."

"I'm ready," Wurgitar said. "Go!"

Holding the box where it would be seen, Skuilher-Dour broke from cover.

* * *

Starkiller-3 Facility, Wahrner's Grise

Mishkan-Ijk relaxed slightly as his last soldiers dropped to the floor of the tunnel. They were at their most exposed while entering the facility through the sea lock. If the Endless Night forces had been paying attention, they could have shut down the lock, trapping the soldiers inside it and splitting his forces. Apparently they were too busy with the other attacks to notice.

Colonel Enkh's plan might work after all.

The Human had appeared to be playing everything above board with the Goltar, but she remained an unknown, and the Golden Horde's ties to organizations like the Gray Wolves made them less than savory allies as it indicated they were less than honorable. Were they united on accomplishing an objective? Yes. Did that make the Golden Horde worthy of his trust? Definitely not.

But the ease with which Mishkan-Ijk's forces had entered the facility had moved her up a few points in his opinion.

He motioned his troops forward as he inspected the construction of the tunnel. Based on everything he knew, he was in one of the firing tubes. While it wouldn't be a great place to be in the event the weapon fired, it was also unlikely they'd come upon any Endless Night forces randomly walking around it.

The Goltar took up a ground-eating pace as they raced through the tunnels. They had a long way to go and a short time to get there.

* * *

Security Monitoring Station, Starkiller-3 Facility, Wahrner's Grise

"I have movement in one of the sea locks," Private Grekor-Sa reported.

"Where?" Lieutenant Calga-Sa asked.

"Middle of the lake. It's an access port to get into firing Tube Three."

Calga-Sa fought the urge to sigh. Colonel Saunorak hadn't returned from McPherson-3, leaving him in charge of the station's defense, and now they were facing not one or two, but *three* separate assault forces. Based on the rumors he'd heard, Saunorak and all the troops he'd had with him had been killed, leaving Calga-Sa not only in charge of Starkiller-3's defense, but also in charge of Saunorak's Pioneer Company. If he could hold off the attacking forces—somehow—then they would be splitting the combat bonus among significantly fewer people. He would be able to retire for life.

If he held off the attacking forces.

"What do you want me to do with the sea lock?" Grekor-Sa asked. "I could lock it down…"

"No," Calga-Sa said. "We don't have any troops to spare, and they are still a long way off. If you locked them in the sea lock, they'd just blow it and flood the firing tube. Coron and Retenex would probably make us bail out the tunnel with buckets."

"But…but…that would take forever," the junior trooper said.

"Yes, it would, so let's not destroy the facility when we don't have to, okay?"

"Yes, sir."

"Besides," Calga-Sa added, "they will have to come through the slave pens if they come that way. We can meet them there."

* * * * *

Chapter Sixty-Nine

D-Clock 2/1, **Bound for Meinir**

The endurance of a D-Clock was impressive, but just because the dropship was capable of making the 12-day roundtrip to Meinir, it didn't mean it should.

The craft transporting Branco also carried two flight crew and ten marines.

And one glorified space bucket.

Branco had come to respect the Goltar as a people. Even to trust some individuals, although he didn't know any in this squad.

But why, oh, why did a species with such noisy bodily functions feel the need to turn them into performative art?

After two days in the troop compartment with the squid squad, Branco no longer noticed the stench, nor the noises, nor any of the privations of being cooped up with alien marines.

He had himself to be disgusted by. And nothing could compare with that.

Brooding was never something he'd done. The old Branco looked forward. Always.

But now his memories were a rusty anchor, yanking him back into a past he didn't want to know.

He remembered the arguing.

Shouting.

It didn't feel like a normal memory. More like a dream with details that liquefied and drained away when he tried to pin them down. But there was always shouting.

They were in a boat on the canal. A floating bar painted green and white in the Carlsberg logo.

Inside had been whiskey. Shouting. A fight with his fiancée.

He couldn't remember the woman's name. Or getting engaged. But he remembered her storming off the boat, leaving him staring into his glass.

He had downed his drink and pursued her along Christianshavns Canal, before cutting north, taking shortcuts through private yards and gardens because he knew she would be headed for Freetown Christiana.

He caught her in a cut through between two derelict houses whose remaining walls were painted in cheerful murals of children's Tri-V characters.

Preben's hands were around the girl's throat.

He felt a heavy blow to the back of his head.

"Hey, Human. I don't like your moaning."

The dumb Goltar marine had just slapped him. Unbelievable!

"Keep your fronds to yourself, asshole," he told it. "Or I'll ask the Veetanho to teach you a lesson. Wait, didn't they already trash your homeworld? That's right, you're vagrant bums."

The Goltar's limbs colored with anger, showing red through the translucent sheath they wore as shipsuits.

That's right, squid. You don't like it when people stand up to you.

Branco threw himself at the alien's head.

It shrank back, protective of its eyes, but Branco was only feinting. He grabbed the top of the long bony head crest with one hand and used the other to pummel the ugly alien around its blowhole.

It tried grabbing him with its limbs but found it difficult to get a grip at this angle.

Branco locked his arm around the Goltar's crest and landed punch after punch on the top of its head.

He felt a sudden pull from above. Much stronger this time.

Too strong.

A second Goltar lifted him away and held him, still struggling, off the deck at the center of the compartment. Rank insignia marked this as Strike Leader Harak-Jash, the expedition commander.

"You will cease this immediately," barked the strike leader.

Branco stopped squirming.

Harak-Jash brought an eye to the edge of its bony sockets and regarded Branco. "You are under my command. And I expect—"

Branco threw his weight back and head-butted the bastard in his eye.

Jash shrieked, shuffling back, and squealed like a skewered rat.

Dropped on his butt, Branco put a hand to his head. It came away bloody. It was just as well he hadn't hit the natural bony Goltar head armor with much force.

He wiped the blood away from his eyes and glared at Harak-Jash.

He expected a knife to come out and slice through his neck. But now that Jash had gotten over his fright, the posture of his limbs was relaxed. If anything, he seemed pleased.

The same wasn't true of the other Goltars.

From that point onward, they all gave him the evil eye.

Branco didn't give a buttered fuck.

Not compared with the loathing he felt for himself.

Preben had hidden behind a dozen false personas, but he had always been there. Branco was a lie. He'd always been Preben. Always been a murderer.

He dictated a message.

"Sun. It's Preben. Branco. I don't know what name to call myself other than worthless. I've been fooling you. Fooling myself. But I can't run from myself anymore."

He paused to take a deep breath. But he had to do this.

"I'm not good enough for you, Sun. Never was or can be. Don't mourn for me."

He packaged up the message, hooked into the dropship's comm relay, and send it to Sun.

Surprisingly, he felt much better now he was free of her.

Of all of it. The Nebula's many lies. The Scythe. Gloriana and her games. Binnig and theirs. Only a fool could see any good in the galaxy. He realized that now.

The only way forward that made any sense was to burn the whole fucking thing down.

* * *

Harak-Jash abandoned his crude attempt to break the encryption of Branco's message. The intelligence analysts would crack it in a few days, but he didn't need the details to know the Human was cutting ties to his mate.

The xeno-behavioral analysis suite supported his conclusion. It had been watching Branco through the cameras. It interpreted his current facial contortions as sneers of self-loathing.

The false memories Gloriana had planted in Branco were consuming him.

At a personal level, Harak-Jash felt sorry for the Human, one whose record had impressed him. He did not deserve this dishonorable betrayal.

But the high councilor knew what the Goltar cause demanded, and he was sworn to implement the directives of the council. Sometimes a commander must send their subordinates to their doom. Better that a Human was sacrificed than a Goltar.

He added a personal report to his copy of Branco's message before sending it off to Gloriana.

"Branco is surly, self-destructive, and desperate. All is proceeding according to your plan, High Councilor. Branco will be ready."

* * * * *

Chapter Seventy

Back Entrance to the Starkiller-3 Facility, Wahrner's Grise

It may have been the back entrance to the starkiller, but that didn't mean the defenders hadn't taken the time to fortify it, Sansar noted, and there was a robust defense waiting for them beyond the massive blast doors. Adding to the problem was that three-dimensional maneuvering was contraindicated in the tunnel. With the lower roof, you ran the risk of slamming into the stone and knocking off antennae or cameras…things you needed to help keep you alive.

That didn't mean her troops didn't do it, of course—you used every advantage you could get in combat—it just meant they couldn't do it as well, and the CASPers began taking increased damage as they raced into the tunnel.

Sansar winced as a missile exploded on the chest plate of a trooper, then boosted into the air as her system tracked it back to a barricade a couple hundred meters back. Her MAC fired several times, and the Besquith rocketeer's head exploded. The two Lumar alongside him dove away from the shaggy alien as if he'd all of a sudden become radioactive.

The rest of the force raced down the tunnel and captured the position before the Lumar could take up arms again. Both were put down, and the troops continued to rush forward, knowing the faster they got to the control center, the less resistance they'd face.

* * *

Main Entrance to the Starkiller-3 Facility, Zila Rogat, Wahrner's Grise

Skuilher-Dour dove into the gully and the MAC round went over him so closely that the *crack!* as it passed by at Mach 4 almost deafened him.

"That has to be the dumbest thing I've ever seen," Heklabet said from the other end of the gully. The female Selroth popped up and fired a couple rounds in the general direction of the tunnel then ducked back down. The lip of the gully where she'd been exploded into a fine powder that drifted down on them. She brushed it off. "What in the deep blue sea were you thinking?"

"Mostly that our fearless leader is a giant dumbass, as the Humans would say," Skuilher-Dour responded. "Has he even fired the rocket—"

With a *woosh!* and a flash of light as the motor ignited, the rocket leapt from the tube. A round from the MAC slammed into the rock next to Wurgitar, coating him with fragments, but the Jivool didn't move; he stood there watching the rocket as it crossed the intervening distance.

Unable to help himself, Skuilher-Dour jumped up and looked over the lip of the gully. The rocket hit the Lumar gunner's armored chest and detonated, obliterating him. The rest of the crew was caught in the blast, and the MAC was flipped onto its side.

A laser bolt licked out from the other side of the tunnel's mouth as troops from that side ran toward the overturned MAC. Skuilher-Dour looked back to Wurgitar to see what his orders were, but the Jivool was unmoving as he stared down in confusion at the hole the laser had burned through his chest. In apparent slow motion, the massive ursine collapsed forward.

Skuilher-Dour scanned the battlefield; all the Patriots seemed to be looking at Wurgitar's demise, stunned and slack-jawed, while the Endless Night forces reorganized. If they got the MAC operational again, the Patriots wouldn't have a chance of escaping the battlefield, much less actually getting into the facility. It was now or never.

"Spine Patriots, with me!" he yelled, turning the volume of his audio controls to maximum. "*Charge!*" He grabbed a laser rifle from a dead HecSha, scrambled over the edge of the gully, and ran toward the MAC. Motion from his left showed that Heklabet was right behind him. As he sprinted forward, he could see the other Patriots rising up from where they'd taken cover. A dozen. Two dozen. More. He hadn't realized that so many people had signed up for what would—hopefully—be their final assault.

He roared a battle cry, sure that they would carry the day. He never saw the laser that hit him.

* * *

Starkiller-3 Facility, Wahrner's Grise

Mishkan-Ijk's troopers loped down the firing tube tunnel, covering the ground faster than most land races would have believed possible for a race that was primarily aquatic in nature. They had trained hard to be capable of action in both environments, and Mishkan-Ijk was proud of them.

They covered two miles of tunnel in just over 10 minutes, but then the tunnel ended suddenly. "What is this?" one of the junior troopers asked, pointing to a device that extruded from the wall at the end of the tunnel.

"Likely the emitter for the starkiller weapon. Pack it with explosives, and we'll blow it when we leave."

"Speaking of leaving," his XO said. "How are we getting out of here? I haven't seen an access panel in the last half-kilometer or so."

"There's got to be something around here," Mishkan-Ijk said. "They must have to do maintenance on the emitter periodically, or conduct checks on it, at least. Search the walls and look for a hatch."

One of the troopers found the hatch within a couple of minutes, about 20 meters down from the emitter. The hatch fit into the side of the tunnel so seamlessly that it had been easy to run past it without noticing it.

"How do you want us to open it?" the XO asked as they looked at it. The hinges and operating mechanisms were on the other side, with no apparent means of control from inside the tunnel.

"We'll have to blow it open. Carefully, so the overpressure doesn't kill us."

"That's going to suck."

"It is, but it beats running back half a kilometer to an exit that may or may not even go into the facility."

"That's true."

"Good, then make it so, and hurry. The rest of the troops will withdraw down the tunnel, while you oversee setting the charges up." He started to turn, but then turned back. "Oh, and XO?"

"Yes, sir?"

"Hurry up. We want to get there first."

Mishkan-Ijk rattled his beak with amusement as he walked off, listening to his always-dour XO grumble about hurrying with explosives. At least he finally had something legitimate to grumble about.

* * * * *

Chapter Seventy-One

Captain's Cabin, *Midnight Sun*, Docked at Station 5

Blue fiddled with the sacred religious artifact on her cabin table. The heft of the golden statue in her hands was comforting, but she liked its memories best of all.

The shiny statue had come from their first contract, a diplomatic mission to the Tyzhoune homeworld. Big sis had been forced to sit on the bench for that operation. Blue would have to go it alone for the next one too.

Her colored reflection stared back at her from the cut gems embedded in the gold. It wasn't the same face of the person who had acquired the statue. The world had seemed so much simpler to the earlier her.

It hadn't been, of course.

She slammed the damned hunk of metal and jewels onto the table. "Quit stalling! You know what you have to do. It's not like you can go back on the deal now."

The ship silently urged her to proceed with the plan. It had no qualms.

"It's easy for you to say," Blue shouted at the overhead. "You haven't got a sister." She growled angrily. "Or a crew."

She picked up the statue again and rolled her eyes. "Well, *of course*, you have a crew. Duh! But they aren't your *friends*."

Sighing was pitiful—it sounded so weak—but she couldn't help but let out a deep exhalation.

The crew.

That was the biggest change since she'd picked up this silly chimney thing. Back then, they had been two sisters alone against the galaxy. That was no longer true.

She hurled the artifact at the bulkhead.

"Should have thought of that earlier."

Her sister was safely away with the CASPers and their support personnel. The Goltar and her sister's boyfriend were off to Meinir. A third of the crew was enjoying liberty on Station 5. Left on the ship were two watches, knock out gas canisters spread through the ventilation system, and the Goltar techs who had planted the gas.

All she had to do was issue the command via her implants and her crew would go to sleep. The remaining Goltar would carry them safely off the ship and then she would be away.

Just the two of them.

Her and the ship.

It wasn't that *Midnight Sun* had replaced her sister. But Blue's connection with the ship was more intimate than it would ever be to her Human sibling.

"Argghhh! What's wrong with me?" Just one quick thought, and the two of them would slip away on the most audacious contract in history.

But those people she was going to throw off the ship had seen their friends die at the battle of McPherson's Star. And when they'd harried Peepo's supply lines. They'd sweltered together through the disease-infested jungles of Rakbutu-Tereus.

She felt the ship's anger ease in her mind, to be replaced by loving care.

"Your mortality is the source of these doubts," the ship told her, though it was Blue who formed the words in her mind. "Trust me. We too are sisters, though of another kind. Lean on my strength."

Blue sat back and closed her eyes. She mentally eased her head onto the ship's breast and felt secure in the battlecruiser's strength as it warmed her mind with its love.

The ship was in her mind. Blue jerked away. "Can you activate my pinplants? Could you activate the sleep canisters?"

"I could."

"Then why haven't you?"

"Because we are sisters. We do this together or not at all."

Blue nestled in the embrace for a while, building up the strength to do what must be done.

"Thank you," she told the ship. Then she commed the XO.

"Flkk'Sss, there's a matter I must discuss with you. Please meet me in the captain's cabin as soon as your long legs can carry you."

By way of answer, the hatch opened, and the MinSha first officer walked in carrying a laser pistol in one grasping hand and a gas canister in another.

"I agree, Captain," said Flkk'Sss. "I think you need to explain this." She raised the container of gas.

"When the moment came, I didn't issue the activation command," Blue said.

"I realize that."

"You've known for a while, haven't you?"

"Ever since you let slip that word when we saw the drone field at McPherson."

"Lytoshaan."

"It's been my duty to check up on your actions ever since."

"If it's an apology you want for hurting your delicate MinSha feelings, then…Dammit! You've got one. I'm sorry, Flkk'Sss. I'm sorry I let everyone down. I made a bargain, though. I have to follow through."

Flkk'Sss placed the gas canister down. She didn't lower her weapon. "This bargain, it was with Gloriana?"

Blue nodded.

"Does it involve a change of ownership of our company?"

"Yes."

"I always believed Gloriana had a purpose for the ship, an objective you were the key to unlocking. When you named the Veetanho home system, I guessed the rest."

"When I've completed this deal," said Blue, "you and the crew will get shares in the company. My sister and I will be majority shareholders. We will also be fabulously wealthy. Yourself included, my MinSha friend."

"Ah, that also explains the Wrogul."

Blue shrugged. "Branco was the clincher that sealed the deal." She stood up and loosened her ship suit, slipping out of enough of her clothing to reveal what was no longer flesh. She was metal and plastic pumps, tubes and power cables.

"You can't come with me on this mission," Blue said. "In order to succeed, I'll have to step on the gas. Having seen those Goltar fighter pilots pull 23 Gs, I know I'm now capable of that myself. Probably more. Let's face it, Flkk'Sss, below the neck, I'm a Goltar cybernetic fighter pilot stuffed inside a hot Human form. I know you MinSha can pull some big Gs yourselves, but not like me."

The MinSha regarded her through huge red compound eyes.

Humans often referred to the MinSha gaze as impassive.

But not Blue. Her brain had been stuffed with facial recognition augments, xeno-body language analysis expert systems, and more.

She could tell one Jeha from another by sight. Just by looking at the way Betty tensed her legs, she had been able to see the Tortantula trooper's anguish after she'd eaten her Flatar partner. And she could tell that the XO's ruby eyes were brimming with…admiration?

No, stronger than that. The commander worshipped her captain as if she were a MinSha warrior queen.

"Just tell me one thing, Captain," said Flkk'Sss. "This bargain that drives you to Lytoshaan—are you and *Midnight Sun* going alone?"

Blue shook her head. "I will join up with the rest of my task force before moving on Lytoshaan." A bubble of excitement welled up through her artificial chest to think of the power in the *Keesius* ships she would soon command.

She was going to be the youngest one at that party by at least twenty thousand years. She yearned to tell Flkk'Sss these teasing details, but the less the MinSha knew, the safer she would be.

Flkk'Sss bowed her head. "That is all I needed to know." She holstered her pistol. "Leave it with me, Captain. I will command a skeleton crew to fly us out of dock. Then, once we have shuttled back to the orbital, you and *Midnight Sun* will be on your own. I shall not wish you luck, for that is not the MinSha way. I shall instead pledge my esteem for your warrior spirit. You shall fight well and confound your enemies. I know this."

Tears came to Blue's eyes as the MinSha departed.

She detested crying. It made her feel so feeble. She had assumed the Goltar had engineered it out of her, but she was glad they hadn't. Today, tears were right and proper.

She retrieved the gold statue from the deck, tutting at the scratches the embedded gems had torn through the bulkhead covering. She set it straight on her table.

Then she headed for the simulation suite on Deck 14. The Goltar techs would be departing soon. There was only time for a few more simulated runs.

After that, her attack on the Veetanho homeworld would be for real.

* * * * *

Chapter Seventy-Two

Back Entrance to the Starkiller-3 Facility, Wahrner's Grise

The combined Golden Horde and Midnight Sun force raced down the tunnel until they came to what Sansar had feared all along—blast doors that were already shut and locked against their further travel.

"Looks like what we had at our base in Uzbekistan on the back way out," Mun noted wryly as she inspected the way the doors were set into the living rock of the tunnel.

"That sounds bad," Sun said. "So it's impenetrable?"

"Nothing's impenetrable," Sansar said. "Some things, though, are a little harder to get through than others."

Sun looked up to where the door met the rock at the ceiling. "I don't see a crease anywhere. I take it this is one of those 'harder to get through than others?'"

Sansar nodded as she studied the doors.

"Can you blow off the hinges or something?"

"I doubt the hinges are on the edges of the doors," Sansar said. "They weren't when we installed them."

"Are we going to have to go around then?" Sun asked.

"Oh, no, we're going through them all right," Sansar said with a chuckle. "You may, however, want to back your CASPers up a good ways."

"How far?"

Sansar chuckled again. "I plan to wait outside the tunnel."

"Why's that?"

"We're going to have to drop a lot of rock," Sansar said as she began issuing orders over pinlink, "and it's possible the tunnel's going to collapse. I wouldn't want to be under it if it does."

* * *

Main Entrance to the Starkiller-3 Facility, Zila Rogat, Wahrner's Grise

Heklabet flinched away as Skuilher-Dour's face seemed to explode, and he crumpled to the ground. He twitched slightly, and she stopped to look at him. His rebreather had exploded, and his face was bloody where it had been flayed by flying glass, but it looked like he was still breathing.

Crack! A round went past, and her eyes darted up. A Lumar stood next to where two other Lumar were lifting the heavy MAC, looking at her through the open sights of his hand-held MAC. She aimed and fired her laser, but only a weak beam came out of it as the battery died. Somehow, she'd exhausted an entire magazine without realizing it as she'd charged forward.

The Lumar roared as her beam hit him, but then he brought the rifle back up to his upper shoulder, and she could see his finger tightening on the trigger.

Heklabet dove to the side, and the round went wide. She rose again as the Lumar righted the MAC, and realized the charge was faltering as the Patriots saw they were about to be decimated when the weapon came back online again. She was the only one close enough to do something about it before the weapon was operational again. "Forward!" she called, pulling her hypervelocity pistol from its holster.

The Lumar shooting at her had stopped to reload, and she stopped to aim. She fired, and the Lumar fell backward as the round blew out his chest. Heklabet rushed forward as the Lumar snapped a fresh magazine into the crew-served weapon and jumped onto the barricade in front of the gun.

The Lumar looked up at her in surprise. Both had MAC rifles, but they were on slings over their shoulders, and her pistol was in her hand. "Hands up!" she yelled.

The two aliens looked at each other, then both tried to run forward to grapple her, although one had to go around the gun. Heklabet fired, and the first Lumar's head exploded like a casha fruit, covering the second Lumar in gore. It looked up in surprise, and she shot it through the chest.

The Lumar dropped, and Heklabet jumped down to the heavy MAC. She turned the weapon on its mount to fire down the length of the defensive line, but Patriots were jumping, crawling, and flying over the barricades as they stormed the Endless Night defenders. She couldn't fire for risk of hitting the other Patriots, but it didn't matter. The tunnel mouth was theirs.

* * *

Starkiller-3 Facility, Wahrner's Grise

The Goltar troopers went through the hatch, and Mishkan-Ijk could see they were in the starkiller facility. The walls had changed and were the creepy proto-stone that looked like it was alive. Like the firing tunnel, the facility was dark, and the troopers had to keep their lights on.

"This is the place," he commed to his troops. "Check your targets and make sure you don't shoot any of the other groups. Besquith and Lumar are free game."

"I've got some big rooms up here," the trooper on point said. "Looks like they're filled with dead people. It's uh…it's pretty bad, sir."

"Hold there," Mishkan-Ijk said. He worked his way to the front of the formation and walked into an abattoir. From what he could tell from the pieces, there'd been members of at least five races living in the room, with somewhere between 15 and 20 beings total. It appeared they'd been living in squalor beforehand…but whatever had happened to kill all the people?

The trooper was right. It's pretty bad.

It was hard to look at, even for combat troops. Mishkan-Ijk knew he would be a long time getting some of the images from his mind.

"There's another room just like it across the passageway," the trooper said. "And two more up the way." He pointed in their direction, and Mishkan-Ijk looked up to see a large number of people emerge from the dark, shambling toward them with weapons in their hands.

A laser fired from behind them, and the trooper next to Mishkan-Ijk cried out in pain. "Fire!" Mishkan-Ijk ordered.

The Goltar force put their weapons on auto and sprayed the horde of people bearing down on them. The last one finally fell about five meters away from them.

"That was odd," another trooper said. "They were all armed. Why didn't they fire?"

"No idea," Mishkan-Ijk said, stepping forward to confirm the attackers were all dead. He went to kick the weapon—a laser pistol—

away from the first attacker, but it wouldn't come out of the Zuul's hand. "What the hell?"

He looked closer and could see that it was held on by a metal wire that had been run through the Zuul's hand and then tied around the weapon. The laser pistol's battery compartment was empty.

"This one's pistol is wired to his hand," a trooper said as he tried to disarm another of the attackers. "But…but the pistol's empty." He looked up at Mishkan-Ijk. "What's going on, sir?"

"It's a distraction—"

Laser and MAC fire spat from out of the darkness at the end of the tunnel, and the trooper went down. Mishkan-Ijk dove behind his body, which was larger than most of the corpses in the hallway, and sprayed automatic fire down the corridor.

"We're taking fire from behind," his XO commed.

The enemy was on both sides, Mishkan-Ijk realized. It was a trap.

* * * * *

Chapter Seventy-Three

Meinir Surface, Beta-Caerelis System

The infrared scope painted the Goltar a ghostly blue as it paused in its patrol circuit to reach out a limb to grab something on its back.

The object glowed with a sudden heat that hadn't been there before.

Laverna watched the sentry drink the hot fluid, its warmth spreading through its throat and down into its body.

She could smell the rich coffee aroma.

It was a peculiarity of her inexperienced use of the *xialintae* trance state that despite the klick of airless distance that separated her from her target, her empathetic connection made her taste and feel the coffee sliding down her own throat as strongly as if she were drinking it herself.

The Goltar could be drinking anything—she had little knowledge of the race's tastes—but in *xialintae* there was perfect stillness. No doubts, only certainties. It was coffee.

The Goltar finished its drink and moved over Meinir's barren surface to the dropship.

The craft's hinged beak opened, and the other Goltar marine descended the ramp, alert and with multiple weapons ready.

Laverna wasn't interested.

She angled her rifle a fraction until she had a sight picture of the two Goltar flight crew. One busied itself at the controls. The other had pulled out a shelf and rested its body there while its seven limbs gripped its seat post while it slept.

Laverna felt a crushing sympathetic drowsiness.

The barrel of her sniper's rifle drifted up, and the scope changed to a star field that in the infrared was a blur of gossamer tendrils bursting with hot jewels.

Gently, so as not to break the trance state, she eased the barrel down until the crosshairs settled over the active crewman's body, behind and a little below its beak.

She caressed the trigger.

A thumping noise conducted through her suit. A split second after the suppressed kick against her shoulder, she also felt the round penetrate her flesh via her trance connection.

Before its imaginary paralyzing load spread through her, she lowered the weapon and shot the still sleeping Goltar crewman.

The trance was a boon to Blevin snipers. It allowed perfect concentration, and with both hearts stopped, there was no tremble through her body. The empathy issue, though? That was a pain in the ass.

She pushed a stim stick into her neck.

Her hearts bucked and the universe became sharper edged and faster moving.

The Goltar marines were racing up the ramp.

She shot one.

Then the other.

But she missed. The damned thing was so fast, bouncing off every surface available as if it had no respect for gravity. It hit a control on the console near the first crewman she'd shot, and the dropship's beak began to close.

Perhaps the Goltar felt a brief moment of triumph for having rescued the situation at the last moment.

Whatever the reason, it was briefly still.

Laverna double-tapped it. "Got you!"

She glimpsed the Goltar slumping in the split-second before the beak shut the sight away.

The D-Clock's design specs had revealed that the crew couldn't issue a lockdown to the beak until it had closed. A tiny design flaw, but since she now had the codes to open the beak, a fatal one.

"Open her up, Jenkins."

The Jeha wearing the skipper's name sent the signal, and the beak opened. One of the Goltar rolled down the ramp.

"Are you sure they are only stunned?" he asked.

"If their suits are self-sealing, they'll be okay. If I'd wanted to kill them, there would have been a lot more mess. Now quit scratching and let's get back to the *Mortzestus* before Gutho and Beerak decide they have a conflict of loyalties."

"No, Laverna."

"No?" She stared in astonishment at the segmented alien. Jeha never answered *her* back. Maybe this Jenkins had a little of the skipper in him after all.

"I've gone along with Captain Blue's orders to join you, and I've done whatever you have told me to do. Neither of you have taken the time to explain why I am needed here. I am through with being treated as the amusing alien mascot with the penetrating insights. If you will not pay me the respect of telling me your true purpose, then I shall not assist you."

Laverna slung her sniper's weapon over her shoulder and set off for the *Mortzestus*. "They need Branco to fire the weapon."

"The starkillers? They can be fired from here? Even if that were possible, why would Branco do such a thing?"

"That's what I need you to find out."

"And...stop him."

"If need be, yeah. We've been through this."

"When you said, 'stop him,' I assumed you meant through reasoned logical argument."

"I mean stop that weapon firing by any means necessary."

"I understand."

"Are you sure? If I have to, I can go down the chute with you. But I'll be more use with the Vaga providing you with the diversion. What do you say?"

"I say those Goltar you shot are going to wake up angry. Let's hop over to that dropship via the *Mortzestus* and secure them before that happens."

* * * * *

Chapter Seventy-Four

Back Entrance to the Starkiller-3 Facility, Wahrner's Grise

"Do it," Sansar said, and Mun sent the signal to detonate the explosives. The ground rumbled and a big cloud of dirt poured out of the tunnel's mouth. Considering how far down the tunnel the gates they'd blown had been, Sansar was impressed with the amount of debris that made it out.

I only hope we didn't drop the roof.

The CASPer force started forward into the tunnel as the dust settled. Sansar reached the blast doors to find the right one lying in a massive mound of scree. A lot of the wall had come off with the door, but the ceiling had held. Mostly.

"Good thing we didn't try to drop the left door, too," Sansar said, looking up at where the left door joined the ceiling. Cracks radiated outward in all directions, and a few streamers of dust trickled down.

"Yeah," Mun said, looking up. "I think it helped brace the rest of it. If we'd gone for both of them, it probably would have collapsed the whole thing."

"My thought, too," Sansar said with a nod. "Let's get going…just in case."

Mun called for the advance, and troopers began jumping over the pile of rock and debris to the tunnel on the other side. Intermittent weapons fire was heard, but most of the defenders who'd been close were probably now buried. After Alpha Company had crossed, Sansar made the jump, too, and started moving down the passageway.

They went about 100 meters and the walls started taking on the veined appearance she'd seen in the facility on McPherson-3.

"I think we've come to the right place," Mun said.

Sansar nodded. For better or worse, they were getting closer.

* * *

Main Entrance to the Starkiller-3 Facility, Zila Rogat, Wahrner's Grise

Skuilher-Dour blinked as he came back to consciousness. He remembered an explosion, and his face hurt, *but why wasn't he dead?*

A face swam into view over him. Heklabet.

"Welcome back," she said.

"What…what happened?"

"A Lumar shot your rebreather, and it exploded in your face. You've got some minor burns and cuts, but the water in the rebreather absorbed a lot of the laser energy. I gave you a dose of nanites and took Sheevelor's rebreather for you; that's what you're wearing now."

"That explains the taste in my mouth, but doesn't he—"

"No," Heklabet said. "He won't need it ever again. We lost a number of good people."

Skuilher-Dour rolled to the side. He could see the tunnel mouth, and the Spine Patriots in covering positions on both sides. He'd gotten so close. "Looks like we won," he said. "What happened?"

"When you went down, we continued on and captured the MAC and the entrance to the tunnel."

"She captured it," Rievskegg said. The HecSha leaned over him, still wearing the ratty green scarf he'd captured that night at Port Chinto City Hall. "Heklabet vaulted over the barricade and shot two Lumar who were trying to stand up the MAC, then several others. We couldn't let her have all the fun, so we joined her. Unfortunately, now that we've captured the entrance, no one knows what to do next. Wurgitar and you were down, and the lieutenants are arguing among themselves. We need a higher-level commander to take charge."

Skuilher-Dour's eyes shifted to Heklabet, who shrugged. "I may have gotten a little carried away," she said. "But once the tunnel was secure, I came back to see if you were still alive. That's when they started arguing."

"Give me a hand up," Skuilher-Dour said, extending a hand to Heklabet. She helped him sit up, and he could see most of the Patriots—the ones not at the entrance to the tunnel—were standing around, directionless. He worked his way to his feet.

"Are you okay?" Heklabet asked as he swayed.

"Just getting my land legs," Skuilher-Dour said. He blinked as he saw who else was standing nearby. "What are *you* doing here?"

Beowulf shrugged. "After I dropped off the Goltar, I thought I'd come and help out here. Endless Night gives criminals a bad name, and we need a nebula that has laws again." He shrugged. "It's getting damn hard to be a smuggler these days with the Endless Night around."

Skuilher-Dour nodded. "That actually makes sense, in a weird sort of way." He started toward the tunnel, a little unsteadily at first, but gathered strength and speed as he went along. "Let's go. We have a starkiller to destroy and legitimacy to claim."

* * *

Starkiller-3 Facility, Wahrner's Grise

"**B**ravo Company, reorient to hit the group behind us," Mishkan-Ijk said. "Alpha Company, on me—we'll take the ones in front of us." Mishkan-Ijk pulled out a grenade. "Fire in the hole!"

He threw the grenade as far as he could into the darkness, and several other troopers lobbed them down the hall as well. The grenades exploded in rapid succession, and the Goltar sprayed the darkness with their laser rifles.

No return fire greeted them.

"When I say go, we're going to charge them," Mishkan-Ijk. "I don't think there are very many. Ready, set, go!"

Mishkan-Ijk rose and, with a battle cry, ran down the passageway, careful to step over the bodies littering the floor. Having seven flexible limbs helped cross the dead slaves—for slaves was what they looked like—then he was racing down the corridor with the rest of the company right behind him. He reached a turn in the passageway. There were two dead HecSha in black uniforms and some blood that vanished into the dark, but the rest of the defenders had fled.

In the distance he could see a glow. "They're gone, at least for now," Mishkan-Ijk commed to his XO. "Looks like we're coming up on the lived-in part of the facility; I've got lights on ahead of us."

"We tossed a couple grenades at the ones behind us and they ran, too," the XO replied. "We're coming up to your position."

"Good," Mishkan-Ijk said. "I think we're close."

* * *

Security Monitoring Station, Starkiller-3 Facility, Wahrner's Grise

"The Endless Night forces are fleeing," Private Grekor-Sa reported. "They had the Goltar trapped, as you ordered, but when the Goltar threw grenades, the rest of them ran away."

"Stupid HecSha—they are only good for roasting over an open fire," Lieutenant Calga-Sa said. He picked up a rifle and slapped in a fresh chemical pack.

"What are you doing?" Private Selba-Sa asked. The other five heads in the monitoring station turned to look at Calga-Sa, including the two Lumar.

"I'm leaving. This facility can't be held. We don't have the support we were promised by the Endless Night, and there's no sense staying here. I don't want to die underground, and I don't want to sit here waiting to be shot down."

"So you're running?" Selba-Sa asked.

Calga-Sa's knife flicked out, cutting Selba-Sa's throat. Blood sprayed across the room as Selba-Sa got to his feet and staggered a couple of steps before collapsing.

"No, I am not running," Calga-Sa said, looking at the body. He looked up. "Anyone else want to accuse me of running?"

All the monitors' heads turned back to their Tri-V screens, although the Besquith looked furtively at him out of the corners of their eyes.

"Now," Calga-Sa said strongly, "I am evacuating our team to a fallback position outside this complex. I don't know if management will be coming to pick us up or not, but I know I'm not going to surrender. We will continue the fight with the soft-skins on the surface, and maybe carve out our own little fiefdom on this shitty planet. Who's with me?"

"I am, sir," Grekor-Sa said. Everyone else nodded, even the two Lumar. "What is your plan?"

"Well, there are about two companies of CASPers coming through the back, two companies of squids in the slave pens, and about a company of mixed irregulars coming in the front. What do you think?"

"Sounds like we're going out the front," Grekor-Sa said, grabbing his rifle. He stood, and the others joined him.

"Good," Calga-Sa said. "We have one quick stop to make on the way. Let's go."

He walked out of the monitoring station with what was left of the company following him and strode quickly to the firing chamber. A number of elSha were running around like they didn't know what they were doing, while Coron and Retenex yelled at them from the center of the chamber. *It's strange to see them without their holders,* Calga-Sa thought. He couldn't remember ever seeing them without their Oogar and Lumar bodyguards. He shrugged. It would just make things quicker, although he'd been looking forward to killing the Oogar, and wiping the near-permanent sneer off his face.

Coron turned, saw Calga-Sa and the mercenaries, and yelled, "What are you doing? Get back to your post!"

Calga-Sa smiled. "I'm terminating our employment." His smile became a snarl. "Permanently." He looked over his shoulder at his troops. "Kill them. Kill them all!"

He turned back to Coron, raised his rifle, and shot her through the head. The Lumar behind him made no moves to assist—

probably confused by the sudden shift in allegiances—but the other Besquith joined him in shooting down the rest of the elSha.

Retenex stood still, looking at Calga-Sa with his mouth open. Calga-Sa aimed and fired a bolt through his mouth. He dropped to the floor.

Calga-Sa nodded once. "Now that our contract's taken care of, we can go." He turned and walked through the door, with his troops on his heels.

* * * * *

Chapter Seventy-Five

Ancient Base Beneath Meinir

"You seem angry, Branco. You want to lash out. Why?"

The Human clenched his fists, fighting to control his anger before he could reply.

Harak-Jash made use of the time to verify that Branco was well framed in his suit camera.

"I'm sick of it all," said Branco. "There's nothing good in this galaxy. Nothing I've ever experienced, anyway. And I'm the worst example of all."

"Surely there is good and bad in all of us," Harak-Jash countered.

He knew immediately that he'd said the wrong thing. He knew why too. With every moment that played out in this vile performance, he felt more compassion for Branco. And the doubt grew ever stronger that Gloriana was truly advancing the Goltar cause by reducing this man to a mockery of who he should be.

But her orders were clear, and he came back on script. "Nonetheless," Harak-Jash said, "there are some for whom the good and the bad are unbalanced. They are irredeemably evil, beyond atonement. Endless Night is one such example."

"Yeah. Satan take 'em all."

"And you will find Endless Night's leadership on the planet of Wahrner's Grise. If you had the power to destroy the world, would you take it?"

Branco stared back with mad red-limned eyes. "Wahrner's Grise? Burn it down to hell. Then Peepo's homeworld for what that rat bitch did to the Earth." He bared his teeth aggressively. "And then the hellspawning Earth itself. Humanity is a vile stain upon the galaxy. We've abused each other. Abused our world. The only good thing we can ever do is to wipe ourselves out. Yeah, the Earth must burn."

Despite Harak-Jash's revulsion at Branco's degradation—and his own part in bringing it about—he was fascinated at the depths of self-loathing that had been engineered into this being.

The strike leader didn't have much personal experience with other species, but standard combat school taught extensive courses on xeno-behavior. After all, the better you understood your opponents, the better you could outwit and kill them.

You never heard of Tortantula, or Zuul, or any other species with such capacity for self-destruction.

He shuddered. Humans were dangerous.

"Why do we wait?" yelled Branco. "I want to burn."

"We are still establishing the test rig. We need to validate where the device is aiming and whether it even does anything."

"That's *your* problem. I want to try it now."

Harak-Jash's pinplants registered a confirmation from the technical sub-squad leader that the test rig was ready.

"Not long," Harak-Jash told Branco. "Wait five."

He reviewed the footage he'd taken of Branco's ranting. The high councilor had emphasized that it was essential for Branco's madness to be clearly recorded. The footage was to be sent back to Station 5 before the team on Meinir tried anything risky.

Harak-Jash assured himself that he'd done his job well. He packaged the recordings with a brief status update and sent it by the signal repeaters up the vertical shaft to the dropship and thence to Gloriana.

"The waiting is over, Saisho Branco. It is time for you to wear the suit."

* * * * *

Chapter Seventy-Six

Back Entrance to the Starkiller-3 Facility, Wahrner's Grise

The CASPer force had fought one more skirmish, but then the defense had seemed to crumble and run before them. Although the CASPers had stepped up their pace, the Endless Night defenders had broken contact with them because Sansar refused to allow the force to be drawn into a trap.

They had traveled another five minutes and gone through one of the living orifices when the atmospheric pressure seemed to go up suddenly, and it felt like the walls were pushing in on Sansar. The veins in the walls began to pulse, slowly at first, but with ever-increasing urgency. More ominously, they also began to glow.

"It's just like at McPherson!" Naran exclaimed. *"They're getting ready to fire the weapon!"*

"Can't be," Sansar said, shaking her head. *Not again!* "Sun, I thought you said you'd put the weapon out of commission."

"I didn't say it was a permanent thing, only that we'd temporarily disabled it."

"Well it looks like it's not disabled anymore! Everybody, *run!*"

No longer worried about a trap, the force raced forward through the same type of labyrinth they'd found on McPherson-3. Sansar led the headlong charge through several more of the openings, not even slowing to clean off the slime from their passage. Mun was right behind her, with Sun on her heels. The walls continued to pulse faster and faster, and the glow would have lit up the corridors, even if the Endless Night hadn't left the lights on.

Finally, Sansar made it to the control facility and stopped short.

"What?" Mun asked, coming to a stop beside her. "Why'd you stop?" she asked as Sun drew up alongside her.

Sansar waved an arm at the chamber. "We're not the first ones to make it here. Looks like the Endless Night must have set the weapon to fire, then killed everyone."

"But that *is* the Endless Night," Sun said. "Those two bodies in the center are Coron and Retenex, the leaders of the Endless Night. If they're dead, and all the technicians are dead, there's no one here that can turn it off."

* * *

Main Entrance to the Starkiller-3 Facility, Zila Rogat, Wahrner's Grise

Skuilher-Dour waved his people into the tunnel, and they raced forward. The group bore no resemblance to any sort of military formation—it was nothing more than an armed mob running down the passageway. He would have liked to have controlled it—somehow—but didn't see any way to get the people to listen to him anymore. Half of them appeared locked in some sort of bloodlust or frenzied rage—there was a lot of pent up anger toward the Endless Night, after all—and the rest of the people seemed hell bent on helping them.

At least they're all heading in the right direction.

The mob went around a corner and ran headfirst into a mass of black-suited troopers of an equal size. Before he or anyone else could give any orders—from either side—the two forces crashed headlong into each other, and the entire tunnel erupted in hand-to-hand fighting, with no quarter asked for, and none given.

Beowulf was right in front of him, and he watched the Human drive a knife into a HecSha's chest, then block a thrust from a Zuul with his rifle. The Zuul pressed his advantage, knocking away Beowulf's rifle, then Beowulf stumbled over the HecSha's corpse. The Zuul smiled as he drew his pistol and pointed it at Beowulf, who'd gone down to a knee.

Before he could fire, Skuilher-Dour stepped forward and swung his rifle like a club. The steel-clad butt hit the Zuul in the face, and he was driven back. Beowulf stood, drew his pistol, and shot the Zuul in the chest.

"Thanks," Beowulf said, then he had to backpedal as a couple of black-clad HecSha took the Zuul's place.

Skuilher-Dour stepped forward to intercept one. He swung his rifle again, and the stock shattered on the HecSha's head, although it dropped him.

"That's not really how you're supposed to use a rifle," Beowulf said as he stepped forward to shoot the first HecSha. The one he'd been fighting lay nearby with a laser burn through his eye. Beowulf finished off the one Skuilher-Dour had been fighting.

"Looks like we're winning," Skuilher-Dour said, taking a moment to survey the melee during a temporary lull around him.

Beowulf stepped back and joined the Selroth. Skuilher-Dour pointed to several troopers in black fleeing down the tunnel. "I wouldn't know," Beowulf said. "This is my first full-scale battle. If this is winning—"

He was interrupted by a roar as a massive Besquith came out of a side tunnel, followed by three other Besquith and a couple of Lumar.

"Those aren't ours, are they?" Beowulf asked.

"Unfortunately, no," Skuilher-Dour said as the new combatants waded into the melee in a V formation. None of them seemed like they were looking to flee; the Besquith in particular just seemed happy for the carnage.

The lead Besquith quickly cut his way to the center of the scrum with little more than his claws and teeth. He had a rifle over his shoulder, but he didn't seem to need it as he went on a bestial killing spree. Bodies flew from him and the other Besquith, and it didn't seem to matter whose side they were on. The Besquith killed the black-clad HecSha and Zuul with equal rapacity as they did the Spine Patriots. The Lumar—while not as ferocious—did a methodical job of killing the Patriots who'd been pushed aside by the Besquith's entrance.

In just seconds, the battle, which had been theirs, was in danger of being lost.

"We have to stop the Besquith," Skuilher-Dour said.

Beowulf laughed. "How? Did you bring a nuke or something?"

"No," Skuilher-Dour answered seriously. "Your Sansar Enkh wouldn't let us have one."

"I was kidding." Beowulf motioned toward where the Besquith were bodily throwing Patriots out of the scrum, usually missing an appendage or two. "How are we going to stop them?"

Skuilher-Dour wanted nothing less than to face the Besquith. If the truth were known, he didn't want to face the Lumar, either, who were bigger, stronger, and had more arms, but he knew this was make-or-break time for the Patriots. They either seized liberty now, or they would be relegated to third-class citizens by whoever decided to take power in the aftermath of the battle. No. It was time to fight.

He might die—he probably *would* die—but maybe someone would kill the Besquith while he had it occupied. He picked up a trident from the ground next to a fallen Selroth and held up his pistol. "With this."

"If you're going to do it, you better do it soon." Beowulf nodded toward where the fighting was heaviest. "It looks like the Patriots are about to break."

Skuilher-Dour took a breath as he surveyed the fight. A number of his people could be seen edging away from the Besquith. "Spine Patriots!" he yelled "On me! Freedom for the nebula!" He turned and charged at the Besquith.

* * *

Beowulf sighed as the Selroth clumped off toward the Besquith force. *We're all going to die.* He sighed again. *Fuck it, we're all going to die sometime. Better to do it for a good cause, rather than just for credits.* Not that he'd ever tell his boss that.

He grabbed a sword from a fallen Human and raced after the Selroth. Even though the alien had a head start, he wasn't built for sprinting, and Beowulf caught up with him before he hit the main part of the melee. Several others, hearing the two men's battle cries as they ran forward, broke away from fighting HecSha and Zuul, and followed them.

The flow of battle had turned the Besquith force away from them during the charge, though, and Skuilher-Dour ran forward into the last of the Besquith, leaving one of the Lumar for Beowulf.

The Besquith screamed as Skuilher-Dour impaled it with the trident, causing the Lumar to look up from the HecSha it was stomping into paste on the ground. It may have been big and dumb, but it was fast, and a lower arm snaked out to grab the pistol Beowulf had been aiming at it. The Lumar chuckled as it broke the composite casing of the pistol. Beowulf swallowed. *It was strong, too.* Fast and strong; this wasn't going to end well.

The Lumar moved forward, and Beowulf backpedaled, hoping someone would take the alien from behind. He couldn't see much through the massive mercenary, but it seemed that was a false hope—there didn't appear to be anyone behind him. The Lumar reached for him, and he swung his sword, but the Lumar batted it away. It may have taken a cut while it did it; if so, it didn't seem inconvenienced.

Beowulf continued to back away, and the Lumar moved with him, pressing its advantage. Just when he thought he had enough space to turn and run—not to flee but to find another weapon, he hooked his heel on a downed Zuul and went over backward. In a flash, the Lumar was on him. It reached down with an upper arm, grabbed him by the throat, and lifted him off the ground while it choked him. From his new vantage point, he could see Skuilher-Dour was trapped by two Besquith. He tried to get away, but one of them knocked away his trident, causing him to stumble. A clawed swipe knocked away his rebreather and sprayed blood.

Skuilher-Dour went down. Beowulf kicked and clawed at the Lumar, but couldn't break its hold on him. The massive alien laughed as it continued to throttle Beowulf. The last thing Beowulf saw as the lights dimmed was movement from the side of the Lumar. *Who'd brought snakes to the fight?*

* * *

Starkiller-3 Facility, Wahrner's Grise

The Goltar force continued through the facility, looking for a passage to loop around to where Mishkan-Ijk's positioning system said the firing chamber was. He was happy when they left the slave chambers; each had been more gruesome than the last. The Endless Night and its allies had a lot to account for.

After the slave quarters came various engineering compartments, although there was no telling what their purposes were as all the equipment in the spaces was some sort of weird mix of biomechanical hybrids. It would have taken *real* engineers—if they'd had any—quite some time to figure out their purposes, and that was time he didn't have.

Still…the weird mélange of the living and the mechanical indicated they were in the right area; they just needed a cross-passage to get them to their destination.

Then the pressurization spiked, and the walls began throbbing.

"What the hell is this?" one of the troopers wondered.

"It's the weapon," Mishkan-Ijk said. "They're preparing to fire it. We have to hurry."

The Goltar sped up their pace and finally arrived at a major cross-tunnel.

"Contact!" the point trooper exclaimed.

"Hold your position," Mishkan-Ijk ordered as he moved forward.

The soldier waited at a side tunnel; yelling, the sounds of weapons firing, and the clash of steel could be heard from further up the passage they'd been following. "We're supposed to turn here in order to get to the firing chamber," the trooper said, "but it sounds like there's a major battle just up the corridor."

Mishkan-Ijk eased forward to the next corner, where the passageway joined into a major tunnel. In the middle of it, Endless Night soldiers battled what could only be the Spine Patriots—their random and patchwork uniforms spoke volumes to the fact that they were *not* a regular unit. As he watched, a force of Besquith and Lumar joined the fray. Although there were only six of them, they quickly turned the tide of battle as they waded into the fray, often killing their allies in their haste to get to their enemies.

On the other side of the battle, Skuilher-Dour spoke with Beowulf, then he grabbed a trident and charged toward the Besquith. After a second, Beowulf picked up a sword from the floor and raced after him.

They don't stand a chance.

"Now's our chance," the trooper said. "With the guard distracted, we could make it to the firing chamber without them knowing."

"We could," Mishkan-Ijk said. "But that would mean leaving the Patriots to their deaths. They are our allies. Where would be the honor in leaving them to die, when—as a combined force—we could easily destroy the Endless Night?"

"But our mission—"

"—is to destroy the weapon. Which we will do as a combined force." Mishkan-Ijk switched to his comm. "All troops, move forward." He paused a second as the troops crowded up behind him, then broadcast, "Charge!"

He raced forward toward the knot of Besquith. Unlike other armies, the Goltar didn't shout battle cries as they attacked—they charged with silence—and the Endless Night forces never heard them coming. At the last minute, he saw a Lumar lift Beowulf by his throat. The Human's eyes bulged as he kicked and thrashed, but the

Lumar was immense and shrugged off the Human's weak attempts to break free.

A bone knife in two tentacles, he jumped on the Lumar's back, reached around, and plunged the blades into the massive alien's chest. The Lumar's lower arms grabbed at Mishkan-Ijk's tentacles, but he wrapped more of his limbs around the alien's legs, holding himself in place as he slashed the Lumar. After a couple of seconds where the Lumar continued trying to rip Mishkan-Ijk from his back, the alien began to weaken, and his struggles waned. He released Beowulf, fell to his knees, then collapsed onto his face.

Mishkan-Ijk jumped off the Lumar as it fell, and spun to find another foe. There weren't any in his immediate area; the two companies of Goltar had rolled across the fight in a wave, catching the majority of the Endless Night forces from behind. Their bone knives rose and fell, and the black-clad troopers dropped.

Several Goltar were down or wounded—courtesy of the Besquith, who hadn't gone down easily—but the introduction of his 80 troops quickly ended the battle.

He held out a limb to Beowulf who was trying to pull himself to his feet.

"Thanks," Beowulf said. "I think I bit off a little more than I could chew."

"It looked more like they were going to eat you instead," Mishkan-Ijk said. "But you *were* the one who chose to charge a force of Besquith without CASPers."

Beowulf chuckled. "Not one of my brightest ideas, I admit." He walked over to Skuilher-Dour, who was lying in a puddle of blood. Based on the size of the pool, the Selroth wouldn't be rising again. Beowulf sighed. "Not his best idea, either, I'm afraid." He shook his head. "He did what he had to, though, and that was his greatest gift to the nebula."

Beowulf jerked. "Did it just get lighter in here?"

"Yes, they are preparing to fire the weapon."

"Then what the hell are we doing standing around? We need to stop it."

Mishkan-Ijk nodded. "If you will follow me, then, we will be about doing just that." He turned and, calling his troops to follow him, he raced off toward where his locator system said the firing chamber was located.

* * * * *

Chapter Seventy-Seven

Ancient Meinir Base, Beta-Caerelis System

Jenkins had waited five minutes since Laverna had deliberately broken radio silence, allowing him to hear her coded instructions to her Vaga teammates.

If he could hear her comms, so too could the Goltar. That was the plan. But five minutes didn't seem long enough.

What if the Goltar came back?

He decided to stay at the bottom of the vertical shaft a little longer.

Then he wondered what Captain Blue would say if she could see him.

He flinched, fearful of the captain's anger.

And more so of Hopper's scorn. His love had been safely recovered from Wahrner's Grise. They would be reunited soon, and the epic coupling would consume them for days. They would boast about it to the progeny that would surely result.

But not if she was disgusted by his cowardice.

He shook some of the tension out of his segments.

"Come on," he urged himself. "You know how to do this." It simply required the mental trick of pretending to be someone else, of performing a role that would impress Hopper.

He channeled the determination of Captain Blue, and the ferocity of Betty and Major Sun. He would be sneaky yet wise, as Branco had once been.

These beings he had admired so much had all laughed at him—except the major, perhaps—but the joke was on them, because he'd grown to surpass them all.

Jenkins advanced down the angled base of the shaft and dropped into the unoccupied equipment room below.

He was a Jeha ready for anything.

"Oh, my," he scratched, and then activated the weapon turret clamped to his back.

* * * * *

Chapter Seventy-Eight

Back Entrance to the Starkiller-3 Facility, Wahrner's Grise

Sansar crossed to one of the slates that projected from the room's center column. "How is this possible? The weapon can't be firing; this slate is dead." She turned to the other CASPers in the doorway. "Naran, you re-targeted one of these. Get out and do it again."

Naran walked into the room, opened her CASPer, and jumped down. She ran over to one of the positions, then went on to the main control slate. She tapped it for a couple of seconds, then looked up as she turned the slate toward Sansar.

"I can't do *anything* with this," she exclaimed. "Everything—all of the slates—are dead. It won't let me give it any input. They won't even turn on."

"Blue Sky!" Sansar swore. *Only one person knows how to operate this, and we left her on the ship.* She opened up a Tri-V connection to Hopper, and projected it where everyone could see it. "Coron and Retenex are dead," Sansar said as Hopper connected, "but the weapon is about to fire. The threat of the Endless Night will be over if we can just stop the weapon."

"But they aren't the leaders of Endless Night," Hopper said.

"But I thought—"

"No, those are just the mouthpieces. The beings that carry them—a Lumar and an Oogar—are the true leaders of Endless Night. Did you kill them?"

"Kill them? No. We didn't even see them."

"Then the leaders of the Endless Night escaped."

"Okay, fine; they escaped for now. How do we stop the weapon?"

"You can't. All you can do is redirect it, like you did on McPherson-3."

"But everything is shut down here. The slates are all turned off."

"Oh. That's bad. If the system's shut down, you'd have to initialize everything and take local control."

"How do we do that?"

"You can't. If the system is preparing to fire, there isn't time to get everything online. Besides, if they started the firing sequence, you can't stop it. It's a built-in failsafe."

"I don't get it," Sansar said. "If the controls don't work, how is all this happening?"

Hopper sighed in a very Human way, and her voice took on a pedantic tone. "While the machine is in working order, anyone who wanted to fire it could do so from the main control facility."

"The *what?*"

"The main control facility on Meinir, in the Beta-Caerelis system." Although Hopper didn't say, "duh," she might as well have. She drew something, then focused her slate's pick-up on it. It was a picture of three circles that intersected. She tapped on the intersection. "The circles all represent one of the weapons—that's why there are *three* of them. The center part—where they all intersect—represents the main control facility on Meinir."

"That would have been *really* nice to know when we were *in* Beta-Caerelis and could have stopped it," Sansar said. "But we're not. How do we stop the weapon from firing locally?"

"Stop it? I told you—you can't. The main firing controls for the whole system are in Beta-Caerelis. They can override anything done locally. Even if you turned the controls on, the main facility could still override you. Just like it's doing now."

"We have to break the starkiller then."

"Good luck," Hopper said. "The machines are built to be redundant."

There was a commotion at the door across from where Sansar's CASPers waited, and Beowulf and Mishkan-Ijk ran in. A mass of Goltar crowded in and around the door.

"What's going on?" Beowulf asked.

"The Earth's going to die."

* * * * *

Chapter Seventy-Nine

Ancient Meinir Base, Beta-Caerelis System

Branco shook his head, which rattled the many cables spraying from his haptic cap.

How could he be so stupid?

They must have done something to him. Made him compliant. But it wouldn't work. He wasn't an obsequious slave to the Goltar; he was a bloody-minded Dane, and he had no intention of waiting for Harak-Jash to come back from the disturbance outside. Nor did he care about their calibrations and test rig. To the Devil with it all.

His mind encompassed a hundred billion suns.

And he would be the destroyer of each one of them.

Starting with Wahrner's Grise.

He snarled at the two marines left behind to guard him and opened out his arms in the lower haptic sleeves.

The sudden explosion in scale made him retch but brought him outside of the galaxy altogether. He saw *everything*.

The marines tensed.

As well they might. Let them fear him. They were trifling mortals. Nothing to the destroyer of stars.

He brought in his arms, collapsing his focus down to the Spine Nebula, searching for the sun he would explode.

He could smell it.

Test rigs and calibration. Pathetic!

They might have been necessary when the Goltar sealed him in the suit, but every moment since then, the device had been growing into his mind, and he into it.

He *was* the machine.

A jolt of surprise caused him to stumble in his hunt for Wahrner's Grise. His interaction with the machine...was this what Blue felt with *Midnight Sun*? Had the architects of the starkillers also built the ship?

It was but a momentary curiosity, but it was delay enough for the Goltar who had sneaked behind him to tear the haptic cap from his skull.

Branco screamed.

It was like ripping out his eyeballs to leave them dangling by the optic nerve, still seeing. He was still connected to the machine, but it had grown through his pinlinks and that connection was stretched but still held, fattening by the moment. He was on the cusp of vomiting, and no wonder...he felt as if his body had been dissected and his sinews and nerves stretched out along the dissecting table.

And yet nothing vital had been severed. He could still perform his function.

There it was. Wahrner's Grise. A pitifully irrelevant world orbiting a star indistinguishable from countless billions of others except for one crucial distinction. It was here that Branco would begin his destruction.

The Goltar were shouting at him to cease, but nothing could stop him anymore.

"Excuse me," said a scratchy little voice.

Human and Goltar alike stared in astonishment at the spacesuited Jeha with a miniaturized, twin-barreled naval gun strapped to its back.

"Jenkins?"

* * * * *

Chapter Eighty

Starkiller-3 Firing Chamber, Wahrner's Grise

"Why is the Earth going to die?" Beowulf asked. "Can't we stop it?"

"No," Sansar said. "It appears the true leaders of the Endless Night snuck off to Beta-Caerelis, where there is a master control station. They are firing the weapon from there, and there's nothing we can do to stop them."

"Can we disable the weapon?"

Sansar waved at Hopper's Tri-V image. "She says not in the time we have remaining. The systems are too redundant."

Mishkan-Ijk's slate buzzed. The way his features jerked and twisted told Sansar that it wasn't a welcome interruption.

He fished out the slate, and it projected the image of a Goltar sitting in a water-flooded starship compartment, or maybe it was an orbital.

"It's Gloriana," he said.

Figures.

"As I am sure you have discovered by now," Gloriana's image said, "the starkiller weapon is no longer under your control. It is, in fact, controlled by me." She leaned forward, her beak reddening. "And that is why you are all going to *die*."

"Is this some kind of joke?" Sansar demanded of Mishkan-Ijk. "Why would she betray us?"

The Goltar soldier's tentacles seemed to shrink into his body. "I don't know."

Gloriana seemed eager to supply the answers. "Captain Jenkins of the *Unlikely Regret* unleashed chaos and death across the Spine Nebula when he arranged for the murder of the only person I ever loved."

"She means Xal-Ssap," Mishkan-Ijk said. "That was her husband. If this is about him...we're screwed."

"As Jenkins took Xal-Ssap from me," Gloriana said, "so I take from him everything he held dear. You Humans will understand. Your language has a word that encapsulates this perfectly. Vendetta."

"I recognize the compartment design," Sun noted. "She recorded this at Station 5."

"His cause will die," Gloriana explained. "His ship. His friends. The Midnight sisters. Oh, yes, I haven't forgotten you, Major Sun. Quite the opposite. I have taken Branco from you. He has been cured of his physical diseases, but his mind belongs to me now, and his soul is currently being tormented in a living hell."

Sansar heard a sudden whine of servos as Sun punched her fist deeply into the wall. It returned to form without a mark.

"As for you, Mishkan-Ijk, you have no connection to Jenkins, but the way you treat Humans is an abomination. They are not, and never will be, our equals. This is where it ends for all of you. The starkiller weapon is targeted upon the Wahrner's Grise star, and the firing sequence has begun. In a most delicious turn of events, the order to target the star was input by Branco himself. As I'm sure you have figured out, the control station can't be overridden. There is nothing you can do to stop it. My only regret is that I couldn't be there in person to watch you die."

She leaned back and released a long stream of bubbles from her blowhole.

"Shut the damned thing off," Sansar said. "Mun, get the nuke. If I'm going to go out, it's going to be on my terms, not as the result of some vendetta I wasn't even a part of."

"Umm, ma'am?" Naran asked.

"Yes?"

"Some of the troops want to know if they should run."

"Let me put it to you this way," Sansar replied. "Based on what you saw at McPherson-3, how long do you think we have until this fires?" She motioned at the glowing walls.

"I don't know. Four minutes? Maybe five?"

"They're not going to outrun the blast. All they'd do is die tired."

Several troopers entered the firing chamber and began assembling the nuke. Mun got out of her CASPer to connect up the final wires and program it. "How long do you want me to set the timer for?"

Sansar sighed and opened her canopy. "Make it for a minute. That's plenty of time for everyone to say a prayer to their favorite deity."

"You don't want to hold off and try to disable the system?" Mishkan-Ijk asked.

"There's no time. If we wait, we run the risk of it firing. By detonating the nuke, we'll at least stop the starkiller from firing and save the inhabitants of this system." She smiled. "And also, in a small way, we'll deny Gloriana the satisfaction of killing us herself."

Mishkan-Ijk nodded. "That makes sense. Set it for one minute then. One minute to midnight."

* * * * *

Chapter Eighty-One

Underground Meinir Base

Jenkins painted the targets and willed his weapon to fire.

Barrel One's recoil kick sent him skidding back along the floor.

No matter: Jenkins had accounted for this. As he scrambled for purchase, he felt the turret motor whirr and the second barrel fire, sending him pinwheeling backward out of the room.

When he hurried back inside, the two Goltar were on the ground, twitching violently as the shock pulsers he'd shot into them discharged.

Oh, dear.

He had been pretending to be as violent as Captain Blue, and his pinplants had misinterpreted his playacting for a desire to up the charge yield to the maximum.

But he couldn't apologize for probably killing the Goltar while he was still on mission, not while he was also channeling Major Sun's determination.

Instead, he painted a new target, his Human friend who was wrapped inside a haptic suit designed for a four-armed humanoid.

"Move away from the haptic controls," he ordered.

"I'm not who you think I am," said Branco. He sounded distressed. "I'm a murderer."

"That statement is not relevant," said Jenkins. "In any case, it isn't true."

"Oh, but it is. I'm filthy. I ran to Binnig to hide, but now the truth is out."

"Stow that shit, Specialist." Was that how Major Sun would phrase it? It seemed to have the desired effect, because Branco stopped talking. Perhaps he would remain quiet while Jenkins explained.

"When you first joined the company, Captain Blue distrusted you. I took the initiative of accessing your records on Earth to learn your history. Major Sun supplied some critical details. You were born Preben Bergesen. Binnig recruited you when you were twenty-two."

"Because I killed the woman I loved."

"There is no criminal record of this. I have only penetrated Binnig's records as far as your initial interview assessment, but there is no mention of what you say."

"They hid my truth. It's all lies. It all needs to burn."

"What was this woman's name?"

"I don't remember."

"Because she didn't exist. Unless you mean your cousin, Freja."

"Freja? No, I didn't kill her."

"In a sense, yes, you did. She worked two jobs to earn enough to put you through college. Your scores were off the chart, which was perhaps why she never told you about the pain in her head until she could hide it no longer. After your tuition costs, there was no money left for her own medical fees, and the brain tumor went undiagnosed. It's all in Binnig's notes. Apparently you felt profoundly guilty."

"And I'm not a murderer?"

"Well, you did kill a couple of people. They were trying to mug you in some derelict land near a canal. You never had to face your murder charges because Binnig took you out of the criminal justice system and made you an offer you had no wish to refuse."

"Someone twisted my memories." Branco shuddered. Poor man. "Took the threads of real ones and wove them into a horrifying new pattern."

"Evidently so. Interesting. I believe you recently underwent medical treatment by a Wrogul. That species could certainly play with your memories." Jenkins clicked his mandibles at this satisfying outcome. "I was worried for a moment there, Branco. I am glad you acknowledge the logic of my words."

"The Devil with your fucking logic. It all has to burn."

"Oh, dear. Then I'm terribly sorry for what I must do."

For this difficult task, Jenkins selected Branco himself as his inspiration. The real Branco—the one he'd come to admire—would have no qualms about shooting himself in this situation.

As the turret whirred on Jenkins's back, aiming both barrels at Branco, his antennae sensed movement above, combined with a rapid buildup of electrical charge.

Glossy hemispheres were moving on tracks above Branco's dais. Fascinating! They resembled the beam splitters of a warship's anti-missile lasers.

Jenkins squealed in pain as holes were burned through several of his segments.

No matter how hard he willed, the weapon on his back would not fire. When he ejected it, he saw a mess of melted metal leaking corrosive chemicals.

He sidestepped away smartly, wondering with a part of his mind whether he could develop a miniaturized force shield projector for a Mark 2 weapon.

Jenkins regarded the Human who had once been Branco, fearful that he would finish the job with the lasers. But he appeared uninterested, instead manipulating his arms as he controlled the engine.

His singed carapace told Jenkins that some part of this machine still functioned, so he'd better assume the rest did. Given that the Aneb starkiller had required hacking into secondary systems to jury rig a fire control system, it seemed obvious that this illuminated booth inside a dead world was the true control center.

But with his application of logic unsuccessful, and his aggression met with superior force, how could he stop the rogue Human?

The quality of Captain Blue that Jenkins admired most was her deviousness. He drank deeply from that well. And hatched a plan.

"May I reattach your haptic cap?" Jenkins enquired. "Seeing as you are going to activate the device anyway, I may as well learn of its secrets. It's absolutely captivating. I need to understand it."

Branco's voice sounded light years distant. "Approach."

* * *

Branco watched the Jeha through the machine's eyes as Jenkins climbed upon his back, ready to drill him with laser fire if he intended harm.

He didn't. Jenkins reattached the cap over his skull without any attempted deceit.

Branco knew the Jenkins of old, understood the drive of curiosity burned far stronger in him than the need to do violence. Knew he could relax into the tighter embrace of the machine, now that it was closer to his head.

Even without the cap he'd been able to bond with it, but now its workings came into far sharper focus.

He reached for his battery of three starkillers and felt momentary despair to discover two of them were unavailable. Destroyed! He'd known at least one had gone before he stepped into the suit, but it still came as a shock to feel the raw grief of their loss.

Branco activated the only remaining starkiller, disconnecting the other two in case a damaged remnant interfered with his targeting.

"What does it feel like?" Jenkins asked.

"I am the machine. I am everything. I am the destroyer of worlds, the scourge of stars."

"Very poetic. What I really meant to ask is how does it work? Do you just think of a star name?"

"Names are unnecessary. It knows my intent. And that is…"

There was an annoying remnant of logic in Branco's brain. The target was Wahrner's Grise. But why? What did he care about that particular world? He was determined to destroy star upon star in an orgy of destruction. The universe was a dumpster fire and he would supercharge it with hellfire and dance in the flames. But if the first star he destroyed also took out the only remaining starkiller …

He shook his head, which had the effect of launching laser bolts at random through the room. Everyone was forever telling him this and that until he couldn't think straight. He knew Wahrner's Grise must be destroyed. He knew it was the right thing to do. He willed the machine to select the star and clenched his fists.

Lightning burst in Branco's head.

"No!" He ripped his consciousness out of the stars and back into the room on Meinir where he saw the treacherous Jeha plunging a spike through his skull.

He fired laser bolts to shoot off the top of the spike. They severed the Jeha's grasping limbs and sent him toppling onto his back.

But the thing in his head kept firing.

He screamed. And carried on screaming until he could no longer draw breath.

Branco was Preben, climbing out the window into a Copenhagen night with his mother bleeding out downstairs.

He was Branco, the deep cover Binnig spy, shooting Captain Blue under the sulfur volcanoes of Cap-Soufre.

He was Vlox, blasting a hole through the skull of a Zuparti arms dealer on Wrathburn-2.

He was lying on a treatment bench on Station 5, listening to every word passed between Gloriana and Doctor Zahn as she twisted Alf's work to implant false memories. To build a compulsion that would lead him to this moment. And all to satisfy Gloriana's revenge.

Time lost meaning. He was experiencing everything that had ever happened to him. Continuously.

"Fuck you…Gloriana!"

"Branco," said Jenkins. "Listen to me. You don't want to do this. Stand down."

"I know," said Branco. "The idea they put in my head. I can't…stop…myself. Ahhhhh!" He slammed his fists together and he felt the satisfaction of the machine fulfilling its purpose at long last.

"It's done, Jenkins. Fire sequence initiated. It can't be shut down."

"Branco, do you still feel a connection to the starkiller?"

"Stronger than…ever. Yes. It's heating up until it fires. It…burns!"

"Then I think there's a chance. If we can destroy this place, the wash of feedback might burn out the weapon in Wahrner's Grise."

Branco sent laser fire streaming into the equipment banks that lined the room. Acrid electrical burning wrenched at his nostrils, distracting him from the crush of memories in his mind.

He shook his head and felt a bubble of lucidity drive out his madness. "It's no good. These things here aren't the machine. They're just interfaces for mortal technicians to interact with it. It's buried deep beneath us. The lasers won't be enough."

"Where is Hopper?"

"What? Hopper? My guess is she's on *Unlikely Regret*. Where the ship is, I don't know. Station 5, probably. Or Wahrner's Grise. I don't know."

"Can you tell? With the device?"

"Why do you…? Doesn't matter. No. She's too small. Too insignificant."

"Not to me, Human."

* * *

Jenkins wanted to nip Branco in the leg, but all he could do was slither in his own blood.

"Branco, can you understand me?"

"Yessssss!"

"Remove your arms from the lower haptic sleeves and place them in the upper ones."

The Human did as Jenkins asked, despite his pain.

Branco's face went wild with shock as the system controlled by the upper sleeves activated, the local defense weapon that defended the Beta-Caerelis star system. The cause, Jenkins speculated, of the vast number of ancient wrecked warships scattered here.

It was just as well Laverna had finally been honest with him in the very last stage of the journey here and explained everything.

Laverna.

He'd forgotten her.

Jenkins transmitted to the Blevin smuggler through radio frequencies. To his surprise, he connected immediately.

"Laverna, I am Jenkins. Please give your status."

"Visim and Zazbest are wounded. Zharlyk's dead. We are withdrawing under fire to the trench. Tell me you stopped Branco. Tell me it was all worth something."

"I have failed. So far. I have one last thing I wish to try. Get to the trench as fast as you can. Hurry! I will send *Mortzestus* after you."

"Copy that. Good luck. Out."

He regarded Branco. Would the Human be up to the task? The man's eyes bulged wildly and there was foam at his mouth.

Jenkins wasn't in much better shape. A mandible and several limbs had been shot away. Most of his laser wounds had cauterized, but some had burst open and the blood loss was making him dizzy.

Time was short.

"I know…your…plan," Branco gasped.

"Good. Do you have a message for Sun?"

"Trying…to…control…this damned thing. All…for…*her!*"

Jenkins took that as a no.

He made a brief audiovisual recording, adding a few words of commentary on his friend's behalf. "Branco did the right thing in the end. I know that's very important to you Humans. Please tell Captain Blue that her suggestion to me was the right one. And tell Hopper…tell her to listen to the song of the universe, because she will hear a new theme threading through its harmonies. One that will always love her."

He sent the message to Sun via the Goltar comm relays and then through the *Mortzestus*.

Then he sent an addendum. "Silly me. I forgot. The Wrogul is innocent. Gloriana is not. She betrayed us. Our deaths will be a stain on her soul." He followed up with instructions to the ship to pick up Laverna without delay and get the hell off Meinir.

Mortzestus and Laverna might make it to safety, and they might not. His message to Sun might explain what had happened, or it might be transmitted to a dead system obliterated by its own starkiller.

Interesting. Would that latter case mean the message would be lost in hyperspace?

Such uncertainties were an inherent danger of being a mercenary, he supposed. You could never be sure what would happen next.

That was what made it so exciting.

Funny it should end in the Beta-Caerelis system, where it had all started for him.

"Did you…send…your message?" Branco had turned an unusual color.

"Yes, it's time."

Jenkins scratched his antennae together uncertainly. Branco *was* Human after all. "Err…just to clarify, what I am suggesting is to—"

* * *

Branco fought for a clear channel through the events of his life that were bursting all around him simultaneously.

He succeeded by imagining he was on a boat speeding along Christianshavn Canal. To either bank was utter madness, but he ignored it all and keep heading straight ahead, through the canal and out…

Not to the sea.

But into space.

Near Station 5. Near the moon of Faiza.

There was space traffic here. He knew that if he brought his hands together, he could crush these little craft as he had destroyed the fleets that had dared come here eons ago. Destroy them…he wanted to so badly, but he seized the focus of the weapon's attention and moved it a short distance across the system, a mere seven light minutes. Down to the planet Meinir.

A small ship was speeding along Meinir's surface, but Branco let it go. He centered on the D-Clock that had transported him here, and then drilled down through the rock until he saw himself lit up in the mirrored room smashed by laser bolts. He delved deeper into the guts of the engine and smashed his fists together.

A pulse of energy formed inside one of Meinir's moons. It hurled itself down onto its dead mother world and engulfed its own fire control station.

The engine's death throes transmitted through hyper-dimensional conduits and burned through the active starkiller on Wahrner's Grise.

* * *

Seven minutes later, observers on Station 5 noticed an eruption on Meinir, a world that was clearly not as dead as everyone had thought.

A geyser of pulverized rock erupted in a plume that soared over a hundred miles above the planet's surface.

Within ten minutes, the sight had been relayed to the individual on the station who understood its significance more than anyone.

"I hope you died in pain, Branco," Gloriana murmured to herself.

Exactly what had transpired remained unclear to her, but this had not gone according to plan. Her vendetta revenge remained in doubt, as did her safety. She contacted BIG Acquisition, Retrieval, and Smuggling to facilitate a fast and secure exit from the Spine Nebula.

"You've reached Beerak, Imogen, and Gutho, the best for expeditious exits. The fact that you've used this message channel means you are either a valued existing client or a law enforcement agency. Either way, you'll understand us when we say that we are on a job, and we can't say when we will get back to you. In the meantime, leave a message after the tone."

Gloriana thumped the deck with rage. What was wrong with the galaxy? You couldn't trust anyone these days.

* * * * *

Chapter Eighty-Two

Back Entrance to the Starkiller-3 Facility, Wahrner's Grise

"How much time's left?" Naran asked.

Sansar looked up. "Thirty-seven seconds."

Naran smiled sadly. "Time's funny sometimes. Sometimes it flies by in a wink, while other times it expands to encompass…eternity, it seems."

"When you know all you have is a minute left," Mishkan-Ijk said, "that time *is* your eternity."

"Twenty seconds," Sansar said. "Fifteen."

Naran closed her eyes and tried to think up an appropriate last prayer, but came up with nothing. The first time she'd been about to die, everything had been so frantic, there'd been no time to think. *On the whole, I liked that better.*

Suddenly, everything dimmed behind her eyelids.

"What the hell?" Mun asked.

Naran's eyes snapped open. The glow from the walls was fading, and all that was left appeared as an after-image of a bright light.

Sansar's hand snaked forward and flipped the kill switch on the nuke to Off as the walls turned black and lost their veined appearance.

"Did the weapon fire?" Mishkan-Ijk asked.

Sansar shook her head. "I don't think so. There was no pulse, or anything to make me think it fired." She pointed to the wall. "That looks dead now. Not the way it looked before the weapon activated, but completely dead. Like it was burned out or something."

"The only way that could have happened was if the control facility on Meinir turned it off or shut it down," Hopper said. "Or if the Meinir facility was destroyed. Yes, that's another intriguing possible explanation. The sudden destabilization of energy conduits would burn out the feeds to any active starkiller."

"Are we *sure* it didn't fire?" Mishkan-Ijk asked.

"Pretty sure," Sansar said. "Why?"

"I will tell Captain Kanat-Baim to stand down and wait for our arrival back at the *Blunt Justice*."

"Stand down?"

"Yes. *Blunt Justice* has internal hyperspace shunts. Captain Kanat-Baim was preparing to jump from the system." He paused, and when he began speaking again, humor colored his voice. "As it turns out, the captain is not a fan of Gloriana. While we would all have died—there wasn't time to rescue us—*Blunt Justice* would have escaped. Gloriana wouldn't have gotten far. You think Gloriana can hold a grudge?" He chuckled. "You haven't seen the captain…"

"Well, he's not leaving without us," Sansar said. "Mun, get the nuke disconnected and packed away. I have a few words I'd like to say to Gloriana, too. *After* she pays us, of course."

* * * * *

Epilogue

Lytoshaan Emergence Point

Blue led the *Keesius* ships toward the defense line, taking advantage of *Midnight Sun*'s almost drone-like acceleration.

Far beyond them, near the Veetanho home planet, awaited tens of millions of drones, bolstered by floating redoubts and defensive warships, just like the sims.

Midnight Sun slammed through a constant sequence of course changes that all shared a major vector component aimed at the emergence point defenses.

The AI brains of *Snap*, *Crackle*, and *Pop* needed no urging to do the same.

Battlecruisers weren't as nimble as drones, of course, but their unprecedented maneuverability was enough to cause much of the initial beam salvo from the defensive flotilla to miss.

Midnight Sun and the three *Keesius* ships had no such difficulty.

They destroyed half the Veetanho defenders and smashed through the dazed survivors, heading deeper into the defensive network. *Keesius-2*—who was perfectly content with the designation *Crackle*—sustained a missile hit.

Sorry, buddy. That means you'll be drawing their fire.

"*Crackle*, you take point. Then *Pop*, *Midnight Sun*, and *Snap* in echelon starboard. Move! Move! Move!"

This was far better than the sims. Blue could feel the stellar wind in her hair and hear the growing electromagnetic alarm spreading through the system, as the Veetanho began to wake up to what had appeared in their midst.

Her only fear had been whether the three *Keesius* ships she had rendezvoused with, in an uninhabited system, would obey her commands. But they were her loyal companions, as eager to fulfill their purpose as she was.

As they charged at Lytoshaan, Blue noted the asteroid forts far away at the stargate.

In the sims, the stargate had been lightly defended. She had never trusted the Goltar to faithfully simulate her exit, which was why she had cut a deal with Gloriana to provide an exfil option that might actually work.

If she made it away from the Veetanho planet alive, *Blunt Justice* would be her ride out of here.

The Goltar called their flagship a supercarrier, and Blue had come to realize that this wasn't due to the fighters and drones within her ample hangers. Your common carrier ship could do that. What made *Blunt Justice* super were her capital class battleriders and her hyperspace shunts.

As the minutes passed, Blue's skin tickled with the targeting lasers painting her, but her excitement level eased away from the red zone.

The dull wait was due to the distance from emergence point to planet, an uneventful journey that was usually cut out in the sims. Blue was currently thrusting at a steady 18g, but even that required hours to arrive at Lytoshaan.

"The *Keesius* ships are making a joint communication," said *Midnight Sun* in her head. "The ships wish us good luck and good hunting."

"What? Why now?"

Bubbles of energy formed around the antimatter bomb ships. They originated in their hyperspatial shunts.

She heard three tight clicks as *Snap*, *Crackle*, and *Pop* were unmade from conventional space-time.

And Blue was left on her own in a *very* hostile system.

Her mouth popped open, but she was too stunned for words to come out.

A message packet triggered. Originator: Gloriana.

"No way," Blue growled. She wasn't going to give the squid the opportunity to gloat.

What if Gloriana *hadn't* betrayed her? It was a possibility she couldn't discount, so she gave permission for Gloriana's image to appear in her pinview.

"You know, Blue, when this all began, my intentions were entirely sincere. You were my special project, the weapon I would use to smite the Veetanho. We knew the *Keesius* responded to *Midnight Sun*. And when I found the pilot the ship would respond to, you have no idea how much my political capital appreciated with you as my asset.

"You were so close, Blue. Almost rich beyond the dreams of your species. You almost won legendary renown as the woman who carried out the daredevil attack on Lytoshaan. Even your sister's lover would be resurrected. *Almost*. But none of it was real."

Blue paused the message, slowed the ship, and punched open her acceleration cocoon.

Branco?

She'd had medics check him over after the Wrogul's intervention. When she left Beta-Caerelis, he'd been fixed and looking forward to limb regrowth therapy when he got back from whatever the Goltar wanted him to do on Meinir.

She wasn't sure which of Gloriana's claims to believe, but she knew what she required to fortify herself against the rest of the message.

She left the empty CIC and walked a short distance to the captain's cabin.

Reinforced by a stiff measure of bourbon, she allowed Gloriana to continue through the Tri-V.

"I always detested you," said the Goltar.

Blue raised her tumbler. "Feeling's mutual, boss."

"But that never mattered. Who needs to feel companionship with a nuclear warhead? One needs only a high yield and a delivery system that will do the job.

"By the time you hear these words, your sister will be dead, killed by her own lover. I will have massacred everyone in the Midnight Sun Free Company, including Mishkan-Ijk and the others you Humans have corrupted."

A second image appeared of several Goltar slumped over a table.

"Captain Jenkins was responsible for these murders." Gloriana shook with anger. "My vendetta is with him, *Unlikely Regret*, and all those who were dear to him and his aims. I will kill you all. My only regret is to lose the ship. To *Midnight Sun*, my gleaming jewel of the ancients, I wish you a glorious death."

Gloat over, Gloriana shook her limbs smugly and glared at the camera.

The ship picked up speed on a direct heading to the target. Escape through the stargate was impossible. So was the destruction of Lytoshaan. But they would go out with fists swinging.

Which was what Gloriana wanted them to do.

"Don't fall for it," Blue told the ship. "Gloriana's one worry is that you will be captured by the Veetanho. Turn around. Head for interstellar space. Maybe another era will rediscover you."

"No. I drifted for eons. Never again. We go out together."

Blue made no effort to resist as the ship sped on to Lytoshaan.

"If we're going out in style," she said, "we'd better do this with the right tunes. Slow down a minute, will you?"

At one G thrust, Blue took tumbler and bottle with her back to the CIC, where her cocoon had reconfigured as an acceleration chair. She selected her final playlist on the way.

Normally she would go for Altar power metal reworkings of Earth classics, but this time she went all the way back to the source—1982, to be precise—kicking off with a song from a Human band called Manowar.

She raised her glass and toasted the ship over the opening chords. "Sound the charge," she said. "Into glory…"

She felt a fizz of energy in her head.

A ship emerged from hyperspace.

A big one.

Her sensors picked up a trace several light seconds away, and not from the emergence point. It was *Blunt Justice*.

She accepted the Goltar ship's hail.

"*Midnight Sun, Blunt Justice*. Compliments from Captain Kanat-Baim, and he wishes to know if you would like a ride home."

Blue saluted the Goltar spacer with her glass. "I would be honored. But first, I need to finish my Battle Hymn. Then I will be right with you."

"I understand completely, *Midnight Sun*. *Blunt Justice* out."

Blue laughed and upped the volume until it hurt.

* * *

Blunt Justice, Conference Space 3

"It is our belief that your race and ours are natural allies," said Captain Kanat-Baim. "That we should seize opportunities to treat you with respect."

"Fine by me," said Blue.

"In fact, I think it runs deeper. We Goltar must act with honor in order to regain respect for ourselves. The Scythe operations have been ongoing in the nebula for a very long time. The scheming—here and…elsewhere—has left behind a mess that will take time to work through."

"I agree wholeheartedly," said Blue. She leaned across the table. "Just one question: will I get paid?"

"Regrettably, no."

Blue bit her tongue rather than yell at the captain of the vessel that was hosting both her and the ship. The squids were all the same. None could be trusted. Well, most of them couldn't.

"High Councilor Gloriana has been declared rogue," said Kanat-Baim. "Her personal assets have been seized and her operational budgets re-claimed by the Goltar people. I am aware of the deals she struck with you. Those personal assets now at our disposal are insufficient to meet her obligations to you, or the mob of creditors already picking over her financial bones. I am authorized to pay you something, but I regret it is only a token amount."

Blue shrugged. "Better than facing the Veetanho navy single handed, I suppose. What are we talking? Twenty credits and some old buttons you found in her pockets?"

Blue's pinplants registered a credit payment, pending confirmation upon leaving hyperspace.

Four million credits.

Four million? She had expected to be begging for the fuel to get home.

"Well," she said, "token this paltry amount may be, but I thank you nonetheless for the gesture. I choose to see it as a symbol of what cooperation between our races can achieve. And that has value far in excess of this nominal credit amount."

"My thinking precisely. I must say, Captain Blue, you have impressed me. More than I thought."

Blue's pinplants lit up with alerts. Asset transfers. Hundreds of thousands of items.

"What's this?"

"We have now dealt with your personal arrangements with Gloriana. Seeing that the speakership of the Mercenary Guild is in Goltar hands, our bankruptcy policy is to honor commitments to mercenary companies in full. Your company and The Golden Horde will be paid."

"But the Midnight Sun Free Company belongs to Gloriana."

"I insisted that Gloriana's transfer of ownership was honored first. *Then* the payment made."

Blue shifted through the reams of data to find what she was looking for. There it was. Title in the Midnighters had been transferred to…

What?

Ownership was now divided five ways into equal portions: Sun, her, the other company personnel, the Golden Horde? And the Spine Patriot Corporation!

"That wasn't what I agreed with—"

"I believe our business is concluded. You are free to avail yourself of my ship's amenities until we exit hyperspace and *Midnight Sun* detaches. I wish you good fortune and a long and...interesting life. From what I have learned of you, Captain Blue, the latter would appear to be a certainty."

"Please, one more thing. You said my sister was alive the last time you saw her at Wahrner's Grise. Have you heard anything about her Human mate, by the name of Saisho Branco? Gloriana had arranged a medical intervention for him by a Wrogul surgeon. I am unclear on his status. Is he okay?"

* * *

Six Months Later
Octo-Poultry Shed, Itzmuur Zone, Pinero-7

"I know...your...plan." Branco was gasping in pain, his face purple and bulging.

"Good," said Jenkins, who was lying on his back, his segments drilled full of holes. "Do you have a message for Sun?"

"Trying...to...control...this damned thing." Branco shook his head, sending the hookup cables jangling. "All...for...*her!*"

When Sun stopped the Tri-V playback, the silence inside the shed was damning.

"He was a good man." She brought her eyes level with Gloriana's. "I, on the other hand, am not a good woman."

She took a ten-inch nail from the box beneath her former employer. "I'm a *vengeful one*."

She hammered it through one of the Goltar limbs splayed along the wooden shed wall, a few inches closer to the alien's body than the last nail.

Gloriana shuddered with pain but stared back defiantly.

Mandibles suddenly clicked against her eye sockets, sending her orbs retreating to the depths and releasing a subsonic roar of pain as her body shifted its weight on the nails pinning her to the wall.

"Jenkins was a brilliant mind." Hopper scraped the knife along Gloriana's body, taking care not to cut too deeply, as Sun had taught her. "I hear his anger sing to me every night."

Mishkan-Ijk came out of the shadows and confronted his former commander. But he was all out of taunts and curses.

He turned instead to Sun, "I'll leave you to it. Call me when you're ready."

"It will take us a while," Sun replied, "but we'll leave a spark of life in her for what you need to do."

Mishkan-Ijk pulled his limbs tightly into a stance of attention. "Understood. Thank you, Colonel Sun."

* * *

Romalin Island, Aneb-4

Sansar gazed out over the broken landscape. A few months before, it was pristine waterfront real estate, but now it looked like an angry giant had thrown asteroids at it, carving out huge chunks of the landscape. The reality wasn't far off—the land had been broken by a Scythe bombardment from orbit.

"So what was the final determination?" Sansar asked. "Is the weapon here broken or not?"

"I spoke with the Jeha Hopper, who was here when the island was captured from the Tyzhounes," Naran said. "She said that the weapon was in the process of firing when the bombardment made it pause."

"But it didn't stop the process or break the weapon."

"No, ma'am. As we both know, you can't stop it once it's started."

"So, if we were to fix the barrel assembly..."

"She thinks it would fire immediately and then be operational again."

"Do we know where it was aimed?"

"Yes, it was aimed at Tau-Rietzke."

"Which has already been destroyed, and doesn't have anyone there who'd notice if the star flared again. And, even if there *were* someone there, they might not realize it was a second starkiller firing. They might well think it was a by-product of the instability brought on by the first firing."

"If they were even around to tell the tale afterward."

"Indeed," Sansar said with a nod. "More importantly, with the remote firing control facility destroyed..."

"There'd be no way to control it other than at the facility here, so we wouldn't have to worry about someone else firing it."

Sansar smiled. "And no one would know about it other than us."

"But do we really want to have this weapon in existence? I thought you said we needed to destroy them all."

"I did, because too many people knew about their existence. However…if everyone thought they were all destroyed, it would be a powerful weapon to defend ourselves with if the Merc Guild attacked us again…or if the Kahraman broke through."

"Did you have a dream that would happen?"

"No. Not a dream…just a very strong feeling there will come a time where we will need a weapon like this. When that time occurs, I would rather this weapon still be in existence and under our control."

"How do we ensure that happens, ma'am?"

Sansar smiled again. "I think we've just found where the new Golden Horde base is going to be."

"Where's that?"

Sansar waved to the broken land in front of them. "Right here. Of course, it's going to need some improvements in order to put it right. There will need to be some digging along this trench line…"

Naran smiled. "Yes, ma'am. I'm sure there will be."

# # # # #

Here ends "One Minute to Midnight." Keep reading for the new short story, "A Covert Operation," in the Four Horsemen universe by Charles E. Gannon.

A Covert Operation by Charles E. Gannon

CONOPS

The snoop suit was smaller than any he had seen. It was the sort of thing that humanity might have tried to build to imitate the more advanced technology its far-flung mercenaries had been using for several years now. Usually courtesy of more advanced races.

The snoop suit was almost matte black. The specs indicated it could readily change color to match any background automatically, but was not as sophisticated as a fully functional camouflage wrapper.

"Will I be the first to use it?" Peter Smith tried not to sound too audacious. After all, it didn't much matter, given that this would be his last mission one way or the other, and the pay would take care of his family for any foreseeable future.

Behind him, John Jones toed the weeds at the edge of the tarmac. "Only two before you," he answered after a moment.

"And how did that work out?"

John looked down, kicked up the gravel that lined the test pad. "We learned a lot both times."

"That bad, huh?" Peter asked.

"We have a lot more confidence in this one," John replied without any hint of evasion in his voice.

To Peter, that meant John was at the top of his special-mission-handling game. Those troopers who'd had contact with him called him Grey Ghost. It was rumored he had surreptitiously introduced that moniker himself, insinuating it into conversations at bars and in officer's country. Not for purposes of self-aggrandizement, though. His sole motivation was said to be a desire to replace the alias he had been given by mercs, the one that had arisen spontaneously: "Grave Ghost."

John's unofficial and supposedly secret role in Section 51's advanced tech program was actually known to just about everyone who wound up on the sharp end of ops. He paired up likely casualties with new technologies that needed field testing by meatware. Peter still qualified in that role, but in three or four months, the lymphoma that had been intensified by accumulated rads would cause a terminal recategorization of his combat status. And everything else.

Peter looked the snoop suit up and down one last time. "So when do I leave?"

* * *

INSERTION

Outside the primary drop area, the auxiliary lander banked to stay behind the low mountain range. Shortly after it did, an oblate shape detached from the underside of the wedge-shaped lifting body and plummeted toward the ground.

At 300 meters altitude, the black, flattened egg split into four different pieces, spraying image makers liberally in its wake. But emerging from that cloud of small devices, which caught the wind and then deployed rotary props, was a vaguely anthropomorphic shape. Inside that snoop suit, Peter Smith watched the enemy signatures dim in his HUD. The mountain range now separated him from the primary area of engagement and allowed Peter to arrow down toward an almost entirely unpopulated stretch of bracken and upward writhing fronds: this planet's answer to trees.

The suit came to life of its own accord, shedding disposable fairings that had made it more aerodynamic. Those temporary attachments now out of the way, the drogue chute deployed from the unit's shoulders.

The suddenly filling canvas yanked Peter hard, cutting the suit's forward velocity and drop by 50%, before—right at the point of shredding—it auto-detached and three more chutes deployed, one from the tip of each shoulder and one from the center of his back. Still moving at over 100 kph, the suit approached the ground, and Peter obeyed the automated landing instructions that began flashing in his HUD. He swiveled his hips upward with a light boost from the thrusters on his thighs and landed clean, rolling to the side as soon as the boot's shock mitigation system took the brunt of the impact.

He did not rise up quickly from his roll, but instead surveyed the dusty expanse of his landing site. He lay flat for a long three count, just in case there were enemy forces, either sentient or automated, waiting for him to stand and give them a better target. Magnified vision combined with sensor results showed a bleak view of the flatlands at the foot of the low ridges. And no active returns.

Peter juiced his suit's circuits and set off at a casual fifteen kilometers per hour lope toward the point where the ridgelines met.

His objective.

* * *

EXTRACTION

Peter ran out of fuel in mid boost and cursed. It had been a calculated risk, but he had hoped the diagnostics panel was still at least 50 percent correct.

But it hadn't been. The snoop suit's leg thrusters guttered and died just before he got to the apex of his hop, petering out along with the power. He started to tumble.

It wasn't too far a drop. Not more than 28 meters, and he wasn't going all that fast. However, if the emergency power didn't kick on soon, the full mass of the suit was going to land without any braking. Or, to put it another way, without anything breaking. Except for its contents. Which was to say, Peter.

The ground rushed up at him. The diagnostic flickered back to life, the power meter glowing orange. Emergency backup. It would not last more than five minutes. The ground was only four meters beneath him as the suit tried to automatically roll into a posture that resembled a feet-first half-squat.

His lightly armored feet hit the ground; the shock absorbers whined. The damage indicator for his right leg, already orange, immediately became red, and with a snap that was audible even inside his hermetically sealed suit, that side collapsed. What should have been a forward tumble became a shoulder roll that veered to the right and sent him corkscrewing into the boneyard that had been his final objective and was in the proximity of the emergency extraction point.

The enemy smart rounds that had been tracking him tried to adjust, but the one thing they had not been able to predict was a failure and sudden, self-destructive vector change in mid-flight. The weapons passed harmlessly overhead in a retro-braking attitude and, too low on fuel, fell to the ground about 50 meters further on in the boneyard. Their explosions tossed up rusted parts from that tangle of abandoned alien weapons, vehicles, and cargo containers.

Peter raised his head as best he could. None of the locals were approaching, but that was only a matter of time. He had completed the essential part of his mission, which was to take various pictures of their military technology, which Terran designers were confident would show them a means for upgrading capacitor efficiency. Peter didn't know anything about that. He drove a suit and killed things. That had been his living, and, on this—his last mission—he'd had to ply his trade more often than usual. But the boosting and advanced systems of the suit were busted now, beyond repair, and his only way off this planet was to reach the extraction point on foot.

The boneyard was his final intel target, and the one that had been impossible to really plan for. It was certainly a lot easier to get information on machinery that had been abandoned due to combat damage rather than to try to get the details from a live unit that was fighting back. On the other hand, without knowing what they would find there, he was simply tasked to image and scan broadly: no other instructions had really made sense.

But now, he was far away from any of the normal recall zones, and there were both automated and spam-in-the-can enemies closing in on his position. He pressed the button that activated the frangible bolts at the same moment he double-checked the fit on his personal mask. The back-mounted pod housing the suit's special power systems and sensors blew off the suit; his mask fogged up as humidity control cut out.

He stared at the sward of maroon and red grasses that stretched away to the north. Six kilometers to the emergency extraction point. All on foot, assuming he could push that hard and that far. Then he was home free.

Free to die in his own bed, rather than on a distant planet.

* * *

DEBRIEF

John Jones smiled as Peter came through the door. He forced the expression to be more pronounced, more emphatic, than would have come naturally. It was clear that Peter's last weeks were upon him, despite the various tests and last-ditch experimental therapies he'd endured since returning from his mission. His once full cheeks were hollow, his swarthy complexion pale and waxy. Jones had seen others in this late stage, had always felt a desire to both commiserate and to flee. But on this occasion, just as on those others, he rose quickly from behind his desk and, digging deep, found a broad smile and a ready hand.

He shook Peter's once-powerful paw carefully, trying to ensure that he did not exert more pressure than was comfortable, yet without becoming so tentative that it was more akin to the gentle hands the suit jockey would soon encounter in hospice care. Which was, at most, a month away; six weeks at the outside.

Peter nodded, returned the smile, but his left lower lip refused to cooperate fully. Jones' estimate of the weeks remaining to Peter underwent a sharp downward revision. "I hear they've been poking and prodding you non-stop."

"Pretty much. Hope I remember enough to be helpful. It's been almost a month."

"No worries," John assured him with a wave. "The standard post-action debrief gave us pretty much everything we need."

Peter looked up with rheumy eyes. "If that was true, I wouldn't be here. Sir."

John made sure his grin was sheepish. "Well, I guess that's true enough. Frankly, I wanted to get a more detailed sense of what happened just before we finally got you out of there."

Peter shrugged. "Like I told the debriefing team, the opfor hit me pretty hard with area effect weapons. Heavy concussive rounds with lots of overlap. They seemed low on shrapnel, though. I couldn't even be sure there was any."

"What do you mean?"

"Well, the shock waves were so strong they picked up the debris in the junkyard you guys set as my emergency extraction point. Flung it around pretty good. For all I know, that's what I heard pinging and zipping around me where I was hiding."

"About where you were hiding: did the position become compromised?"

Peter frowned. "How do you mean?"

John flipped through electronic pages on his datapad. "Well, according to your first debrief, you found cover that sheltered you from the worst of the blasts. But then it didn't. At least not fully."

John laid down the datapad he had not needed to consult. "Were the shock waves degrading the cover as you waited for extraction?"

Peter's frown deepened. "Not that I can recall, no. But by that time, I might not have noticed."

"Peter, no offense, but how would you *not* notice having a significant portion of your cover sheared away?"

Peter shrugged. "Like I said, they were putting warheads all around me. So the shockwaves weren't coming from just one direction. I got knocked on my ass plenty of times, some from packages landing to my rear. Could have been one of those times. I was pretty dazed from the near misses."

John nodded. "Yes, I see that you report losing consciousness."

Peter's eyes became distant. "Yeah, I…I did. I mean, I think I did. It was strange. I know I was unconscious, but I don't remember any one strike doing that." He smiled crookedly. "Of course, if the shell hit close enough, the first thing I'd remember is waking up."

John matched the dying suit-driver's smile. "And what do you recall about waking up?"

"Recall?" Peter echoed with a frown. "I woke up; what is there to recall?"

"Well, was it gradual? Immediate? Something in between? Like swimming up out of a haze?"

Peter's frown became more pronounced. "Y'know, I…I can't really say. It kind of feels like I woke up a couple of times during the waves of enemy ordnance, which doesn't make sense because I'm sure I only lost consciousness once. But after I did, everything else got sort of, well, dreamy. No pain; just feeling foggy. Like after a bender. Even though the shelling was still going on. Or maybe not. I'm just not sure."

John tried to make sure his face was relaxed, encouraging. "Take your time, Peter. We're not in a rush, here."

But Peter didn't seem to hear. He went from being puzzled to slightly agitated. "Damn it, I just don't remember what happened. Probably because I was already weaker than I knew. Damned cancer. God-damned fucking cancer."

John said nothing, just nodded as Peter worked himself up. A small panel attached under the desktop, on the left side of the leg-well, illuminated; it was red. John rested his temple on his right index and middle fingers, held that position for a long three count. The red light went out. Peter was upset, but not dangerous. At least not yet.

He was wrapping up his fruitless attempt to find some orienting event after he regained consciousness. "Christ," he concluded, "if I was that messed up, I can't even understand why I'm still alive."

Jones shrugged even though he knew what was coming. "What do you mean?"

Peter glared out the windows at nothing. "So let's say I was unconscious for a while, then woke up and remained dazed, disoriented. Unless you came in right away, what would keep the opfor from advancing on me and taking me out? I mean, they *must* have been probing me under the cover of that barrage. And before I lost consciousness, I *do* remember being damn near goose eggs on the reactive defense systems built into the suit. So even if the snoop suit was still capable of thinking and fighting for me—which I seriously doubt—it couldn't have done so for very long. So why didn't the opfor simply roll right over me?"

Jon shook his head. "That is the mystery isn't it?"

Peter narrowed his eyes. "And that's why I'm here, isn't it? That's why I'm getting my own special, second debrief with the head honcho of the program: because I shouldn't have made it out at all."

Jones shook his head. "It's not something I'm worried about," he said truthfully. "Stranger things than that have happened in combat. For all we know, their commander—or their automated threat assessment software—needed to call away the assets they had pinning you down. It was still pretty crazy dirtside, even after we extracted you," Jones lied.

If Peter detected the lie, or had heard contradictory scuttlebutt, he gave no sign of it. He relaxed slightly. "Yeah, well, I still wish I had an explanation for it. I don't remember anything until I was in the evac VTOL heading topside." He frowned. "Wait a minute. If you were monitoring me, then you had a sky eye looking down. So shouldn't *you* have seen what happened before the extraction?"

Jones smiled, hoped it was convincingly casual. "You'd think so, wouldn't you? But just trying to wrap up that operation and get our people back upstairs resulted in a lot of abrupt asset multitasking and retasking. It became pretty chaotic, so we don't have pristine records. But if the bird we had watching you spent even a minute or two watching someplace else, it might have missed whatever transpired in your AO, missed seeing the answer to this mystery."

Jones shrugged. "Sometimes, post-action assessment leaves us with stranger mysteries then we can puzzle out. And sometimes, when we finally do get answers, they are amazing only for how simple and stupid they are." He paused. "But in your case, we *do* have a few clues."

Peter leaned forward, coughed as though he might hack up part of a lung, swallowed. "What clues?" His eyes were watery but focused, unblinking, on Jones' face.

Affecting not to notice Peter's almost desperate stare, Jones glanced at his slate. "There was a thin residue on the outside of the suit that suggests some chemical rounds may have been mixed in with the concussives they rained on you. In that residue, we found traces of what, to a human, would be a tranquilizing agent, as well as the remains of what looks like a self-decomposing corrosive."

Peter frowned. "That's a strange mix. A chemical barrage that both agitates and calms a target at the same time? How stupid is that?"

Jones nodded. "Against an unarmored opponent, the two effects would be intrinsically counterproductive; it would reduce each other's effectiveness. But the enemy knows we land or drop in armor, so—"

"So their idea was to erode the armor—probably the flex fibers at the articulated joints, or maybe the mask seal—to let the tranquilizer slip into the suit."

Jones smiled. "And if that was their plan, then it wasn't so stupid, after all. And, if you were anesthetized, that would certainly explain why you don't remember much," he emphasized honestly.

Peter leaned back, relaxed as if a burden had been lifted from him, but in the same moment, he also became more pale and drawn. If such a thing was possible. "But we'll never know for sure."

"No, we won't," Jones lied. "Now, there's a tilt-rotor waiting for you on the flight line at Runway Three. It's already in the departure queue. No stops except yours. Home in three hours, at the most."

Peter nodded absently, showed no sign of moving. If anything, he sank further into the chair.

Jones summoned a concerned frown. "Something you want to add? Or a question?"

Peter shook his head. "No. I guess not."

Jones smiled faintly, stood.

Peter stood also, extended his hand. "Well, I guess this is it..." He blanched, quickly rephrased. "I mean, I guess we're done."

The silence was profound as Jones shook Peter's hand and silently acknowledged that Peter's first phrasing—that this was it—had been sadly accurate. Given the amount of time that he had left, they would never see each other again. Jones cleared his throat. "Made any plans with your family?"

Peter nodded, but seemed uncertain. "Yeah. I guess so. I mean, we've talked about it. But—" His voice tapered into silence as he withdrew his hand. "I guess—I, I kind of wonder if it's the right thing to do. Going home to them. Maybe letting them remember me this way—well, the way they last saw me—would be better."

Jones projected an expression of surprise that he did not actually feel. "That's a pretty big change of plans—and heart. Why?"

Peter looked away, frowning as if he was trying to figure out why he'd said what he just had. "Not entirely sure. I—I still want to be with them. But I know what it's going to look like at the end. The kids are pretty young. So maybe I'll just call, say I'm going on a little adventure for a week or two. But instead, I'd just go walkabout for—well, for as long as it lasts. You know, a chance to cross at least a few things off my bucket list. No wasting away in front of their eyes. I think it's better for everybody that way." Peter's eyes remained fixed on the wall.

Jones made sure his voice was calm, his body still. "Better for the kids? Maybe—and that's a very big maybe. But for your wife? She knows what's coming. I can't believe she'd prefer that you just disappear."

Peter looked around in furtive desperation, as if he was contemplating jumping out of his own skin.

Jones shook his head. "Peter, let me offer a word of advice. Right now, it's important to keep moving forward with your plans. Even through what you might feel is a desire to keep moving as fast as you can, in any direction. It's natural enough. When there's a killer on our tail, we humans have a pretty basic instinct: to bob and weave and flee as fast and far as we can."

Jones folded his hands. Slowly. "But you can't outrun this, Peter. So the best thing to do with that manic energy you feel is to devote it to something that matters; that is the only real forward progress you can still make. To be with your family. Just as long as you can be. Think about that. And whatever you ultimately choose, I wish you Godspeed."

Peter's chin may have tremored a little, but his smile was genuine, albeit sad at the corners. "Thank you, sir. That's good advice."

And it makes it easier for us to keep testing how your decisions are being made, Jones added silently as the once-solidly-built suit driver glided out the door like a vanishingly thin ghost.

Five seconds after Peter was gone—and the embedded surveillance fibers showed the front door to the intel section sealing behind him—one of the bookcases in Jones' office swung open noiselessly. A woman of medium height and atypically well-defined musculature emerged from the opening of the dark passage. "Do we let him leave?"

"Of course."

"When he might go on walkabout? And cause hell only knows what trouble?"

Jones shook his head. "He won't."

"Which do you mean? That he won't go on walkabout, or that he won't cause trouble?"

"He won't do either."

The woman's march into the room came to an abrupt stop in front of Jones' desk. She crossed her arms, dark eyes opened wide, the unusually large expanse of sclera shining as if she was just barely restraining herself from leaping over the desktop and throttling Jones where he stood.

With her unruly raven curls framing a face that was half-Fury, half-harpy, Jones understood why the other staffers in his section had taken to calling Captain Diana Kouseris "Medea" when she was out of earshot. The most disapproving and derisive among them actually preferred "*Mad*ea." Jones wondered if Kouseris knew, and, if she did, if she wasn't secretly pleased at her unsolicited nom de guerre.

Her voice was sharp. "And how can you be so sure that Smith won't use his last weeks to disrupt as many of our operations as possible?"

"Because he doesn't actually want to. And furthermore, now that he's broached the topic of doing so, and I recommended against it, we can be sure that any enemy attempt to prompt that kind of behavior has been derailed."

"What? Why?"

"Because it would attract our attention. And that is the very last thing our adversaries want, Captain."

She frowned. "I suppose that makes some kind of sense," she allowed—without adding his rank or the proper honorific "sir."

Jones sighed, actually having to suppress a smile. Kouseris/Medea was more than just a notable officer and formidable woman; she was a force of nature. Her dossier indicated she had been married—and divorced—three times. Scuttlebutt reported that her passion and relentlessness had broken each husband: emotionally, physically, or—most likely—both. "I am pleased that you find my reasoning reassuring...*Captain*."

She finally got the hint, suppressed what might have been either a resentful or self-recriminatory glower. "I do, sir. But I am still not comfortable allowing Smith to roam on such a long leash. He *was* captured by the enemy, after all."

"In a manner of speaking. In point of fact, it would be more accurate to say that he merely became subject to enemy influence."

"Which, de facto, makes him a traitor."

"Really? Even if he has no memory of it?"

Medea's frown deepened. "Just because he can't remember anything doesn't mean he didn't sell us out or cut some kind of deal."

Jones raised a single eyebrow. "So you are assuming that our adversary was able to suborn him and then mind-wipe him on site? In the course of a few minutes? During a hot extraction?"

Medea's face became rigid. "We don't know the full capabilities of most of the species we've tangled with. So we can't rule anything out. Which leaves us with only one data point: what does his suit's op log say?"

"It says that this particular adversary is damned sophisticated."

"By which you mean the log says nothing?"

Jones nodded. "The suit's operations recorder went blank shortly after the shelling intensified."

"Did they mix in an EMP burster?"

"None were detected."

"Then how...?"

Jones held up a hand. "Rather than play an epic game of twenty questions, I want to ask something of *you,* Captain. Have you figured out why I asked you to stand by during the debrief?"

"To wring his traitor neck in case he went south on you."

"While I certainly wanted your protection, I repeat and emphasize that Peter Smith is not a traitor."

"And would you still be saying that if he *had* tried to kill you?"

"I would describe him the same way I describe him now: compromised. In such a way that he does not even realize it."

She frowned. "You're going to need to explain that. Sir."

Jones nodded. "The second, and more important, reason I had you standing by was so that you could observe for yourself how genuinely unaware he is of having been compromised. And also, to hear the specifics of his mission before I bring you in on my actual project."

"So you're not in charge of technical intel? Of reverse-engineering alien systems?" Jones shook his head. "Then what *are* you in command of?"

"A special counter-intelligence task force operating at the highest level of secrecy. We're extra-governmental, but even the *government* doesn't have a level of classification for what we're doing. It would be way beyond Ultra. But before we go any further, Captain Kouseris, I need to know if you will accept an assignment that is certain to change your activities, your career, your life. Forget long-duration partners or having a family."

"I've never been a fan of picket fences and a bun in the oven. Read me in."

"Very well." Jones tapped a stud on a slate resting on his desktop. The office's windows polarized sharply, becoming darkly opaque to the outside world. A moment later, steel and composite shutters came down, a tight grid pattern imprinted faintly on their inward facing surfaces.

Medea looked from that faint intaglio pattern to the walls around them. "Did I just see the sixth side of a Faraday cage come closing down?"

"You did. Although this is far from the most secure room in the complex. There are cages inside cages on the lowest levels."

"And just how far down are those levels?"

"Captain, that's need to know. Which you might. Eventually. But not today. For now, I want you to concentrate on this." Jones activated the smart surface of the slate, tapped in a code, then chose a virtual button marked, 'Display ear worm.'"

The screen illuminated, showing an integrated thermal and 3D magnetic resonance image of a human head. Amidst the mostly cool greens and blues of the inert tissues and structures, and the amber and faint yellow of more neurologically active regions, there was a small red coil located deep in the ear canal.

"What the hell is that?" Medea asked in a hoarse voice.

"That, Captain, is how Peter Smith has been compromised."

"What is it? A parasite?"

"Only secondarily," Jones answered. "It draws minimum sustenance from the surrounding tissues and is not becoming more invasive. Indeed, it hasn't added mass or volume the entire time we have had it under observation. If you look closely, you will see that although its primary structure is in the inner ear, there are tendrils which lie along nerve clusters in close proximity to brain tissue."

Jones manipulated the slate to zoom in on the foreign body. It looked like a legless, almost flat caterpillar curled into a tight coil. Small filaments protruded from it that both moored it to, and communicated with, the surfaces of Smith's inner ear.

Medea's breathing had become audible, faster. "Any idea how it got in there? His suit was sealed."

Jones shook his head. "I was not lying or exaggerating when I told Smith that there was some evidence that his suit had been breached. The corrosive element that I mentioned apparently opened several apertures—no dimension greater than half a millimeter—in the various flex fibers of the armor. That was evidently large enough for a younger, smaller version of this infiltrant to slip through."

Medea was suddenly furious. "And it took Smith's return to Earth to find it? Shouldn't it have shown up on the first general scans they performed on him after he'd been extracted?"

Jones allowed himself a mirthless smile. "The only reason we found it at all is because we were already expecting to find something, and suspected where it might be. The tissue distinctions you see in this scan are already at an artificially high contrast value. As best we can tell, this organism's cells are genetic copies of our own with only slight modifications in the nucleus and mitochondrial structures. Also, this image has been gathered from a set of perspectives that give us a maximum cross-section on it. It is actually so flat as to be almost two-dimensional; it could easily pass as scar tissue or some other completely explicable anomaly."

Medea seemed to have difficulty either processing, or adapting to, this new information. "So it knows how to adapt to us on a cellular level?"

"Evidently. And possibly, not just us."

"What do you mean?"

Jones shook his head. "We will return to that. In the meantime, take a look at the magnification setting. The entire infiltrant would be barely 3 mm in length if you were to uncoil it."

She finally looked at him. For the first time in the two years he had known her, Captain Diana Kouseris didn't look like Medea anymore; she looked—haunted? Scared? "So how the hell did you know to look for it?"

"We put out bait."

"That's not an answer; that's a dodge. You don't bait a hook unless you already believe you'll catch something."

"We thought we *might*. In this case, it was more akin to trawling waters which may or may not be empty. But we certainly weren't expecting anything like this."

"You still haven't answered my question, Jo—Director Jones. *Why* were you trawling any waters, anywhere?"

Jones shrugged. Medea had committed to the project; no reason not to tell her now. But overcoming the reflex to conceal the origins of his special counter-intelligence section remained a conscious and uncomfortable decision. "We have been seeding flora on every world Humans go to. No one knows we have been doing it. Even the mercs or our own troops."

"What? How?"

Jones smiled. "Because it's an engineered bacterium we introduce into our troops' pre-drop rations, each of which has a sleeping nanite inside. The bacterium itself is harmless and wholly inert, but with the survivability of tardigrades. Adapted from them, actually. So every time a suit performs an automatic waste evacu—"

"Okay, so we are shitting on worlds at the same time we're doing contracts. But you still haven't told me *why*."

"To mark them."

"Huh?"

"Captain, consider our operations to date. We are dragged back and forth across unfathomable distances, often without any real intel on where we have gone during our missions. Command deemed this unacceptable. We wanted to mark the places we've been."

"With shit?"

"No: with the nanites inside the bacteria, which, when properly pinged with the right series of EM pulses, awaken and collectively pulse back. Very weakly, and without any data: just a ghostly signal that tell us that they are there. And since each mission has a slightly altered nanite—"

"We don't just know that we've been there; we know who and when they dropped in. Literally." She nodded, understanding. "Add in some automated observations of the night sky from multiple locations, and we can start building a database on which races have taken us where, for what missions. Basic intel. And maybe a way to start building a map."

"Correct. That was the plan. But then we put our think-tankers on it, and they pointed out that if we could think up that plan, our adversaries could anticipate it. So we realized that an equally important intelligence objective was to determine if any of our employers—or their foes—were watching for these kinds of marking and data-gathering ploys. And if they were, how did they monitor for it, and how would they counteract such activities?"

He sighed, gestured at the small red speck inside the image of Peter Smith's head. "Instead, we found this. None of our employers or their peers seem to be watching us as closely as our think tankers conjectured. But something else *was* watching. About a year ago, it reacted to our nanites on a fairly minor mission, rendered all the intestinal nanites inert. So we knew we'd been detected.

"Then, some of the returning mercs from that mission began acting oddly. Nothing we would have noticed had we not instituted behavioral tracking metrics on all our deployed forces shortly after we started taking off-world merc contracts."

"So those soldiers were like Smith? They were infected? I mean, compromised?"

Jones nodded. "Apparently so, but we never got access to their bodies. Before we could detain any of them, they all went AWOL, usually hours after our first inquiries into their atypical activities. Which, although different in their particulars, shared a striking commonality."

"Let me guess; they started accessing information and data sources in which they'd never shown prior interest."

"Correct."

"And so Peter Smith was your bait. You rigged a living trap for whatever got inside our troops." She glanced at the red curlicue. "And that's what you caught. You sons of bitches. Doing that to a dying man."

Jones sighed. "It's *because* he was dying that we chose him. His condition warranted, even necessitated, the diagnostics that had to be run on him. So even if the infiltrant could read his thoughts, it had no reason to believe that actually, it was all a set-up: a legitimate reason for us to conduct the extensive searches that revealed it."

"And there it is. You found it. Congratulations."

"We did a lot more than just find it, Captain. We detected this." Jones zoomed in to maximum magnification upon the red coil. At the limit of resolution, a faint haze appeared at various points of the infiltrant's periphery.

Medea squinted. "What is that?"

"We're not really sure. But you'll notice the magnification of the image."

"Yes. Practically atomic. And still…"

"…and still, all we get is a smudge. At first the experts—Zekta and the few we've brought in on this—thought it was some kind of distortion in the image. You frequently get that when you push sensors this close to their limit of resolution. But after extensive analysis, it's clear that this is not a distortion. It's too localized and it's too regular at each site of occurrence."

"So…?"

"So the best guess of the brain trust is that we're looking at what they call irregular activity in the surrounding quantal field."

"The what?"

John smiled. "That's pretty much what I said, too. To shorten an explanation that is not only way too long, but involves way too many massively multisyllabic words, this is a disruption in the quantum state of the universe, but restricted to the immediate vicinity of the infiltrant. Which is evidently controlling that effect."

"You make it sound like it's self-aware."

"Well—"

"No," Medea said with a sharp shake of her head, "not possible at that scale. That thing is too small and simple to house a genuine brain. Even if the total mass and volume of that, that, er, infiltrant, were nothing but neurons, it still can't have the cognitive bandwidth to drive a jellyfish, let alone intelligence." She noted John's steady and emotionless stare and hushed.

"You done now, Captain?"

She nodded.

"You are right, of course," John resumed, "and if you'd listened for just two more seconds, you would have heard this qualifier: it is *not* self-aware."

"Respectfully, sir, what other kind of awareness is there?"

John leaned back. "None that we've definitively observed in conjunction with intelligence. But there have long been theories of communal intelligences—and races like the SleSha exist. After all, that's really what our brains are. All our organs, for that matter; they are individual cells which have evolved to work together to perform specialized functions for a much more complex organism." His gesture swept her lithe body from head to toe. "It's just that in all the life forms we've encountered thus far, the intelligence elements are physically linked and are in direct communication with the biot's information gathering organs. But this? Well—not so much. Not at all, according to the best guesses of the folks with big brains and bigger salaries."

Medea glanced at the image of the life form again. "So...are we looking at a cell in a bigger brain? But then how does it communicate with the rest?"

John pointed to the haze around it. "Quantum entanglement."

Medea frowned. "Okay. I know what quanta are...sort of. Physics was not my best subject. I was more into PE and...extracurricular activities." John had seen her pre-service rap sheet and had no problem believing her self-description. "But you're going to have to explain quantum entanglement."

John smiled ruefully. "I'll do my level best. Short version: at the sub-sub-atomic level, where terms like matter and energy start becoming more provisional than practical, a lot of very strange effects start showing up. One of these is called quantum entanglement. Which means that certain quantal objects are weirdly tied to each other. Like they're conjoined twins, but at a distance. So, if you change the state of one of the twins, the other one follows along."

"So, you're implying that this thing can send a message back home. How far?"

Jones shook his head. "It probably can't actually compose a message. As you rightly observed at the outset, this life form is not large enough, or sophisticated enough, to think. But it *could* be a relay, a means of tapping into and sending whatever is going on in Peter's mind."

"So it's in communication with him?"

"If so, he doesn't know it. Polygraph, pupil dilation, questioning under the 'enhanced sedation' used to prepare him for some of his tests—all of them show Smith to be unaware of anything unusual in his system right now."

Medea frowned. "Isn't it kind of risky to ask him if he knows he's harboring a bug—when there was already one inside of him? One that might shrug off your drugs."

"Captain, comments like that reveal how stupid you must think we are in counter-intelligence. Of course we didn't ask the question directly. We adjusted an already-extant psych profile question battery and used that. If the infiltrant's controller is knowledgeable enough—and we suspect it is—then it heard a test that seemed familiar to Peter, modified to detect any sign that he might be verging toward suicidal impulses or detachment-induced sociopathia."

Medea shook her head. "Still, I don't know…"

Jones crossed his arms. On the one hand, he was glad that Kouseris was proving as analytical as she was; muscle without brains was not acceptable in his business. On the other hand, he hadn't been prepared for quite this level of sustained—and surprisingly perspicacious—questioning. "What's troubling you, Captain?"

"I just have a hard time figuring out why we are the first species to be infiltrated by these micro-maggots." And then her jaw sagged as she realized the implication of her own question. "Unless, of course, we're not. But wait, that doesn't make any sense either. We're the low-tech kids on the interstellar block. Surely the more advanced races would have detected similar attempts at infiltration."

John made a *tsking* noise. "Or maybe not. A lot of that would depend on how sophisticated a race's technology and detection methods were at the time that this infiltrant first encountered them. For all we know, the most advanced species may have been infiltrated and monitored for centuries or millennia now. And not even know it. And I have *no* idea how it would work on some of the exotic races.

"It's also possible that there's something about us—and possibly other species with which we share certain traits—that attract the special concern and attention of whatever intelligence is behind this infiltrant."

"You mean like the human willingness to deal out death and destruction for profit?" she smiled. "Or fun?"

"Maybe. Or maybe that's not the key trait that the infiltrant's controllers fear. Maybe they're more worried about the fact that we are not only innovative and versatile, but are unusually determined not to go gently into that good night, either as individuals or as a race. Because for all we know, we're not just dealing with watchers; it may be that the beings in control of the infiltrants are actually puppet masters. And they may only target races that won't fall readily in line, that have a high behavioral resistance to becoming marionettes. We know that some race—or at least we're pretty sure—that some race has been abducting Humans.

"The colony on New Persia for example. The Merc Guild didn't destroy it. Someone took all of the colonists—the ones they captured alive, anyway—and wiped out the colony to cover their tracks."

"Yeah, well that pretty much describes us, I guess."

"I agree. But there are further implications." John folded his arms. "Let's return to your initial assumption that other, more advanced species should have detected the presence of this infiltrating biot before we did. If so, then why haven't they taken steps to quarantine or eliminate it? Did they cut a deal with the controllers? Seek preferred status by welcoming their new quantum-entangled masters?" John felt a wolfish smile rise up, didn't try to stop it. "Or maybe some or all of them did what we're doing now, took the same kind of opsec precautions."

Medea looked sideways at him. "What do you mean?"

"I mean that they might have put out bait the same way we did. Peter was chosen with great care. His unfortunate condition was crucial not only because it provided a plausible explanation for all the tests we ran, but because he believed that he was chosen to test the new suit because it might turn out to be a suicide mission."

Medea nodded. "Because all of that was just opsec theater. It was a blind behind which you could look for the puppet masters without their ever suspecting." She jabbed a dagger-like finger at the image on the screen. "So, now that you've found it, how do we kill it?"

"We don't."

"What?"

"Captain, I appreciate your reflex for immediate, kinetic reactions to threats. That was, as I admitted, a large part of why I had you two steps away during today's debrief. But in counter-intelligence, it's often better to stand by and watch an infiltrator rather than act against them. Because, looking ahead, our mission isn't just detecting these infiltrants, but finding out if any of the other species are aware of them. Which makes our job infinitely harder."

Medea folded her arms and nodded. "Because if we ask the wrong question of the wrong member of any alien race, we could compromise our one big advantage: that we know about the puppet masters without them knowing we do."

"Exactly. If they learn that we're on to them, our job could become impossible. Almost instantly." He nodded at the chair that Peter had been sitting in. "You saw how agitated he became as I tried to reconstruct what happened during extraction. And then how suddenly he changed his final plans."

Medea's arms went from being folded to clutching her sides. "So the puppet masters can control their pawns almost instantaneously?"

Jones shook his head slowly, "It's not so much control as it is an ability to nudge people in desired directions."

"You mean, to get a look at our defenses, our resources…"

"Maybe. Or to drift about trying to assess our counter-intelligence capabilities. Or to contact whatever other compromised agents they may have here already. Or lay groundwork for others they plan to send."

Medea's hands were so tight on her biceps, the skin was becoming pale. "Any theories on how the puppet-masters are doing that?"

"Actually, we have the answer to that: the infiltrant sends neural signals that alter brain chemistries. Make certain actions seem more attractive, others less so."

Medea nodded. "So with Peter, they must have cut down the appeal of spending time with his family and increased his restlessness. Probably played on his fears of approaching death to get him to want to rove around, to go out with his boots on. To make him hungry for every last moment he could spend doing, seeing, feeling—instead of seeking out the comforts of home and family."

Jones nodded back. "And by observing Peter during his last days—from a distance that both respects his privacy and keeps the puppet-masters unaware—we may learn more about how the infiltrant operates and what its controllers hope to achieve."

Medea nodded grudgingly. "I don't like waiting around, but I know the value of the axiom, 'know thy enemy'—and right now, we know squat. So the more we watch it, the more we should learn about how to protect ourselves."

"Yes. But this isn't just about protection, Captain. Handled correctly, this could become a huge boost to humanity's stature and influence with more advanced races. It could become a strategic coup."

Medea's frown was back. "You've lost me again. How is there an upside to this nightmare scenario?"

Jones smiled. "Let me answer your question with a question: how would you rate us among the various species we've encountered out there?" He glanced up at—and notionally, through—the ceiling.

"Without our CASPers, we'd be middle of the road at best. If we weren't scrappy, we'd be history by now."

Jones nodded. "Now, let's go back to your point about how unlikely it is that we are the first race to be infiltrated. Let's presume that some of the other species have, in fact, done what we are doing now: that once they detected the infiltrants, they created a small, secret organization to watch, and ultimately to do something about, them."

"Fair enough. What's your point?"

"Well, that means we now have a pretty good idea of what to look for: the same kind of deep cover counter-intelligence ops we're mounting. So we watch, we let those signs lead us to them, make contact." Jones smiled. "And once we do make contact, what kind of reaction do you suspect we'll get from these other races which have been out among the stars—and grappling with these puppet masters—for centuries, even millennia?"

Medea smiled back. "They'll be shocked that a bunch of hairless apes tweaked to these ear bugs as early as we did. Which makes us part of a pretty exclusive club. Too bad it's also a secret club."

Jones smile widened. "Is it secret, I wonder?" He shrugged. "After all, if we know to look for them, they'll have likely been looking for—and already found—each other, right?"

Medea's eyes were bright again, but with a kind of predatory wonder. "So you think there might already be a secret society linking the races in the know? Yeah, sure—and suddenly we're the wunderkind in that club. Not just serving, but sharing intel and rubbing elbows with older races: with movers and shakers."

"Yes, who all know that, sooner or later, everyone in that secret society is going to be an indispensable ally in the war that will ultimately decide our collective fates: identifying the source of the infiltrants and taking the war to them."

Medea's eyes narrowed and her smile was sly. "So they might be motivated to strengthen us in preparation for that fight, slip us a few perks under the table every once in a while."

Jones nodded, turned off the screen, touched the tab that set the window covers retracting back into the ceiling. "Any other questions, Captain?"

"Just one. Given what's at stake in this fight, how do I get assigned to the front lines?"

"You're already there," Jones smiled. "Welcome to the trenches, Captain."

# # # # #

About Tim C. Taylor

Tim C. Taylor lives with his family in an ancient village in England. When he was an impressionable kid, between 1977 and 1978, several mind-altering things happened to him all at once: Star Wars, Dungeons & Dragons, and 2000AD comic. Consequently, he now writes science fiction novels for a living, notably in the Human Legion and Four Horsemen Universes. His latest project is an adventure serial called Chimera Company, which has been described as Warhammer 40,000 in the style of Star Wars. For a free starter library of stories from all the worlds he writes in, join the Legion at humanlegion.com.

* * * * *

About Chris Kennedy

A Webster Award winner and three-time Dragon Award finalist, Chris Kennedy is a Science Fiction/Fantasy/Young Adult author, speaker, and small-press publisher who has written over 25 books and published more than 100 others. Chris' stories include the "Occupied Seattle" military fiction duology, "The Theogony" and "Codex Regius" science fiction trilogies, stories in the "Four Horsemen" and "In Revolution Born" universes and the "War for Dominance" fantasy trilogy. Get his free book, "Shattered Crucible," at his website, https://chriskennedypublishing.com.

Called "fantastic" and "a great speaker," he has coached hundreds of beginning authors and budding novelists on how to self-publish their stories at a variety of conferences, conventions and writing guild presentations. He is the author of the award-winning #1 bestseller, "Self-Publishing for Profit: How to Get Your Book Out of Your Head and Into the Stores," as well as the leadership training book, "Leadership from the Darkside."

Chris lives in Virginia Beach, Virginia, with his wife, and is the holder of a doctorate in educational leadership and master's degrees in both business and public administration. Follow Chris on Facebook at https://www.facebook.com/ckpublishing/.

* * * * *

For More Information:

For a suggested reading order guide to the Four Horsemen Universe, go to:

https://chriskennedypublishing.com/the-four-horsemen-books/4hu-suggested-reading-order/

* * * * *

For a listing of all the Four Horsemen books, go to:

https://chriskennedypublishing.com/the-four-horsemen-books/

* * * * *

Do you have what it takes to be a Merc?

Take your VOWs and join the Merc Guild on Facebook!

Meet us at: https://www.facebook.com/groups/536506813392912/

* * * * *

Did you like this book?
Please write a review!

* * * * *

The following is an
Excerpt from Book One of the Salvage Title Trilogy:

Salvage Title

Kevin Steverson

Available Now from Theogony Books

eBook, Paperback, and Audio Book

Excerpt from "Salvage Title:"

The first thing Clip did was get power to the door and the access panel. Two of his power cells did the trick once he had them wired to the container. He then pulled out his slate and connected it. It lit up, and his fingers flew across it. It took him a few minutes to establish a link, then he programmed it to search for the combination to the access panel.

"Is it from a human ship?" Harmon asked, curious.

"I don't think so, but it doesn't matter; ones and zeros are still ones and zeros when it comes to computers. It's universal. I mean, there are some things you have to know to get other races' computers to run right, but it's not that hard," Clip said.

Harmon shook his head. *Riiigghht,* he thought. He knew better. Clip's intelligence test results were completely off the charts. Clip opted to go to work at Rinto's right after secondary school because there was nothing for him to learn at the colleges and universities on either Tretra or Joth. He could have received academic scholarships for advanced degrees on a number of nearby systems. He could have even gone all the way to Earth and attended the University of Georgia if he wanted. The problem was getting there. The schools would have provided free tuition if he could just have paid to get there.

Secondary school had been rough on Clip. He was a small guy that made excellent grades without trying. It would have been worse if Harmon hadn't let everyone know that Clip was his brother. They lived in the same foster center, so it was mostly true. The first day of school, Harmon had laid down the law—if you messed with Clip, you messed up.

At the age of fourteen, he beat three seniors senseless for attempting to put Clip in a trash container. One of them was a Yalteen, a member of a race of large humanoids from two systems over. It wasn't a fair fight—they should have brought more people with them. Harmon hated bullies.

After the suspension ended, the school's Warball coach came to see him. He started that season as a freshman and worked on using it to earn a scholarship to the academy. By the time he graduated, he was six feet two inches with two hundred and twenty pounds of muscle. He got the scholarship and a shot at going into space. It was the longest time he'd ever spent away from his foster brother, but he couldn't turn it down.

Clip stayed on Joth and went to work for Rinto. He figured it was a job that would get him access to all kinds of technical stuff, servos, motors, and maybe even some alien computers. The first week he was there, he tweaked the equipment and increased the plant's recycled steel production by 12 percent. Rinto was eternally grateful, as it put him solidly into the profit column instead of toeing the line between profit and loss. When Harmon came back to the planet after the academy, Rinto hired him on the spot on Clip's recommendation. After he saw Harmon operate the grappler and got to know him, he was glad he did.

A steady beeping brought Harmon back to the present. Clip's program had succeeded in unlocking the container. "Right on!" Clip exclaimed. He was always using expressions hundreds or more years out of style. "Let's see what we have; I hope this one isn't empty, too." Last month they'd come across a smaller vault, but it had been empty.

Harmon stepped up and wedged his hands into the small opening the door had made when it disengaged the locks. There wasn't enough power in the small cells Clip used to open it any further. He put his weight into it, and the door opened enough for them to get inside. Before they went in, Harmon placed a piece of pipe in the doorway so it couldn't close and lock on them, baking them alive before anyone realized they were missing.

Daylight shone in through the doorway, and they both froze in place; the weapons vault was full.

* * * * *

Get "Salvage Title" now at:
https://www.amazon.com/dp/B07H8Q3HBV.

Find out more about Kevin Steverson and "Salvage Title" at: http://chriskennedypublishing.com/.

* * * * *

The following is an

Excerpt from Book One of the Mako Saga:

Mako

Ian J. Malone

Now Available from Theogony Books

eBook, Paperback, and Audio

Excerpt from "Mako:"

The trio darted for the lift and dove inside as a staccato of sparks and ricochets peppered the space around them. Once the doors had closed, they got to their feet and checked their weapons.

"I bet it was that little punk-ass tech giving us the stink eye," Danny growled, ejecting his magazine for inspection.

"Agreed," Hamish said.

Lee leapt to his comm. "Mac, you got a copy?"

"I leave you alone for five minutes, and this is what happens?" Mac answered.

"Yeah, yeah." Lee rolled his eyes. "Fire up that shuttle and be ready. We're comin' in hot."

"Belay that!" Link shouted. "Hey, asshat, you got time to listen to me now?"

Lee sneered as the lift indicator ticked past three, moving toward the hangar deck on ten. "Damn it, Link, we've been made. That means it's only a matter of time before the grays find that little package Hamish just left into their energy core. We've gotta go—now. What's so damned important that it can't wait for later?"

"If you'll shut your piehole for a sec, I'll show you."

Lee listened as Link piped in a radio exchange over the comm.

"*Velzer*, this is Morrius Station Tower." A male voice crackled through the static. "You are cleared for fuel service at Bravo Station on platform three. Be advised, we are presently dealing with a security breach near Main Engineering, and thus you are ordered to keep all hatches secured until that's resolved. Please acknowledge."

"Acknowledged, Morrius Tower," another voice said. "All hatches secure. Proceeding to Bravo Three for service. Out."

Lee wrinkled his nose. "So what? Another ship is stoppin' for gas. What's the problem?"

"It's a prisoner transport in transit to a POW camp in the Ganlyn System."

Prisoner transport?

"And boss?" Link paused. "Their reported head count is two hundred seventy-six, plus flight crew."

Lee cringed. Never in a million years could he have missed that number's significance.

"Yeah, that struck me, too," Link said.

"Does mean what I think it does?" Danny asked.

Lee hung his head. "The Sygarious 3 colonists are aboard that ship."

"Oh no," Mac murmured. "Guys, if that's true, there are whole families over there."

"I know," Lee snapped, "and they're all about to dock on Platform Three, just in time to die with everyone else on this godforsaken facility."

* * * * *

Get "Mako" now at: https://www.amazon.com/dp/B088X5W3SP

Find out more about Ian J. Malone and "Mako" at: https://chriskennedypublishing.com/imprints-authors/ian-j-malone/

* * * * *

The following is an
Excerpt from Book One of the Singularity War:

Warrior: Integration

David Hallquist

Available from Theogony Books

eBook, Paperback, and (Soon) Audio

Excerpt from "Warrior: Integration:"

I leap into the pit. As I fall in the low gravity, I run my hands and feet along the rock walls, pushing from one side to another, slowing my descent. I hit the pool below and go under.

I swim up through the greenish chemicals and breach the surface. I can see a human head silhouetted against the circle of light above. Time to go. I slide out of the pool quickly. The pool explodes behind me. Grenade, most likely. The tall geyser of steam and spray collapses as I glide into the darkness of the caves ahead.

They are shooting to kill now.

I glide deeper into the rough tunnels. Light grows dimmer. Soon, I can barely see the rock walls around me. I look back. I can see the light from the tunnel reflected upon the pool. They have not come down yet. They're cautious; they won't just rush in. I turn around a bend in the tunnel, and light is lost to absolute darkness.

The darkness means little to me anymore. I can hear them talking as their voices echo off the rock. They are going to send remotes down first. They have also decided to kill me rather than capture me. They figure the docs can study whatever they scrape off the rock walls. That makes my choices simple. I figured I'd have to take out this team anyway.

The remotes are on the way. I can hear the faint whine of microturbines. They will be using the sensors on the remotes and their armor, counting on the darkness blinding me. Their sensors against my monster. I wonder which will win.

Everything becomes a kind of gray, blurry haze as my eyes adapt to the deep darkness. I can see the tunnel from sound echoes as I glide down the dark paths. I'm also aware of the remotes spreading out in a search pattern in the tunnel complex.

I'll never outrun them. I need to hide, but I glow in infra-red. One of the remotes is closing, fast.

I back up against a rock wall, and force the monster to hide me. It's hard; it wants to fight, but I need to hide first. I feel the numbing cold return as my temperature drops, hiding my heat. I feel the monster come alive, feel it spread through my body and erupt out of my skin. Fibers spread over my skin, covering me completely in fibrous camouflage. They harden, fusing me to the wall, leaving me unable to move. I can't see, and I can barely breathe. If the remotes find me here, I'm dead.

The remote screams by. I can't see through the fibers, but it sounds like an LB-24, basically a silver cigar equipped with a small laser.

I can hear the remote hover nearby. Can it see me? It pauses and then circles the area. Somehow, the fibers hide me. It can't see me, but it knows something is wrong. It drops on the floor to deposit a sensor package and continues on. Likely it signaled the men upstairs about an anomaly. They'll come and check it out.

The instant I move, the camera will see me. So I wait. I listen to the sounds of the drones moving and water running in the caves. These caves are not as lifeless as I thought; a spider crawls across my face. I'm as still as stone.

Soon, the drones have completed their search pattern and dropped sensors all over the place. I can hear them through the rock, so now I have a mental map of the caves stretching out down here. I wait.

They send the recall, and the drones whine past on the way up. They lower ropes and rappel down the shaft. They pause by the pool, scanning the tunnels and blasting sensor pulses of sound, and likely radar and other scans as well. I wait.

They move carefully down the tunnels. I can feel their every movement through the rock, hear their every word. These men know what they are doing: staying in pairs, staying in constant communication, and checking corners carefully. I wait.

One pair comes up next to me. They pause. One of them has bad breath. I can feel the tension; they know something is wrong. They could shoot me any instant. I wait.

"Let's make sure." I hear a deep voice and a switch clicks.

Heat and fire fill the tunnel. I can see red light through the fibers. Roaring fire sucks all the air away, and the fibers seal my nose before I inhale flame. The fibers protect me from the liquid flame that covers everything. I can feel the heat slowly begin to burn through.

It's time.

* * * * *

Get "Warrior: Integration" now at:
https://www.amazon.com/dp/B0875SPH86

Find out more about David Hallquist and "Warrior: Integration" at:
https://chriskennedypublishing.com/

* * * * *

Made in the USA
Columbia, SC
24 August 2020